D0633617

~

Praise for Terry Frei's Previous Books

Horns, Hogs, and Nixon Coming

"We had a few friends over who thought we had lost our minds as we whooped and hollered through a football game so exciting it was billed as the Game of the Century. For a few hours, we were innocent again, totally caught up in the contest. The game and its cultural contexts have been beautifully chronicled by Terry Frei in his book *Horns, Hogs, and Nixon Coming*."—Bill Clinton in *My Life*

". . . one of the better—and most readable—books of social history published in recent years."—Paul Greenberg, Pulitzer Prize–winning editorial writer, *Arkansas Democrat Gazette*

". . . a superb blending of sports, history, and politics."—Si Dunn, *Dallas Morning News*

Third Down and a War to Go

"Many times you hear athletes called heroes, and their deeds and accomplishments on the field are characterized as courageous. After reading *Third Down and a War to Go*, I am embarrassed to have ever been thought of as brave or courageous. . . . Enjoy this adventure in history, life, and courage and take it from a so-called tough guy—keep the hanky close by."—*Dan Fouts, Hall of Fame quarterback and CBS sportscaster*

"Brings to life, in shades of black and blue and blood red, the idea that certain things are worth fighting for."—Rick Morrissey, *Chicago Tribune*

"Mythology is nice. Truth is better. What a powerful piece of work . . . a telling detail in the great portrait of America at war, young men and women who saw their duty and did it no matter how much it scared them."—Dave Kindred, *The Sporting News*, and author of *Sound and Fury*

'77: Denver, the Broncos, and a Coming of Age

". . . a must-read for fans of the NFL, of the 1970s, and of the American West. You didn't have to live through it in Denver to appreciate this account of the flowering of a franchise and its love affair with a town, but this book takes those of us who did straight back to those thrilling days of yesteryear in unforgettable fashion."—Michael Knisley, senior deputy editor, *ESPN.com*

"Ahh, the memories. And they all happened right here in the forgotten time zone. Those magical moments came back with a rush last week reading *'77: Denver, the Broncos, and a Coming of Age*. What a fantastic read. . . . '77 is more than just a Bronco football memoir. It was a time when our Centennial State exploded on the national scene. . . . [T]hanks to Terry Frei's wonderful work, we get to live that magical moment all over again."—Dick Maynard, *Grand Junction Sentinel*

"No one knows more about Denver and its sports than Terry Frei does, and here in '77, he describes nothing less than the transformation of a city with a special focus on Denver's most magical team. To know why and how the Mile High City exists as it does today, this is essential history."—Sandy Clough, sports talk host, Denver's FM Sports Radio 104.3, The Fan

The Witch's Season

"Events carry the story forward swiftly, and that alone would make it a good read. But Frei has a larger point to make. It's during times of upheaval, when the very foundations of normalcy are being shaken, that personal courage, honor and the willingness to stand fast on principle matter most. All of the central characters in Frei's story will have to decide whether to make that stand, and if so, how to make it. Frei has written three nonfiction books, most notably *Horns, Hogs, and Nixon Coming*. This book proves he can write fiction too."—Ken Goe, Portland *Oregonian*

Playing Piano in a Brothel

"For every story, there's a story behind the story, and Frei's book captures hundreds of them. Frei provides never-before-read tales of legendary athletes, monumental events and games behind the games, as well as his own opinion of newspaper sports journalism as a whole—and its future . . . A must-read for every sports fan."—Doug Ottewill, *Mile High Sports* Magazine

Olympic Affair

Also by Terry Frei

Nonfiction
Playing Piano in a Brothel
'77: Denver, the Broncos, and a Coming of Age
Third Down and a War to Go
Horns, Hogs, and Nixon Coming

Fiction
The Witch's Season

Olympic Affair

A Novel of Hitler's Siren and America's Hero

Terry Frei

TAYLOR TRADE PUBLISHING
Lanham • New York • Boulder • Toronto • Plymouth, UK

Town of Vail Public Library
292 West Meadow Drive
Vail, CO 81657 / 970-479-2184

Published by Taylor Trade Publishing
An imprint of The Rowman & Littlefield Publishing Group, Inc.
4501 Forbes Boulevard, Suite 200, Lanham, Maryland 20706
www.rowman.com

10 Thornbury Road, Plymouth PL6 7PP, United Kingdom

Distributed by National Book Network

Copyright © 2012 by Terry Frei

All rights reserved. No part of this book may be reproduced in any form or by any
electronic or mechanical means, including information storage and retrieval systems,
without written permission from the publisher, except by a reviewer who may quote
passages in a review.

British Library Cataloguing in Publication Information Available

Library of Congress Cataloging-in-Publication Data

Frei, Terry, 1955-
  A novel of Hitler's siren and America's hero / Terry Frei.
    p. cm.
  Includes bibliographical references.
  ISBN 978-1-58979-698-0 (cloth : alk. paper) — ISBN 978-1-58979-699-7 (electronic)
  1. Morris, Glenn, 1911-1974—Fiction. 2. Decathletes—United States—Fiction.
3. Motion picture actors and actresses—United States—Fiction. 4. Riefenstahl,
Leni—Fiction. 5. Women motion picture producers and directors—Germany—
Fiction. I. Title. II. Title: Hitler's siren and America's hero.
  PS3606.R4477O49 2012
  813'.6—dc22

                                                                2012017148

∞™ The paper used in this publication meets the minimum requirements of
American National Standard for Information Sciences—Permanence of Paper
for Printed Library Materials, ANSI/NISO Z39.48-1992.

Printed in the United States of America

To Dr. Morris Ververs, for his considerable help and his
quest to keep alive the memory of Glenn Morris.
To Tony Phifer, for his friendship and for planting the idea.

During a break in the decathlon competition in Berlin, Leni Riefenstahl reaches out to Glenn Morris. Other decathlon competitors, from left, are German Erwin Huber and Americans Bob Clark (farthest back) and Jack Parker (head turned). Courtesy National Archives, Photo No. 242-HD-245-1.

1

~

Leni's Visit

The cook squinted at the ticket on the wheel facing him, pretending to be deciphering the handwritten lunch order.

"What language is that?" he asked softly.

"English," said the perky teenaged waitress, pointing at the ticket with her pen. "Can't you read?"

"No, I mean—"

"I know what you meant," she said impishly, nodding almost imperceptibly over her shoulder, in the direction of the man and woman conversing in a window booth. "German, I think. Or maybe Spanish."

Though her platinum hair unmistakably was dyed, the woman looked to be in her early sixties. Her smart pantsuit and haughtiness made her seem unwilling to concede anything beyond mid-fifties, even to herself. On the other side of the table, the skinny young man with shaggy blond hair was deferential, sipping his coffee as the woman animatedly made a point with both hands and a Teutonic torrent. Werner Vass had just turned thirty and he was accustomed to listening.

The only customer at the four-seat counter, a middle-aged regular who owned the Simla Grocery next door, devoured the final bite of a hamburger and wiped his mouth with the paper napkin.

"Kristy," he called out to the waitress. "Half cup for the road, will ya?"

As she poured the coffee, he told her bitterly, "It's German, all right. I hope I made her a goddamn widow."

1

Kristy sneaked a look at the booth, where the woman continued her monologue, oblivious.

The grocer raised his cup, took several swallows, and then slammed it down on the counter. He dropped four one-dollar bills on the counter and marched out.

As the cook finished assembling the Germans' sandwiches and slapped them on the plates—there were no "presentation" issues at the Simla Café—a stocky man in a dark suit, with a chauffeur's hat tucked under one arm, entered and approached the booth. The Germans made no move to make room for him.

"All gassed up," he said.

The woman responded in clipped and accented English. "How long will it take us to travel to the Denver airport?"

"About two hours, ma'am."

Werner Vass looked at his watch and rattled off something in German to the woman. She nodded emphatically. Turning to the chauffeur, Vass said, "After we finish here, we would like to tour the area a bit more before leaving for Denver."

"Yes, sir. I'll be outside."

Kristy delivered the food, sliding the plates in front of them. Then she stepped back, put her hands together and smiled. "Is there anything else I can get you?"

The woman's return smile wasn't warm; it was a formality. It was a smile offered in accompaniment with a request. "Perhaps some information," she said. "How long you have lived in Simla?"

"All my life," Kristy said. "Except last year at CU . . . at college." Self-conscious, she added, "I'm taking this semester off. Going back next . . ."

The woman cut her off. "Are you or the cook aware of Glenn Morris?"

"The Olympics guy, right?"

"That's correct."

"Well, Eddie just moved here a couple of years ago. So I don't think he does. But there's a display case about him at the school and they always cover him in Modern American History. Won a gold medal in something at the Olympics in the twenties somewhere in . . ."

Kristy's pause was momentary, but something was clicking.

" . . . in Germany."

"Berlin," the woman said, scolding. "The decathlon. And 1936."

"I guess that's why I only got a 'C,'" Kristy said lightly.

The woman didn't smile.

Kristy squinted. "Didn't he just die, too?"

"In January," the woman said flatly. "In California."

"Did you know him?"

"Ye-e-e-e-s." The woman drew out the word, as if she was deciding whether it would be the final one or she'd keep going. She didn't keep going. Kristy interpreted the awkward pause as an excuse to leave and let them eat.

When Kristy dropped off the check, Vass perused it and said, without looking up, "You say there is a display honoring Glenn Morris at the town school?"

"Outside the gym."

"Where is this school?"

The waitress pointed north. "A block up Caribou, right on Pueblo, up the hill and you can't miss it. Gym's the first thing you come to. School just started today."

A few minutes later, Vass stood back as the German woman, transfixed, looked over the glassed-in display. A bell rang and students scurried past. A sign in school colors, blue lettering on yellow background, stretched above the cases.

GLENN MORRIS
1936 Olympic Decathlon Champion
Berlin, Germany

Pictures from his youth established that Glenn had been a student leader and star athlete, both at Simla High and Colorado Agricultural College in Fort Collins, and handsome even then. Front pages from Colorado newspapers told of Morris's Olympic triumph ("GLENN MORRIS CAPTURES DECATHLON CROWN") and his tumultuous welcome home to Colorado. The woman lingered at each.

A front cover of a German tabloid showed Morris, dark-haired and lean, yet chiseled, wearing a USA sweatshirt, smiling slyly at the camera, resting on one elbow as he lounged on grass. He was featured so prominently, his head even covered up part of the newspaper name. The editors apparently believed their readership didn't need to be reminded of the title, but wanted to see the American star.

Finally, she came to a newspaper picture of Morris in a dark USA pullover sweater, and a white collared shirt underneath, sitting on the edge of a bed and writing a note on the adjacent tiny desk. A framed picture of a prim young woman, her hair tied back, was next to his writing pad. The picture's headline and caption proclaimed:

REMEMBERS THE GIRL HE LEFT BEHIND
Glenn Morris, the Colorado boy who is America's hope in the decathlon, takes time out to write his girl back home.

The German woman lingered.

Vass solicitously placed a hand on her shoulder.

"Er sollte bei mir übernachtet," she snapped.

She pulled away from his hand and moved toward the school doors.

They hadn't noticed that three boys had stopped behind them. It was as if a pedestrian looked up at the sky. These kids wanted to take a closer look at what was drawing the strangers' interest.

Starting in pursuit of the woman, Vass bumped one boy. "I'm sorry," the German said. "Excuse me."

The kid pointed to the woman storming off. "What did *she* say?"

Vass slowed and turned. Backing up, he told them, "She said . . . 'He should have stayed with me.'"

With no orders pending and only three customers in the cafe, the cook poured himself coffee, gathered up a couple of sections from the *Denver Post* piled by the cash register, sat at the counter, lit a cigarette, and started reading.

In the front section, he skimmed pieces summing up the early days of the Gerald Ford administration and Richard Nixon's hermit-like existence since his resignation. In sports, he checked on the status of Denver Broncos quarterback Charley Johnson's wobbly knees. On the cover of the Rocky Mountain West section, he read of the freshman cadets reporting to the Air Force Academy fifty miles away in Colorado Springs and laughed at the pictures of hair shorn as barbers showed no mercy. He opened the section, flipped a couple of pages and came to the beginning of the "Arts and Entertainment" pages.

The lead story startled him. Above the headline were three face shots of the woman who a few minutes earlier had been sitting in the booth behind him. All three were from the same interview session. In the first, she smiled. In the middle, she was pensive. In the third, she decisively was making a point with her hand.

The cook read the story twice.

"Nazi" Controversy Mars Telluride Film Festival
By Steven Garrison
Western Slope Bureau

TELLURIDE—By most standards, the inaugural Telluride Film Festival at the historic Sheridan Opera House in this southwestern Colorado mountain town was a spectacular success over the weekend, drawing marquee names, producing overflow crowds, and establishing itself as a can't-miss stop on the festival circuit.

Talks from acclaimed "Godfather" director Francis Ford Coppola and iconic actress Gloria Swanson were popular, but the appearance of German filmmaker Leni Riefenstahl, noted and criticized for her connection to Adolf Hitler and the Nazi Third Reich, drew the most attention.

Showings of two of the famed director's works—"Blue Light," a 1932 drama Riefenstahl also starred in, and Part 2 of "Olympia," a documentary about the 1936 Olympics in Berlin—were respectfully, even reverentially, received in the showcase evening's session. Many "Olympia" viewers were surprised to note that Riefenstahl placed a spotlight on a photogenic Coloradoan, American decathlon gold medalist Glenn Morris.

Riefenstahl was given thunderous standing ovations after both films, and also when she was awarded a silver medallion as one of the festival's main honorees. Her reaction was akin to those of prima ballerinas or opera sopranos, with her blowing kisses, repeatedly mouthing "thank you," and accepting flowers.

A showing of her most famous film, "Triumph of the Will," the documentary about the 1934 Nazi Party Congress in Nuremberg, was slotted for 1 a.m., drew a smaller crowd and surprisingly little reaction—positive or negative.

During the weekend, security was tight. However, protesters numbered less than a dozen and their actions didn't disrupt festival events.

Festival organizers, as they had earlier, noted that Riefenstahl never had been a member of the Nazi party.

Riefenstahl, still a striking woman at age 72, consented to interviews with individual reporters in her suite at the Manitou Lodge before the festival began, reiterating her claims that her films were the work of an artist and that she was neither philosophically nor politically aligned with Hitler and the Nazis.

"I am independent, always," she said. "Hitler said about me that 'Leni is as stubborn as a donkey.'"

She denied she ever had been romantically involved with the Nazi leader. "Because I am a woman and because he admired my work, people who were jealous or were looking for a good romantic story say I was his lover," she stated. "I was never Hitler's lover. We talked a few times on artistic things. Never politics. He didn't talk politics with artists."

Pointing out she was a successful actress and director before turning to documentaries, she asserted she made "Triumph of the Will" only after much convincing from Hitler, who told her that if his propaganda ministry oversaw the project "it would bore everybody." She said she told Hitler she was ignorant of the inner workings and militia designations of the Nazi Party, but that Hitler saw that as a positive, not a negative. She scoffed at the notion the film was propaganda. "It is a documentation, a newsreel done artistically," she claimed.

Swanson, the star of film's silent age, especially seemed incredulous that some considered Riefenstahl's presence deserving of criticism. "Why?" she asked. "Is she waving a Nazi flag? I thought Hitler was dead!"

The cook called Kristy over, gestured at the stool next to him, slid the section over on the counter to be in front of her, and asked, with eyebrows raised: "Recognize anyone?"

"That's her!"

"Sure is. Read it."

The cook returned to the kitchen. Soon, Kristy poked her head next to the order wheel.

"Okay, I've read it," she announced. "And it figures."

The cook asked, "How's it figure?"

"She left a quarter tip."

The grocer burst in, brandishing the same *Post* section, opened to the story.

"See!" he demanded, slapping the page with his free hand. "See!"

"Matter of fact, we did," the cook said dryly.

"I was guessing she was a Nazi bitch, all right," the grocer said. "Like all those others. We buried our buddies, we liberated the camps, we saw the human skeletons, then we heard about the Kraut bitches saying they had no goddamn idea what Hitler had in mind so give 'em and their kids food and feel sorry for 'em! But man . . ."

Pausing, he shook his head.

Then he continued, "This is *The* Nazi bitch. What did we do to deserve this honor?"

The cook shrugged. "Wish we could ask Glenn Morris," he said.

2

~

Glenn's Trials

Milwaukee: Saturday, June 27, 1936

Don't fall down.

Just finish.

As he reached the cinder track's final turn at the Marquette University stadium, Glenn Morris tried to ignore his aching legs and the sudden shortness of breath.

Two hundred meters more.

Then . . .

A hundred more.

The crowd cheered on the dark-haired runner in the Denver Athletic Club uniform. On the infield, his coach from Colorado State College of Agriculture and Mechanic Arts in Fort Collins, good, ol' Harry Hughes, yelled: "Don't let up!"

Almost there.

He made it across the finish line, and then slowed to a lurching walk, drawing his hands up behind his head and trying to gulp in air. A man with a stopwatch put his hand on Glenn's shoulder. "Third place," he said, "4 minutes, 48.1 seconds."

Glenn thrust one arm overhead, fist clenched.

Berlin, here I come!

Hughes, craggy-faced and graying at the temples, charged up and clamped him in a bear hug so enthusiastic, the coach's hat flew off. "World record!" the coach said excitedly.

All Glenn understood was that, unless everyone's computations had been way off, his time in the concluding 1,500 meters meant he had just won the decathlon at the U.S. Olympic Trials. All the hard work, all the dreaming . . . it had paid off.

"World record!" Hughes repeated. "You beat Sievert!"

Glenn turned. "You sure?"

"Meet director said you needed 4:50 . . . and you beat that!"

Soon, confirmation came: Glenn Morris, nine days after his twenty-fourth birthday, had set a world record. It was only the second decathlon of the former college football and track star's life; his first was only three months earlier, at the Kansas Relays in Lawrence. His 7,880 points at Milwaukee in the two-day, ten-event test of speed, strength, stamina, and versatility bettered German Hans Sievert's two-year-old mark. Bob Clark, best known as one of the nation's top broad jumpers, was second at 7,598, and Jack Parker, who had just finished his sophomore year of college in Sacramento, was third, at 7,290.

The top three would represent America at the Summer Games in Berlin.

During the Olympics-style awards ceremony, Glenn was on a higher platform in the center, between Clark and Parker. They accepted their ribbon-style medals and congratulations from Avery Brundage, the head of both the Amateur Athletic Union and the U.S. Olympic Committee, known for his rimless spectacles, his conservative and expensive suits, and his dictatorial manner and arrogance.

The decathlon men were the only Americans competing at the two-day meet who knew they had their Olympic spots clinched. The rest of the meet was the Central portion of the Olympic trials qualifications, coinciding with the West competition in Los Angeles and the East meet at Harvard. At the three regional meets, the top two finishers in each event qualified for the final U.S. Olympic trials at the new stadium on Randall's Island in New York on July 11 and 12. The grueling decathlon test took so much out of the decathlon athletes, organizers believed the Olympic team selections would need extra time to recover before Berlin. Plus, there weren't enough men crazy enough to compete in the decathlon to make regional trials necessary to thin the field.

After the formalities, Brundage called them off the stand for a private conversation. He said, "As you know, I competed in your event—and the pentathlon, too—in the 1912 Olympics . . ."

Glenn thought: *You did?*

". . . and I know you boys are going to represent us well in Germany." Brundage checked his watch. "I need to get to the train station now," he said.

"But I've got a suggestion." He reached into his inside breast pocket, pulled out a postcard-type advertisement and handed it to Glenn. "Since you know you're going to Germany, this is the place to have dinner and celebrate. Make sure you say I sent you and you'll be taken care of."

The card plugged the Café Brandenburg and displayed its motto: "You'll Think You're in Berlin."

⌁

When the three decathlon men and Hughes picked up their keys at the front desk of the hotel section at the Milwaukee Athletic Club, the clerk also handed the athletes stacks of telegrams. Glenn's was the thickest.

CONGRATULATIONS DARLING
LOVE KAREN

YOU MADE US PROUD
MOTHER & FATHER

ALL MEMBERS SALUTE YOU
DENVER ATHLETIC CLUB

HOW COME YOU'RE SO MUCH
BETTER AT THIS THAN FOOTBALL?
CONGRATS! RED WHITE

When Glenn chuckled at the last one, Clark gave him an inquiring look.

Glenn handed him the telegram, saying: "Our passer with the Aggies. He always said if I had any hands, he would have been an All-American."

Harry Hughes peeked over Clark's shoulder.

"Well, Red's got a point," the Aggies' football and track coach said.

Glenn tried to convince Hughes to join them for dinner, but the coach passed. "You guys go out and blow off some steam," Hughes said. "No coaches." He laughed and added, "No adults."

At the Café Brandenburg around the corner, the mustachioed maitre d' indeed perked up when they mentioned Brundage.

"Ah, the decathlon men! Herr Brundage said you might be coming."

He led them to a booth in the corner of the dining room nearest the bar. They ordered a round of beers.

Parker, who had just turned twenty, assured his elders he could drink them under the table, but added he was going to let them off the hook.

Glenn hadn't told his fellow decathlon men he rarely drank, in part because he'd learned the hard way it didn't take much beyond one beer to get him sloppy. In fact, many of the stories written about him in Colorado repeated the exaggeration that he was a complete teetotaler who greeted the end of prohibition three years earlier with complete indifference.

When the beers arrived, they clanked steins and agreed that one of them would win the gold in the decathlon for America . . . or they'd all die trying.

Clark pointed out the poster in a corner for a German American Bund rally scheduled for the next weekend in Grafton, Wisconsin, wherever that was.

"Guess we better get used to it," Clark said.

On the way to the bathroom, Glenn stopped to look at the Bund poster, and then noticed several movie posters next to it. The first was for *Das Blaue Licht*, and the detailed artwork showed a barefoot beautiful young woman in a ragged red dress, with a straw basket in her left hand, seemingly leading, or running away from, a mob of angry-looking bearded old men. Another for *Der Heilige Berg* featured a huge shot of a snow-capped mountain with cut-in pictures of the stars, including one who looked to be the same woman. The third was for *Die weisse Hölle vom Piz Palü* and again showed the actress, perched on top of a ridge in high boots. Glenn looked back over all three and figured out the actress's name: *Leni Riefenstahl.* It rang a bell, no more.

The maitre d' joined him.

"I assume you don't speak German?" the older man asked, smiling.

"No, sir," Glenn said. "A little French. That's it."

One by one, the maitre d' pointed at the three posters and translated the names. *The Blue Light. The Holy Mountain. The White Hell of Pitz Palü.* He turned his palm up in a presenting gesture, toward the caricature of the running woman on *The Blue Light* poster. "All, of course, starring Leni Riefenstahl," he said.

"She's very pretty," Glenn said.

"She also is, as you would say, a very tough cookie. She wrote and directed *The Blue Light*, too. But now, of course, she has her other sort of film work."

Noticing Glenn's blank look, he moved to another poster down the wall.

It showed a stern young German man in uniform—some sort of uniform— holding a red flag with a black swastika on a white circular background. Behind him loomed a castle-type building and a rendering of the Nazi state's eagle perched on a swastika. The lettering below the drawing:

Triumph
des Willens

Reichsparteitagfilm der N-S-D-A-P
Gesamtleitung—Regie—Leni Riefenstahl

The maitre d' explained, "'*Triumph of the Will*, a film of the National So-cialist Party Congress, producer and director Leni Riefenstahl.'" He paused. "It just came out last year."

"She's a Nazi?" Glenn asked incredulously.

The maitre d' was offended by the question. But he answered it. "No, she hasn't joined the party," he said. "Not many woman have. She also makes it clear she is a very independent artist."

On the way back to the table, Glenn stopped and looked again at *The Blue Light* poster. The woman in red. *Leni*.

Although he could have gotten by without doing so, he made two more trips to the bathroom before they left. On the second, he also noticed a front page of the *Milwaukee Journal* sports section, from a week earlier, taped to the mirror behind the bar. The blaring headline and huge pictures com-memorated German heavyweight Max Schmeling's shocking twelfth-round knockout of Joe Louis at Yankee Stadium.

The bartender noticed Glenn's interest and called out. "And we thought Herr Schmeling's best days were behind him!"

When the check came, Clark looked it over, his eyebrows raised.

"So much for Brundage's pull," he said, pointing. "Full bill. Not even a beer free." He reached for his wallet. "Start digging, boys."

As they were leaving, the maitre d' smiled at Glenn and held out a maga-zine.

"Here, young man," he said. "I found this in the back."

It was the February 17 issue of *Time*. On the cover, a woman in a modest swimsuit was on cross-country skis, climbing uphill at the site of the 1932 Winter Games. The caption under the picture announced:

HITLER'S LENI RIEFENSTAHL
At Garmisch-Partenkirchen, woman's work is never done

In his room, he skimmed the story about the Winter Olympics until he came to the passage on the filmmaker. It noted that she was twenty-eight and the daughter of a Berlin plumber. She had been a ballet star; a movie star, impressively doing her own dangerous stunts; and then the writer, director, and star in *The Blue Light*. The story reported Hitler and Riefenstahl had met in 1934, and the Nazi leader considered the actress a German womanly ideal even before commissioning her to make a documentary of the Nazi Party

Congress at Nuremberg. Answering an obvious question—one Glenn was asking, too—the writer said Hitler was a "confirmed celibate" and wasn't involved with Riefenstahl. It made light of Riefenstahl skiing at the Winter Games site in a swimsuit, as pictured on the cover, to work on her tan.

Glenn was gratified to catch the implication that she wasn't a Hitler mistress. But she had done so much. Ballet. Acting. Directing. And she was an athlete of sorts.

He thought of the contrast to Karen, a home economics and education student a year behind him. She was from Sterling, in northeastern Colorado, and her father was a chemist for a sugar company. They'd met at a dance in 1933, when the Fort Collins school was known as Colorado Agricultural College before its 1935 name change, and were known as a "serious" couple within a year. Karen supervised Glenn's diet during his training, emphasizing proteins and red meat. Glenn's affable landlady, feeling a part of the quest, went along with it, good-naturedly grousing that she should add ten dollars to his rent a month to cover the high cost of meat. Other times, Karen came over and did the cooking, either before or after she often held a stopwatch and timed Glenn in his workouts on the outdoor track or in the field house.

Glenn nodded each time someone said of Karen, "Oh, she's such a nice girl," implying, of course, that he was lucky to have her and she was the sort of upstanding young woman he should consider himself lucky to settle down with. She went fishing with him and held her own, and turned many heads on the dance floor.

As Karen neared graduation that spring of '36, she mentioned they should make "plans." When Glenn said he needed to devote all his attention to making the Olympic team and winning a gold medal, Karen looked hurt.

"Oh, honey, don't take it that way," he said, hugging her. "I just mean it's not the right time to make those kinds of decisions. We have plenty of time."

Three days later, she quietly told him that she had accepted a teaching job for the 1936–37 academic year at the high school in Fountain, just south of Colorado Springs. As Glenn headed for Berlin, their relationship seemed "solid," but getting too specific about their future was taboo. At least that's what Glenn thought.

He resolved to send her a return telegram from the train station.

In the morning, he packed the magazine at the bottom of his suitcase, under his clothes.

He forgot to send the telegram.

3

~

Leni's Truth

Berlin

Leni Riefenstahl never lied. Whatever she said became Leni's Truth. She believed it whenever she said it . . . until she needed to say something else.

So as the thirty-three-year-old former dancer and actress immersed herself in preparing for the making of a documentary about the Berlin Games, Leni's Truth was that Hitler and the National Socialist Party leadership had little to do with the project.

Leni's Truth was that the commission came from Dr. Carl Diem, the secretary-general of the German Olympic Organizing Committee, and that the International Olympic Committee signed off on the assignment.

Leni's Truth was that she lined up the funding from a German film company, Tobis, and formed her own Olympia-Film, in partnership with her brother, Heinz, specifically for the project.

As with many contrivances, there were shards of reality in it.

Leni emphasized to all who would listen, and some who wouldn't, that Diem saw *Victory of Faith* and *Triumph of the Will*, her films about the National Socialist Party Congresses in Nuremberg and aggressively pursued and lobbied her to make a documentary about the 1936 Games.

Of course, it wasn't Leni's fault that *Victory of Faith*, about the 1933 Congress, was withdrawn from theaters and banned from further distribution because of a minor inconvenience. Ernst Röhm, the leader of the *Sturmabteilung*, the SA Storm Troopers, was one of the "stars" of the film, seemingly inseparable from Hitler. But responding to the perceived threat of the SA's independent militancy, Hitler had Röhm murdered in mid-1934 in the "Night of the Long Knives" purge of SA leadership. The good fortune for Leni as a filmmaker was that *Victory of Faith*—relatively amateurish given that she had to put together a crew hurriedly and did little preparation—turned out to be a trial run for her.

Leni's Truth was that Diem saluted her adroitness in making them compelling films without allowing them to become propaganda pieces. She was an independent artist, a filmmaker, not a shill! She wasn't a National Socialist Party member! Speeches in the films, even Hitler's, were brief, and dogma was absent! These were chronicles of events and men, not of party doctrine! Hadn't Diem been heard to say that Fraulein Riefenstahl had the body of an actress, the grace and sensuality of a dancer, the intellect of a scholar, and the eye of a painter—all combined in a peerless filmmaker?

Diem excitedly outlined a plan to light the first of many magnesium torches with a flame at the original Games site at Olympia in southwest Greece, transport the flame in a relay of many runners to Berlin, light the flame in the Olympic Stadium during the opening ceremonies, and keep it burning through the sixteen days of the Games. Leni mulled the cinematic possibilities of following the flame. Inspired and intrigued, she knew that if she made the film, she had her title.

Olympia.

Leni's Truth was that she finally gave in, excited and deciding that she would take daring risks. *Olympia* was being made for the world, albeit with Germany in the spotlight as the host nation. She *believed* all that when she said it. In fact, however, the Third Reich's propaganda ministry funded and, because of that, at least implicitly controlled the project. "Forgotten" were her frequently distasteful negotiations with Dr. Joseph Goebbels, the propaganda minister, to secure the Third Reich funding. When meeting her a couple of years earlier, the club-footed philanderer had acted like a teenager with a crush, telling her he waited outside the Berlin theater at the 1926 premiere of *The Holy Mountain*, starry-eyed and trying to see her on the way out. He gushed about her work, especially *Triumph of the Will*, in public and was willing to take credit with the Führer for aiding it. Leni fought off his advances and ignored his threats that if she didn't become his mistress, she would regret it. Other actresses had been smart enough to give in; surely Leni would do so, too.

The slimy Goebbels was living proof that Leni's opportunism had limits.

Still, in August 1935, Goebbels approved a lush budget of 1.5 million reichsmarks for the film, all coming from the Reich treasury, with the funds dispersed to Leni in four installments, beginning in November 1935 and ending in January 1937. Leni's fee of 250,000 reichsmarks was to include her own expenses. She briefly considered the possibility that Goebbels was buying her silence about his clumsy advances, but quickly realized his response would have been to laugh in her face. Magda Goebbels knew of Goebbels's affairs. So any threat to disclose his misbehavior to his wife would have drawn snide laughter from Goebbels, and he would have said Magda had a good life and wasn't going to protest his indulgences; and also that Hitler didn't care. So in reality, while *Olympia* wasn't the Nazis' idea, they quickly discerned its potential advantages for the Third Reich and arranged to pay for it. Leni's company, Olympia-Film, was incorporated in December 1935, long after the deal with Goebbels was closed, and then only as a dodge to camouflage the Third Reich's control. Under terms of the agreement between Leni and Goebbels, Olympia-Film eventually would become the Third Reich's property.

It was ludicrous to portray Leni operating as independently in the making of the film as if, say, a Canadian had been commissioned by the International Olympic Committee and the German Organizing Committee to produce a documentary of the Berlin Games. Yet that's what Leni tried to do. That was Leni's Truth. And now, with the opening of the Games only a month away, after over a year of research and planning how to deploy her forty-five cameramen, plus rehearsal shooting at other sports events, she was desperate to get her way on several key issues. Otherwise, her vision for *Olympia*—and her dream for her future—would be threatened. The *Time* story during the Winter Games had reminded her that the world's view of her was distorted and unfair, and for it to be corrected, she would need to come up with a project appreciated in Great Britain and America.

Leni didn't mind that the magazine parroted the most extreme of her varied claims about her age, making her five years younger than she actually was. She wasn't bothered that *Time* also didn't have her meeting Hitler for the first time until 1934, a year after his ascension to power. Actually, their first encounter was in 1932. Leni went to hear Hitler's rant about the ineffectiveness of President Paul von Hindenburg, wrote him a letter of appreciation, and then was astounded to be invited to meet him. At that audience, Hitler confessed that he, too, was a fan of her on-screen work, especially *The Blue Light*.

Those inaccuracies in the *Time* story bought into Leni's Truth, but what bothered her was the article's sarcastic tone and that it influenced worldwide opinion. The cover and article seemed to imply that she was at the Winter Games on a skiing holiday as an honored Hitler guest. Rather, she was a true winter sports fan who also was there with her top six cameramen to ponder and again practice the techniques that she and her crew would use in following the athletes at the Summer Games.

The Blue Light made it to some American theaters, and the gushing letters from America proved she had English-speaking fans among niche, big-city cinema enthusiasts. *S.O.S. Iceberg* was supposed to add to that, but the English-language version of the film for America's Universal and studio czar Carl Laemmle was a badly put-together embarrassment. She wanted to be given a fair chance in America with films she could be proud of.

She was determined that when she directed and starred in her next film, it would be as an artist whose work deserved worldwide exposure and respect. For that, she had to use *Olympia* to completely dispel, not add to, her undeserved image as a documentary maker under the control of Nazi leaders.

In her third meeting with the handful of German men who served on the Berlin Games' Athletics Organization Committee, she opened on the offensive in the ongoing argument over camera placements in the Olympic Stadium for the featured track and field competition.

"This is ridiculous," she said irritably. "You have to have the courage to stop saying it's not within your power to make these decisions. I went through all the channels to find the right people at the International Amateur Athletic Federation and the International Olympic Committee and by the time we'd gone back and forth and wasted weeks, they said, 'We will need to see what you have in mind once all the officials and participants arrive!' I can't wait that long. I must set up!" She gestured at Diem, next to her. "Dr. Diem has made it clear he is supporting me on this!"

"Within reason, within reason," Diem said.

Leni considered which role and cards to play.

"I must have saturation camera coverage from imaginative vantage points, not just a camera or two we hope isn't blocked at the wrong time. My cameramen must have access to the entire floor of the stadium. We must be able to start digging our camera pits. We must be able to set up the rail along the track to slide our camera on, following the runners. We must be able to erect the four tower cameras at the corners of the infield. No more 'Maybe this, maybe that.'"

"We have heard this all before," one official said.

"Yes, you have. I do not do anything halfway. Nothing by halves! If I must, I will shut down this project. That wouldn't sit well with those who want the international exposure and respect this film would provide for this nation. Everyone would benefit, including . . ."

She stopped. *Surely these imbeciles got the message. Everyone would benefit, including the Führer.*

The head of the committee, a lean fifty-something physician, sighed. "Fraulein, I will try to explain this to you again."

Leni glared. "I know it pains you to be speaking to a woman as an equal, Herr Görter, but don't speak to me as if I am your maid."

"Fraulein," Görter said wearily, "we are trying to help you. It will not help you if we say you can put your people and cameras in areas, but then everyone—coaches, athletes, heads of delegations—is horrified when they get there and see what you have in mind. If they protest and you are made to remove your equipment, fill in your pits and remove your towers, that would set you back. And it would be embarrassing for all . . . including you, correct? And including . . ."

He let it hang there, knowing even Leni understood he meant . . . *including the Führer*.

He tried to sound conciliatory. "Are you *sure* you can't wait until the teams and officials begin to arrive?"

"No! We must allow enough time for everything to be ready by the time the competition starts."

Diem clasped his hands in front of him. "All right, scuttling this project is not an option, for many reasons. Waiting to confer with the foreign delegations and IOC and IAAF officials apparently is not an option, either."

Leni shook her head. No, it wasn't.

Diem continued, "Then we must come to a compromise agreement here. What can we all support in the stadium—and, more important, continue to stand behind if there are objections?"

Görter sighed. "I can guarantee you that there will be objections to the camera catapulting along the track on that rail. As you describe it, Fraulein, it is very ingenious, but very distracting. And eight pits for the cameras will be too many. We'll have people saying athletes will be falling into them all over the place. I don't completely understand the necessity for the cameras and the photographers to be at or below ground."

"Angles and background," Leni snapped. "Shooting up, the sky becomes the background."

"You are the artist. I suppose that makes sense. But eight pits? *Eight?*"

"For the various events," Leni said, as if there could be no dispute.

Another man cut in. "And if you want to be shooting up, how do you explain the four towers?"

"Different angles, shooting down. Variety. Again, not the standard shots."

Twenty minutes later, Leni had accepted a compromise of six below-ground camera pits, strategically placed around the landing areas in field events and near the track, and two towers in the infield. She agreed that she would demonstrate the unmanned camera following the runners on the rail along the track for International Olympic Committee officials before the Games began—and remove it if they objected. She agreed to have no more than six cameras in the stadium at any given time. And the committee agreed it would treat the terms as a fait accompli. They emphasized they couldn't guarantee the IOC and International Association of Athletics Federations (IAAF) would accept everything, but they would make a point of saying Leni had accepted many compromises and even rejections.

After handshakes all around, Leni accompanied Diem to his office down the hall. Diem's assistant, Werner Klingeberg, who hadn't been in the meeting, was waiting for a report.

Diem shook his head in wonderment for ten seconds. Finally, he said, directing his comments at his assistant, "She's amazing."

"Thank you," Leni said, smiling.

"I keep waiting for someone—on the Games committee or even in the Reich Chancellery and Gestapo—to say having the *Hindenburg* above the stadium with Fraulein Riefenstahl's camera is an intrusion, or a security risk. Nothing."

"It is a tribute to German ingenuity," Leni said.

Diem continued, still ignoring Leni, "She goes in saying she'll ask for eight camera pits and settle for four. She got six."

"Yes, I did," declared Leni.

"She goes in saying the sliding camera along the track is expendable, so she lets them say maybe on that, acting as if she has made the biggest concession of our times," Diem said.

"It worked at the national championships," Leni said, shrugging. "But I don't have a lot of faith in it."

"She said she could get the job done with six cameras in the stadium," Diem said. "She got six."

"Oh, I'll have more than six. You think anyone's going to be counting?"

"And I still assume there will be *some* objections, and you still might have to remove some of these things."

"I know that. If most of it stays, I will be satisfied."

Klingeberg offered his hand to Leni. "Congratulations," he said. "We could have used you at Versailles."

4

~

Dempsey, Runyon, Morris

By the time Glenn arrived in New York to watch the final Olympic Trials and train, he was far better known nationally than even when he secured a spot on the American team and set a world record. That was because many sports scribes jumped on the "Morris story" after the Milwaukee meet, reasoning it was a "safe" angle. Most of the rest of the team wouldn't be determined until the meet at Randall's Island, and the Trials ended only three days before the U.S. delegation's departure for Berlin on July 15.

One piece by Associated Press sports editor Alan Gould ran in many newspapers across the land, including in the *Fort Collins Coloradoan*. Gould quoted Amateur Athletic Union secretary-treasurer Daniel J. Ferris, who raved about Glenn's chances to win at Berlin. "Morris combines extraordinary speed with the technique and stamina so essential to sustaining a high average of performance in the ten-event test," Ferris said. "In 1912, Jim Thorpe had great speed and agility but was weak in some field events. Four years ago, Jim Bausch capitalized on ability in the weight events and the pole vault to achieve a world record victory at Los Angeles." Gould also wrote, "No decathlon performer ever has shown the Coloradoan's speed at foot-racing or hurdling, and at the same time managed to keep up with the leaders in the field events." Gould did concede Glenn's potential Achilles' heel in the pole vault, where his best in his two competitions was an anemic 11 feet, 4 inches—or nearly 2 feet under what Bausch cleared in Los Angeles. He also noted what many considered the strangest aspect, worthy of second-guessing, about Glenn's decathlon style: Although he was right-handed in all other things, he pole-vaulted "left-handed," holding and carrying the pole to his left, with his left hand on top as he vaulted. But that seemed the most natural to Glenn when he first tried it, and his attempts at vaulting "right-handed" were disastrous.

The Denver newspapers also profiled him, but the writers didn't talk with him. Glenn told his friends at first that he had no idea where the scribes got some of the malarkey in the stories, but Harry Hughes explained that the Denver Athletic Club, his sponsor, was across the street from the Denver Press Club, the watering hole for Denver newspaper writers. The two memberships mingled. Stories were made up and kept getting better each time they were retold. And some of them ended up in the papers.

However, Glenn realized he had no right to complain about the DAC. The club again came through, raising money for a travel fund, and there was enough for Glenn to ride the train and be in New York on July 6, a full five days before the final Trials. The reasoning was that he could get in hard training at the Randall's Stadium site before the Trials started, continue to work out as he watched the other athletes attempt to secure their spots on the team, and try to be in peak condition before boarding the SS Manhattan for the trip across the Atlantic. At his first workout at Randall's Island, he met with USA team assistant coach Brutus Hamilton, who won the decathlon silver medal in the 1920 Games and now was the track coach at the University of California. Hamilton declared he would be there to help, not interfere with Glenn's training program—especially since he knew and respected Harry Hughes. "The scary thing is that you're not even close to your peak in this," Hamilton told him. "We're going to do what we can in the two weeks there before you compete, to get you as close to that peak as possible after the boat ride."

Once the Trials began, U.S. team head coach Lawson Robertson often spotted Glenn, called him over and asked, "Say, have you met . . . ?" He had met many of the top athletes at Milwaukee or earlier, but he especially enjoyed again talking with the ace middle-distance man, Glenn Cunningham. The former University of Kansas runner was the much-admired fourth-place finisher in the 1,500 meters in the 1932 Games, and the world record holder in the mile. By the end of the meet, Glenn had shaken hands with the majority of his future Berlin teammates, and he was especially thrilled to meet renowned Negro sprinter and broad jumper Jesse Owens.

Glenn also made sure he talked with the three pole-vaulters—Earle Meadows, Bill Sefton and Bill Graber—who made the team. Meadows and Sefton both were University of Southern California students, while Graber, in his mid-twenties, was a graduate of the same school. So there were a lot of USC sweatshirts and other gear around the pole vault pit. The discus also was a decathlon event, and Glenn had room for improvement there, too, so he made sure to find the American aces. Ken Carpenter was another USC product and Gordon Dunn was from Stanford. Glenn also found himself talking a lot with the third qualifier, Cornell man Walter Wood, and the Easterner's self-effacing sense of humor was refreshing.

George Whitman, head of the DAC's sports committee, came to New York to officially give him a good-luck sendoff, and he lobbied Glenn about the advantages of moving to Denver, sixty-five miles south of Fort Collins, after the Games.

"But I need to eat," Glenn pointed out.

"If you're in Denver, our people will be able to take care of you," Whitman said. "I can guarantee right now you could be a buyer for the department store. As long as you're representing the DAC, we'll make sure you have time to train properly. I think we can take care of you better than those hayseeds up in Fort Collins."

Whitman's smile took some of the edge off that, so Glenn didn't react. The "hayseeds" in Fort Collins always would have his gratitude for stepping up when Glenn was a greenhorn kid from Simla trying to scrape his way through college. He and Whitman left it that they'd talk about it again after Glenn returned, and they both understood what was left unspoken—the higher he finished in the decathlon, the more in demand he would be.

On the day after the track and field trials ended, the Olympic teams in all sports assembled at the plush Hotel Lincoln on Eighth Avenue, between 44th and 45th Streets. They had forty-eight hours before their departure for Berlin. Glenn was gratified to discover that his assigned roommate, at the hotel, on the SS *Manhattan*, and in the Olympic Village in Berlin, was the good-humored Cornell discus thrower, Walter Wood. They spent the first afternoon in lower Manhattan with many of their track and field teammates, obtaining passports. They had been told their Olympic ID cards would get them into Germany and back into the United States, but they needed to get passports, too, in case they participated in the post-Olympic exhibition meets in Europe. Glenn also waited in line in a huge meeting room to pick up his team and Olympic ID cards, plus a stack of information that included an Athletes' Handbook, outlining what was acceptable—and not acceptable—from here on. During the conversations with teammates, Glenn quickly learned the athletes' traditional tongue-in-cheek name for all AOC officials: Badgers. Nobody was quite sure how it came about, but it had been handed down. Badgers this, Badgers that . . .

When Brutus Hamilton wandered by, Glenn asked him about the post-Olympic meets. Nobody seemed to be willing to be specific about the possibilities.

Hamilton said, "The one I know about is London—a dual meet with the Brits—and that's even the day before the closing ceremonies. But Brundage keeps talking about negotiating with a lot of other places, too, for after that. That's why you guys don't have definite return dates. And it's why you're supposed to sign those 'leave of absence' forms in your packet there, so you've officially signed up to participate."

"I heard that."

"We might be coming back in several groups on separate ships. Some of the rich kids will stay over there until Christmas or something and then pay their own way back."

"How many of those do you think there'd be?"

"A few."

Hamilton laughed and said a couple of his teammates on the '20 team at Antwerp didn't return home at all. "I guess they met Belgian girls and decided to stay," he said.

"Can't imagine that happening this time," Glenn said.

Hamilton's eyes widened. "Have you *seen* many German women?"

Glenn thought of the *Blue Light* poster. But he said, "I don't mean that. I mean all the things going on there now."

Hamilton shrugged. "Leaders come and go."

At the sendoff banquet, Glenn and the decathlon men were pleasantly surprised to find themselves placed at a table near the dais with, among others, retired heavyweight champion Jack Dempsey. It had been nine years since Dempsey's final fight, the "long count" loss to Gene Tunney. On an exploratory walk around the Times Square area earlier in his visit, Glenn had ducked into the new "Jack Dempsey's Broadway Restaurant," ordered a sandwich, and looked at pictures and souvenirs from the champ's career. He was disappointed to find that Dempsey wasn't in the restaurant at the time, and he hadn't dreamed that he soon would be sitting next to the champ at dinner.

"They were going to put me with the boxers," Dempsey roared, enthusiastically pumping Glenn's hand. "I said I wanted to be with the boy from Colorado I've been reading about."

"Thanks, sir."

"Call me Jack, for Chrissakes."

"Yes, sir."

Dempsey asked, "Did you know I was from Colorado, too?"

"Sure," Glenn said. Grinning, he added, "The Manassa Mauler!"

The table's Badger host referred to a sheet as he made the introductions. The table's guests included the three decathlon men, three rowers, Dempsey, a Broadway producer, a publisher, and the president of Fordham University.

Dempsey gestured for Glenn to take the seat next to him. Glenn caught Parker and Clark's grins, amused rather than jealous, he decided.

"First question," Dempsey said. "Where the hell is Simla?"

Glenn told him.

"Hope that didn't offend you," Dempsey said, "but nobody knows where Manassa is, either."

Glenn knew the lore of a young Dempsey brawling his way through the Colorado mountain mining towns on his way to boxing glory, and he was fairly certain Manassa was somewhere in the Rocky Mountains.

"Everybody thinks it's in the mountains somewhere," Dempsey said.

"It isn't?" asked the Broadway producer.

"No, damn it," Dempsey said disgustedly. "It's in the San Luis Valley, over by Alamosa. It was my family and a bunch of Mormons. Me and my brothers and sisters loved it. I was fishing and hunting on the Conejos before I was old enough to go to school! We all cried—well, at least I did—when we moved, but we ended up in Uncompahgre, and that was fun, too. Anyway, we were so poor, we didn't even know any better."

Glenn told the champ about growing up on the family farm in Simla.

Eventually, the conversation opened up, with Clark and Parker joining in to explain the tricks of the decathlon—maximize your points in your best events and avoid disaster in your worst—and the rowers surprising the trackmen by explaining the U.S. crew was the team from the University of Washington in Seattle, taken en masse after winning the Trials.

As they finished their slices of apple pie, Dempsey spotted an approaching emaciated man in round eyeglasses and with a Turkish Oval cigarette hanging from his mouth.

"Here's a sight!" Dempsey exclaimed, jumping up and blocking the man's path. The other man seemed more concerned that he wasn't going to be able to get to the bathroom within the next minute than he was impressed that the former heavyweight champion of the world was greeting him.

Dempsey gestured at the rest of the table. "To those of you who haven't had the pleasure . . . this is Pueblo, Colorado's own Damon Runyon, the man who nicknamed me the Manassa Mauler."

"They stopped claiming me in Pueblo long ago," the famous writer said with a tight smile.

Dempsey wasn't going to take a crack at getting all the names of the men around the table right, but he turned and gestured at Glenn. "Jesus, three guys from Colorado within spitting distance of Times Square," Dempsey said. "What are the odds of that?"

"All life is six to five against!" Glenn said, surprising even himself.

Flattered that Glenn remembered an often-quoted line from the story "A Nice Price" in his most recent collection, Runyon reached out to shake his hand.

"You must be 'The Simla Sensation,'" Runyon said.

After Runyon left, the publisher said, "It must pain Runyon to be here."

"Why?" asked the host Badger.

"He was against sending a team to Berlin," the publisher said. "Ranted against it for months. The Nazis and the Jewish business."

"So why *is* he here?"

"Free whisky?" asked a rower.

"He hasn't had a drink in years," the Broadway producer said. "Doesn't want to ruin his image by talking about it, but it's true."

Dempsey said, "I'll tell you why he's here." He looked at Glenn and the other athletes. "The boat's leaving tomorrow, right? You're going to be on it, right? The debate's over. Now it's time to get behind you. Put all the other bullshit aside."

"Amen," said the publisher.

"Thanks," Dempsey said. "And the best way to shut up the Nazis is to win all the gold medals, right?"

Glenn smiled uneasily. "We'll do our best," he said.

Five minutes later, Bob Clark grinned at Glenn. "Hey, Simla Sensation, . . . pass the sugar, will ya?"

After the banquet ended, and Glenn stood by his table, he noticed a chunky man of perhaps forty approaching, with a hand up to get his attention. The man had dark sharply parted hair, wore big glasses and had a pipe in one hand.

"Hi, Glenn," the man said, extending his hand. "I'm Paul Gallico of the *New York Daily News*."

"Hello, Mr. Gallico," Glenn said.

Another famous writer!

"It's Paul," Gallico said.

"Okay . . . Paul."

"I'll be on the ship with you folks, and I'm wondering if we can sit down tomorrow after we shove off and chat."

"An interview?"

"Yes . . . I want to tell my readers about you. I think it'll be good if they feel like they know you when they hear about you competing over there."

"I guess that would be all right."

"Good, I appreciate it. I'll find you tomorrow and we'll talk."

Dempsey had been shaking hands and signing autographs, but he noticed Gallico and joined them.

"Oh, my God, watch what you say to this guy!" the fighter said to Glenn, joking. He "punched" Gallico in the shoulder. "Did he tell you about sparring with me so he could write about it? Now he's telling people that he kicked my ass for three rounds."

"My memory's going, Champ," Gallico said, smiling. "That's how hard you hit me."

Gallico peeled off, waved at Glenn and said as he moved, "See you tomorrow!"

The Broadway producer broke off from conversation with friends, too, and shook Glenn's hand again. "Good luck, Morris. You can do me two favors over there. First, win the gold medal." Glenn waited. The producer leaned closer and said, "Second, stick it right up Hitler's ass."

Glenn smiled. "I'll see what I can do . . . about winning it, at least."

5

~

Bon Voyage

In the middle of the Hotel Lincoln lobby, the pot-bellied small-time lawyer in an ill-fitting American Olympic Committee blazer bellowed through a megaphone. Sweat dripped down the Badger's face despite the early-morning hour.

"Gentlemen . . . and ladies! Have your Olympic identification card out. Show it when you get on a bus, so we can check you off. From here on out, you have to assume nobody's going to recognize you or take your word for who you are! That's everywhere, but also, if Mr. Hitler is around, the more likely they'll be to react and ask questions later. So when men in strange uniforms tell you where to go or where not to go, do what they say."

Glenn thought of the Broadway producer's suggestion the night before and smiled. Then, looking at the Badger in his funny suit, he laughed. An elbow dug sharply into his ribs. Next to Glenn, his eyes narrowed by fury, was the spunky Jewish sprinter from New York City. *Barely out of high school. Looks more like one of these corner newsboys hawking New York papers than an athlete. Glickman. Marty Glickman.*

"What's the idea, Marty?"

"You think that's funny?"

"Think *what's* funny?"

"The Nazis' bullshit."

"Hold on," Glenn said, pointing at the Badger. "I was just thinking about *him* warning us to put up with a bunch of guys in funny uniforms over there. That's all we've been doing for the past two days here!"

Not wanting to sound too cocky, Glenn didn't bring up the producer's suggestion for what to do after winning the gold medal.

"Do you even *know* what the Nuremberg Laws are?" Glickman asked sharply.

"Absolutely," Glenn said.

"You're comparing the Nazis and some guys telling us to get in line to pick up a handbook?"

"You're reading too much into this," Glenn said. "Way too much."

Jack Torrance, the huge shot-putter beloved as "Baby Jack" and "Baby Elephant," stepped between them. Glickman needed to stand on his toes and lean to the side to even see the six-foot-two Morris; and that made, first, the decathlete, and then the sprinter, laugh. If anything was going to foil Torrance in Berlin, it was that the world record-holder and former football player at Louisiana State University had gotten fat and flabby after leaving college while serving as a Baton Rouge policeman. The rumor was the scales at the physicals couldn't even handle him, and that he was up to at least 325 pounds.

"Now boys," Torrance drawled. "Need I remind you we're all on the same team from here on?"

"Honest, Marty," Glenn said, "I didn't mean anything by it . . . except against the Badgers."

Shaking his head, Glickman said, "Sorry. I guess all this has me a little on edge. I'm going to the *Olympics*, but it doesn't feel right. I'm starting to wonder if Brundage insisted we go over there just so he could hug Hitler and tell him what fine ideas he has."

"I understand, Marty," Glenn said. "Or at least I'm trying to."

"Good," Torrance said. "Now shake hands . . . or no more throwing lessons for you, Morris, and I'll accidentally drop a shot put on your toes, Glickman, about the time we're passing Greenland."

Torrance stepped aside, letting them shake hands, and then said. "So we're square? From here on out, it's all red, white, and blue, one for all, and all for one."

Glenn felt old, telling himself: *When I was Marty's age, "the world" was the globe in the corner of Old Man DeWitt's history room at the high school . . . and I didn't know much about it.*

Outside the hotel, as a small band played "Stars and Stripes Forever," New York policemen on horses formed a corridor for the athletes to pass through on the way to the buses. Other officers on motorcycles waited to give them an escort to the docks.

Several curious Olympians already were by the buses, gathered around the revolutionary Harley-Davidson VLH chase models, asking questions of the policemen drivers. Others emerging from the hotel were making a beeline for the motorcycles, too. Instead, Glenn stopped at the line of horses, patted the face of a light bay beneath a burly cop and asked its name.

"Golden Boy," the cop said.

Glenn laughed. He leaned close to the bay's ear as he continued to pet. "Golden Boy," he said softly. "Hope that's an omen."

The cop reached in his pocket and held out a carrot to Glenn. "Be careful," the cop said. "Don't want a bite to knock you out of the Olympics."

"Oh, don't worry," Glenn assured him. "I know horses."

"You a country boy?" the cop asked, smiling, and then he nodded as Glenn answered the question with his hand, holding it flat so the horse could nip the treat from his palm.

"Well, guarantee you," Glenn said, "you've never heard of my hometown."

"What is it?"

"Simla, Colorado."

"Can't say I have. Maybe you'll put it on the map."

"Oh, it's on the map. But nobody knows where to look."

The bus rides were short enough to make many of the Olympians grumble that it would have been easier to walk. At Pier 60, at the end of West 20th Street, the SS *Manhattan*, 705 feet long and less than five years old, was draped with red, white, and blue bunting. Newsreel photographers crowded together to document the athletes' gawking reactions as they got off the buses and started the walk to the ship, carrying suitcases.

"I'm getting seasick already," Walter Wood complained.

"It's all in your head," said Glenn.

"Keep telling yourself that . . . until you throw up."

Judging from the yells at the dock, a lot of the athletes—mainly those from the East, Glenn supposed—had friends and family members gathered to see them off.

A man marched up and down the pier, carrying a sign announcing: "Boycott Germany, Land of Darkness." He was noticed, but ignored.

As Glenn was about to step onto the ramp leading up to the deck, a taxicab screeched to a stop nearby, sending band members and well-wishers scrambling. A young woman jumped out, jamming a white cowboy hat on her head. She wore a stylish outfit of billowy white slacks and a white jacket over a blue blouse. That, plus white cowboy boots.

She called out, "You didn't think you were leaving without me, did you?"

A couple of the male swimmers broke ranks to greet her, and one even grabbed her suitcase from the taxi driver. An impeccably dressed man got out of the other side, skirted the back of the cab, then grabbed the woman, planted a huge kiss and didn't let go. It knocked his breast-pocket handkerchief askew, but he didn't seem to mind. The swimmers and others hooted.

"I assume that's Eleanor Holm," Bob Clark said dryly.

"Eleanor Holm Jarrett now," said swimmer Al Vande Weghe, who hadn't joined the mob. "That's her husband, the bandleader." He chuckled. "I hope."

Eleanor's reputation was known to even the most sheltered members of the Olympic entourage. The Olympic Committee put up with her because at age sixteen, the New York girl turned down the Ziegfeld Follies to give swimming a try ("I've always had gold-medal tits!" she liked to brag); at age eighteen, won a gold medal in the 1932 Games in the 100-meter backstroke at Los Angeles; was an actress on a $500-a-week retainer at Warner Brothers without much success; and now, as a twenty-two-year-old "veteran," continued to draw considerable attention to the Olympic program. Even more important, she was favored to win again in Berlin. The swimming coaches *encouraged* her to go her own way, hoping she wouldn't "contaminate" the younger girl swimmers. She bragged about paying only casual attention to swimming as she sang with her husband's band and bragged of training on "champagne and cigarettes." At the Olympic Trials, she easily qualified for a return trip to the Games, then responded to the first writer who asked how she felt: "Got any hair of the dog?" The word among the athletes was that she actually trained hard around her singing stints with her husband's band, and had given in to the coaching of sportswriters to go along with the exaggerations. But there also wasn't any doubt that she had a good time along the way.

Watching her over his shoulder, Wood laughed. "Think she's in tourist class with the rest of us?" he asked. "Looks like she could afford a cabin ticket."

"At the team meeting the other day, she said that's what she was going to do," Vande Weghe said, falling in stride with them. "But the Badgers said everybody had to be in third class. I give her credit, though. She was mad at first, but then she said, what the hell, it'd save her a hundred and eighty-six bucks. A hundred and eighty-six bucks! And she said nobody was going to stop her if she went to see her friends in first class. But she said if Clark Gable or Fredric March are on the first deck, don't look around for her and don't believe the rumors."

Most of the 382 members of the American Olympic team were on the passenger list, and they were ticketed to stay on the two lower decks. On the ship, roughly another 400 passengers were coaches and officials, family members, and journalists bound for Berlin, too. That left about 300 passengers considered "outside" the Olympic traveling party. While there was no mention of Gable or March, the buzz the night before at the sendoff banquet was that their fellow passengers would include famed actress Mary Astor, plus playwright Charles MacArthur and his wife, Helen Hayes, relaxing following the recent withdrawal of the alienation of affection lawsuit filed against Hayes by MacArthur's first wife.

Once aboard, Glenn let Walter Wood check the sheet with their room assignment and the map and lead the way. Comparing notes among the decathlon men and the discus throwers, they discovered that their three rooms were together. Discus throwers Ken Carpenter and Gordon Dunn were in one room, Glenn and Wood in the middle, and decathletes Jack Parker and Bob Clark in the third. So the six of them set off together.

After a few minutes and a lot of steps and turns, Dunn, the Stanford graduate, wondered, "Hey, guys, you think it's a good idea to let a Cornell guy read a map?"

"Should be just around the corner, then at the end of the hall," Wood insisted.

Jesse Owens was in a doorway, wearing a smart dark blue pinstriped suit. He grinned. "Welcome to third class, boys, where *you're* colored, too! Know your place!"

Glenn stopped. Smiling and pointing, he said, "Nice suit, Jesse. You're putting the rest of us to shame."

Owens responded, "The fifth time you see me wearing this, you'll figure out . . . it's the only one I've got!"

Glenn laughed. "I got my first for my high school graduation," he said. "I got my second for my college graduation. Don't know when I'm going to be able to afford a third one, either."

Owens said, "Brundage already asked me where I got this. Pretended he just thought it was nice and wanted to know where it came from. But I know the way he thinks. Dress too nice and he just assumes we're taking money under the table."

"He was laying that on thick in Milwaukee," Glenn said. "We must be 'pure' amateurs and 'sportsmen,' untainted by professionalism."

"I hope to be 'tainted' pretty damn soon," Jesse said. "As tainted as I can get. I have a wife and a kid to support."

As they turned the corner, Ken Carpenter said to Glenn, "He's going to win three gold medals . . . right?"

"Four, if they put him on the relay."

"Sounds like he thinks he'd be set for life."

"Anything wrong with that?" Glenn asked.

"Hell, no," Carpenter said. "But I wonder if he'd have offers coming at him like he thinks they will. You know . . . this still is America. For better or worse."

Glenn wondered, too. This trip and the Olympic experience, in fact, would be his first extended interaction with Negroes. There hadn't been any in Simla, and while there were rumors of a few attending college in Fort Collins, he had never seen any, and his teammates in every sport had been white boys. It had taken track and field to introduce him to Negroes, and he surprised himself with his acceptance of the sport's integration. He was used to the questions from friends about competing with, or against, "monkeys," "gorillas," and "niggers," and even the impertinence of whether he had to shower with the "bucks." But judging from what he had seen and felt in New York, he was convinced being on an integrated team wouldn't be a monumental issue.

Their cramped room reminded Wood and Glenn of a residence hall room for a couple of college freshmen, with small beds, two little writing tables that doubled as nightstands next to them and a shared closet. A box was on each bed, one with Morris's name, the other Wood's. On top of each box was a little white booklet. On the cover, "AMERICAN OLYMPIC TEAM" was above the U.S. Olympic shield and the notation, "S.S. MANHATTAN, JULY 15, 1936."

They both opened their booklets.

WELCOME OLYMPIANS

We are proud and happy to have you aboard this ship and we extend a hearty welcome to every member of the 1936 American Olympic teams, to their officials and to their friends. We feel honored in being the link that bears you on your journey across the Atlantic. We will make every effort while you are aboard to help keep you fit and happy and ready for this greatest of sports events.

The captain, the officers and the crew of the Manhattan, as well as the staff ashore, extend you welcome and wish you Godspeed, joy and victory.

UNITED STATES LINES

Inside, pages listed the crew, headed by Commander Harry Manning, and the members of the Olympic traveling party, in alphabetical order, and not differentiating between athletes and Badgers.

Suddenly, Glenn realized what must be in the box.

"Our uniforms!" he exclaimed, ripping open the flaps and first pulling out a white double-breasted serge coat, with a red-white-and-blue shield on the left chest pocket. Another jacket was blue. The two pairs of slacks in the box were white and patterned gray. Wood watched, making no move to his own box. "Think it's all going to fit?" he asked, the doubt evident in his voice.

"Why wouldn't it?" Glenn responded. "They measured us five times!"

"Exactly. The more the Badgers do, the more they have a chance to get wrong!"

Glenn pulled on the coat. It was a little snug.

"See!" Wood chortled.

"Aw, it'll work," said Glenn, leaving the coat on and digging into the box, while Wood took a look at his own.

Their official team outfits, for the opening ceremonies and other appearances, also included white shirts and red-white-and-blue ties. They each had two long-sleeved sweaters—one white, one red—with USA across the chests, and a white sleeveless sweater with the USA Olympic emblem on the chest. Their two pairs of warm-up suits consisted of sweatshirts and sweatpants with innovative zippers down the outside of the ankles. When they came to the white satin uniforms they would wear in competition, the sensation was as if they were walking on the track in Berlin. The trunks had skinny red, white, and blue stripes running down the side; a tri-color sash ran across the front of the sleeveless shirt.

Bob Clark and Jack Parker were in the doorway.

"Hey, let's go back up to the deck," Clark said. "We're about to shove off!"

Dunn and Carpenter joined them, too. As the six athletes squeezed into spots at the rail, the captains on the tugging steamboats sounded their whistles and a band on the docks played "The Star-Spangled Banner." The SS *Manhattan* moved out into the waters of the Hudson River. The men, women, and children on the dock—and the flags many of them waved—got smaller. Then so did the buildings on the Manhattan skyline.

Walter Wood and Glenn lingered at the rail the longest. The Coloradoan was thinking about what might happen before he saw America again when he felt a tap on his shoulder. It was Paul Gallico.

"Glenn, have a few minutes?"

"For . . . ?"

Gallico laughed. "Poker?" When Glenn didn't get the joke, Gallico added, "Our interview. We do it now, that's one less thing you have to worry about."

"I guess that's all right," Glenn said.

Gallico gestured toward a couple of nearby deck chairs. They sat down and Gallico put his pipe down on a little table. He opened his notebook, put it on his thigh and said, "Let's start with this: Everything I've seen says you're from Colorado, but the roster says you were born in St. Louis."

"My dad was in the feed business in St. Louis," Glenn said. "He wanted to be a farmer. We moved to Simla when I was three."

Gallico scribbled a couple of words, no more, and then asked, "Why Simla?"

"It was a maintenance stop on the railroad. Dad knew some guys who had worked there. They told Dad there were a lot of farms available to work."

"What'd you raise?"

Glenn laughed. "I didn't raise anything," he said. "My parents and my brother—Jack, two years older than me—raised pinto beans. Our place was about three miles outside of town. I had my chores, I worked, but I killed more beans than I helped grow. I got carried away with the plow sometimes, let's just say."

Glenn explained that he and Jack had four sisters—Wilma, Theda, Virginia, and Betty, plus a younger brother, Wayne—so the house was crowded and bedrooms shared.

"I went to a country school—one room, all grades—out by our place for a year, maybe two, and then when that closed, went in town for school. But we did move to a little town called Quapaw in Oklahoma when I was in sixth grade. Dad managed a grocery store. I liked it there. It was just big enough to have a theater, and we saw a lot of cowboy movies. Not sure I know the whole story, but we went back to the farm and Simla after a year."

Gallico laughed. "Back to the snow? That okay with you?"

"It was back to my friends, so, yeah, I was fine with that. And the snow was bad only a couple of times a year."

"That's all? But you were in the mountains!"

"The mountains? Simla?"

Glenn decided Gallico was serious. It didn't shock him, though, because he quickly learned over the previous three months that arrogant Easterners thought the entire state of Colorado was one massive mountain range from border to border, north to south, east to west.

"Mr. Gallico, Simla's pretty much on the plains. Northeast of Colorado Springs, maybe fifty miles."

The writer didn't seem embarrassed. "How big of a town?"

Glenn chuckled. "Small. Great people, great place to grow up. Drive in on the highway, slow down for the stop sign, keep going . . . and that's it. But you might want to say in your story, though, that my parents have moved to Washington State—near Seattle."

Gallico offered a gentle nod that wasn't a promise before asking, "How'd you get started with sports?"

Glenn thought back. He loved to run around the property, hurdling whatever he could use as barriers. During his jaunts, he pictured himself as a football halfback or end leaping over, skirting, stiff-arming or running through tacklers to reach the end zone. He didn't mention all that, though, sticking with: "You can run around a farm a lot. That got me going, I guess."

"Do all the sports in high school?"

"Football, basketball, and track, yeah. Not baseball." He laughed. "I always liked the track guys when I was a kid. They had neat uniforms and they got to go to Colorado Springs and Denver for meets. I didn't have a very good year in football my senior year because my hip was hurt, and I got more serious about track that year."

Even took five first places in the state junior AAU meet!

"Any other interests?"

"I was the editor of the school paper." Glenn grinned. "I had a good staff."

"Did you at least like to write?"

"Oh, somewhat."

"I take it you like to read, too."

"Probably no more than average."

Actually, he devoured the "Rover Boy" and Horatio Alger books as a youngster, and he was one of the few students in Simla who treated the assignments to read *The Red Badge of Courage* and *Tom Sawyer* with eagerness, not dread. A love of reading wasn't something you advertised at Simla High, though. In Simla, that was for the homely girl who edited the yearbook and was destined to be a spinster teacher, not the star athlete. And now, he still enjoyed reading novels.

"Were you always going to go to Colorado Agricultural College?"

Glenn chuckled. "I thought I was going to have to go to work on the railroad," he said. "Nothing wrong with that, but I—we—just didn't have the money for college."

"How'd you get there, then?"

"I thought if I was going anywhere, it was going to be to Greeley—Colorado State College of Education—where my brother was," Glenn said. "But our basketball coach wrote a letter to Harry Hughes—he was the coach in both football and track at CAC—recommending me. He lined me up with a group called the Drugstore Quarterback Club that helps out athletes, and this really great man in it—Sparks Alford—pretty much sponsored me. They expected me to work, though, which was fine with me. I worked at the college's printing plant. Did deliveries on a bike at first, and then operated a printing machine."

"Played football four years?"

Glenn nodded, as he did to the next series of questions that took him through his career, as an all-league choice in football as a senior in 1933, and helping lead the Aggies to a share of a conference championship. In track, he set school records in both the high and low hurdles. He also earned the Aggies a few points when Hughes pressed him into service in the javelin and shot put during the '34 spring season, and the coach tossed it out: If Glenn concentrated on full-time training in track for the ensuing two years, he might have a chance at the '36 Olympics. "I've heard people say we were targeting the decathlon from then on, but that's not true," Glenn said. "We thought my best chance was going to be in the 400-meter hurdles. I was a good hurdler, a good quarter-miler, and that seemed to make a lot of sense."

Looking confused, Gallico said, "But the Denver paper said you went to the Games four years ago in Los Angeles, saw Jim Bausch win the decathlon and told anyone who would listen that you could do better than that. You're saying you weren't thinking of the decathlon that far back?"

Glenn shook his head. "I went to L.A. with my buddy Red White and his family, and went to the track for a couple of days," Glenn said. "That's true. But that's about it. I mean, four years ago, I couldn't even have told you the ten events. I don't know where that stuff about Jim Bausch came from."

He didn't mention the Denver Press Club.

Next, Glenn told Gallico that his academic disorganization worked to his advantage. His grades were good, but he had taken light loads some quarters and spread out his credits across departments, taking several English Literature courses before moving toward economics and sociology. Hughes helped him plot out a fifth year of study that would enable Glenn to graduate in June 1935 with a double major, and he assured Glenn the Drugstore Quarterback Club would continue its support.

"I saw that you were the student body president, too," Gallico said. After Glenn nodded, Gallico grinned and added, "Tough campaign?" Glenn shrugged. "Well, I went to the fraternities, sororities and the dormitories and stuff and made a couple of bad speeches. I was in the Alpha Tau Omega fraternity, and that helped." He smiled. "I didn't tell people I couldn't afford to live there, though. I always was in the boarding house. Only five bucks a month!"

Gallico asked if Glenn could hold on while he made a bathroom visit. During the break, Glenn thought back to that student election campaign. One of the appearances was at a sparsely attended "candidate's fair" at the student union building. His opponent, a bespectacled, pimply future engineer from Denver, outlined an eighteen-point plan to make student government more relevant, including saying it should take positions on world and national events and stage forums on such things as the Germans' drumbeating and maltreatment of Jews under this queer new leader, Hitler, and how it might affect the European order. Glenn was even more sheepish when he ran into his opponent in the Student Union after the election, and the future engineer politely congratulated him and dryly said Glenn obviously was more in tune with the student body. He still could feel the bruises left by his opponent's disdain—and remember his response.

"Jews in Europe don't matter to any of you," the opponent said. "There are maybe twenty Jews on this campus, and they're damn near the only ones who care."

"I don't even think of it that way," Glenn told him, genuinely exasperated. "I don't think, 'There goes a Jew.' I'm from the country, this is the big city to me, and it took people to tell me it was supposed to be an issue for me to even know who's Jewish. If that makes me some farm boy idiot, I'm a farm boy idiot."

Glenn—then and now—also was thinking of the Aggies' game his freshman year against Colorado Mines in football and several of his teammates were talking about needing to shut down "The Jew"—and it took them to explain to him that they meant Berg, the big Mines fullback.

Gallico was back from the bathroom. "Where were we?"

Glenn smiled. "You tell me . . ."

"That extra year at school?"

Glenn explained that he not only served as student-body president, but also finished up his requirements for a degree and helped coach in both football and track, while spending much of his time training. He told Gallico that as his graduation approached in the spring of '35, he sat down with Hughes on the South Field House steps. "He told me that if I wanted to try for Berlin, everything we had done to that point would seem easy compared to the next year," Glenn said. "I said that sounded good to me. But we still were thinking the 400 hurdles first."

"How'd you support yourself?"

"I coached some and the Denver Athletic Club agreed to sponsor me," Glenn said. "When I had time, I helped sell Fords at a car lot. It wasn't easy, but it was good enough."

Gallico looked at his notes again.

"What did your girlfriend think about all of that? Karen, is it?"

Glenn nodded, then said, "She was all for it."

"So last year, all the AAU meets?"

"Yeah, but in the 400 hurdles, mostly. Didn't do that well. I decided God was telling me that I should give the decathlon a shot. It worked out for the best."

For a few seconds, Gallico pondered what to bring up next. Deciding, he said, "But when you were trying to decide which event you would try to make the team in, we were talking about boycotting Berlin altogether. What were you thinking about all of that?"

The truth was, Glenn was elated when the Amateur Athletic Union's national convention in December '35 ultimately voted   barely   to endorse sending a U.S. team to Berlin. "I would have respected any decision we made," Glenn said carefully. "But I still want to believe that the Olympics—no matter where they are—can bring us together."

Gallico perfunctorily nodded. He checked his notes, then looked up again. "So anything else you want to tell me?"

Glenn thought a moment. "There's one other story I keep hearing that isn't true," he said. "The Denver guys keep saying I've been carrying around Hans Sievert's picture and pull it out and say I was going to beat him in Berlin."

Gallico feigned shock. "You mean that's *not* true?"

"No!"

"Glenn . . . good stories sell papers," Gallico said. "Even if they're only stories." Then, suddenly, his tone darkened. "But it's that kind of bullshit—it's what people expect—is helping drive me out of the sportswriting business."

Glenn was incredulous. "You get paid to go to games and you're going to quit?"

"Yup," Gallico said. "There're other things going on, too, with a wife trying to clean me out in the divorce, but I'm tired of this racket."

"What are you going to do?"

"Don't laugh . . . write fiction. And don't say that I already do."

"Well, good luck with that," Glenn said.

"In the meantime, it's up to you to give me something good to write about in Berlin."

"Have you been to Germany before?"

"Bunch of times," Gallico said. "I speak the language okay . . . at least I will after I get some practice for a few days. But between you and me, the way things are going over there, it might even be more handy to not let anyone know I speak it . . . and just listen."

6

~

Onboard Bonding

The decathlon and discus men joined their track teammates on the open-air sports deck the next morning. They'd been ordered to wear their Olympic uniforms at the first workout so the photographers could load up on pictures. The massive shot-putter, Jack Torrance, and the universally respected Glenn Cunningham led the warm-up stretching exercises and calisthenics.

The coaches watched, ready to pitch in with suggestions. But they had made it clear that he and the staff wouldn't interfere with individual training programs.

The Negroes started out leisurely running together, with Jesse Owens leading. Nobody, including Glenn, seemed to think much of it. That was the way it was. Then Glenn Cunningham joined the Negroes. He didn't say a word; the former University of Kansas star just ran with them. His story was universally known, at least among the American athletes. His badly scarred legs were reminders of the horrific Kansas schoolhouse fire that had killed his brother and left him facing a life in which even walking would be a miracle. He had done much better than that.

By the second lap, the group was about thirty—including the Farm Boy from Simla and several women runners, too. As they trotted, Glenn saw the glares and sensed others, including from a few of the athletes from other sports on deck, and, even more so, many "public" passengers. The pack took care to avoid the passengers indulging in morning walks or merely peering out over the water along the rail. The tennis net and flying balls in the middle of the deck were obstacles, too, and Glenn's first injury was the bruise on his calf from an errant serve.

Owens started slowing near the end of the fifth loop, and the others followed his lead and gradually came to a stop. As they stood around, some with their hands on the back of their heads and others just waiting, it was as if all were thinking: *What next?* Cunningham was as winded as if he had walked to the refrigerator to fetch a milk bottle. He stepped into the middle of the group. Glenn Morris at least had broken a sweat, and he ran his hand across his forehead and then back through his hair as Cunningham started talking.

"Now," Cunningham said. "It's time to get something important on the table."

He paused. As if on cue, Jack Torrance arrived at the edge of the group. Torrance always made it clear to anyone who asked about his shot-put training routine that it didn't include running, even slowly.

Cunningham continued, "I know this won't be the first time you've all heard something like this."

Glenn Morris noticed Cunningham's look in Torrance's direction and realized the spirited discussion in the hotel lobby the previous morning qualified as "something like this."

"This is an individual sport, but we're a team, and we're all representing our country together," Cunningham said. "Negroes, whites, Jews, Christians, guys, gals. All of us. Right?"

Glenn Morris nodded, too.

"But that's a two-way street," Cunningham said. "Jesse Owens, they were trying to make a point—and some of us were in on it—when they planned out the dinner seating last night and assigned you to sit with three Southern white boys."

Hurdlers Glenn Hardin and Forrest Towns, plus Torrance, raised their hands slightly. It was a roll call, not a request to speak. Three Southern white boys.

"But you decided you didn't want to sit with them and went to another table," Cunningham said. "Why?"

Owens looked around. "Want me to be honest, don't you?" he asked.

"Of course," Cunningham said.

"I thought if I sat down, they'd get up and leave."

Cunningham turned to Torrance. "Jack?"

"Hell, we *suggested* it, Jesse," Torrance said. "I wanted to back up something I'd said at the hotel. We weren't going to leave the table."

"Towns?"

"That's right," responded the University of Georgia student.

"Hardin?"

"I was going to ask for starting tips, for Christ sake," drawled the Mississippi native and former Torrance teammate at LSU.

That triggered nervous laughter.

Cunningham said, "Remember, when we get to Germany, the thing Hitler and his thugs can throw back in our faces is that we don't practice what we preach because of the way we treat Negroes in our country." At that, Owens and many of the Negroes nodded. "If we're acting like we're two teams—one black, one white—we're leaning into the punch," Cunningham said.

Other trackmen, wondering what was going on, were gathering on the perimeter of the discussion. "Everybody!" Cunningham announced, raising his voice, "I can't *tell* anyone who they should play shuffleboard with on this ship or who you should be friends with, but we have to be a team."

Ralph Metcalfe, a lanky Negro sprinter expected to challenge Owens in the 100 meters, spoke up. "You're forgetting something."

"What's that?" Cunningham asked.

"There *are* some people on this team—and, for sure, some of the jackass Badgers—who think Hitler's right. There's a master race . . . and then there's the rest of us."

There were murmurs of assent.

"Anybody?" Cunningham asked. "Thoughts on that?" He looked around and settled on Glenn Morris.

"Morris?"

Oh, Jesus, don't say anything stupid.

"I played college football, too," Morris said. He paused, thinking of how far to step out on the limb.

"Keep going," Cunningham said.

"I don't miss being banged up all the time. I don't miss the broken noses. I miss that feeling that everybody in the locker room is depending on each other. If I dropped the pass or I didn't make the block, somebody else looked bad. We had to root for each other; we had to depend on each other. That's what I miss. We're all out there on our own. We need to change that, I think."

"That all sounds good," said young Negro sprinter Mack Robinson. "But I don't get your point."

"My point," Glenn said, "is that we should start acting like we're a team."

"All agreed?" Cunningham asked.

At least there were no objections.

Cunningham turned to high jumper Cornelius Johnson. "Corny, you were on the team in Los Angeles, too, even though you were twelve or whatever it was."

Smiling, Johnson corrected him. "Eighteen."

"Wouldn't you say that we would have done even better if we had bonded better as a team out there? I think since we were home, it was like we all were on our own. Just a bunch of individuals thrown together."

"Absolutely," Johnson said.

"So I'm saying now that we're going to Germany, it's going to take more of acting like a team"—he nodded at Glenn Morris—"like a football team, even, to do as well as we're capable of doing."

"I'll go along with that," said Torrance.

"Me, too," said Jesse Owens.

As they broke up, the sprinters began working on their starts, running sprints in each direction at the side of the deck, from one chalked line to another. The other sprinters stretched.

Glenn wandered over. *Time to match action with words.*

"Can I join you?" he asked of nobody in particular.

Owens gestured at the slightly wavy starting line with his hand.

"On your mark," he said, grinning.

They all ran a few sprints, and at one point, Marty Glickman waited for Glenn and asked if he could talk to him privately. Over here, he gestured.

"First off," Glickman said, "I'm going to play football at Syracuse, so I identify with you."

"Thanks," Glenn said.

"The other thing you should know . . . well, you were at the Trials, weren't you?"

Glenn nodded.

Glickman continued, "So you know, I'm looking over my shoulder a bit here, too. We ran that 100-meter final and they told me I was third—behind Owens and Metcalfe. So I'm being interviewed on the radio, and they're saying I'm the boy who's going to be running with them in the 100 meters in Berlin, and while I'm talking, the judges come and tell me I've been bumped down to fourth behind Frank Wykoff . . . and *then* they say I was fifth, behind Foy Draper, too. So I've gone from running in the 100 at the Olympics with Jesse and Ralph to just being on the team and hoping we stick to the way it's been done in the past so I have a spot in the sprint relay. The two guys they suddenly placed ahead of me in the 100 run for Cromwell at USC. So . . ."

Dean Cromwell of USC was the American team's assistant coach, nominally in charge of the sprinters.

"How do they pick the relay?" Glenn asked.

"It's always been that the top three from the trials run the 100, and then the next four run the relay. So if they stick to that, it should be Foy Draper, me, Stoller, and Mack Robinson. But there are no real rules, so I'm at their mercy now. Mack doesn't care all that much because he's running in the 200, but for me and Stoller, the relay's our only chance. Writers already are saying the coaches are telling 'em nothing will be decided until we're in Berlin. Maybe not until the last minute."

Glenn was incredulous. "How could they take you and not let you run?"

"They might. They said we'd at least run in the exhibitions over there after the Olympics. And . . ."

Glickman suddenly was a bit self-conscious.

"What else were you going to say?" Glenn asked.

"Well . . . look, we've talked about this, but the Germans would prefer there aren't any Jews competing at all. The Badgers know that, too. I'm not saying they'll screw us because of that, but I'm wondering. We'll just see what happens." He paused, and then added, "Come on, let's run."

After a few more sprints, Glenn found himself next to Owens.

"Hey, Jesse, how do you divide up your training?" Glenn asked.

"Been meaning to ask you the same thing," Owens said. "I've got three or four events. You've got ten!"

"Well, the stuff from the coaches is that it really comes down to trying to work one set of muscles one day, another set the next."

"That's what *they* say . . . what do *you* think?"

"I've never figured out which muscles are in which group," Glenn said. "*I* think you have to trust what your body tells you. Every day."

They each ran another "sprint"—Glenn first, Jesse following. By then, they had drawn a crowd. Gawking women holding umbrellas to shield them from the sun, other athletes, scribes and photographers all gathered near them. AP's Alan Gould wore a suit and a bowtie. He called out, "All right, boys, which one of you is going to be called 'the world's greatest athlete' after Berlin?"

"Can't it be both of us?" Jesse asked.

Another scribe, Joe Williams of the *New York World-Telegram*, wondered: "Have you gentlemen decided what's smaller—Jesse's Oakville, Alabama, or Glenn's Simla, Colorado?"

"Nothing's smaller than Simla," Glenn said.

Owens reached out his right hand.

"Wanna bet?" he asked.

"You're on!"

Gould laughed and said he would do the research and get back to them with the verdict.

As Glenn finished up his workout and picked up his sweat suit, Gould approached him again and asked if he could come to Glenn's room that afternoon with his photographer. "We might have gotten a good picture here of you in your uniform, but the bosses and papers want something of you alone, in street clothes and all cleaned up," Gould said. "We are, you know, the world's largest news-gathering organization."

"Okay," Glenn said, "after our meeting."

No more than five minutes later, as Glenn drank a glass of water procured from the on-deck bar, Joe Williams caught up with him and introduced himself. *This is getting ridiculous*, Glenn thought.

"Hey, Morris, just want you to know one of the Denver papers—the *Rocky Mountain News*—is running my stuff and throwing a few bucks my way to do a separate piece or two about you." He chuckled. "Especially if you win, of course. So when I'm asking you questions or trying to set up an interview, it's for your folks back home in Colorado, too. I'll be like Gould and the news-service boys, too, that way. Did he give you the 'world's largest news-gathering organization' pitch?"

Glenn laughed. "A couple of times now," he confessed.

"Well, there are going to be a bunch of us after you, you know," Williams said. "Just make sure you keep your head on straight."

"That won't be a problem, Mister Williams."

Avery Brundage presided over an all-team gathering in the social room. "I know some of you, and this team in general," he said, "are about to accomplish feats that will set the standards for American Olympic teams for many decades to come!"

Around Glenn, many of his track teammates cheered lustily.

"Now, here's something very important, people," Brundage said. "A lot of you said you didn't like the 'training-table' lunch and dinner yesterday."

The grumbles confirmed that.

"All right, we'll make a deal," Brundage said. "We'll get the ship's regular menu for you . . ."

He held up his hand to quiet the cheers.

". . . as long as it's understood that you have to be careful about it. If all you do is say keep it coming and shovel it in, you're going to balloon up and your Olympic clothes and uniforms won't fit by the time we get to Berlin."

"What if they don't fit now?" a weightlifter asked.

The head nodding from many of his teammates confirmed that the Badgers doing the measuring had been inaccurate with others, too.

Brundage ignored that. "So we're agreed on food?"

The nods, claps, and yells were his answer.

"All right, second point," he said. "The Olympic tradition is that delegations dip their flags to the host nation's head of state and Olympic officials in the opening ceremonies. It's part of our U.S. Army regulations that the flag never dips, and we as Olympians are obligated to follow that. We need to decide an alternative gesture of acknowledgment."

"Why?" Marty Glickman asked loudly.

"Excuse me?"

"You're talking about Hitler. Why can't we just ignore him?"

"We can't do that," Brundage said.

Glenn Cunningham raised his hand. "Well, the Winter Olympics were in Germany, too, right?"

"That's correct."

"What did we do then?" Cunningham asked.

"No flag dip," said Brundage. "It was 'eyes right' . . . everybody looked over at his box as the team passed by. It didn't go over very well. So we're going to try something a little different in Berlin. Here's my suggestion: Eyes right again, but men doff your caps, and put them over your hearts. It's a salute to the flag you're walking behind, not the man you're looking at."

At first, Glenn was shocked that Brundage was consulting them, but he quickly decided that it was a way to spread out the blame.

"Why do we have to decide now?" asked a basketball player. "We've still got two weeks before the opening ceremonies. Can't we all think about it?"

"No," said Brundage. "We need to start preparing people for what we're doing. Unless there is something else—and I mean something else reasonable—anybody wants to throw out there, we're going with the eyes right and hats over the hearts."

"I can go along with that," Jesse Owens said.

"I still think we should just ignore him," Glickman said.

"That's *not* an option," Brundage snapped. "Besides, it's not just Hitler in the reviewing box. You have to look at it like you're acknowledging both the host nation and the Olympic tradition—not just one man. So is that agreeable?"

No response.

"All right," Brundage said with a tone of finality. "That's what we're do-ing."

He then announced that all but the track and field athletes could leave, because the final order of business involved only them.

"Think this is going to be good or bad?" Bob Clark asked Glenn.

"Don't know . . . but I'll vote for bad," Glenn replied.

Brundage panned the remaining group. "Okay, as I think many of you know, we're continuing our tradition of having a fun meet with Great Britain after the Games. This time, it's going to be in London—White City—on the 15th. Some of you will go there."

Glenn Cunningham spoke up firmly, but with some diplomacy. "Sir, that's before the closing ceremonies in Berlin. Wasn't there any way that meet could be later?"

"No, Cunningham, that's the date they wanted to do it . . . and we had to go along."

There were a few grumbles, and Brundage, glaring, let them die down.

"Also," he said, "most of you consented to be part of post-Olympic meets and exhibitions . . ."

"Like we really had a choice," one trackman near Glenn muttered.

Brundage continued, "We're still hearing from European promoters who say they're interested in hosting some of you. We might ask a few of you to go somewhere *before* London, but I would assume that for the most part, it will be after. If it's a bunch of places, we'll divide you into groups. We expect these offers to keep coming in after the Games start, because what you do will build excitement and interest in seeing you compete in person. So some of this—a lot of this—might be arranged at the last minute. I'd apologize for that, but it's unavoidable."

Jack Torrance raised his hand.

"Yes, Mr. Torrance?"

"With all due respect, sir, I take it you're getting a cut of the gate, right? What are *we* getting out of it? Shouldn't we at least have more choice about who goes where?"

A few gasped at the big shot-putter's impertinence. Many mumbled their agreement with his implied point.

"Absolutely, Torrance, we will get a share of the box-office receipts or guarantees, or both, wherever any of you are sent," Brundage said. "Mister Ferris, the AAU secretary-treasurer, will attempt to consult with most of you to discuss the possibilities as they unfold. But what *you* get out of it, first, is a chance to see more of Europe. What you get out of it, second, is the satisfaction of knowing you're helping the organization that sent you to Berlin—the American Olympic Committee—fund programs down the road . . . including the 1940 Olympic teams. We can't just pull money out of a hat, as you saw when we barely came up with the funding to send *this* team."

Glenn gave Brundage credit: The official was smart enough to realize they all had been reading about the frantic last-minute fund-raising, and the pronouncement shortly before the Americans' departure that the goal had been reached.

"What places are we talking about besides London?" pole-vaulter Bill Graber asked.

"Well, so far . . ."

Brundage looked up at the ceiling, jogging his memory.

" . . . several other German cities, plus Scotland, Finland, Czechoslovakia, Austria, Sweden, Norway. They'll be watching what goes on in Berlin and gauging the demand before they finalize anything with us."

Torrance muttered, "That means they're haggling over their cut."

Gould and his AP photographer knocked on Glenn's door five minutes early. Glenn was dressed in a USA sweater and lounged on the bed, with Thomas Wolfe's latest novel, *Of Time and the River*, open on his chest. He jumped up and, with his index finger marking his page, let in the AP men.

Gould took note of the book.

"Wow," Gould exclaimed, "you really reading that? Wolfe? I tried *Look Skyward Angel* and couldn't get past page two hundred."

"*Look Homeward, Angel*," Glenn corrected. "And yeah, I made it through it for a class. The professor wanted to turn it into more than it was, I admit. I read it like it was his life—no more than that."

"You're the only one I know who read the whole thing," Gould said. "I thought it was one of those books everybody bought and nobody made it all the way through—but wouldn't admit they gave up. Congratulations! How's this one?"

"Pretty much more of the same," Glenn said, grinning.

"Is that good or bad?" Gould challenged.

"Good," Glenn said. He laughed and added, "Mostly."

Gould pointed at the book. "How long's this one? A thousand pages?"

Glenn turned to the back pages and checked. "Close," he said. "Nine hundred twelve. I'm on . . ."—he looked at his finger bookmark—"ninety-two."

"No way you'll make it."

"I'll try." Glenn thought a second and added, "Hey, if you're writing anything, you don't need to mention that stuff. I don't want to make people think I'm claiming to be some egghead or something. I just like to read."

Spotting the picture of Karen on the little desk, Gould asked, "That your girl?"

"Yeah," Glenn said.

"What's her name?

"Karen."

"Back in Fort Collins?"

"Well, she's in Sterling—Sterling, Colorado—now . . . for a little bit."

"Been going steady a long time?"

"Three years. She just graduated."

"Heading for the altar, sounds like."

"At some point, I s'pose so."

After the interview, Gould said he had another idea for a picture. "You sit there, on the bed. Here's a pen. Here's some paper. Start writing to her. People love that stuff, Morris."

Glenn played along, actually starting a letter to Karen. The photographer took about ten pictures, both with Glenn's head down and with him looking up and smiling at the camera.

When the AP men left, he kept writing.

7

~

Fire and Fury

Finally, the months of painstaking preparation would begin to give way to action.

Leni and several staff members boarded a Junkers "Ju 52" plane, a seventeen-seater, heading for Greece and the Olympic torch lighting. On the way, they stopped in Belgrade, where Leni was greeted as a great woman of the cinema, meeting with reporters at the airfield and delivering a preview of her Olympics film.

"This will be like nothing else I've done," she said as photographers, including her own, shot pictures of her speaking. "It's the beauty of the human body and athletic competition, all against a backdrop of the Games' roots, which we'll salute in the filming in Greece."

At the Royal Palace, she had an audience with both Prince Paul, the Kingdom of Yugoslavia's regent; and his nephew, King Peter II, who was only eleven years old and had succeeded his assassinated father, Alexander I, in 1934. Prince Paul was far more cordial than young King Peter, and Leni chalked up the boy's attitude to shyness. She tried to break through by presenting the boy monarch with her standby for such occasions—a copy of the portrait of her as Junta in the opening scene of *The Blue Light*. It didn't work. The young king thanked her, but remained distant.

"A strange one that boy is," she said in the car on the way back to the airfield.

She was with Ernst Jäger, the former journalist she had hired as her publicity man on *Olympia*. Jäger was on the trip mainly to answer questions about the project for the entourage of German reporters and radio announcers covering the torch relay. But Leni trusted his instincts enough to use him as a sounding board. After all, his work history included a stint as editor of *Film-Kurier*, the German movie trade publication that had raved about much of Leni's work as an actress. His editor's career was derailed because his wife was Jewish, but Leni realized he could help her. His malleability was proven when, under Leni's name and her line-by-line approval, he wrote breathless copy for the picture-laden booklet, *Behind the Scenes of the National Party Convention Film*, issued in early 1935 to coincide with the release of *Triumph of the Will*.

"Leni, he was probably just scared of you," Jäger said. "You can be very intimidating to a boy whose voice is about to break." He chuckled. "Or anyone else."

"How can he be intimidated? He's a *king*!"

"He certainly is, but . . ."

Jäger paused, seemingly having decided not to continue. Looking at his watch, he said, "We should get to the airfield by . . ."

Leni cut him off. "What were you going to say? But what?"

"But he's a boy!"

"That's *not* what you were going to say."

Jäger thought for a moment. Slowly, he said, "Well, one of the reporters told me the king's being told by some who have his ear that he needs to worry about the Third Reich and its intentions for his nation. If all of that is true, perhaps he extended that wariness to you."

Leni shook her head. "Why does everyone want to bring me into affairs of state?"

"You have to face it, Leni. To many, you're no longer the actress playing Junta or any other role. You are . . ."

He paused to set it off.

". . . Hitler's filmmaker."

Leni snapped, "I should send you back to Berlin right now!"

"I'm sorry, but that's the truth," Jäger said. "If you want someone to only flatter you and lie to you, you need someone else. You know I can be practical—in my situation in our country now, I have to be—but if you want me to serve you well in this position, I have to be able to be blunt with you." He let that hang for a moment. "Respectfully, of course."

Leni sighed. "I know you're right," she said. "That's why, after this film, I have to return to acting, too, in my own dramas. I need to open doors, not close them!"

After ten minutes of less serious discussion, Leni put her hand on Jäger's knee. "Ernst, you understand I wasn't saying there's anything wrong with being"—a change in her tone set off the next two words, just as he had done—"'Hitler's filmmaker.'"

"Oh, for God's sake, I am not a plant to test you," Jäger said sharply. "You hired me, not Goebbels, and I am grateful for that, especially under the circumstances. I'm not taking notes."

"I know that. But . . . well, I just need to make that clear." She paused. "I don't want to be known as *only* that."

After spending the night in Athens, Leni's entourage rode in cars to Olympia, to film the torch lighting and then the start of the runners' relay to Berlin. They were catching up with another of Leni's photographers, Willy Zielke, who spent two weeks in June with a crew shooting footage for what Leni envisioned as the opening scenes of the film at the Acropolis in Athens. Trusting the temperamental Zielke was risky, but he was an ace with his film camera, and as a director and cinematographer of his own works.

Repeatedly in preliminary planning meetings and informal discussions with her cameramen, her mantra about *Olympia* was: "Film, not newsreel." She said it so often, staff members saw it coming and mouthed it as she said it. They understood one of her goals was to connect the modern Games to the Olympics' roots in antiquity. Plus, she insisted on portraying the events in Berlin as a celebration of youthful vigor and the beauty of the human body. That wasn't newsreel. She also emphasized she would have many men with still cameras shooting, also, for supplementary material to go with the film—publicity and a picture book.

Her vision of the Prologue was to begin with the Zielke's panning of the ancient sites at the Acropolis and at Olympia, 350 kilometers to the west of Athens; and move to shots of many sculptures and copies, from several sites, including those of Medusa, Aphrodite, Apollo, Achilles, Paris, Faun, Alexander the Great, and, ultimately, Myron's *Discobolos*—or the Discus Thrower. She didn't know if it would work, but she wanted to try it, and her idea was to fade from the Discus Thrower statue figure to a modern, live athlete—perhaps even a real Olympian!—in the same pose, wearing only a loincloth, and then uncoiling and throwing the discus. Then, at least in the outline in her head, she would move to shots of the torch lighting at Olympia and the start of the runners' relay. If necessary, she said without self-consciousness, they would supplement the footage of the torch lighting and relay with their own "alternative" staging, probably at the ruins at Delphi after the torch relay passed through that site, too. Her staff stifled smiles, knowing that one way to trigger her ire was to mention accusations that she had "re-created" scenes in her previous documentaries—accusations which were true, but which she always denied.

They drove to Olympia to catch the torch lighting. There, Leni leaned forward behind the huge upright cameras and got a sense for what the lens was seeing as her crew filmed. She held up her hands, put her thumbs together as the horizontal bottom of the "frame" and raised her index fingers at the sides of the shot. Over a dozen Greek women in smocks watched as sunlight, channeled through magnifying glasses, kindled a fire, and one of the women lit a torch from it. Next, the Greek maidens emerged from the original stadium site to light a fire at an altar. After speeches by German and Greek dignitaries, a band played the German national anthem, and "*Die Fahne Hoch*," better known as the "Horst Wessel" song—a Nazi tribute to those who fell in battle with "reds and reactionaries." Leni watched impatiently. Her cameras, including one with sound, were rolling, but she already had made up her mind that the speeches and music wouldn't be part of her film. That would be too much like her Party documentaries. This was for rehearsal purposes and also to humor Dr. Diem and the German organizers. No more.

Finally, Greek runner Kyril Kondylis reached out to the fire, lit another torch, turned, and started running with it held aloft. He wore shoes and shorts. Nothing more.

Leni slid into a Mercedes convertible, joining a Greek driver and Ernst Jäger. In front of them, cameraman Heinz von Jaworsky—Leni's former personal assistant who had learned the photographer's craft and earned both a promotion and her trust—rode in another convertible and shot footage of the early runners with his handheld camera.

As the relay continued, heading east toward Athens, Leni realized she had been right to assume that the relay wouldn't fit her vision. Some runners wore traditional Greek outfits, including tunics, skirts, leggings and vests. Worse, she saw a backdrop of modernity—police barricades and officers who stopped and delayed her and the crew; motorcycles; automobiles; and the vehicles belonging to the reporters and following German radio crew, transmitting intermittent reports back to the homeland.

"Shit," she said sharply. "That won't do. This is all useless. Useless. Boring, staged ceremony. Then this!"

"Well, how much do you need of this?" Jäger asked. "With all you'll shoot at the Games, you'll have more than enough to choose from."

"I want the Prologue to be at least fifteen minutes. Fifteen minutes to put my stamp on this."

"But then you'll run out of time for the athletics."

"It probably will be two films, Ernst. Maybe three."

"*Two* films? How long have you known this? Have you told anybody?"

"When the time comes, I'll proudly announce it."

"Then you can't do all the editing alone. You do it the way you did it on the other films, the premiere won't be until after the *next* Olympics! You can't bring them out one at a time, either. They all must come out at once. And you will age ten years!"

"I'll handle all that when the time comes."

Jäger gestured at the chaos around them. "Use this to your advantage!"

"*How* would I do that?"

"You go from Willy's artistic shots and tight on the first runner lighting the flame"—Jäger's "artistic" was a bit sarcastic—"to the contrast. To this. You start with mist in the peaceful and deserted Acropolis. That's what Willy shot there, right? With all those smoke pots?"

"One hundred and eleven smoke pots. Every one of them fifty reichsmarks against the budget."

"So, you show that! So quiet. Peaceful. Isolated. And then . . . tight on the runner lighting the flame and turning. Maybe we follow him for his first steps. And then . . . modernity! He . . . or one of the next men . . . is running in the modern world!"

"And what would that accomplish?"

Jäger was undeterred. "You establish the connection between the Olympic Games' ancient roots and their place in the modern world! To 1936!"

Leni patted his knee. "Ernst, if I had listened to you, we'd have set *The Blue Light* in modern Munich, not the Alps in 1866."

He played along. "Well, at least you wouldn't have had to climb that damn mountain barefoot all the time."

"I'll concede that," Leni said, smiling. "But what I what I want to do here is set the mood of ancient Greece and stick with it until the flame is out of Greece."

Near the village of Pyrgos, twenty kilometers from Olympia, she spotted her star. The dark-skinned runner had long and wavy hair swept back above his ears and across his temples, flopping on every step. He was perhaps twenty. Although he was in a billowing and traditional Greek outfit, Leni was able to picture him as a statue on display in Florence. "He looks like a Pericles!" she exclaimed.

When the runner finished his segment, Leni ordered the driver to stop. "I *must* meet that man."

Like so many of Leni's staff, Jäger had heard her say *that* many times before, too. In fact, a few of them had been ensnared in the web of the driven artist—the woman who, when she indulged in her desires, often treated sex as enthusiastic recreation, as she had dancing or skiing, but also as a means to an end. Strong men wouldn't put up with her demanding terms. Weaker men in awe of her went along with her, but then she took them for granted and eventually became bored with them.

Along the way, she came to consider her image as part of her power. Finding them useful more than slandering, she did nothing to diminish the exaggerations about her, such as that she directed her sex, too: *Action! Cut! Next!* She had fallen hard a few times, most notably for her longtime cameraman Hans Schneeberger and skier Walter Prager. Those men had moved on to other women, but remained Leni's friends. Schneeberger wasn't available for *Olympia*, and Leni regretted that. It would hurt the film. However fleeting the affair, her lovers always could be used. Forever. Producers, actors, cameramen, bankers . . . she disarmingly acted as if an ultimate level of trust had been established and should continue in their work, even when the sex didn't.

Standing beneath a tree as he waited to be picked up by the runners' bus, the young torch runner sensed their approach and turned. He responded with the familiar look Leni always—accurately or otherwise—interpreted as an undressing. Introducing herself, she reached out. He shook her hand lightly, but his gaze was blank. She signaled to their Greek driver, hired because he spoke several other languages, including German. He joined them, and Leni asked him to explain to the boy who they were. But the boy's understanding of Greek was minimal, his responses halting. The driver switched to another language. *Russian*, Leni thought. The boy spoke in a flurry. The driver turned to Leni.

"He is from Russia," he said, gesturing with an open hand at the boy. "I am very sorry, it's not my best language. His family fled here. Something political."

"What is his name?"

The driver asked.

"Anatol," the boy said. He smiled at Leni and added to her, "Anatol Dobriansky."

Anatol knew more French than Greek, and the driver more French than Russian, so that became the language. Leni could follow it. Between her gestures and the relayed words, she was able to get it across that she wanted Anatol to serve as the torch carrier in her reenactment of the lighting and the early stages of the relay. In a film. Her film. Not here. At Delphi. They would go to Athens, spend the night, then all head to Delphi. And in case she wanted to take him back to Germany for more filming, did he have a passport? No, he said, again bewildered. Leni said they'd figure that out, that she might be able to have one sent to the border. Finally, Anatol got it across that he needed to at least go to his home in Pyrgos to pick up clothes and inform his parents.

An hour later, Anatol walked out of his family's tiny home with a small suitcase—and his father. Lean and graying and in his late forties, Anatol's father made his wariness clear through gestures, but when Leni handed him a stack of Drachma notes, he turned more enthusiastic. Leni assured him, or thought she did, that Anatol would return home soon. At their Athens hotel, Leni showily announced that Anatol would stay with Jäger in his room.

The next day she discovered that her advance scouts had been right: The ruins at Delphi were perfect supplemental settings for her Prologue. The official torch relay was scheduled to pass through the next day, doubling back from Athens, and Leni's crew would remain behind to shoot it just in case, although she was all but certain she wouldn't use any of that film, either. On this day, Delphi was deserted and the late-afternoon and early evening provided perfect backdrops. Anatol proved to be an eager actor, wearing only a loincloth and lighting the torch at a raised hearth. It took several takes to satisfy Leni, but he eventually got it perfect, turning slowly to his left, looking into the flame, as if he was marveling at what he was holding and what he was about to do. Then Leni had the cameras set up farther away, and they shot several takes of Anatol stepping down two stone stairs to begin his run down the slope, and through the ruins.

Anatol seemed to be enjoying himself more with each step.

8

~

Most Handsome

Surprising himself, Glenn didn't get seasick during the storm on the second night out, when Walter Wood threw up twice and complained that he thought the Greek gods behind all this Olympics business were supposed to be protecting them.

As the voyage continued, running on the deck got old, and the rain and cold made even that limited work difficult. Glenn felt sluggish. His pre-trip rough outline of a training regimen, designed in consultation with Harry Hughes, proved unrealistic. He picked up and fooled around with the javelin, shot put, discus, and vaulting pole, handling them and hoping not to completely lose the feel for them.

When the weather was tolerable, the group running continued. Also on the deck, the Olympians organized bowling games, using Coke bottles for pins and oranges for balls. Glenn gave up when his orange curved more than a Carl Hubbell screwball and he couldn't even hit the Coke bottles, much less knock any of them down. He and Glenn Cunningham also got into golf putting duels on the deck, trying—only occasionally successfully—to control the balls on the shuffleboard deck. There were also a volleyball net and table tennis table, but they were constantly in use, and Glenn only was a spectator. In table tennis, the best mixed doubles team—hands down—was Jesse Owens and a tiny swimmer, Mary Lou Petty. Happenstance threw them together, and they were such fun to watch, all demanded they remain partners. In shuffleboard, Owens's partner was javelin and discus thrower Gertrude Wilhemsen, and they were formidable, too.

Beyond the recreational games, there were temptations. Glenn heard the rumors, too, of the lifeboats being turned into the nighttime rendezvous points, whether for Olympic team couples—in most cases, the athletes in different sports had just met and attractions were common—or a male athlete and a "civilian" female passenger.

The fourth day out, Avery Brundage called another U.S. squad meeting—in shifts—in the social hall/dining room. His message: He and other officials weren't deaf, dumb, and blind. They were seeing and hearing of athletes drinking and partying, and often cavorting on the first-class level, at the bar, or even in private cabins. He said nothing about lifeboats, though.

"This is no joyride!" Brundage declared. "If President Roosevelt was on this ship and he invited you to have a highball or two in the first-class lounge, you'd still be subject to the rules in the handbook. We've warned some of you who aren't paying any attention to them. There will be no second chances from here on. None. Don't test us. If we have to drop any of you off in Ireland at the first stop and send you home, we'll do it."

Referring to a sheet of paper, he added, "I remind you, you all signed the forms agreeing to, and I quote, 'maintain strict training during the voyage and until my competition in Berlin is completed,' unquote. And that you would, quote, 'refrain from smoking and the use of intoxicating drinks and other forms of dissipation while in training,' unquote."

Marty Glickman, standing behind Glenn, raised his hand.

"Yes, son," Brundage said.

"Are you saying we can't go to the first-class level, even if we're invited? I know I've met some nice people—older couples—who've invited us up there. They're not parties. You must know that. You and all the Badg . . . and all the officials . . . are in first class, right?"

Brundage glared.

"I'm saying don't abuse our trust," he said. "We're not monitoring you twenty-four hours a day. If you go up there, that's your business. But don't make fools of yourselves and, by extension, of us."

After Brundage left, Jack Torrance smiled wryly at Glickman. "Marty, I think you're on his list now."

"I already was," Glickman said darkly.

Glenn asked Torrance, "What was that all about? Who's been out of line?"

"The weird thing is, it's mostly the girls," Torrance said. "Eleanor Holm has been up there, drinking and playing dice with the sportswriters and a bunch of the upper crust. Like William Randolph Hearst Junior."

Runner Archie San Romani, the 1,500-meter man who had become notorious among his teammates for spending most of his time in his room playing his cornet, grinned. "Maybe she won too much money from those boys and somebody complained."

"Hell, the way I look at it," said Bob Clark, "playing dice is a lot better than blasting away on a horn!"

The way he said it, though, made it clear he was teasing. San Romani hadn't played more than three hours a day and no later than 9 at night.

⌣

The next day, Glenn was on the deck, catching his breath after a few laps when he heard a woman's voice behind him.

"Glenn?"

He turned and was looking at Eleanor Holm Jarrett, in an opened robe over a wet swimsuit. She reached out and, smiling, introduced herself.

"Glenn Morris," Glenn responded as he lightly shook her hand.

"I'd figured that out," she said, giggling.

They really are gold medalists, Glenn decided, and he could tell she noticed his appraisal.

"How's your training going?" Eleanor asked.

"Just trying not to get too out of shape. How about you? I hear the pool isn't that great."

"That's putting it nicely," she said. "It's too short, the water shifts with the boat rocking, and really the best thing to do is have someone tie a rope to you and try to swim in place." She laughed. "I know there are some people who think I'm not training at all, though. Okay, so I'm not sitting in my room and knitting. I'm not apologizing. But speaking of that . . . there are a lot of folks in first class who say they'd like to meet you."

"I'm out here every day," Glenn said.

"No, they mean up there, in first class on 'A' Deck . . . at night. You don't have to get wild, just show up, shake hands, have a beer and make some friends. Why are you such a loner?"

"A beer? You know the handbook says we're not supposed to have any alcohol."

"Shit, Glenn, half your team runs laps and then goes right over to that window."

She pointed at the little window where a man in a bowtie served beer. And Eleanor was right: Many of Glenn's teammates replenished fluids with a visit to that window. "So come up with me to first class tonight."

Noticing his reluctance, she added, "You look like a movie star . . ."

He started to raise a hand.

"Oh, don't even try to give me that humble bullshit," she said sharply. "You know you do. But I'm not jumping your bones, all right? I'm not going to drag you into a lifeboat and tear your clothes off." She laughed and added, "We'd have to chase Jesse out of there, anyway."

He didn't react to that. He'd also heard the rumor that morning that when she hadn't been able to sleep, Helen Stephens had taken a walk in the middle of the night, heard noises coming from a lifeboat, and seen Jesse Owens and then a woman non-Olympian lift the canvas and emerge. Of course, Helen had confided in another runner and sworn her to secrecy, meaning it took at least an hour for the story to reach all corners of the Olympians' tourist-class quarters.

Eleanor said, "Look, just meet me up there on the 'A' deck. If nothing else, you'll have fun. You might even meet a rich widow or an heiress!"

"I don't know . . ."

"Glenn, trust me, and now I'm being serious, so help me God, these are the people who can *make* you after you win."

"*If* I win, you mean."

"There you go again. You're going to win and you know it. They can help you turn a gold medal into real gold!"

"I've talked to the sportswriters plenty."

"It's not just them. I'm talking about people like Hearst's son, actors, actresses, tycoons . . ."

"But Brundage warned us."

"Hell, he gave me the speech personally, too," she said. "He's lecturing me, but I also could tell if I'd said, 'Avery, why don't we just go back to your cabin and talk this over for a few hours in bed,' he would have led the way—and then said all was forgiven. He's a creep. Trust me, I know. One 'yes' from me and none of this bullshit would have happened the last four years. He wouldn't have tried to take my amateur standing away after Los Angeles because I was trying to be an actress and he certainly wouldn't be giving me shit now."

Glenn was getting self-conscious, and not only over embarrassment over what she said about Brundage. Several of his track teammates had walked by and leered, even giving him the high sign.

"Eleanor, I just don't think it's a good idea. The Badgers are mad and I can't take that risk." He paused. "Don't you think you should be a little more careful, too?"

"Brundage is just bluffing," she said disdainfully. "He knows I know too much, including about him and his zipper. Besides, he wants to win so he comes off as this organizational genius and inspiration and all that bullshit."

"Okay, but I think I better stay out of first class, just the same."

"Your loss."

"No hard feelings?" Glenn asked.

Eleanor made a show of staring at his crotch.

"Doesn't look like it," she said, raising her eyebrows.

Noting his embarrassment, she reached out and lightly slapped his arm. "Look at you blush! They *told* me you're still a country boy. They were right. You really are!"

She started to walk away, then turned. Looking him directly in the eyes, she said, "The offer's always open."

⌒

As the voyage entered its final days, Badgers handed out paper ballots at lunch. The men got to vote for women in a "Beauty Contest" and for "Most Popular" among their male teammates. The women's ballots listed a "Most Handsome" category for men and "Most Popular" among the women. They were asked to list first, second, and third choices for each.

At another team "ball" in the social room, Brundage went to the microphone to award little cups to the winners. With a handful of other track athletes, Glenn was at the back of the room, near the doors. Tiny Katherine Rawls, who competed in both swimming and diving, was most popular among the women. The behemoth shot-putter, Jack Torrance, brought down the house by picking her up with one arm and carrying her to the stage to receive her award.

"No trophy for this, sorry," Brundage said, "but for the record, the runner-up was Betty Robinson."

Glenn clapped loudly at that one, knowing—as everyone who voted for her likely did—that the sprinter, a gold medalist in the 100 meters way back in 1928 in Amsterdam, had recovered from a near-fatal plane crash to make the Olympic team for the third time as a member of the 400-meter relay team.

Glenn Cunningham won for most popular among his teammates. No surprise there, and Morris and his teammates responded with a long ovation.

"Second was Jesse Owens," Brundage announced.

That got a nice hand, too, and Owens waved.

"Now, the beauty contest," Brundage said. "The winner is . . . Joanna de Tuscan." The pretty fencer, who like Eleanor Holm Jarrett, was married, accepted the cup and held it overhead, but otherwise seemed to ignore Brundage, who was rebuffed in his attempt to deliver a congratulatory kiss on the cheek.

"No trophies again," Brundage said, plowing on, "but the runners-up are Betty Robinson, again, and Alice Arden, both track and field."

As had many of his teammates, Glenn had developed a bit of a crush on the cute and curly-haired Arden, the high jumper from New York, and voted for her as the runner-up to Eleanor, so he joined in that ovation with extra enthusiasm, too. But it also hit him as he heard the comments around him: How could Eleanor not win? Then Eleanor was storming toward Glenn and the doors.

"The bastard rigged the voting," she said to another swimmer trying to stay with her. Eleanor spotted Glenn. "See?" she asked angrily. "This is the only real way he can get back at me!"

And she was gone.

"All right," Brundage said, "the award for most handsome, voted on by the women . . . Glenn Hardin, track."

Amid the cheers, plus a few shrieks from the women, Brundage peered out, looking for Hardin. "No Hardin? Going once, going twice. . . . All right, then the runner-up moves up. That makes the winner . . . another Glenn! Glenn Morris."

Others patted him on the back and shook his hand as he made his way to the stage.

"Congratulations, Morris," Brundage said, handing him the cup and gesturing at the microphone.

Geez, what to say?

"I'm accepting this for Glenn Hardin," he said. "Not for me."

A voice came from among the women. "And he's modest, too!"

When he was back with the trackmen, he tried to turn it into a joke. "Besides, I don't like finishing second!"

9

~

Queen of the Castle

Back in Berlin, Leni confronted another logistical challenge. She needed to place cameras, at least one large enough to be capable of recording sound, in Adolf Hitler's loge box at the opening ceremonies in the Olympic Stadium. From close up, she had to get footage of him stepping to the microphones at the temporary rostrum, pronouncing the Games open.

She called his adjutant, Wilhelm Brückner, at the Chancellery, and made an appointment. A sign of her status was that she had to wait only ten minutes. Hitler greeted her by grasping one of her hands in both of his. With no additional preamble, he said, "Let me ask you first, now that we're so close, do you still think this is going to be worthwhile for the Third Reich?"

"My film?"

"The Olympic Games themselves!"

"Oh, I think so," Leni assured him. "My mind hasn't changed. We will show the world the wherewithal and the hospitality of the German nation . . . and what we can do when challenged. That is what I'm going to get on film."

Hitler said, "I told Speer cost was no object, that we wanted the biggest and best stadium and other facilities the world had ever seen! We inherited this, but we need to stage the best Games ever. The display of our resolve and strength is worthwhile. But I find it repulsive that we are stepping away, however briefly, from the reordering of our society."

As had most Berliners, Leni had noticed the disappearance of the signs declaring, "NO JEWS" or "JEWS: YOUR ENTRY IS FORBIDDEN." She understood why: Among those coming to Berlin were high-profile and influential figures from around the world, including journalists. They would form independent judgments rather than allow themselves to be manipulated by the British and American correspondents based in Berlin turning out censored, but still untrustworthy, dispatches about Hitler's Germany. For the visitors' benefit, temporary subtlety in the Reich was appropriate. She also had heard of the jailing of petty criminals—or actually, those who even *looked* like petty criminals—to lessen the chance of street hustlers victimizing foreign visitors. Also, Gypsies were rounded up and removed to Marzahn. So while one aspect of the reordering was delayed, she thought, others were accelerated. Yet Hitler wouldn't care about the side issues. For him, it was about the Jews.

"It is unfortunate—disgraceful!—that we are allowing our visitors to dilute our determination, ever so briefly," he growled. "Once the boycott movements were quashed, they could not have withdrawn the Games from Berlin even if we had remained completely on track in our treatment of the Jews. Roosevelt would have paid lip service to the Jews and bluffed about ordering the Americans not to come, but they would have been here, too. I am afraid I have let Goebbels brainwash me."

Hitler walked to his desk and picked up a copy of the propaganda ministry's *Der Angriff*. Locating a passage, he read aloud with disgust: "We are not only going to show off the most beautiful sports stadium, the fastest transportation, and the cheapest currency. We must be more charming than the Parisians, more easygoing than the Viennese, more vivacious than the Romans, more cosmopolitan than London, and more practical than New York."

He slammed the magazine down. "Practical? *Practical?* Is mongrelizing *practical?* The Americans will be coming here with their vermin and primitive beasts and we are to be so *practical* as to act as if they could be so impressed with our hospitality they will want to remain behind and become citizens of the Reich!"

He ranted on in that vein for about ten minutes, pacing the room, before pausing and then moving back behind his desk, but not sitting down.

"But you, too," he said finally, "are going to tell me we now must be hospitable for our guests, that it will be a step forward for the Reich in the long run to do so. Correct?"

Leni stayed silent. With the Führer, she knew the best strategy was to bide her time.

"I know that's what we must do," he conceded reluctantly. "We must be seen as firm, but reasonable and civilized. If it requires holding our noses a bit, even letting a Jewess wear the German uniform, we will have to accept that for the greater good. I know that." Pounding his desk with each word, he repeated, "I . . . know . . . that. But those who mistake our hospitality for weakness will do so at their own peril!"

Suddenly, as if she had just walked in and he had five minutes before a staff meeting, he announced, "What is so urgent?"

Now.

As quickly as she could, avoiding any pauses, she explained she needed his blessing and his orders to others to allow the two cameras in his box at the opening ceremonies. Both cameras would photograph him during the entrance of the athletes, nation by nation, and then show him close-up and record him as he stepped to the microphone and declared the Games open.

"Is that all?"

"Some thought you would object."

"You have my permission. I will make that known."

"Thank you," Leni said gratefully. "I know you will enjoy the Games!"

"Oh, I don't intend to be there much after the opening ceremonies," he said dismissively.

Leni was genuinely incredulous. "You don't?"

"Athletics, sports, such irrelevancies. I truly have more important de-mands on my time, you understand. And from what I am told . . . I have been braced for this . . . I will be reminded that sport is not always the true measure of worth. I'm told the Americans will turn it into a niggerfest."

Leni said carefully, "The German team is expected to make us proud."

"Let us hope so," he said. "And let us hope many winning athletes from other nations will represent the Aryan ideal, too!"

As Hitler took a step toward the door, a sign Leni recognized as dismissal, she said, "From what I understand, some white Americans will win, too."

"I can handle *that*," Hitler declared. "Especially if they are impressed enough to go back and tell Roosevelt and those of his ilk that America needs to keep its crooked nose out of our affairs! We will need the young men of their generation to speak up, to say the affairs of Europe are not their own."

Leni reached for the door handle.

"Or even better," Hitler added, "we need those young white Americans to tell their countrymen and their leaders that we are right."

Leni's next stop was the men's Olympic Village in Döberitz.

The two guards at the circular drive entrance stepped in front of the Mercedes convertible. Extending the Nazi salute, the young guard on the driver's side held a clipboard in the other hand. Then he gazed directly at Leni in the back seat and said deferentially, "Welcome Fraulein Riefenstahl. It is an honor."

"Thank you," Leni said with a half smile, acknowledging the compliment but making it clear it was both expected and commonplace.

"The supervisor is expecting you."

He directed her to a large administration building to the left of the main entrance. There, she was impressed with all the luxuries the organizers were providing for the athletes—a post office, bank, stores, laundry, and travel agency. She marched into the superintendent's private office alone. The superintendent, Lieutenant Werner von und zu Gilsa, gushed his welcome and said he hoped she took it as a compliment that he couldn't help but think of her first as *The Blue Light*'s Junta, not a director.

"Unlike Junta, I'm wearing shoes now," Leni said, smiling. She paused, and then abruptly adopted a businesslike tone. "I wanted to meet with you to be assured that I and all on my staff will be granted universal access here at the Village."

"We've been told to accommodate you, of course," von und zu Gilsa said. "You and your people won't be impeded, within reason, of course. Visitors must be 'authorized,' as you can imagine. And women? Well, officially, this is off limits to women, so you might encounter some surprise if you visit us. And there will be areas you probably will not want to go."

Leni snapped, "I am not planning on storming the shower rooms, so I don't see that as an issue."

She didn't mention that one of her ideas was to shoot athletes nude but in the mist, in the camp's sauna.

The superintendent seemed to be calculating his next words.

"What is it?" she asked sharply.

"The forested area by the lake will be guarded."

"Who's there?"

"Before the Games start . . . women of fine German, Aryan stock. As I understand it, some are sports instructors, carefully selected by the Gestapo to be suitable and attractive. Others are from the Band of German Maidens."

"The Maidens? *Children?*"

"Fraulein, these are the older members or former members. They are old enough to be women. Regardless, these women will have passes and they are only to be in the woods by the lake over there." He gestured to the east. "It will become known to the athletes—the Aryan athletes—where these maidens are."

"For?"

"For . . ."

He shrugged.

Leni scoffed. "Do you have cots set up out there? Or do they just roll around in the leaves?"

"I have not been involved in the planning, Fraulein. I do know that the women are to have only one encounter, and they are to ask to see their companion's Olympic identification and write down the information. In case . . ."

"You are not going to chase down these athletes later and foist a child on them, are you?"

"Oh, no, it's so the state knows who the Aryan father is, if that is the result, as the state cares for the child. That's all. Otherwise, there are no questions asked and we aren't here to make judgments."

"And in another twenty years or so, we have German Olympians?"

"I have heard that possibility raised, but I don't believe it's the purpose."

"So you are telling me to stay away from the forest?"

The superintendent smiled. "Unless you are shooting a very different kind of film than what I have been told."

Leni had used the editing rooms at the Geyer Film Laboratories, in the southeastern Berlin borough of Neukölln, as far back as *The Blue Light*. So she was in a familiar setting there as she went through the footage from the Greece trip with Stephan, her young, but already balding, editing assistant and clerk. With Stephan hovering around to do her bidding, she made no decisions about what she would use—that was a long way off—but she wanted to get a rough idea of what they had, from both the real ceremony and torch relay and from her own versions that paid more homage to antiquity.

The raw, developed Prologue footage from the Acropolis was confirmation for her: Willy Zielke was brilliant, both as a director and cinematographer. His work would set the tone and the foundation for the remainder of the filming. Still, she had the gnawing feeling that something was missing, a bridge between the shots of the ruins and the sculptures in one segment and Anatol's torch lighting and her restaged relay segments in the next. Then it hit her: *Muses! Sirens! Show beautiful nude women dancing, perhaps with a body of water behind them. And then go to the torch lighting and runners!* She resolved to corner Willy during the Games to discuss shooting that sort of additional footage for the Prologue in the coming months. Willy was a strange fellow, but she didn't think he would rebel about shooting nude women, perhaps even in an exotic location.

With that weight off her mind, she felt buoyant as she returned to planning the filming of the Games. She had worked with most of the cameramen on other projects. One reason she consented to do another film on the 1935 Party Congress was that she could use it to put together a staff for *Olympia* and practice for the monumental task ahead in Berlin. *Day of Freedom* was only twenty-eight minutes long and saluted the career military men of the Wehrmacht, all but ignored in *Victory of Faith* and *Triumph of the Will*. It mollified the Wehrmacht, which she knew could only help her. In the finished film, she ignored the announcement of the monumental Nuremberg Laws, which stripped Jews of virtually all their rights as German citizens. She did that for two reasons: One, she considered the film a supplement to the two previous Party Congress films and didn't want to go over old ground, however justified the message. To Germans, even the Nazi hierarchy, she could say: *It was time to give the Wehrmacht its due*. Two, as she sought to return to acting and directing dramatic films, she was fine with producing a film that allowed her to say to the rest of the world: *See, I don't get involved in dogma*.

The Reich's *Olympia* budget was so extravagant that Leni had no problem rationalizing the huge expense of renting and renovating Castle Ruhwald, an old and unused building in a park on the Spandauer Chaussee, as the Olympia crew's headquarters. Castle Ruhwald was only eight kilometers from the Reich Sports Field, the site of the Olympic Stadium, swimming stadium, and most of the competition venues.

All three hundred Olympia-Film employees moved in, including Leni, who temporarily left behind her plush fifth-floor apartment on the Hindenburgstrasse in Central Berlin. Married or unmarried, all the film employees knew they would be working long hours at the event sites and attending late-night planning meetings, so it would be easier to be at the company's temporary headquarters. Plus, there was a band-together mentality among the filmmakers, carpenters, electricians, drivers, message runners, and even the cooks and janitors, as if the Castle were their own Olympic Village. Leni had the only private bedroom, isolated in one corner. Other sleeping quarters were both in separate rooms—six or eight per room—or barracks-style in vast halls. Lavatory and shower facilities were plentiful. Equipment could be stored, maintained, or repaired in several large shops. Food was served cafeteria style.

Anatol Dobriansky had his own bed among the runners and drivers. Leni's Truth was that she gave in to the young Russian's entreaties to be brought to Germany, much of them pantomimed, and that she told him he could work as one of her message-runners during the Games . . . but then he must go back to Greece. Anatol was enthusiastic, tireless, and now—after settling into Berlin and being excited by what he saw, including the power of her fame—infatuated with Leni.

With morning light showing between the small crack in the curtain, Leni awakened, looked at the clock and lightly nudged the slumbering Anatol. He moaned, turned back toward her, and then reached for her with one arm. Leni ducked under it, quickly kissed his forehead and rushed out of bed.

Looking down at him, she smiled indulgently. "Oh, you're a fun boy, but I just don't have time."

After she bathed and was dressed, she shook him awake again. "You need to be dressed and out of here in ten minutes." She pointed at her watch and at Anatol, and pantomimed his exit. "Understand me?" Sitting up, he nodded, but still had a vacant look. Leni told him, "When you walk into the cafeteria, you will act like nothing happened."

Anatol nodded again.

"And this is going to be the last time for a while," she said.

Maybe ever.

He understood well enough to look hurt.

Leni thought: *I'm going to be too busy to babysit.*

She said, "And if anyone asks you where you were since last night, you just look at them like you're an idiot and you don't understand a goddamn word they said."

Starting to walk away, she laughed darkly. Without turning, she added, "You won't even need to act."

As she waited for the stragglers to arrive at the staff meeting, Leni stood next to a meticulously constructed scale model of the Reich Sports Field and looked at the men—all men—seated around the long table in the long, skinny room. Perhaps some changes would have to be made, but as of this moment, she considered the official roster of cameramen—Leni was always thinking of how the credits would look—to be forty-five. Most had assistants, too, so the room was jammed.

So many old friends, mostly trusted, both personally and professionally—includ-ing Hans and Guzzi, who have shared my bed. Hans Ertl, her lover as recently as three years earlier, when both worked on *S.O.S. Iceberg*, was the mechanical genius. Suggest something and he found a way to do it, as he would show soon when shooting both above and below the water with the same camera at the Olympic pool. Guzzi Lantschner was a handsome skiing star who won a silver medal in the Alpine Combined in the Winter Olympics earlier in the year. Appearing in the mountain movies, he learned how to work the cameras—and was becoming one of the best in the business. Among the others, handsome Walter Frentz was the perfect man to work from the pits at the track and field and know how to shoot the same things as others but get better images. And Heinz Jaworsky, so patient and professional, was such a good soldier in Greece! Most of the rest were veterans, too. She trusted them to adapt to the unpredictable and unscripted nature of the athletic events, such a contrast to either scripted stories or the plodding pageantry at the Nuremberg rallies.

She handed out sheets with assignments for each of the crews for the week leading up to the Games. The goal would be to become familiar with the sites and, as the athletes began showing up and practicing, to get a better feel for how to film specific events. Plus, they would compile film of likely medalists as they trained, accumulating the sort of close-ups not easily attainable in the real competition. Referring to a notepad, she ran down her list of strategic points. They had heard much of the spiel before, but she wanted it fresh in their minds.

"We'll also be shooting material next week at the Olympic Village, both training and in the living quarters, so be on the lookout for anything that gives the film more of an international slant and proves we are not fixated on our own athletes . . ."

"Once the Games start, shoot everything taking place in front of you. When in doubt, keep shooting . . ."

"Always wear the all-access armband, but also wave your Olympia-Film card, if necessary, and act as if anywhere you want to go, you belong there. Don't take no for an answer and tell them to take it up with me . . ."

"Remember: Film! Art! Not newsreel . . ."

"Don't shy away from the winners . . . no matter who they are. We'll worry about who they are later . . ."

"Remember, Rolf here"—she pointed at Rolf Lantin, who had one of his cameras on the table in front of him—"will be with me most of the time to shoot still photos for a booklet or other material about the making of the film."

"When runners give you communications from me, even if I am being critical, don't be defensive. Act! As we move along, the best assignments will go to those who are doing the best jobs. . . ."

"We will hope to assemble here each night at eleven o'clock. We'll go over general issues, and then I will meet with each cameraman individually to go over plans for the next day. Clearly, some of you will have to wait a long time, so I am asking for your indulgence . . ."

A half hour after the meeting ended, Ernst Jäger knocked on her half-opened door and came in. "The Olympic programs just came in!" he said excitedly. "They put an American on the cover."

"Not one of the Negroes?" Leni asked incredulously.

"No, no, no," Jäger responded. "They wouldn't have been that stupid."

"Who then?"

"Decathlon man. World-record holder. They needed to decide on the cover a month ago, and they told me the Americans picked their decathlon men before the rest of the team, so they were able to get a picture."

Jäger returned soon with a copy. Entranced, Leni looked at the dark-haired, chiseled American throwing the shot put on the cover.

"Glenn Morris," she said slowly, reading.

Jäger mused, "Put him in a uniform, and he could have been in *Triumph of the Will.*"

"I don't know about that," Leni said. She thought of Luis Trenker, her striking costar—and former lover—from her early "Alpine" films and added, "But in *The Holy Mountain*, certainly. He's more handsome than Trenker!"

Jäger said, "You know the winner of the decathlon is declared the world's greatest athlete, correct?"

"I didn't know that," Leni said, distracted.

I must meet that man.

With the Games so close, Leni considered politely declining Air Minister Hermann Göring's invitation to hear American pioneer pilot Charles Lindbergh's speech at the Air Ministry, and then attend an afternoon tea honoring Lindbergh put on by Lufthansa, the national airline. But she decided that the opportunity to meet the first man to fly across the Atlantic solo was too compelling to ignore.

Lindbergh ostensibly was in Germany to represent the U.S. Army Air Corps and inspect Luftwaffe facilities. The growing tensions between the nations didn't preclude openness, and in fact made displays of strength and preparedness prudent. But Leni had heard the hints that Lindbergh in private moments sounded as if he were carrying a National Socialist Party membership card in his wallet.

Reporters stood in the back of the room as Lindbergh began his speech at the luncheon—a speech he gave a sentence or two at a time before allowing a well-dressed, middle-aged civilian translator to pass along his message in German. Leni was one of the few women in the room. At first, she wondered if the notes in front of the American were his own, or he was following instructions from his military leaders. She quickly decided, no, the pilot's thoughts were his own—and nervy, considering his audience. It sounded as if he were speaking directly to the portly Göring, the Great War flyer now in charge of the German air forces.

Air power in the Great War had led to significant destruction, Lindbergh noted. But that would be nothing compared to what could happen in future wars, given the advances in bomber aircraft and weaponry. He said "those in aviation" should attempt to avoid the unnecessary unleashing of the new forces of unprecedented destruction, and he called for a "new security founded on intelligence." Leni interpreted that as praise of the Reich's openness on his tour, and as a challenge to continue it—and even for his own nation to reciprocate. Around her, though, the reddened faces and squirming of Luftwaffe men made her wonder if they thought Lindbergh was merely chiding his hosts.

A little later, as she waited in the reception line at the Lufthansa tea, Leni noticed that Lindbergh was uneasy as he shook hands, seemingly intent on avoiding any communication that would require the interpreter at his side to become involved in something other than introductions. When it was Leni's turn, the Luftwaffe adjutant held out the introductory card for the interpreter, but he ignored it. He didn't need it. He had seen *The Blue Light* four times.

"Fraulein Leni Riefenstahl," the interpreter said. As Lindbergh took her hand, the interpreter added in English, "Our renowned actress and filmmaker."

Smiling, Lindbergh said, "Oh, I know Miss Riefenstahl's work. Please tell her I very much admire it."

Leni cut off the translation. "Thank you," she said in English. She continued, "Thank you for your message. I agree our nations need to be open with each other."

"Yes," Lindbergh said solemnly. "With communication and candor, peace is possible."

The Luftwaffe officer behind Leni was being shoved along, so she smiled again and left Lindbergh. As she walked away, Leni wondered if he had seen her on-screen as Leni, the actress, or simply been shown one of the documentaries in his briefings. Then she decided that Lindbergh's smile was his answer. That was the smile of another man who was meeting Junta.

A balding man with a moustache and in glasses strode toward her, catching her attention with a slight wave. She recognized him as American journalist William Shirer, well known in the Reich Chancellery circles and considered an influential—and often challenging—voice in the portrayal of the Reich for the American readership. Two years earlier, he had just arrived in Germany as a correspondent when he covered the Nuremberg rally, which was the basis for *Triumph of the Will* and later told her of the film: "I wanted to stop watching it because of what I was seeing, but I couldn't. It was that mesmerizing. And frightening."

She had interpreted that as at least respect for her work, but as Shirer's antagonistic reputation spread, she wondered if he had been playing the role of a nit-picking critic.

"Good evening, Fraulein Riefenstahl. I'm William Shirer, Universal News Service," he said.

"Of course, Mr. Shirer," she said neutrally. "I remember you."

"I'm wondering how your preparations are going for your Olympics film," he said.

"Very satisfactorily, Herr Shirer. It will be a tribute to beauty, competition, and the Olympic ideal."

"Have you have been instructed to downplay the accomplishments of American Negroes if they are successful here?"

Leni remained calm. "As you saw in my previous work, I am an independent artist," she declared. "I am a filmmaker. I do not have preconceptions when I begin a project. I document what we see. We will simply have to see how events unfold, won't we?"

Shirer asked, "Shall I interpret that as a 'no'?"

Leni's eyes flashed defiance. "Interpret that as a 'no, no one tells me what to do.'"

10

∼

Zehnkampf! Zehnkampf!

As the SS *Manhattan* traveled up the Elbe River toward Hamburg, the word spread through the American athletes that Avery Brundage had just kicked Eleanor Holm Jarrett off the Olympic squad.

Glenn didn't know whether to be mad or sad. He could still hear Eleanor saying of Brundage: "Oh, he's just bluffing."

One of her young swimmer roommates seemed to know the most, and more trickled in from the athletes' grapevine. The word was that Eleanor had played dice with the sportswriters the afternoon before and later partied in first class and had been loud when walking around the deck before going back to her room. The stories differed, depending on who was telling them or how many times they had been passed along, but most agreed that the swim team's chaperone, Ada Sackett, had confronted Eleanor during the evening, suggested she go to bed, and was told to mind her own business. This morning—when Eleanor hadn't been in bed long—Sackett took the ship doctor to wake her up and examine her. The doctor declared her in the throes of acute alcoholism. The swim coaches made all the girls on the team go to Eleanor's room and see how sick she was, and then reported her to Brundage. And a few hours later, Brundage had passed judgment: Eleanor was off the Olympic team.

Glenn and Walter Wood were on the deck later when Joe Williams hustled over to them.

"Hey, boys, can I get your comment on Mrs. Jarrett's suspension?"

"Mister Williams, I don't know enough to comment," Glenn said. "You know more than I do. All I know is she is off the team and that's sad."

"Wood?"

"Put me down for the same thing, Mr. Williams."

After Williams left, Walter nudged Glenn.

"That was weird," Walter said. "But you sure were right about him knowing more than we do."

"I hadn't thought of it that way," Glenn said, realizing what he meant.

They had both heard that Williams and Paul Gallico were among Eleanor's favorite drinking buddies, and that many writers were treating the crossing as a nine-day party. Glenn wondered if that helped explain why Williams, who was supposed to be chronicling the Colorado athlete for the *Rocky Mountain News*, hadn't yet asked him about anything else.

Before the Americans were to go ashore the next morning, Brundage called another team meeting. Glenn was trying to figure out if these lectures would be a common occurrence in Berlin, too. He hoped not.

"Ladies and gentlemen, I understand that dispatches in American newspapers have said this trip over was hijinks on the high seas, with parties going on around the clock," Brundage said. "You've been slandered. Human nature being what it is, some people will believe what they read. I'm suggesting that when you write home, correct them."

A swimmer near Glenn quietly said, "We got that straight, boys? All we did on the way over was work out, eat, and read the Bible!"

Brundage moved on to a spiel about representing America and being polite to officials, spectators, and even fellow competitors.

"Remember we are representing the greatest country in the world and we are here to win for the honor of our country and the glory of our sport. If I'm not able to address you all after we arrive . . . good luck to you all."

The athletes cheered—as much because his speech seemed to be over as in reaction to its sentiment.

Beating Walter Wood back to the room, Glenn finished packing and, as ordered, put on the blue blazer, tie, slacks, and white hat. Because of the uniforms and clothes they had acquired during the trip, they were issued a duffle bag they could use along with their own suitcase. As he was about to leave, he stopped in the doorway and looked back. In the nine days of the crossing, it had become home, the spot where he would lie on the bed and look at the ceiling or close his eyes and picture his dreams for

Berlin. Clearing 12 feet in the pole vault. Doing so well in the 100 meters and the broad jump, Jesse Owens congratulated him and said he was glad Glenn was in the decathlon and not the "regular" events. Plowing along in the 1,500 meters until he knew he had the gold clinched. Accepting the gold medal. Looking at the American flag and hearing "The Star-Spangled Banner."

All in his third decathlon ever.

Glenn shut the door and headed for the deck. At the rail, he had mixed feelings as he stood among his teammates, with his suitcase at his feet. A huge banner, in English, at the Hamburg dock announced: "WELCOME TO GERMANY." A band played "Stars and Stripes Forever." The American flag was next to the German flag. Along the shore, Germans welcomed them—with the Nazi salute.

Next to Glenn, Marty Glickman said, "That just doesn't look right. That shit, with our flag."

Walter Wood joined them. "Hey, Glenn," he said. "You forgot something in the room." He reached into his duffle bag, pulled something out, and handed it to Glenn.

It was Karen's picture.

⁓

As the Americans filed onto the dock, a huge crowd welcomed them, despite the drizzly weather. At first skeptical, Glenn tried to spot evidence that it all was scripted, rather than genuine, but the warmth of the smiles and the greetings, and the outreached hands, won him over. He was shocked to see that many, especially the children, were eager to touch the Negroes. The displays of friendliness continued during and after the ride to the beautiful and historic Hamburg City Hall, where dignitaries not only welcomed them, but also insisted on all—the American athletes included—joining in a toast of friendship with orange juice and sherry.

"Where's Eleanor when we really need her?" Jack Torrance asked.

"They say she's going to be on the train with us to Berlin," swimmer Al Vande Weghe said.

At the Hamburg train station, as they were waiting to board the express to Berlin, sprinter Mack Robinson voiced what had been running through the minds of Glenn and many others. "I know the Germans are supposed to hate me, but they're sure not acting like it," he said.

Sam Stoller snorted. "They look down on you Negroes. They *hate* us Jews. But they aren't sure which ones we are."

"You know what I'd like to think?" Glenn asked. "When nobody has time to tell the regular German people how to act, when they're just reacting naturally, maybe they're not so bad."

"Keep dreaming, Morris," Marty Glickman scoffed.

"I agree with him," declared 400-meter runner Archie Williams. "Think they'd let us in the City Hall in Birmingham?"

"Hold on. It's all a charade from now on," said sprinter Ralph Metcalfe. "They're trying to fool us—and the world."

Jack Torrance asked, "Don't you think we've figured out what the Nazis are? They don't have us fooled. For Christ's sake, we almost skipped their Olympics!."

"And they're not *all* Nazis," Glenn reminded.

Stoller said, "What you're forgetting is that your 'regular' German people have less say every day. The thugs are taking over. It doesn't matter anymore how many decent Germans there are. Besides, more of *them* are deciding to go along with this bullshit every day."

Walter Wood nudged Glenn and pointed. In another area of the terminal, a group surrounded Eleanor Holm. Glenn and Walter wandered over. "At least I won a hundred bucks in the crap game," she told the group sarcastically. "If you want to do it, I won't stop you, and I'm grateful. They said I could come on the train and they'd at least listen to me. I'll tell 'em I'm sorry, I'm done drinking, and ask for another chance . . . but if that asshole Brundage thinks I'm gonna beg—at least beg *him*—he's got another guess coming."

In the half hour left before the Americans boarded the train, some of the athletes circulated, seeking signatures on handwritten petitions asking for Eleanor's reinstatement. When tiny swimmer-diver Katherine Rawls approached Glenn's group of trackmen, he waited as others signed. "The coaches don't know how much she helps the rest of us," she said. "She's really a nice person. She deserves another chance."

Glenn decided he needed to take a last-second trip to the bathroom.

"What was that all about?" Jack Torrance asked him when he returned. "Sure looked like you didn't want to sign."

"She already had her second chance," Glenn explained. "I've had Brundage up to here, too. If they let her back on the team, fine, but all they did was tell her to tone it down a bit. She wouldn't even do that."

"All true," Torrance conceded, "but it couldn't have hurt to sign the petition."

"Well, if Katherine still was here when I got back, I might have signed it. Not with a lot of enthusiasm, though."

"You can probably catch her . . . or any of the others with a copy," Torrance noted, gesturing at the girl about fifty feet away.

"That's okay. It can succeed or fail without me."

Glenn didn't leave his window seat as the express train passed through the countryside on the three-hour trip from Hamburg to Berlin. Everywhere they looked, there were young men in uniforms—Glenn couldn't, and didn't want to, keep them straight—and the swastika flags. Spotting the train as it traveled past, many of the Germans, and far from only those in uniform, gave the Nazi salute. Glenn wondered if a wave back qualified as acknowledging the salute and what it stood for.

The Berlin station was jammed.

"Think they do this for Norway?" Torrance asked dryly.

"Listen up everybody!" hollered a Badger at the door. "Step off and stay on the platform. They've got a little ceremony planned for us. Then we go to the buses."

As they stood in the aisles and waited to climb off, Glenn could see Brundage leading the way onto the platform, where a delegation of Germans in civilian suits waited. One man, apparently in charge, not only shook hands with Brundage, he also kissed him on the cheek.

"Did we just see that?" Glenn asked Walter Wood.

"Afraid so. At least there was no tongue."

When they all were wedged on the platform, Brundage's pal stepped to a microphone and introduced himself—in English—as Dr. Theodor Lewald of the German Organizing Committee. He welcomed the Americans and said he hoped the Games strengthened the bonds and increased understanding between the two nations. A band played "The Star-Spangled Banner," with the Germans through the station standing respectfully at attention, and then Brundage got his turn, alternating with the interpreter.

"We are happy first because we know the great disappointment Germany suffered when the 1916 Games were postponed because of the World War," he said. "And secondly, because the Olympic call has been answered so splendidly around the world that more than fifty nations will participate in what probably will be the finest competition in the history of sport. Conditions in Berlin are the finest ever provided in modern sports competition. We in the United States who pride ourselves on being the first in so many fields cannot equal the facilities provided here."

The crowd loved that.

The Americans headed to the vehicles outside. Young Germans both reached out to touch the Americans and to plead for autographs. Much to Glenn's amazement, the clamor for Jesse Owens again was enthusiastic and unrestrained. "Ow-ens! Ow-ens!" young boys hollered. Jesse slowed and tried to sign on the move.

Then as Glenn started through the line, he was even more amazed.

"Morris! Morris! *Zehnkampf! Zehnkampf!*"

He recognized the German word for decathlon. That much, he had learned. In the next five minutes, he signed more autographs than he had in four years of college sports competition. Many of them were on his huge picture on the cover of a German newspaper. As he signed one for a pretty young German woman, a javelin thrower looked over Glenn's shoulder. "What's that headline say?" he asked Glenn, good-naturedly. "'Beware, the Simla Sensation'?"

Glenn winced. The nickname had gotten around.

The javelin thrower snatched the paper from Glenn when he was done signing and handed it back to the girl, saying: "*Ich liebe dich. Du bist schön.*"

The girl smiled shyly. "*Danke.*"

"What was that?" Glenn demanded.

The javelin thrower grinned. "I said, 'I love you. You are beautiful.'"

Outside the station, as they waited to climb into the charabanc-style, or open-topped, buses and open cars that—according to the schedule on the sheet Glenn checked again—would take them to the Unter den Linden for a short parade to Rotes Rathaus, the city hall, for another welcoming ceremony. Sam Stoller raised his hand and called out: "All right, this is Germany now! All Negroes . . . know your place. You walk behind."

"You don't think we're used to that?" asked 400-meter man Jimmy Lu-Valle. "Just like home!"

"Yeah, but here's the difference," Stoller said. "All us Jews, get under the wheels!"

"Damn it, Stoller," a guy Glenn didn't recognize growled, "are you going to be this way the whole time? We're here to compete, not bitch, okay? If the Germans treat *you* like shit at the Village or anywhere else, and the same with our Negroes, I'll be the first in line to back you. But until that happens, why don't you do us all a favor and shut up! If you're going to hate this so much, you shouldn't have come, made your point that way and left a spot for someone who wanted to be here."

"Hey, I've got an idea," Torrance shouted. "Why doesn't *everybody* just shut up!"

That triggered applause and cheers.

Glickman and Stoller sat behind Glenn and Wood on a charabanc. As they headed to the Unter den Linden, the Germans waved and cheered from balconies, sidewalks, and windows. Swastika and Olympic flags were attached to light poles and flagpoles.

Glenn spotted the English-speaking German army man—introduced to them as Colonel Hauptmann—assigned to escort them to the Village.

"What does Unter den Linden mean?" he asked.

"Under the Linden," the man said. "Under the Linden trees."

Glenn waved. "Where are they?"

Earnestly, the German explained, "They had to be removed for the subway construction. Others will be planted to replace them later. But our visitors will thank us as they travel around during the Games."

As the Americans walked from the buses to the city hall, thousands of cheering and chanting Germans lined the now-treeless boulevard. Hammer thrower Donald Favor drew cheers when he traded hats with a Berlin policeman. Paul Gallico found Glenn. They had to holler to be heard.

"So, Morris, what do you think of the receptions today?" the writer asked.

"Very impressive," Glenn said.

"Have you heard about Sievert?"

"Hans Sievert? What do you mean?"

"The Germans say he's hurt and if he competes at all, it might just be in the shot put—but not the decathlon. So your stiffest competition is out. I need to get a comment from you."

"Well, if what you say is true . . ."

"It's true," said Gallico.

"If what they *tell* you is true," Glenn said, amending, "that's too bad. It's never good when someone isn't able to compete. I know how I'd feel if I couldn't. But it's still the same. Jack, Bob and I hope that one of us wins the gold for America."

"You know how to say all the right things!" Gallico said, teasing.

"I believe 'em!" Glenn declared. He paused. "Let me ask *you* something. Did you hear anything more about Eleanor Holm?"

"They turned down her appeal," Gallico said. "She said she'd never drink again if they gave her another chance, and I think that might have hurt her cause more than it helped because nobody believed her. I'll tell you one more thing if it's between just us for now."

"Okay."

"She's blasting all the Olympic Committee folks, saying they were partying all the way over, too, so they have little right to look down on her. She said at least a hundred other of you athletes drank, too."

"That's nice of her," Glenn said dryly.

"No, she said there's nothing wrong with that. She's saying she was treated differently, and I have to say I agree with her. That's going to hit all the papers back home. And she's already been signed up to do a column for Hearst—for the International News Service—from over here, so they're not going to be able to shut her up."

"She's writing?" Glenn asked.

"Well, her name's going to be on top of it," Gallico said. "A bunch of the guys will take turns ghosting it. Writing it for her."

"Tough work!"

"Hearst's boy helped get her drunk every night, so it's the least he can do."

11

~

The First Looks

The women's Olympic living quarters, the Friesenhaus, was on the grounds of the Reich Sports Field. In addition to being close to the competition venues, the American women—including the sixteen track and field competitors—also had the advantage of being within walking distance of a temporary train station and the huge Strength Through Joy Village, built for the Games, with restaurants and cavernous beer halls. They were about eighteen kilometers, or about eleven miles, west of Central Berlin.

The men's Olympic Village, in Döberitz, was another fifteen kilometers to the west. The Badgers asked Glenn Cunningham and some of the other veterans in the other sports if they wanted to visit the Reich Sports Field, with its various venues, on the way to the Village, or wait until the next day, and the answer was decisive: *It's on the way, isn't it? Let's do it now.*

The buses pulled into the Glockenturm Plaza, next to the tall, brick Great Bell Tower. The American teams from different sports separated, with the trackmen heading across the vast May Field to the Olympic Stadium. Badgers kept hollering that the buses would be leaving again in an hour.

Glenn and his teammates filed past the security guards and walked through the gap—the so-called marathon gate—in the west end of the cavernous bowl. The lower bowl and the field were carved out below ground level, so the stadium looked far bigger from the inside than it did from the outside. The Americans looked down wide stone stairs to the track and its infield. Directly below them, a tunnel opened onto the track.

Glenn Cunningham was in front, and when he stopped part of the way down, it created a brief logjam.

"I didn't think anything could be better than the Los Angeles Coliseum," Cunningham said, awed. "This is."

The sheer magnitude of everything stunned Glenn Morris, too. "Wow, it's huge," he marveled.

Jesse Owens and several of the Negroes caught up with them. "And it makes the track look tiny," Jesse said. "Like it's about two hundred meters around!" Glenn had to smile. Jesse had his track shoes, with the laces tied together, hanging around his neck.

About fifteen workers were mowing and trimming the grass, tinkering with runways and pits, and lining the lanes.

High jumper Cornelius Johnson waved an open hand, palm-up. "But what's with the holes?"

Now they all noticed the trenches. About four feet deep, they were reinforced with metal rails on the outside. Cunningham waved down the English-speaking man from the German Organizing Committee who had met them and followed them in. He asked the German what the holes were for.

"They are for the cameras," the man said. "Motion picture cameras."

Owens asked, "We're going to be in the movies?"

"Yes, Mr. Owens. Leni Riefenstahl is making a film of the Games."

Bob Clark blurted, "A whole movie on just the Olympics?"

"That's the plan," the German said. "The German Organizing Committee and the International Olympic Committee picked her. She and her people have been here quite often, making arrangements and setting up. I don't see them now, though."

Wait. That name . . .

"Did you say Leni Riefenstahl?" Glenn Morris asked.

"Yes," the German said. "Fraulein Riefenstahl has stated she will shoot perhaps a million meters of film at the Games for her movie."

Jack Torrance was incredulous. "*Fraulein? She?*"

He was startled when the answer came from Glenn Morris.

"Leni Riefenstahl . . . their Katharine Hepburn and John Ford rolled into one. She was an actress. Now she's a director. But she's still real young, under thirty."

"How do you know all that?" Torrance challenged.

"She was on the cover of *Time* a few months ago," Glenn said, shrugging.

"She a hot number?"

"I guess you could say that."

When they arrived on the track, Glenn kneeled and felt the cinders. The surface seemed fast and, at least if dry, conducive to top-flight performances. As soon as he had decided that, Owens trotted past him, with his track shoes on. He at least had placed his blazer on the barrier between the track and the seats.

"What you think, Jesse?" Glenn called out.

"A-okay!" Owens responded, not turning.

Standing again, in the corner of the track, Glenn looked at the upper deck and imagined a spectator in that far corner, looking down on him as he ran the 400 meters. He wondered how small he would look from way up there, and he wondered what he would look like in Leni Riefenstahl's film. He knew it would seem different when the seats were filled and the noise was deafening. Then he noticed the distinctly different seating area in the lower bowl, at mid-track. The area was cordoned off from the general seating sections, and was divided into boxes, as at a racetrack or a ballgame. At the top, between the façade of the upper deck and the boxes, a seating ledge—almost a mini-plaza—protruded.

The man from the German Organizing Committee got Glenn's attention. He was with a well-dressed older man, introduced to Glenn as Ernst Jäger. He was a writer, the German explained, who now was working with Fräulein Riefenstahl as a publicity aide on her Olympic film and needed to take Glenn to another part of the stadium.

Strange. Glenn was wary, even before checking his watch. "But the buses are leaving in forty minutes . . . from way over there," he said, gesturing in the direction of the May Field.

"We will get you to the Village in a car, if that is necessary," the German committeeman said. "Fräulein Riefenstahl would like to meet you."

"Wow," Glenn blurted. "Me and who else?"

Jäger, whose English was excellent, also said, "Only you. She believes the decathlon will be an important part of her film and she has been told that you are the likely champion."

Glenn thought: *I wish everyone would stop talking like that . . . it might jinx me.* "But why now?"

"Fräulein Riefenstahl is thorough. On anything, drama or documentary. This is the way she works. We were having meetings here, they told us the Americans had arrived, and she said, 'I must meet the decathlon man.'"

Halfway down the front stretch, Glenn and Jäger walked off the outside of the track, down a couple of stairs through a small plaza-type area and through one of the several doors in a wall mostly made of glass below the dignitaries' boxes. There was a small lobby and another set of double doors on the far side, and Jäger explained that the room beyond the doors was the lounge for dignitaries to gather before heading to their seats in the loge. The double doors opened and about ten men filed out, several of them carrying hand-held cameras. Several of them took in Glenn's Olympic wardrobe and nodded; others took no notice as they left. Jäger led him into the doorway, gestured to go ahead and then walked away.

At a long table on one side, a woman sat, scribbling furiously in a notebook. She was smartly dressed, in a white jacket and blouse, and a small jaunty hat that still allowed her hair to show. Frozen in the doorway, Glenn was transfixed. Sensing his presence, Leni Riefenstahl turned and, seeing him, stood. She was wearing baggy trousers, but her movement was so graceful, it made it even easier for him to imagine her great legs. From underneath her notebook and stack of papers, she pulled out the Olympic program. Holding it up, with his picture on the cover, she smiled and said, in English, "You are Glenn Morris."

"Yes . . . and you are Leni Riefenstahl."

Leni felt strange. This was not how it worked for her, and she wasn't quite sure how to handle it. She was often attracted, but that could be cold and clinical. She was rarely excited at the same time. This time, she was excited, even—and for the first time in years—a bit nervous.

The silence lasted only seconds, but seemed minutes to Glenn. Leni left her paperwork on the table, approached him and offered her hand held straight out, her palm parallel to the floor. Glenn reached out, too, and placed his hands above and below hers. The touch was electric, her look intoxicating. She wasn't flirting, yet that was more alluring than if she had been. She seemed not at all self-conscious about her obvious attraction. Glenn was used to women flirting; what made this different was Leni's lack of coyness. Or could he be imagining things? He released her hand; she didn't move.

"I've wanted to meet you ever since I saw the program," Leni said. "And read that you'll be our gold medalist. As perhaps Ernst told you, I am doing a film on the Games."

"The man from the organizing committee told us first. He told us what the trenches were for."

"Do you know who I am? What I do?"

Glenn didn't know how uncharacteristic it was for Leni to ask that in this tone. For once, she wasn't demanding. She really needed to know if he knew.

"Sure," Glenn said. "I saw you in *Time* magazine . . . on the cover, too. And I've heard about your films. Even seen some posters."

"Have you watched any of the films? They've been shown in a few of your cities."

"No, I'm sorry, I haven't." He smiled. "Where I'm from, we're lucky to see many *American* films. We're just now getting to the 'talkies.'"

"We might have to take care of that," she said suggestively. "And I mean the films I'm in, not the documentaries I was *ordered* to do. Despite what your magazine said."

He caught the "ordered."

Glenn pointed at the program, on top of the stack. He teased, "That the first you had heard of *me?*"

He was amazed at how easy that had come out, how quickly he had lowered his guard.

"I have to admit, yes, it was," she replied. "You dislike me for that?"

"Not at all," Glenn said. "Nobody in American knew who I was until a month ago."

"My film will make you famous, around the world," she declared. "It is about the dignity of the human body and the beauty of competition, and the decathlon will be a key passage."

Glenn asked, "What were you doing here today?"

"We were here early to check our camera placements and sightlines. We are trying to be different. This will not be newsreel." Pointing up, she added ominously, "And we also wanted to check the Führer's box."

"Hitler will be here?" Glenn asked.

"If he comes to the competition, his box is at the top of this area."

Glenn thought: *That ledge.*

Leni continued, "All we are sure about is the opening ceremony. He definitely will be here for that." She gave him a little wave. "Here, follow me."

They walked up a long, wide stone stairway, with hand railings on each side. At the top, after they passed through a small reception room, Glenn discovered that Hitler's small open-air box didn't have chairs or seats in it. A clear barrier about three feet high was at the front, with a rail across the top, but Glenn was shocked to see the box was otherwise open. At most, Glenn estimated, a dozen men could sit here, if they bunched into two rows.

"There will be a temporary rostrum and microphones there at the rail," Leni said, gesturing. Then she pointed to the sections below. "The dignitaries from the other nations will be down there. The Führer and his guests will be here." She smiled, letting him in on the joke. "I assume someone will bring them chairs."

Two men, one of them young, the other older, were in the box, looking down at the Americans on the field. Glenn's teammates were moving toward the marathon gate to leave, so he realized he didn't have much time.

Leni ignored the men. The young one was Anatol Dobriansky. Glenn didn't notice his glare.

"Wow," Glenn marveled. "This is where Hitler will be. I assume you know him?"

"I do," she said matter-of-factly.

"And? What's he like?"

Leni seemed to weigh her answer, taking a quick look at the other two men in the box.

Glenn said, "I'm sorry, that was a stupid question."

"No, that's all right," Leni assured him. After a few seconds, she added, "He is a complicated man."

A whistle sounded down on the field. Halfway up the marathon gate steps, Lawson Robertson waved at the athletes lingering on the field. He blew the whistle again and turned his back, walking up the stairs.

"I have to go," Glenn announced.

"Let me show you one other thing first," suggested Leni. She led him into the little room behind the box. They were alone, but Leni lowered her voice. "You Americans are accustomed to saying whatever you want. That can be a problem here. Even in English."

"For me or you?"

"For me, certainly. For you?" She shrugged. "I can't say."

After a few seconds, as the two men entered the room, she brightened and spoke louder.

"We have drivers if you want to stay longer," Leni said. "We could get you to the Village."

"We haven't been there yet, so I probably need to go in with the team," Glenn said.

She accepted that. Ernst Jäger suddenly appeared in the room, too. Leni turned to him and spoke German. Jäger nodded.

Leni said to Glenn, "Ernst will get you back to the field. I myself haven't learned where all the tunnels are in this place and where they go."

As Glenn started to follow Jäger, Leni called out. "One more thing. I will have a crew at the Village tomorrow to film some training. Will you be there?"

"I think so. But why film training?"

"So I have a better idea of what each event looks like, for planning," she said. "Also, so my photographers can acquaint themselves with the competitions, too. There might be close-up-type shots I can cut into the actual Olympic competition later, if need be."

Leni held out her hand again. Glenn's hold was tighter this time. "I probably won't be able to be there with the crew, though," she said. She smiled. "Administrative details, you understand. I will look forward to seeing you again . . . very soon. We will talk more."

Reluctantly, Glenn broke away.

12

Max Schmeling, Center

Their long white building was one of one hundred and forty identical dormitories for the athletes on the Village grounds. Thirteen rooms were in each. Walter Wood and Glenn's double room was at one end, nearest the bathroom area and the showers, and farthest from the large sitting room at the other end. The morning after their arrival, Glenn stepped on the scale in the bathroom area—he was shocked to see it registered in pounds, not kilos—and discovered he had gained eight pounds since leaving New York.

Starting today . . . eat light and train hard!

At the crowded Village practice track, along with Japanese, French, and British athletes, among others, Glenn ran several laps with Bob Clark and Jack Parker to warm up, with Brutus Hamilton watching. Then Hamilton called the three decathlon men together and asked each, in turn, their practice plans for the day. Since Clark also was competing in the regular broad jump, his routine was slightly different. "That all sounds fine to me," Hamilton told the three athletes. "I'm here if you need me from now on, and if you need anything, ask. But I'm not going to be in your hair, either." He paused. "As near as I can tell, you've got a real shot at finishing one, two, three. I want all three of you walking away thinking you did as well as you could. My goal is to let the medals fall where they may, as long as all three of you are on that stand. So you need to be helping each other out, too. Right?"

Clark said, "I think that's been our attitude all along, coach."

"Good," said Hamilton. He reached out with his right hand, palm down. Glenn and the other two decathlon men piled their hands on top of Hamilton's for a few seconds.

After Hamilton left them, Walter Wood wandered over from the discus ring. "Should we start calling you the Three Musketeers? All for one and one for all?"

A little self-consciously, Glenn said, "Our goal is to push each other to a sweep!"

Wood laughed. "Well, Mister Morris, I agree you'll get a medal unless your roommate smothers you with your pillow some night because you won't stop talking in your sleep!"

"He talks in his sleep?" Clark asked with a laugh.

Knowing he did, Glenn shrugged.

Wood said, "Not every night . . . or at least I haven't noticed it. But some nights." He grinned. "Don't worry, nothing juicy yet."

One of Glenn's first missions was to make sure he hadn't completely forgotten everything he knew about the pole vault in the previous two weeks. He joined the Americans' three pole-vaulters—current USC men Earle Meadows and Bill Sefton, plus former Trojan Bill Graber.

"You know what the worst part of the decathlon is at something like the Olympics?" Glenn asked Meadows as they stretched.

Meadows played along. "And what might that be?"

"Practicing with 'regular' people who are better than you in each event." He gestured at three nearby Japanese, picking up their poles and preparing to take practice vaults. "Those guys won't know who I am, and they'll be saying how could America send such a horrible vaulter here?"

Meadows laughed. "Glenn, I hate to burst your bubble, but once they see you try this, they'll *know* you're not a regular vaulter. They'll *know* you're in the decathlon."

Graber said softly, confiding, "You could learn by watching the Japanese guys, too. All three of 'em have perfect form. We're more athletic than they are, but they jump the same way every time." Graber pointed at the oldest Japanese vaulter. "Nishida was second at Los Angeles . . . yeah, two spots ahead of me. So he's an old man, too. But as near as I can tell, he's a good guy." Then he pointed at the other two, in succession. "Oe . . . Adachi . . . both of 'em could medal, or even win, too."

Glenn took his first few vaults—designed both to bolster his confidence and enable him to work on his form—at a paltry 3.0 meters, or not even 10 feet. The other vaulters seemed to be locked in at 3.4 meters, or about

11 feet, 2 inches, the opening height in the regular competition—a height Glenn would be giddy to accept in the decathlon. They made it look easy.

As the Japanese vaulters continued to work, Glenn sat down on a bench with Meadows and Graber.

"What do you think?" Glenn asked.

"It's not too late to switch back to right-handed," Graber teased.

"I'd show you how bad I am at it . . . except I might hurt myself, and that'd be on your conscience," Glenn replied.

"We'd at least get a laugh out of it, though," Meadows deadpanned.

"All right, let's be serious," said Graber. "From what I've heard, all you have to do is clear *something* and you've got the gold medal."

The accented voice came from behind them.

"That is what I believe, too."

The Americans turned. A squat, muscular blond man in the Germany warm-up suit skirted the bench and reached his hand out to Glenn. "Glenn Morris, I am Hans Sievert," he said warmly. Surprisingly warmly, Glenn thought.

Still shaking Sievert's hand, Glenn stood up. "Wow," Glenn said. He turned to the vaulters. "This is Hans Sievert . . . the Germans' best decathlon man."

Smiling, Sievert said, "I am the *former* world record holder." He gestured at Glenn. "This man broke it. And I expect him to beat his own record here."

"What about you?" Meadows asked Sievert.

"Alas, I won't be in the decathlon," said the German. "I have an injured leg and can't run. I'm competing, but only in the shot put." He laughed. "I'll be fortunate not to finish last."

"So it's true," Glenn said.

"That I won't compete? Yes, it is true," said Sievert. "But our Erwin Huber is a fine veteran!"

"I'm really sorry you won't be in it," Glenn declared.

"You are?"

"Absolutely. I really want to see how good I am against the very best."

"I hope that whatever man wins the gold medal—you, Huber, the other Americans, anybody else—does so with a score I know I couldn't have beaten. That way, I won't feel as badly. So I'll be rooting for you all."

Glenn thanked him.

"I also have to ask you if you will do something for Fraulein Riefenstahl's Olympic documentary film crew," Sievert said.

Glenn hoped his excitement didn't show. "What is that?"

"In about forty-five minutes, when the others should be done, come over to the ring and let them take film of you putting the weight," Sievert said.

Glenn realized he meant throwing the shot put. "I guess so," he said.

"Should we call you 'Hollywood' Morris?" Meadows asked, teasing.

Sievert seemed to catch the gist of that. He said to Meadows, "I believe they might do the same thing with you at your event later in the week. Fraulein Riefenstahl and her people are thorough. And I need to ask the same of your other decathlon men."

"That's better," Meadows said.

After more small talk, about the great dining hall food, the Village cabins, and the Americans' reception in Berlin, Sievert shook hands all around again. "See you in a little while," he told Glenn, and then headed off to find Clark and Parker.

Meadows said, "His English sure as hell is a lot better than my German."

"Kind of embarrassing sometimes, isn't it?" Glenn mused. "And then all these boys in uniform here . . ."

They'd all noticed the uniformed boys from the Reich's Honorary Youth Service stationed at the Village as stewards, all trained in various languages. At least half spoke English fluently and already had served as guides and aides for many Americans in their brief time on the grounds. The Americans had two English-speaking military men assigned to them—Captain Hauptmann from the Army and Captain Dierksen from the Navy. It didn't seem right to ask their first names, so nobody ever learned them. Glenn and the Americans also had been told they could ask for the use of guides if they wanted to take sightseeing or exploratory visits into Berlin. The debate was whether it was wise to take along the guides, or to prefer the privacy of being unescorted.

Graber said, "I think it's kind of scary."

Meadows asked, "Scary? How?"

"There's a little too much of that over here," Graber said. "For one thing, they sound smarter than we do. I mean, when was the last time you heard anyone say, 'Alas'?"

Glenn smiled, because he had been thinking the same thing.

Graber continued, "Did you see *All Quiet on the Western Front?*"

Glenn said, "Yeah. Great film."

Graber said, "It's like I'm watching that again. German soldiers speaking English."

"Sievert's *not* a soldier," Glenn corrected.

"He will be," Graber said. "They *all* will be. And so will we."

"Thanks, mister gloom and doom," Meadows said, shaking his head. "You think even if another war starts over here, we'll be in it again?"

"Another war's going to start and yeah, I do," Graber said.

"Hope you're wrong," Glenn said. "On both counts."

Glenn, Clark, and Parker arrived at the shot put ring at the same time. Sievert introduced them to Erwin Huber, who turned out to be leaner than Sievert and physically more impressive, and was dark-haired with a cleft chin and an engaging grin; and to cameraman Albert Kling, who—it quickly became apparent—didn't speak a word of English. With Sievert watching, and the cameraman prone just outside the front of the shot put ring with his huge film camera, Glenn went first, throwing the shot put *over* Kling and his camera. He hoped he didn't "scratch" or step out of the ring, trip over the man and fall awkwardly. Glenn imagined the headline: "Morris Breaks Arm in Camera Accident, Knocked Out of Games." Kling filmed from the side for a third throw. Then he nodded, indicating he had enough film of Glenn, reached out, shook his hand again and said, "Thank you." He'd been trained to say that much.

Clark, Parker, Huber, and Sievert went through the same routine.

When they were done, Glenn turned to Sievert. "Can you ask the photographer what it's like to work for Leni Riefenstahl?" Sievert turned to Kling and rattled off a question with "Fraulein Riefenstahl" in it. Kling answered back.

Sievert reported, "He said, 'She works very, very hard, and expects the same from her crew.'"

Glenn was genuinely curious. "Does she know what she's doing?"

Sievert squinted. "I'm sorry, I don't understand."

"Is she knowledgeable about the technical things, or does she just watch everyone work?"

Sievert asked and Kling answered decisively. Sievert interrupted him in bursts to translate, with the cameraman figuring that out and pausing in appropriate places. Sievert turned to Glenn. "He says she has blinkers when she works. . . . She understands everything. . . . Her instructions are very precise. . . . She says what lens to use . . . what focus length . . . how many frames to run . . . what filter to apply. . . . If cameramen have not worked with her before . . . they start out thinking they know more than her . . . then they discover that she teaches them things. . . . All who know her well say . . . she studied everything during the filming when she was an actress . . . soaked it all up like a . . . sponge."

Glenn nodded. He had sensed as much.

"Glenn Morris!"

Glenn turned. The yell had come from Coach Lawson Robertson, near the broad jump pit. Robertson was with a couple of well-dressed older men, but they had started to walk away. The coach waved Glenn over.

"How much longer you working out?" Robertson asked.

"Maybe an hour," Glenn said. "Just want to run a while now."

Robertson looked at his watch. "Okay, that'll work out fine. When you've showered, put on one of the USA sweaters—over a tie, maybe—and slacks and be in the entrance plaza at 3." He gestured at the men he had been talking with. "They say there's going to be a big wheel visitor, and they want you to meet him and have your picture taken with him."

"Who is it?"

"They wouldn't tell me."

"Well," Glenn said hesitantly, "this won't get me in trouble, will it?"

Robertson grinned. "I think they would have said if it was Hitler."

Glenn couldn't keep his mission secret from his roommate, so Walter Wood came with him. The photographers were set up and waiting in the plaza, just inside the front gate. Glenn recognized the familiar men from Associated Press, Alan Gould and his photographer, but there were others, mostly German. He was about to ask if they knew who was coming when the entourage came into sight. As the group got closer, Glenn spotted the man in the middle. He was wearing a stylish three-piece dress suit, complete with the handkerchief fashionably showing in the outside breast pocket. His walk was leisurely, but he didn't need to swagger to have one.

It was the man pictured on the front page of the *Milwaukee Journal* sports section behind the bar in the Café Brandenburg—Max Schmeling, the former heavyweight champion of the world and Joe Louis's recent conqueror. The boxer was with Dr. Theodor Lewald of the German Organizing Committee. Spotting Glenn near the photographers and writers—the USA sweater made him hard to miss—the German official waved Glenn and Schmeling together, as if he were a referee about to give them their pre-fight instructions in the middle of the ring.

The boxer didn't wait to be introduced.

"Ah, the program boy! The decathlon hero!" Shaking Glenn's hand warmly as the photographers did their work, he added, "It's a pleasure to meet you, Glenn Morris."

"Thank you, Mr. Schmeling."

"Max!"

"Congratulations on your victory last month . . . Max."

"Did I surprise you, too?"

Glenn smiled. Uncomfortably feeling as if the whole world was listening, he added, "Well, yes, you did. Joe Louis is a great fighter."

"I know that. He is a credit to his nation."

Schmeling asked Glenn if he had his legs back after the boat ride across the Atlantic, and Glenn said it probably would be a few more days.

"That's why I take the *Hindenburg*," said Schmeling. "Only takes a couple of days. And I . . ."

He turned to a German and in a quick exchange, sought help for a word in English. Turning back, he said, "I vomited only once."

Glenn introduced Walter Wood, who shook Schmeling's hand as if he wasn't going to let go.

At the first lengthy pause, Gould spoke up. "Max, can we get a picture of you and Morris running—like you're in training?"

Schmeling nodded.

"Walter, too?" Glenn asked.

Gould looked at the photographer. "Sure," the photographer answered. "Better picture with one on each side."

Glenn's smile was genuine as they walked about a hundred feet down the cement pathway and then turned and "ran" back toward the cameras. He was enjoying himself. Imagine, he thought, he had met Jack Dempsey and Max Schmeling—two former heavyweight champions—in the last two weeks, one on each side of the Atlantic. The two American athletes flanked Schmeling as they trotted up to, and then past the cameramen.

The conversation at dinner got around to sex. Several Australian and New Zealander trackmen crashed one of the American dinners, joking that since they arrived in the first week of July, their goal was to eat in each of the thirty-eight cafeterias within the huge dining hall building. "Don't know how anyone eats that Japanese gruel, though," one said. "Everything else has been great, though." They were at the table with Glenn and a dozen Americans.

The word already had gotten around about the Aussies and New Zealanders' encounters with the German maidens at the lake—and, in theory, the similar opportunities that awaited the Americans or any other "Aryans."

"It's kind of creepy, actually," said one of the Aussies. "Policemen are guarding the area. Couple of Gestapo types had to wave me past. Then the girl had to approve me, too. Had to hand her my Olympic badge and she wrote down every goddamned word on it. It was like she was filling out a form at the doctor's office. She said no way could I use a wrap. And she bled all over."

"Would you do it again?"

The Aussie laughed. "I said I wouldn't, but . . ."

"I can guess what's going to happen," said an American Glenn didn't recognize. "Everybody's gonna say no way will they do that . . . but we'll all be out there before this is over. And there are going to be a bunch of babies born next spring or so who look like us."

A New Zealander said, "Ah, but the big question is . . ." He nodded to the table where most of the American Negroes were eating. Only then, he continued, ". . . what if any of them try to get in on it? Not that I have anything against it, but these Nazis sure do."

The Aussie laughed and leaned forward, trying to keep his voice down. "From all I hear, your Negroes don't need help getting sex," he said.

Glenn remained silent as he finished his roast beef and potatoes. When he was done, got up, and approached the doors, Archie Williams was waiting for him. At first, Glenn was worried that Williams had gotten wind of the conversation with the Aussies.

"I understand you met Max Schmeling," the 400-meter runner said.

Glenn's first reaction was to be relieved. "Yeah, Walter Wood and I did."

"They say you told him it was great that he beat Joe Louis."

Glenn no longer was relieved. "I congratulated him. That's all. He won. I congratulated him. What's wrong with that?"

Williams said, "He's German. Joe Louis is American. You congratulated the German? Did you give him the Nazi salute, too?"

"Come on, Archie! I didn't mean it that way. Really. I didn't!"

Williams looked him in the eyes for a few seconds. "All right, I'll take your word for it."

As they started walking again, Williams confessed, "They introduced him to Jesse, too. Schmeling even shook his hand. Told Jesse he knows he's going to win a bunch of gold medals."

Walter caught up and unsuccessfully tried to recruit Glenn to head to the Hindenburg Hall, the community building with movie theaters and a concert hall, to hear the Berlin Orchestra.

"You Cornell guys . . ." Glenn teased. "Noses in the air."

"Hey, it's relaxing," said Wood. "You should try it!"

"No, thanks!"

With Walter gone, Glenn wrote a brief note to Karen. Then he realized he owed a letter to his Denver Athletic Club benefactor, George Whitman. In it, Glenn summarized the trip over and the team's arrival in Berlin, then finished up with:

> Maybe I shouldn't have been so surprised that Schmeling wanted to meet me. They look at the decathlon a little different over here. The people in Germany think a decathlon man is about tops in athletics, so I have been the target of autograph seekers, movie cameras and the curious element. Hans Sievert seemed surprised when I told him I was sorry he couldn't compete. I mean it. I wish he were competing so I can see if I really am the superior. I know I'll have some tough competition as it is, but I'm going to be ready. I'll not let you down if it's humanly possible to win. I'm going over 8,000 points or die. I hope all three of us American boys do that, in fact, and we're all standing there on the medal stand watching three of our flags go up. I hope I'm in the middle, of course, but we want to make America proud of all three of us and maybe get more people to realize they should pay as much attention to our event as the sprints or the distance races, and not just once every four years.

As Glenn finished sealing the envelope and placed it on his nightstand, there was a knock on his door. It was the young steward from the Honorary Youth Service assigned to the building. He handed Glenn a small envelope. "A letter for you, Mister Morris," the boy said in his precise English. "It was left for you at the gate, not posted, and they called for me to come get it right away."

A few letters had been waiting for Glenn when the team arrived, but he still enjoyed seeing the address on the envelope, as if it were confirmation that he really was at the Olympics:

> Mr. Glenn Morris
> American Olympic Team
> Olympic Village
> Berlin

The return address, though, was what really got his attention:

> L. Riefenstahl
> Olympia-Film
> Castle Ruhwald
> Berlin

"I am to return in thirty minutes to see if you have a return note for me," the boy said. "The driver is waiting, I am told."

Excited and a bit confused, Glenn thanked the boy, closed the door, then opened the envelope and read the handwritten note on Leni's stationery. She wrote that it had been a wonderful experience to meet him. She thanked him for allowing her crew to shoot him putting the weight that day. She told him that before the Games began, and they both became so busy, she would enjoy getting to know him better, since he was so likely to be featured in the film. She would have her car pick him up at the front gate at 19:45 (or 7:45) the next evening, and he would be brought to a dinner in Central Berlin—unless, of course, he had a previous commitment or otherwise was unable to leave the Village. If either was the case, she would understand. She said she hoped whoever delivered the note had asked him to write her a return note and send it back via her messenger. And she said that for many reasons, she asked that he not tell the other Americans of the meeting. She closed with: "Come hungry."

Glenn read the note four times, trying to read between the lines. Was this as blatant as it seemed? She was a world-famous actress, for God's sake, four years older. Or was it truly only a social gesture, "a dinner," one that would find him dining with Leni and seven other members of her crew—or even with her and her lover of the moment, whoever that was? Was he imagining things, including the intrigue and even a hint of danger?

This is like Claudette Colbert asking you to dinner! You've never met a woman like this in Simla. Or Fort Collins. How your world has changed in the past few weeks! And this, before the Olympics have even started!

Glenn again used the Olympic Village stationery supplied to the athletes.

"Thank you for the invitation. I will be at the gate. Sincerely, Glenn Morris."

After the steward picked up the note, Glenn had trouble getting to sleep. Then, at some point in the middle of the night, when he was dreaming of Leni in the costume on the movie poster cheering him on in the pole vault, he suddenly was awake. He was awake because Wood, who had turned on his desk light, was standing over Glenn and shaking him.

"Jesus, this time, you were talking to beat the band!"

Glenn, still groggy, just stared.

"Sorry," he said, finally.

Wood went back to bed and turned out his light. A few seconds later, he spoke up in the dark. "You must be pretty stoked to be in that Olympics movie. Or be all horned up to chase after her."

"Why you say that?" Glenn asked, dreading the answer.

"Shit, it was 'Leni this,' 'Leni that,'" Wood said. He laughed. "Don't worry, as near as I can tell, you weren't tearing her clothes off or anything. Or you weren't screwing her over there by the lake with the Australians watching."

Glenn was almost asleep again when Wood's voice again broke the silence. "You know, don't you, she's probably got a general for a boyfriend or something," he said. "Or even . . ."

Wood didn't finish the sentence.

Glenn pretended he didn't hear. *He might be right about the general. But until I know different, I'm going to assume* Time *magazine knew what it was talking about when it said she wasn't fucking Hitler.*

When he was asleep again, his dream was of being on one side of a restaurant booth, with Hitler and Leni, looking cozy, on the other.

If he talked, though, Wood didn't tell him about it the next morning.

13

Sauerbraten, Champagne

At the Village track, Glenn ran several "sets"—racing 100 meters three times, 200 meters twice, then 400 meters and 800 meters. Then he started over. "Whoa, you're going to leave it all here," Brutus Hamilton lectured him. But he kept it up.

As he cooled down, trotting slowly around the outside of the track as others went harder on the inside lanes, he thought: *That's probably five pounds right there!* Marty Glickman had worked out hard, too, and they found themselves warming down together. As they gathered up their sweat suits, Marty admitted that he still didn't know what was going on with the relay. He explained that Lawson Robertson, the head coach, was being paid to allow a press service to distribute a ghostwritten column under his name from Berlin. Problem was, in the latest dispatch—or so Marty was told—Robertson outlined a plan to have Jesse Owens, Ralph Metcalfe, and Frank Wykoff all on the 400-meter relay, with the fourth spot determined in a "runoff" competition among Glickman, Sam Stoller, and Foy Draper. Robertson was claiming to the runners that the writer "ghosting" the pieces after talking with him misunderstood. "I'm not sure I believe him, though," Glickman told Glenn. "Interesting how the only two Jews on the team would be going after one spot—and against Draper, too."

Glenn was gratified that Glickman now seemed to be considering him a confidant.

As Glenn, wearing his blue USA Olympic team blazer and the gray patterned slacks, passed through the gate area, a tall, middle-aged man in a
chauffeur's uniform was waiting.

"Mister Morris?"

Glenn reached out his hand. "Glenn Morris," he said.

The chauffeur already had turned. "This way, please," he said.

Glenn followed him to a big, black, four-door car. The driver opened the
back door on the passenger side and leaned in, then pulled out a black suit
jacket. Glenn didn't notice the jacket at first, though, because he couldn't
resist going to the front of the car, checking out the grill and the Mercedes-
Benz ornament above it.

He called out to the driver, "What model is this?"

"Mercedes-Benz D 260 limousine." He had a little trouble saying the number, but his English otherwise was good.

The driver held out the jacket. "Fraulein Riefenstahl suggests that you
change into this, rather than your Olympic jacket," he said.

Glenn slipped off the blazer and tossed it in the back seat. With the driver
still holding open the back door, Glenn donned the black jacket. "Fits perfect," he told the driver, who shrugged. Glenn leaned down to start through
the back door, and then stopped. "Do I have to sit in the back? Might be able
to see more in the front."

"Sir . . . please," the driver said, nodding at the back seat.

As car pulled away, Glenn asked, "Where are we going?"

Still looking straight ahead, the driver said, "Café Halder. On Unter den
Linden."

Twenty minutes later, despite attempts at small-talk conversation, Glenn
had gotten little out of the man except his name—Kurt. As the limousine
approached the café on a corner, Glenn noticed the Olympic flag hanging
outside, amid all the huge swastika banners on the poles up and down the
street. As he stepped out of the car, he smiled as he thought of spotting the
Café Brandenburg's motto in Milwaukee a month earlier: "You'll Think
You're in Berlin."

I really am in Berlin!

"The maitre d' will escort you to your room," Kurt told him.

"My room?"

"The private dining area."

The stuffy and plump maitre d', in his mid-forties perhaps, didn't seem to
change expression when Glenn said simply, "Glenn Morris."

"*Amerikaner, sehr gut,*" the man said. "*Komm mit mir.*" His gesture made
it clear: Follow him. They walked between tables, past booths, past well-

dressed couples and groups of men, through a door and into a small room decorated with what seemed to be expensive paintings. There were four booths, but none were in use. The maitre d' gestured at a booth—*sit!*—and left. Glenn was alone. He didn't have a menu to look at to kill time. But a couple of minutes later, he heard cheers and applause out in the main room. Leni slipped through the door and then slid into the booth, on the other side, reaching out. Glenn took her hand. She wore an elegant dark gown.

Well, this isn't going to be me and a bunch of others, too.

"I hope you didn't have to wait long," she said.

"I didn't."

"We had to go over the final arrangements for the airborne cameras."

"Cameras . . . in the air?"

"In the *Hindenburg* airship, in an airplane, and in balloons," she said. "The organizers and the Gestapo, too, wanted to know what to expect—and not to expect—over the stadium. I am getting close to being ready, but from here on, it will get even more demanding."

"I understand."

"For both of us, of course," she said. She nodded in the direction of the café's main doors. "And shall I assume that Franz out there was rude to you?"

"Well . . ."

"He was, then. I am very sorry; I had forgotten that he still is very bitter. He often talks of the Battle of Belleau Wood in the Great War. He was in it. Lost a lot of his friends, he says. The more he drinks, the more he tells."

"That battle was against us? The United States?"

Leni's look made it clear she was trying to decide if he was serious. "Yes, but such a disagreeable subject, I am sorry. Enough. No more talk of war."

Leni lifted her hand. A waiter appeared out of nowhere. Leni spoke to him. He nodded and left.

"We'll start with champagne," she told Glenn. "If your training allows it."

"We're really not supposed to, but nobody really pays attention to it," Glenn said. " I'm not much for drinking, though, I have to admit."

"You're not one of those crusaders, are you?" Leni asked. "What did you call it? The ban?"

"Prohibition," Glenn said. "And no, I didn't care one way or the other. Now, I just know myself. I stop at one . . . of anything. So one glass."

"Whatever you say," Leni said with a grin.

Glenn couldn't resist asking, "Is anyone else coming?"

"I hear you met Max Schmeling, so I thought of inviting him and his wife—she is an actress, also—but I didn't." She grinned. "So you will have to make do with only me."

"I didn't mean it like that," Glenn said. "I was just curious."

For a moment she looked down and, for the first time, seemed almost sheepish. "Now, everyone out there at the tables is trying to remember who—if anyone—walked in here ahead of me," she told him. "They will try and stall to see who comes out with me."

"Nobody will recognize me."

"Don't be so sure. They have been selling the Olympic programs for weeks now. And your picture has been many places."

Glenn for a second thought of the reaction if American writers got wind of this dinner . . . what was it, a date? Or even the German writers. He pondered the reaction in Colorado if the reports filtered back, especially to Karen. He would write: *This woman is making a movie about the Olympics and we talked about it.*

"Unless you object, we will have *sauerbraten*," Leni said.

Before it arrived, he also had a second glass of champagne. He got a little lightheaded. Leni had four. She was unaffected.

Glenn was amazed that the waiter's timing was perfect. He was there for the emptied glasses and the last bites, and the courses arrived at pauses in the conversation.

Early on, Leni apologized for her English.

"I was about to compliment you on it," Glenn said. "I understand you better than some of the Southerners on our team."

"Still, I am trying to make it better," Leni said. She lowered her voice, and Glenn could barely hear her. "If I am to break out of this box, I must do that."

Leaning back, she looked him in the eyes. *Understand?*

"So, now tell me," she said. "Is Simla a big city?"

"It's tiny," Glenn said. "After New York and then here, it seems smaller all the time."

"But you went to university."

"College, yes. I played football. Our football, not your football."

"My researchers say you are new at the decathlon. How can that be?"

"In our country, nobody starts out a decathlon man. The decathlon finds you. You can do a little bit of everything, and somebody says, 'Why don't you give it a try?' America pays attention to it only every four years."

Leni touched his hand. "I'm sorry," she said. "I'm interviewing you. You must think I'm like a fat journalist with bad breath smoking a cigarette and holding a notebook."

"Oh, I don't think *that*," he declared.

They both laughed.

"But I have to ask," Leni said. "Why was your champion swimmer eliminated from the team? It couldn't have been just . . ."

She lifted her champagne glass.

". . . this, could it?"

Glenn said, "It was because she did it so openly, even after they warned her to not flaunt it." He sensed Leni had a reason for asking, so he continued. "Why, what did you hear?"

Leni leaned forward. "I heard that your officials said she was telling other women athletes that at some point during the Games, they needed to make some very public protest against the treatment of Jews in the Third Reich. That she had said it was going to have to be up to the women because you men didn't have the courage."

Glenn thought for a few seconds.

"I never heard that," he said. "I also think that if it was true, and that's why she was thrown off, she would announce that and have much of the American public on her side."

"Would she? Are you *sure* of that?"

"Yes," he said emphatically.

"And *you* would be on her side?"

"Absolutely. I hope that doesn't offend you."

She dismissed that with a wave.

Glenn said, "But the main thing is that Eleanor has been blasting Brundage and our Olympic folks, anyway. So that's another reason why if she was tossed for trying to lead a protest, she'd be telling the world that. She has no reason to hold back."

Leni said, "Well . . ."

"What?"

"Your Mister Brundage told our Olympic people if she brought the Jewish issue into it, there were maybe some things she had done on the ship she wouldn't want her husband to know about. Things *they* knew about."

"I don't think that's true," Glenn said. "She did a lot of drinking and flirting, but I didn't hear of anything else."

The offer's always open, Eleanor had said. *Well, except for that.*

Glenn continued, "I think once the stories got started about her, people couldn't stop—and the stories about her got out of hand."

Leni laughed darkly. "That sounds familiar."

After Leni and Glenn finished dinner, the waiter cleared away the plates—and that would be the last they would see of him for the next twenty minutes.

Glenn plunged. "What do *you* think of the Nuremberg Laws?" he asked.

"I filmed that Party Congress last year for yet another documentary," Leni said. "I didn't mention the laws. Does that answer your question?"

"Not really," Glenn confessed.

"Glenn, I have been in the film business since I was very, very young," she said slowly. "I have worked with many Jews. Your own Universal Studios put up a lot of the money for *S.O.S. Iceberg*, one of the last films I was in, and many in that company are Jews. What difference does it make what you are if you advance the art? None!" She laughed. "Mainly, the only Jews I don't like are the critics. But that is not because they're Jews. It is because they're critics. Most of the critics, whether Jews or not, are . . . how you say it . . . 'assholes,' anyway. But the Jewish issue, here in Germany now? Many of us believe that this is more posturing by the National Socialists than it will be policy."

"I'm sorry for being so dense," Glenn said.

"What's 'dense'?"

"Being a small-town boy who's still trying to figure out the world. I told somebody the other day—one of the Jewish fellows on our team, in fact—that I wasn't brought up to look around and take note of what everyone was. Some people would make cracks sometimes, but most of us really didn't think that way. In the country, we were all the same, anyway. I didn't even see a Negro in person until a couple of years ago. So if I'm ignorant about some things, I'm . . . well, I'm not sorry, I'm just trying to explain."

"Something tells me you're more worldly than you admit," Leni said, taking the sting away—while also teasing—with a caress of his hand. "They say you were president of your university."

"Of the student body, yes. But they voted for me because I was a football player. A few months ago nobody recognized my name outside of Colorado. And now . . . I'm in what looks like a famous restaurant . . ."

Leni smiled. "Oh, it is famous."

Glenn continued, ". . . with a famous actress and director."

Leni smiled and shrugged.

Glenn said, "But now it's your turn."

"What do you mean?"

"To answer. The *Time* magazine story about you said your father was a plumber in Berlin. Were you born here?"

"Yes, but your American writer misunderstood. My father . . ."

Glenn interrupted. "What's his name?"

"Alfred," Leni said. "He started out as a plumber, but he became involved in construction projects, mostly the improvement of existing buildings and larger homes with modern sanitation and ventilation. He was *not* fixing toilets. He did well until our currency was worthless, and then as everyone did, we went through difficult times when I was very young after the war. But we—my parents, my younger brother and I—survived. Father is doing well again now. You might see his trucks—Riefenstahl Heating and Sanitation."

"And you were a ballerina?"

"Yes, but I was mostly on my own, recitals and performances."

"How'd you start dance?"

"I convinced my mother to allow me to take lessons, but she knew my father would be against it, so we had to keep it secret from him." She smiled. "My *mother's* name is Bertha, in case you needed to know that, too."

"Thanks," Glenn said wryly.

"She and I had to plot. Father believed that he had to approve everything we did, every mark spent. There were to be no surprises. He believed dancing, even ballet, was decadent and frivolous, not something a young lady did."

"I thought ballet was the opposite of decadent," Glenn remarked.

"That was a time of wildness, especially here in Berlin, and he thought anything in the arts was part of that."

She explained that when her father got wind of what was going on behind his back, he threatened to divorce Bertha and soon tried to get Leni away from the corrupting influences of Berlin by enrolling her in boarding school. But she practiced dance there, too, and eventually came back to the city. Finally, even Alfred came to accept that she had a talent for dance—legitimate and artistic ballet.

"He could see that I was successful, that this wasn't some frivolous pursuit," Leni said. "Soon, I was giving one-woman concerts all across Germany—Munich, Cologne, Frankfurt, Dresden . . . and many more. And Austria and Switzerland."

"You must have been really good!"

"I was . . . then. But I hurt my knee. I was able to recover, but I realized I shouldn't rely only on dancing. I had many pursuing me to try films. So I did. I still was able to dance a little in some. Arnold Fanck—a famous director—found that I was suited for the kind of stories he loved, these silent mountain films like *The Holy Mountain* and *The White Hell of Pitz Palü*. Then I had the idea for *The Blue Light*, wrote the summary for the story, and we turned that into a script. I produced and directed it, also. It showed for many months in London and Paris, too. Then I was in *S.O.S. Iceberg*, so difficult for all of us to shoot in Greenland. My God, we all thought *The Holy Mountain* and *Pitz Palü* were dangerous, but they were easy compared to *Iceberg*! It was a miracle none of us were killed. I promised myself I would only do films I also directed after that."

"But then Hitler *made* you do his films?"

"It was more complicated than that, but yes. He never threatened me. He didn't have to. By now, we Germans understand that saying no comes with risks. To your careers, at least. Perhaps to your families."

"What if you *had* said no?"

"I would not have worked again," she declared. "He would have said he understood, but the second the door closed, he would have made sure the Reich Film Board was told to let it be known I was not to be touched, not as an actress, not as a director. Not as anything. Financing for my future films would have been impossible to secure. My father's business would have been in danger. So, yes, I had a choice—but not much of one."

"You could have left Germany. You are known around the world."

"Known, with some successes in other nations. But not completely accepted yet. I want to have international success, yes . . . but from here. I am German. I want to stay. I make no apology for that. Even if I could have left, my family still would have been here and been subject to reprisals."

"But you've never become a Nazi."

"They have let me take the position that it would diminish my work for them if I were not truly independent. At the party gatherings, I was an artist capturing on film the National Socialist men and message as they were. For better or worse. That film was not propaganda. It was documentary."

"I think I'd much rather see you on the screen than Hitler. In *The Blue Light* or any of those."

Leni's smile was warm—and warming. "I will see what I can arrange," she said. She thought for a second. "What is your schedule tomorrow?"

"Training. At the Village."

"Of course. All day?"

"Four hours, maybe. It's still over a week until our competition. I need to get back in shape and then start tapering off."

"Can you be done and ready to leave the Village by 13:00?"

Glenn mused, "One in the afternoon . . . I suppose so. Why?"

"If you are agreeable, I'll have a car pick you up again . . . and we will go to the movies!"

He grinned. "Popcorn?"

"If you want."

Suddenly, she slid out of the booth and was standing above him. "I will be right back," she said. "Then we will go."

She headed to the bathroom in the back of the private room. Glenn still was trying to figure out what that meant—*go where?*—when she returned and slid into the booth next to him. She put her hand on his knee and smiled, but her tone was far from lighthearted. "Only one rule," she said.

Glenn waited.

"You never, ever repeat what I said about . . . about the Führer and his policies," she said. "And how I came to be involved with the Nuremberg films. I shouldn't have been so careless. Even with you. I have shown a lot of faith in your discretion. Already. I hope you are flattered and aware of what that means."

Tough Leni Riefenstahl, the whirlwind, suddenly was touchingly vulnerable and afraid.

"You can trust me," Glenn said.

She kissed him. It was soft, but very real. Then she said, "Don't save my notes, either—the one from last night or any future notes. Promise me that. You will tear them up and get rid of them. I also said too much in that first one. I won't . . . I can't . . . do that again."

She paused and gestured around the room. "Coming here was probably a mistake. I wasn't thinking of secrecy, more of privacy. But as I said in the note last night, it probably would not be wise to tell others about our friendship. The staff here knows not to talk. But someone might place us together. So if anyone asks, this was a business dinner to talk about the Olympics film."

Funny, that's just what I was thinking . . .

She said, "I have to go back to Castle Ruhwald now to speak to the cameramen and go over the plans for tomorrow."

"I was going to ask you about that," Glenn said. "You have a *castle?*"

"It's the building where we all—all of us working on the film—are staying now, through the Games. It's not where I normally live. I have an apartment in Central Berlin. I have been gone so often, there is not much reason to have a villa. Maybe soon."

"So no drawbridge and moat?"

"Pardon?"

"That's what we think of when we hear 'castle.' A drawbridge and a moat, and maybe men with bows and arrows and swords on the top of the wall."

"So you read of King Arthur?"

"Sure did!" Glenn said excitedly. "The junior-high English teacher in Simla made everyone read it every year. Came to figure out later that he was too drunk to teach anything different. So that meant three years in a row for us. But I didn't mind."

"Glenn Morris, you are a very interesting man. Part small-town boy still—you don't mind me saying that, do you?—and yet a man who will become more famous every day. You certainly aren't like the movie men I have to deal with . . . and not like the politicians and functionaries I have been made to work with the past few years. Many of them are assholes." She winced. "There I go again. Forget I said that."

And she certainly is not like Karen.

"I'll be at the swimming pool in the morning to make sure we're ready there," she continued. "Hans Ertl, one of my best cameramen, and I have devised some approaches for the swimming and diving we need to test. But I can take a break in the afternoon. It might be good for me, in fact."

"Same for me," Glenn said.

Leni kissed him again and Glenn kissed back. After a few seconds, Leni pulled away and quickly stood. When Glenn tried to stand, too, Leni gave him a gentle nudge back into the booth.

She said, "I ask that you wait here for Franz to come and get you, and he'll take you to a door—not the front door—where your car will be waiting."

"All right," Glenn said.

Then she was gone.

In his limousine on the way back to the Village, Glenn again wrestled with himself and tried to interpret the signs. The mutual attraction was unmistakable. But what was she saying? What was she offering? He conceded to himself that he hadn't been a saint since he and Karen started going together. In the past few months, he had ended up in bed with the waitress in Lawrence at the Kansas Relays and then with the daughter of a Fort Collins insurance executive who bought a car from him. He had felt guilty each time, at least, and it was fortunate that the daughter of the insurance man was attending college out of state and didn't seem to have illusions. He rationalized it as a few wild oats before settling down. But this was different. This was a world-famous woman, not a woman whose name he couldn't be certain of as he looked back a week later, as with the waitress (Betty? Barbara? Bernice?).

But at least now he was certain Leni was neither a whore nor a Nazi. Remembering Wood's words, though, Glenn conceded to himself he needed to find out if there was a general—or someone—in the picture.

14

The Blue Light

Leni's early morning meeting was with two executives of the Reich Film Board to go over her plans for the Olympics film and make sure they would support her. A young assistant was with them, and in the ensuing minutes he took notes only when told to write down something specific for future reference. But he was so attentive, he seemed to be soaking up every word.

After Leni was assured of that support for the Olympics project, she also brought up the terms for the future national rerelease of *The Blue Light* to theaters across Germany, most likely in conjunction with the release of *Olympia*. She was planning to head to the swimming stadium after the meeting.

"So how many Jews are we talking about here?" asked the portly board president.

"Three," Leni said. "Balazs as a director and writer, Mayer as a writer, Sokal as a producer. All were in consultation and subordinate to me, of course."

"Their names cannot remain on the credits, you understand."

Leni laughed. "You are not expecting an argument, are you?"

"Well . . ."

"They are Jews," she snapped. "They got more credit than they deserved. That was, and is, my vision, my story, my film. Sokal put up some money and as a Jew, he wanted more in return and I am sure, as a Jew, he swindled me. To give him any credit mocks the creative process. The other two helped me, I admit, but to claim that it was anything more than that is ludicrous. And they have made those claims."

The president asked, "And you were surprised by that?"

"Nothing Jews do surprises me," Leni said with disgust. "At least not now. I admit there was a time when I was naïve, but I am smarter now. The Führer helped me see things for how they are. I'll never again let Jews manipulate me. Good riddance. The credits without them will be more accurate with the spirit of how that film was made—and who made it."

"Then I think we're all on the same page."

Inside, she was gleeful. *The Blue Light* would become even more her film—and hers alone—from now on. Harry Sokal, forceful and astute as a banker, but pathetic and easily manipulated as her lover, was in her past. She had been embroiled for three years in a battle with writer and director Bela Balazs, who had the gall to expect to be paid for his help with the script. He should have been honored to help a great actress spread her wings! Now, for certain, he wouldn't receive a reichsmark for it. Somebody also had to tend to nominal directing duties when Leni was on camera, but a trained monkey could have pulled it off after Leni had laid out what she wanted. Deep down, even she had to admit Carl Mayer was a capable writer who had done good work—but as far as she was concerned, he also just had offered advice on how she could turn her idea for the story into a script. *Her* script.

Good riddance . . . all three.

Ecstatic in the wake of the meeting, Leni watched at the swimming stadium as Hans Ertl demonstrated the ingenious procedure he had come up with to shoot film of the diving. This was the official day of practice when the competitors could become accustomed to the venue, and Ertl was in the pool, in a swimsuit and with his Sinclair camera, encased in a protective cover. He shot the divers, both men and women, coming off the three-meter board and ten-meter platform, and then went underwater himself to follow them.

As Leni watched from the side of the pool, a gray-haired official confronted her. "You realize, don't you, that we will not be able to allow this during the competition?" he asked.

She didn't give him the satisfaction of confirming that was *why* Ertl was filming the training as if it were the real thing. If nothing else, they could splice in these shots among the real competition. "We can worry about that when the time comes," Leni told the official. "But, look, the competitors seem to be enjoying this."

Ertl had already told her that before her arrival, his major problem was that some of the divers were making faces at the camera or waving as they moved back toward the surface. He finally had told Germany's best diver, Hermann Stork, and the Army man attached to the American swim team for the day to ask them to treat this as the real competition.

A tiny American girl approached Leni, waved over the Army man and said, "Can you please ask her if—"

"I speak English," Leni said.

Wide-eyed, the girl asked, "You're really the director?"

"I am," she said.

"This is Fraulein Leni Riefenstahl," the Army man snapped. "She is famous in our country as an actress and director. Our country, and beyond!"

"Wow!"

Knowing she—or Ertl—needed the cooperation of the divers, Leni smiled and willingly shook hands as the girl introduced herself.

"I'm Katherine Rawls. Katy."

"Where are you from, Katy?" Leni asked solicitously.

"Fort Lauderdale," she said. "That's in Florida."

"You are a tiny thing," Leni said.

Rawls grinned impishly. "That's why they call me 'The Minnow.'"

"How old are you?" Leni asked.

"Nineteen."

"I thought you were younger," Leni said, genuinely shocked. "I hope you accept that as a compliment."

Grinning, Rawls pointed at the other side of the pool to another American.

"That's Marjorie Gestring," she said. "She's only thirteen!"

Rawls breathlessly explained she competed in both swimming and springboard diving, and even had won a silver medal in diving four years earlier in Los Angeles. "We were right next to Hollywood," she said, "and nobody did anything like"—she gestured at Ertl in the pool—"that. Or even filmed us at all, from what I can remember."

Leni laughed. "See what we women can do if they let us?"

"I didn't think they let women do anything in Ger . . ."

Rawls caught herself, and then said, "I'm sorry, that came out wrong," Leni waved if off.

"I guess there aren't many women directors in our country, either," Rawls conceded.

"I don't believe there are any," Leni said.

"Was it hard to get them to let you do it?"

"They didn't let me . . . I just did it. I wouldn't take no for an answer. They wanted me to be just a face on the screen and I said I wanted to do more. So I did it. But I also want to return to the screen, too . . . after *this* film."

A U.S. diving coach hollered from his spot near the board.

"Katy! Any day now!"

The little diver smiled, lifted a hand in farewell as she backed away, then turned and trotted to the board. Leni looked at her watch and decided that since Ertl was on the right track, he could continue without her.

〜

The same driver, Kurt, at least shook Glenn's hand this time. He took Glenn to an impressive apartment building in Central Berlin. "This is the Hindenburgstrasse," Kurt explained. "A very desirable location."

The ride was long enough that Glenn's hair, wet when he climbed in, was dry by the time they pulled up.

"The lift operator is expecting you," Kurt told Glenn as he held open the limousine's back door and gestured at the main entrance. "He will take you to the residence."

Leni was casually dressed in trousers and a blouse as she greeted him with a chaste kiss on the cheek and then grabbed his right hand with her left. With her right, she gestured at the huge living room.

"Welcome to Cinema Riefenstahl," she said, smiling.

"Wow!" marveled Glenn, surveying the ornate furniture, paintings, a framed picture of Leni herself, sculptures of Greek figures, and a large movie screen set up and opened along the back wall, in front of the fireplace. Then he noticed the projector, too, and asked, "So this is our theater?"

"Is that acceptable?"

"Well, the driver didn't tell me anything. I thought we were going to that castle. Or I was meeting you at a theater."

"No, this will have to do," Leni teased. "I'm staying at the castle, like all my crew, but I was able to get away after the filming at the pool. You have some very cute divers especially. But they are girls. Children!"

She led him into the adjacent formal dining room area. A tray of meats and cheeses was on the table, with several bottles of Coca-Cola.

"Are you hungry?" asked Leni.

Glenn was stunned to see the soft drinks. "You've got Coke here?"

"Your American company is trying to make inroads and sent over many free cases for the Olympics, both the Winter Games and now."

"The stuff in it keeps me awake," Glenn said. "Cocaine, caffeine . . ."

Leni chuckled. "Nobody seems to like it at the Castle. So if you fellows need a few extra cases, let me know."

As they ate a light lunch, Leni told him about the morning at the pool. "My cameraman there has taken my innovations and done very well with them," she said.

Glenn laid out his training regimen in the morning. "At least I was pretty much left in peace," he said. "But I feel sorry for Jesse Owens. It's like he's on display. And everybody's being nice to the Negroes. I'd make fun of your people except I know it would be the same thing in Simla, and the athletes from the other nations are acting the same way. It's like everyone is saying, 'Come see the Negro!' He's spending half his time signing autographs. Even for the Germans who work there! Hope nobody gets in trouble!"

After an awkward silence, Leni jumped up. "Movie time!" She led the way back into the front room. "I'm sorry I forgot to arrange for your popcorn."

"That's all right," Glenn said. "Bloats me, anyway."

She gestured for Glenn to sit on the couch, but out of the way of the projector's path, and moved off to close the curtains, darkening the room.

"What are we watching?" Glenn asked.

"You'll see. One of my favorite films."

"Better than *Mutiny on the Bounty?*" Glenn joked.

"Much better."

She turned on the projector, skirted the couch and sat next to Glenn. Lifting his arm, she draped it around her shoulders, and leaned against him. "Now don't get any ideas," she said with a laugh. "We *are* watching this film."

As he suspected, it was *Das Blaue Licht.* "The Blue Light," she translated, needlessly. When he spotted her name in the opening credits, Leni asked pointedly, "You asked me about the Jews? Half the people involved with this film are Jews. I told you, I work with them. I am fine with that."

Children played in a village. A horn sounded and an open car pulled into the courtyard, outside a building with a sign that announced: *Osteria.* The driver was a man, his passenger a woman. A young couple.

"An inn in Santa Maria," Leni said. "Present day."

Glenn laughed. "Shush and watch!"

She tapped him with a finger. "All right . . . unless you want translations for a while."

"Yeah, you better."

On the screen, the children crowded around the car as the man and woman climbed out. They squealed and held out huge crystals, offering them for sale. Then one little girl reached out with something else—a little framed picture of Leni, or whomever Leni was playing. It was a miniature version of the picture on Leni's wall. As the couple entered the inn, the young woman scanned the room and noticed several more framed copies of the same picture of Leni. Moments later, the couple was eating with the inn proprietor and, finally, the woman spoke.

Leni began her soft translations. "Who is this person Junta?"

"Ernst, come in," the man called out. When a little boy entered, the man directed, "Bring in the book about Junta."

In a few seconds, the little boy soon returned with a huge book, seemingly almost as big as he was. Leni's picture—the same one—was cut into the book's cover, which said:

Historia Della Junta
1866

"Horst," the innkeeper told the young man, "now you get to read about the Blue Light on the mountain."

Raising her voice, Leni said, "Now we go back . . . to 1866."

A hand reached out and picked up a huge, shiny crystal. Then, onscreen . . . Leni, as Junta. Kneeling in the mist from a nearby waterfall. Ragged clothes, wet hair.

The woman on the poster.

Junta heard a stagecoach on the road below. It stopped and a man climbed out and gathered his belongings. "Vigo, a German painter," Leni explained.

In the next few minutes, Junta hurried down the mountainside and entered the village. Villagers, approaching the church, glared and shunned her.

"Some of them are real villagers," Leni said. "Living in the past. It's Foroglio, in Switzerland. It was like going back in time."

Junta's face, fearful and vulnerable, filled the screen several times. Even the minister, seeing her from a window balcony, seemed wary of her. She ran away, down stone stairs, through the village.

Then the villagers, plus Vigo, were eating in a square. Vigo said to the innkeeper, "You are not so joyful here."

The innkeeper explained: "There is a curse on our village. . . . When it is a full moon, there is a blue light shining on the rock. . . . Each time the young boys want to go up, and each time, one more falls and dies. . . . I planted a cross for my youngest son."

Suddenly, Junta was on-screen again, on the pathway next to the square. She offered flowers from her basket. Nobody wanted them, but children ran up behind her, taunting, and knocked the basket out of her hand. As the contents fell out, the huge crystal she had just found was on the ground, too. The fat local trader saw it, too, and walked over to pick it up. Looking it over, he reached into his pocket with his other hand to pay her for it. Junta tried to take back the crystal, but the trader wouldn't let go. She bit his hand, grabbed the crystal and ran away.

Vigo asked the innkeeper, "Why are you so against that girl?"

The innkeeper railed, "She is not normal. . . . How can she climb toward the blue light on the steep side of the mountain, while the young boys fall down every time? . . . This Junta, she's the damned devil's witch!"

Tonio, the innkeeper's older son, ran after her. Eventually, he dragged her into a darkened alley, and off camera, they wrestled. Junta pulled back out of the alley and ran off, heading through a stream and water and trees, arriving at a ramshackle cabin at the foot of the mountain.

"Monte Christallo," Leni explained to Glenn. "It's really the Crozzon di Brenta in Italy."

That night, with the full moon out, another village boy, Silvio, tried the climb and was killed. When grieving over the boy's retrieved body the next morning, his mother spotted Junta and accused her of being a witch. With Vigo emerging and trying to stop them, the townspeople chased after her and she fled back to her cabin. She called out for Guzzi, a young boy shepherd, and he joined her. Even Glenn could tell that as Junta finally spoke, it was in Italian. Leni converted that, too, into English for Glenn.

"I was on the street, early this morning," Junta told the little boy as goats and a dog were around them in the cabin. "All of a sudden, I saw a crowd in front of Maria's house. I heard Maria shout, 'Junta! Junta!' I was afraid and ran away. Then I saw the crowd. They ran after me with sticks. They threatened me with their fists and they shouted! They threw stones at me. I was running but they came nearer and nearer. Then a man jumped from a window." She raised her arm. "He stood there like this and shouted: 'Stop!'"

When the dog started barking, warning them that Vigo was approaching their cabin, Junta stopped talking. So did Leni.

Most of the rest of *The Blue Light* was a blur for Glenn. At best, he might have been able to offer a broad outline.

Vigo was smitten with the beautiful Junta and, like a puppy, followed her around. Junta went back up the mountain, to the grotto with the crystals, on the night of the next full moon. Vigo believed he was doing a favor for her and the village by disclosing to all her "safe" path to the top. But when the villagers followed Vigo's map, they looted the crystals, and Junta was distraught when she discovered that. So distraught that she, previously such an adept climber, fell to her death.

By then, Leni and Glenn's clothes had been on the floor for nearly an hour. Glenn was on his back, with his head tilted sideways, again watching the film. Leni lay sideways on top of him, turned to the screen as well.

Earlier, he couldn't help but notice that as Leni was on top and riding him, she not only had her eyes open the whole time, she also was looking at the screen, at least out of the corner of her eye. Glenn was surprised that, rather than being offended, he discovered that added to the excitement and thrill. He also spent much of the time after caressing her small, but firm breasts, which she had told him with a giggle "are perfect for ballet dancing . . . not always for the cinema."

As the film ended, Leni looked down at him asked, "How was that?"

Glenn laughed. "Couldn't you tell? I haven't done it like that much . . . and never like *that*."

"I meant the film."

"I really liked it," he said. "You were . . . are . . . beautiful."

"And?"

"Want a review? Is that what you're saying?"

"Yes. From an American view. The film, not just me."

"It was a really pretty movie. Those mountains. The light. It even *looks* different, and I can't explain it."

"Very perceptive! It was a new kind of film stock. We could make day look like night, among other things."

"Is it a fable of some kind—with a moral?"

"I thought of it as a story. Others think of it as a fable. That is the wonder of storytelling. And filmmaking. It can be different things to different people."

"I'm thinking it was saying that being different isn't necessarily evil. And that it's good to leave well enough alone."

Leni laughed. "That's as good as anything. But I didn't know you were paying that much attention."

"Not sure you could get away with an ending like that in America, though," Glenn mused. "We like happy endings."

"Yes, I have heard that you Americans are in dreamland."

In bed later, after more lovemaking, Leni's head was on Glenn's chest.

Glenn broke a long silence. "Been meaning to ask you . . . Leni's not your real name, is it?"

She laughed. "For as long as I can remember, it has been," she said. "But, yes, you are in bed with Helene Amalie Bertha Riefenstahl."

"Pleased to meet you, Helene Amalie Bertha," Glenn teased.

"Now you know why I'm Leni," she said.

She lifted her head and looked down, into his eyes. "A woman could fall for you."

"I'm just amazed I'm here," Glenn said. "And with you."

"So are you proud that you fucked a movie star?"

"No, it's not that," Glenn said.

She laughed darkly. "And you already told me it wasn't your first time, so that's not it. So when *was* your first time?"

"Really want to know?"

"Unless it was with a goat out there in the country."

"Just a girl in Simla. Her parents weren't home." He paused. "Pretty boring, huh? Not in a car, not outside, not with my science teacher or the minister's wife. Had crushes on both of them, I admit, but . . . It was just a girl. And she cried for an hour." Embarrassed, he said, "Okay, what about yours? Your first time?"

Leni turned somber. "Well . . ."

"This doesn't sound good."

"Otto Froetzheim. Germany's best tennis player. I was dancing then and well known already, but I still was young and stupid. He invited me over, I was silly enough to go and I hadn't been in his apartment twenty seconds when he threw me down and took me, right on his couch."

"He raped you?"

"I said no, but I didn't put up a fight. I cried, too. When I came out of the bathroom, he said he had to leave, dropped one of your twenty-dollar bills in front of me and said if I got pregnant, I could take care of it with that. That's when our money was worthless, and twenty dollars American was like a gold bar. Maybe I should have been complimented. I wasn't. Thank God, I wasn't pregnant."

A tear dripped from Leni's right eye. Years later, Leni's Truth had transformed her own calculated deflowering—she had gone to the famous tennis player's apartment *because* of what would happen—into rape. And Leni's Truth disregarded that after that, she was Froetzheim's lover for several years. At least she hadn't rewritten the twenty-dollar-bill part of the story . . . that had happened exactly as she described, with Froetzheim cold and in a rush. At least the first time.

She switched gears. "I take it you have a girl—or girls—back home."

Glenn didn't say anything right away.

Leni said, "Oh, for God's sake, you're not going to offend me. Unless you're married and didn't have the decency to tell me."

"Oh, no, I'm not married."

"Close?"

Glenn laughed. "She thinks so. I don't."

"Spoken like a man."

"She's just out of college and will be teaching school this fall in Southern Colorado. I don't know what'll happen. She's a nice girl. But there's no ring, no promise, no plans."

"I think you're overlooking something," Leni said.

"What?"

"Your life is about to change. You're going to have other opportunities. Will she fit in all of that?"

He thought of Eleanor Holm. "A lot of people are telling me that. I've got to win first. Nobody chases a silver medalist. Then I'll see."

"You could even be an actor," Leni said.

Glenn laughed.

"I mean it," she insisted. "Handsome, nice voice . . . and that smile!"

"So that's what this was? An audition?" He was part serious, part joking, half-offended, half-flattered.

Leni snapped, "Stop that! I was attracted to you when I saw the program cover. There was just something. I thought I was right at the stadium. I knew I was right at the restaurant. And I'm certain now." She paused and noticed Glenn's look. "My God!" she exclaimed. "You're embarrassed!"

"No, just a bit in shock still, that's all. Not long ago, you were a movie star on a poster to me."

"Did you at least fantasize about me?"

"Well . . . yeah . . . I did." He was shocked he admitted that.

"See?" Leni asked. "Dreams can come true!"

"Hey, your turn again," he said, switching the subject. "You're almost thirty. How come you're not married?"

"You say that like there's something wrong with it," Leni said.

"I just mean . . ."

"I know what you meant. I've been in love, but not what you call *love*."

"What about now? Have a guy now?"

"Think you'd be here if I did?"

"I just told you I had a girl . . . and I'm here. Does that make me a bad fellow?"

"It makes you human," Leni said. "And there's something here, too. I know that. You know that."

"Yes, I know that," Glenn said tentatively, still trying to believe all of it.

"I don't know what it says, but both men I'm talking about both have remained my friends. Mostly, it's that I'm so busy and I'm gone so much. Last one was a ski instructor. Very nice, very handsome, very intelligent, very tender. It lasted almost two years. But when I was editing *Triumph of the Will*—and I admit I was preoccupied and obsessed; it is the only way I know how to work—he took another lover. When I was told about it, he confirmed it so matter-of-factly . . . he'd kick her out and we would go right back to the way we were. I said it wasn't that simple. And that was it. So, see, I can be hurt, too!"

Glenn asked, "Just two?"

"Just two what?"

"You said 'both.' Been in love only twice?"

"Is this a test?"

"No, but you are in the movies . . ."

"Let me tell you something," she snapped. "The film business is no different than anything else. You get ahead as a woman, they say you've fucked everyone in the business . . . whatever the business is. In film, you're seen shaking the hand of someone important, they say you've fucked him. You act opposite a leading man, they say you've fucked him. You've gotten a part from a director or backing from a producer, they say you've fucked him. It happens. I know it happens. That's not how I've gotten where I am, and I've stopped worrying about what people think or say. My God, I know there are idiots out there who think I fucked Hitler . . . or Goebbels . . . or both."

"I know."

"You said that a little too quickly," she said. "You know that's not true, right?"

He paused, and that was too long for Leni.

"I should make you leave right now!"

"Look . . ." He took a deep breath. "What I was worried about was if you had *any* boyfriend I needed to worry about. And worse, if he's powerful, jealous, and maybe carries a gun." He hadn't intended to be funny, but as it came out, it made him laugh.

Leni didn't appreciate that, either. "This is *not* a laughing matter," she snapped. "But so you know . . . no lover now, powerful or otherwise. And, no, never Hitler or that snake Goebbels or any of those Nazis. They were, and are, film subjects to me. No more."

"Of course," he said. "I wouldn't be here or be like this"—he gestured down, noting his nakedness—"if I didn't know that."

"Good."

Mainly, he was relieved. "You don't hear much about Hitler and women, anyway," he said.

"That's the way he wants it," Leni said. "There is a woman, but everyone knows it is not to be discussed. His only love is supposed to be the Fatherland. And the other thing . . . I thought about this after last night, and probably the less we talk about the Führer, the better."

Glenn tried to take the edge off the conversation. "Why, is there somebody hiding in the closet?"

She was grateful for that and returned the grin. "Don't be silly." She pointed at her huge closet. "That's why I keep the closet door open."

Glenn was on a chair and starting to put on his shoes when Leni, fully clothed, sat on his lap and put her arms around his neck. She kissed him, and then leaned back. Looking at him, she asked, "Will you be impressed with yourself if I tell you I am dizzy?"

"No, I suspect you'll get over it pretty fast."

"And you're not dizzy?"

"Of course I am. But it sure looks to me like you're going to be working twenty hours a day from here on, or something."

"Perhaps so," she shrugged.

"I'm not sure how much I'll be at the stadium before the decathlon starts," Glenn said.

"We will figure something out," Leni said with certainty.

"The head of our committee, Brundage, warned us about this, but they're putting together plans to send us to meets all over the place after we're done here. We all signed these forms saying it was okay with us. There's a meet in London on the 15th, but I doubt they'll send me to that. It's only one day, no decathlon—thank God. There'll be others after that, and we're supposed to go where we're told." He laughed darkly. "So we have no idea what we might be doing after we're done competing, before we head home."

"Let's just see what happens," Leni said. "You must let me contact you. The world will not end when the Games do, either. Remember that. But same thing still is true. It will be better for both of us if this is our secret."

"You'll be at the stadium when I'm competing, won't you?"

"Oh, yes," Leni said. "But let me take the lead about whether we know each other and all that."

"Why?"

"It's just best. Including because of all the reporters looking for stories. You don't believe the American athlete and the German actress together would be a big story, a . . . splash?"

"I guess so."

There was a part of Glenn excited by that prospect; and another part of him horrified by it because of all the explaining he'd have to do to the folks back home . . . including Karen.

"Even tomorrow, I'll be at the stadium," she said. "Dress rehearsal for the opening ceremonies. We have to make sure we're all set for the real thing."

"How can they have a dress rehearsal without us?"

"Hitler Youth taking your place. They even know how many to assign to each nation, behind each flag."

"Hitler Youth behind the American flag?"

"Yes."

"Make sure they don't dip it. If you're looking for realism."

Leni jumped up, walked to the door and waited. "You don't need to see me get all misty. Come on, Glenn Morris. Go. The car will be out there."

"What about you?"

"I'll be five minutes behind you . . . just long enough."

She gave him a lingering, deep kiss and then quickly shoved him out the door.

15

Aren't You Thomas Wolfe?

Glenn's usual way of sorting out everything was to ask himself questions, then answer them—as he ran, or walked, or put off trying to get to sleep. On the way to the dining hall in the morning, he tried it again.

Did Karen deserve this—again? He felt guilty that he didn't feel more guilt. Leni was a star, a famous world figure, but the Games would be over in two weeks and—no matter what happened in the decathlon—he most likely would be going back to Colorado. At some point, perhaps soon, that life probably would include marrying Karen, who hadn't laughed at his quest to make the Olympics in this weird event and postpone entering the real world. Rather, she supported him, everywhere from the field house during training to the kitchen. He wasn't ready to commit to when that marriage date would be, and he hadn't been above taking advantage of those other sexual opportunities, even before Leni. But Karen was reality. Being with Leni was a fantasy—a fantasy lived out, an experience he never would forget, but a fantasy nonetheless. In a few years, he and Karen would be middle-aged parents posing with their three kids, and Leni would be his little secret. He knew that's the way it was, the way it would be, the way it had to be.

As he worked out in the discus ring later, he shut out all of that. Walter Wood watched intently as they took turns throwing. Ken Carpenter and Gordon Dunn, the other discus men, already had finished their work. After Glenn's third toss, Wood stopped him as he came out of the ring. "Your release is a tad bit early in your arm whip, seems to me," Wood said. "You're losing the last bit of snap."

On the next throw, Glenn made a conscious effort to keep his release in-dex finger on the discus a split second longer. The result was his best throw of the day, by about five feet.

"Hey, thanks!" he told Wood.

"Least I can do," Wood said. "That picture with Schmeling's probably go-ing to be my biggest moment of glory here. Unless about ten discus throwers get sick—including two of ours." He thought a second. "Or unless I run into Greta Garbo tonight and she's impressed by my Cornell ring."

Thinking of Leni again, Glenn laughed. "And where might that happen?" he asked with eyebrows raised.

"Downtown," Wood said. "A big group's going in to Berlin tonight. You should come, too. Last fling before we get serious."

Glenn was surprised that he was so eager to go, but he decided the last thing he wanted to do was sit around the room and continue the debates with himself. About thirty Americans—half of them trackmen—were among the athletes on the two buses. The German guides meeting them at the stop near the Brandenburg Gate emphasized in several languages—Span-ish, English and Japanese—that buses would load up and leave from this spot at 23:00, 24:00, and 01:00.

"The ones unfortunate enough to miss the buses will be on their own to get back to the Village," one guide warned in English.

"You mean the ones lucky enough!" an Australian runner said jauntily. "Lucky enough to have found an hospitable fraulein!"

"You're dreaming," another Aussie said. "If you miss the last bus, you'll be passed out in the gutter."

Glenn loved hearing the Aussies' banter at the Village. In fact, even when they were talking about the mundane, just passing the word about a team meeting time, they could sound like they were teasing each other.

The Olympians went several directions, and the Japanese took off to-gether. Most of the Americans, plus a few Australians and Spaniards, fol-lowed Jack Torrance, trusting him because he claimed the Germans working out at the Village track had recommended a spot—at least as a starting point. The Essen Haus turned out to be a giant hall with long tables. The German customers spotted them, but other than the raising of steins in their direction for welcoming gestures, left them alone at first. None of the German men were in uniform, though, which surprised Glenn. Up to this point, it had seemed as if half the men in the country wore uniforms. Gradually a handful of men—all in their twenties, it seemed—wandered over. One of them just started talking to Torrance, as familiarly as if this was a corner bar in Denver and everyone knew each other. Or as familiarly as it could be when half the conversation was in a second language. Because of the noise, only those closest to Torrance could hear, but Glenn was part of it.

"Americans, correct?"

"Most of us," Torrance said. He gestured up and down the table. "Australian and Spanish, too."

"Welcome," the German spokesman said. He raised his glass, and his German friends did the same. Glenn reached out and tapped a few of the Germans' steins and glasses. Smiles all around.

Another German, skinny with floppy light brown hair parted in the middle, materialized at Glenn's side. Glenn was starting his second beer, and had just told himself he would stop there.

"What do you think of our country?"

"So far, it's very impressive," said Glenn. "Everybody seems nice."

The German smiled. "Not what you expected?"

"I wouldn't say that."

"There are a lot of lies being told about us," the German said.

An Aussie broke in. He wasn't challenging, asking it almost breezily. "Like what?"

"Like . . ."

The German stopped.

The Aussie asked, "You mean like . . . how you treat your Jews?"

The German waved his hand. "I'm sorry to have raised this. There is no need to talk about such serious matters. These Games should be about friendship . . . between your nations and ours."

Before long, the Aussies announced they liked the Essen Haus just fine, so there was no need for them to move on to another tavern. The American trackmen, Glenn included, decided to walk back to the Unter den Linden and wander a bit before picking out a spot for another round . . . or a nightcap. As they made it clear they were about to head out, the German who had mentioned "lies" approached again and leaned in close to Glenn. Now Glenn noticed that he seemed to be on his own, not with the other Germans.

"You fellows misunderstood," the man said.

Glenn peered at him quizzically.

The German continued, "The lie is that by now, we are all Nazis. We are not. And even many who have joined the party for reasons of pragmatism do not advance the party principles."

"I think most of us know that," Glenn said.

"Do you? Then tell your journalists to stop saying 'Hitler's Germany' or 'Nazi Germany.' It still is the Fatherland. Deutschland. Germany. There are many of us who love our country, but are not Nazis. Remember that during the Games."

Glenn smiled. "I'll try to."

The German said earnestly, "No, I am serious! During all the salutes of Hitler, please remember that. Some Germans are doing what they have to do—not out of enthusiasm, but necessity and duty. It is no different than if you were a member of your President Roosevelt's opposition party, acknowledging he is your head of state. I've read that many in America believe his policies are against your nation's traditions."

"That's true," Glenn said. "They're called . . . Republicans."

"It's much the same here."

"But Americans can openly disagree. Can you?" Glenn challenged.

The German leaned even closer. "No. We can't," he said conspiratorially. Then he backed off and reached out. "It is a pleasure to meet you, Morris. Good luck in the Games."

Suddenly, he was walking away.

"Hey!" Glenn called out. The German gave a half-wave over his shoulder. Glenn had wanted to ask how the German knew his name, but then he suddenly realized his face had been all over—or, if that wasn't the reason for the recognition, someone else could have disclosed his identity. At least that's what he thought until they were on the street, and hurdler Forrest Towns caught up with Glenn.

"Wow, Long sure looked like he was telling you something important," Towns said.

"Who?"

Glenn was thinking he meant another American, and he didn't know of a team member named Long.

"The German you were talking with," Towns said. "You don't know who that was?"

"No," Glenn admitted.

"Geez, I thought you knew . . . That's Luz Long. The German. Only man in the world who *might* be able to beat Jesse Owens."

Glenn was genuinely confused. "In what?"

"Broad jump," Towns said. "If Jesse gets too tired because he's doing everything else, too, that guy'll beat him!"

Glenn's first instinct was to pass along what Long had said, but then quickly realized that would be betrayal. He was reminded by that, too, when they were back on the Unter den Linden, draped with the huge swastika banners hanging on long poles from the front of the buildings amid moving spotlights. Then Walter Wood, in charge of picking a second spot, called out, "Next stop, Café Wilhelm!"

The spacious café and bar was sedate, at least compared to the beer hall. The Americans settled at several tables, near the back. Glenn was with Wood, Torrance, and Towns. Soon, they noticed a huge man loudly speaking English at a nearby table. His back was to the athletes and he hadn't noticed them. He wasn't as big as Torrance, but even seated, he appeared to be strikingly tall and burly. His companion, facing them, was a smartly dressed blonde young woman who, judging from her accented attempts to respond during his rants, was German. The man was drunk, that much Glenn could tell. He also seemed familiar. Turning slightly, he looked up at the waiter and announced, "Your country is magical! If there weren't a Germany, someone would have to invent one! If your publishers were just a little more honest in accounting for royalties, it would be perfect!"

Publishers?

After the waiter left, Glenn walked over to the American's table. "Excuse me . . ."

The man looked up.

"Yes?"

"Aren't you Thomas Wolfe?"

"Now why in the hell would you confuse me with that fat hack?" Noting Glenn's embarrassment, the man laughed and added, "Of course I am."

"I'm a fan," Glenn said.

"Of course you are."

Wolfe didn't seem interested, so Glenn began to back away. "Just wanted to say . . ."

The writer turned. "You want an autograph." It was a statement, not a question.

"That's all right. You're busy."

"Oh, don't mind me," Wolfe said. "Just been a long day, getting here and right away meeting with Ambassador Dodd—I must have signed a book for everyone in the embassy—and doing the interview with the newspaper in my suite. And now Thea here"—he gestured at the woman—"has gotten me very drunk on this exquisite *Pfalzer* wine."

Wolfe had turned slightly to keep Glenn in his sight, so he caught sight of the other Americans at the back tables. "You boys all Americans?"

"Mostly," Glenn said.

"Well, I'll be damned . . . you're our athletes!"

Glenn grinned self-consciously. "Right."

"Well, how come you're not in bed? Or drinking milk somewhere? Or putting yourself to sleep by reading Sinclair Lewis?" He laughed at his own jokes and gestured at one of the extra chairs. "Sit down!" he roared.

"Just for a minute," Glenn said. He introduced himself. Wolfe's handshake was firm. He seemed genuinely pleased when Glenn told him he had started *Of Time and the River* on the SS *Manhattan*, was making steady progress and was enjoying it. Glenn thought about asking, but didn't, if Wolfe was offended if readers skipped some of his painstaking description and philosophical rants to get on with the story. After doing that some in *Look Homeward, Angel*, Glenn was doing more in *Of Time and the River*.

"Enjoying it is good," Wolfe said. "But are you *appreciating* it? Appreciation is the lifeblood of an author."

Glenn couldn't resist. "I thought it was selling books," he said. "Lots and lots of books. Which you seem to do."

Wolfe chortled. "That, too." After a pause, he asked, "What sport are you in?"

Thea leaned forward and told Wolfe, "He is your decathlon man."

To Thea, Wolfe said, "How do *you* know who he is?"

"His picture was on our front page this week," she told the author, and then smiled at Glenn. "*Berliner Tageblatt*," she explained. Offering her hand, she added, "I am Thea Voelcker."

Wolfe told Glenn, "Thea is the newspaper artist. Drew my picture, and I am sure it is wonderful, for the story that is in soon and will send my German edition sales soaring even higher! For that, she has earned the right to shortly return to my suite."

Thea shrugged. Glenn wasn't sure if that was confirmation or denial.

"Did you come for the Olympics?" Glenn asked.

"Two birds, one stone," Wolfe said. "I was here a year ago and loved it. I was going to come over sometime for promotion and to check on whether I'm being robbed, and we agreed this would be a good time, with all the journalists and other influential folks here. I'll be meeting with some of them. Plus, I'm working on six books and I decided a break would do me good."

"*Six?*"

Wolfe shrugged. "Give or take."

Glenn asked, "You going to any events?"

"Dodd said I could use his box whenever I wanted. Said I could look behind me and see Hitler." He paused. "So let me ask *you*, since you have shown yourself to be a man of fine judgment and terrific literary tastes . . . how do you like Berlin so far?"

"What we've seen is great," Glenn said carefully. "The stadium is stupendous, and, well . . ." He made a sweeping gesture that might have described the café . . . or all of Berlin. "Who wouldn't be impressed with all of this?"

"New York has its charms," Wolfe said, "but it's filthy compared to this. This is so wonderfully cool and clean after New York! Did you see the cobblestones on the street? They look like they're scrubbed two hours a day! And now, the energy!"

Glenn nodded. "But our Village is way to the west, so we really have to work to get in here." He thought of Leni and his earlier visits: *If he only knew.* "And I'm pretty sure it's going to be the Village and the stadium only for us from here on out . . . at least until we're done with our events."

Wolfe asked Glenn when he was competing. Glenn told him, while being fairly certain the novelist wouldn't remember the days.

"I'll leave you alone," Glenn added. "I just wanted to say hello."

Ten minutes later, as the Americans were ordering what they promised each other would be their final round, including a beer Glenn would only sip, Wolfe and Thea passed by, heading out. Glenn had briefed his teammates about both the author and his companion.

"Win lots of gold, gentlemen!" Wolfe bellowed.

Thea, strikingly tall herself, looked over her shoulder, and it seemed to Glenn that she was trying to make it clear she was just putting up with him to his door—and not beyond.

"That dame is gorgeous," Torrance said, voicing the obvious. "And she even *looks* smart. So . . . what's she doing with that asshole?"

Towns reacted in mock horror. "Wait," he announced to Torrance, "you are belittling a true Southern gentleman of arts and letters, one of the finest craftsmen in the history of American Literature, a titan of the written word!"

Torrance gave him a withering look.

Towns laughed and added, "Our Modern American Literature professor called him all that, and I was brought up to believe that if an LSU professor says it, it must be true. So I just went along with that and I got a 'B.'"

"I'm glad I didn't take *that* class," said Torrance, the fellow LSU grad. "The guy's still an asshole."

Glenn cut in. "Now we'll be in his next book," he said. "He writes about his own life, you know. Just changes the names of the people and places. Instead of 'Baby Elephant,' you'll be 'Moose' or something like that."

"Just so I win the gold," Torrance said with mock solemnity.

They caught the midnight bus back. *That's why you don't drink. Much.* Glenn berated himself for trying to keep pace with the boys—at least until the last round. He wasn't drunk; he just felt light-headed and on the verge of nausea.

In the room, Glenn grabbed *Of Time and the River*, hoping to make it through another fifty pages. He tried to picture the huge man from the café, no longer just the man whose picture was on the book cover, at a typewriter, writing the words on the pages in front of him.

After about twenty pages, he caught himself nodding, and gave up.

As he went to bed, he told the picture on the desk: *Night, Karen.*

As he closed his eyes, he wondered: *What did Leni do tonight?*

Leni's day was a whirlwind of going to the outlying competitive venues and rechecking her crews' setups there, then returning to the stadium to watch and film the opening ceremonies rehearsal. Finally, she went to the Geyer Lab to look over the "rushes" to make sure the angles and lighting would be appropriate for the real thing two days later. Stephan, her editing assistant, was a marvel, usually reading her mind about what she would want to see, or being able to quickly adjust to the unpredictable.

During the viewing of the film, Leni realized she wished Glenn Morris were with her. All night. It was a yearning she hadn't felt for over a year, at least not since Walter Prager. And it added to her attraction that she was starting to wonder if there might be a way he could aid her career, helping her broaden her appeal in America.

16

~

Helpless American

It was Ernst Jäger's idea to make Leni available to reporters at the Olympic press center in downtown Berlin as the opening ceremonies neared. Jäger shepherded her through a back door into the huge room set aside for the session. Peeking through a curtain, they could tell that although the announced time for the session still was ten minutes away, the room already was jammed. "Sometimes I forget you're a cinema star," Jäger said. "Directors and producers never draw this many reporters."

Jäger had told her that roughly 1,400 writers—half German, half foreign—were registered to cover the Games, and it seemed to Leni that a majority of the total had decided to show up to hear her. As she waited, she quickly skimmed the story in the morning *Berliner Tageblatt* that described Joseph Goebbels's welcoming speech to the Olympic journalists. He denied that the Games involved propaganda motives for the Third Reich, but also challenged the writers to ignore the lies previously spread by others and to explore and chronicle the New Germany "as it actually is." Leni agreed with Goebbels this time: Outside reporters, especially British and American, too often saw and heard only what fit their preconceptions. In her case, she needed them to be open-minded enough to accept her independence as a filmmaker.

Jäger began with German and English introductions and said that for the first part of the session, he would allow the Army man assigned to the press center to do the translations as needed. Leni emerged from behind the curtain and moved to the rostrum. For the next twenty minutes, she fielded unsurprising questions about the size of her crew, deployment of cameras, envisioned volume of film shot, *Olympia*'s likely release date, and even how she came to be connected with the project. She patiently waited through the translations, into English and, if it was requested, into French. She rattled off Leni's Truth about Carl Diem's pursuit of her to make the documentary, about its backing from the International Olympic Committee, and about its financing.

Then a British journalist asked, tentatively, in German: "Is this going to be another propaganda film for the Third Reich and Hitler?"

Leni wanted to give him credit for trying to speak German, but she nonetheless was perturbed. "I just told you," Leni snapped, "this film has been commissioned by the Olympic movement powers, not by the German government. This will be about the Games, not the nation hosting them. This will be about the athletes in them, from around the world, not about the setting."

A man introduced himself as Louis Lochner, head of the Associated Press bureau in Berlin. He spoke German.

"Yes, Mr. Lochner," Leni said with a smile. "Nice to see you again."

"It's nice to say that the Olympics are above politics," Lochner said. "But doesn't the withdrawal of Spain's athletes after war's breakout there emphasize that not even the Olympics can be immune to such considerations?"

Leni replied, "I wish all athletes from all nations were here. I will film the ones who are."

From the side of the podium, Jäger suggested that the next segment be conducted in English before they finished off with an all-German series of questions and answers.

Leni thought: *Practical!*

The only other woman in the room raised her hand. Expecting a sympathetic question, Leni pointed at her.

"Sigrid Schultz, *Chicago Tribune*," she said. "I'm wondering how much opposition and difficulty did you encounter as a woman in making progress in the documentary film business in today's Germany, which seems to see a woman's role as having children?"

Even some of the other American journalists groaned.

Leni smiled wickedly. "There are many American journalists in this room," she said. "How many are women? One. You. So I suspect I have encountered no more opposition and difficulty as a woman filmmaker than you have as a woman journalist."

Several reporters laughed, not so much because of what Leni said, but because hard-bitten journalists always respected a quick comeback.

Joe Barnes, Berlin correspondent of the *New York Herald Tribune*, noticeably had to struggle to avoid laughing as he gave his name and affiliation. Then he turned serious. "Many of these athletes you mention from 'around the world' are Jews and Negroes. Are you committed to documenting their presence—and even their successes—as part of this film?"

Leni responded, "I will show the most compelling stories of the Games. Whatever that turns out to be, I will show. This film will be for New York and London and Paris and Tokyo as much as it is for Berlin."

Barnes persisted. "Does Herr Hitler know that? Or Doctor Goebbels?"

Leni turned to Jäger and said in German, "Are German reporters this rude when they are in New York?"

Jäger shrugged.

Turning back, Leni said, in English, "This is, and will be, the world's film. Ultimately, the decisions and the responsibilities are mine."

A tall, gray-haired man in a hat spoke up. "I'm Grantland Rice, Mister Barnes's compatriot from the *New York Herald Tribune*. As perhaps you know, the opening ceremonies will take place on the twenty-second anniversary of the beginning of the Great War. Are you going to attempt to pay symbolic homage to that, and to the Games as perhaps a vehicle for international understanding?"

Leni responded, "I'm sorry, sir, my English is not *that* good . . . I don't understand you."

A young American reporter raised his hand and offered, "Don't feel bad. A lot of *us* can't understand him, either."

That brought sympathetic laughter.

Rice was agitated. "Translate for her, please," he said, gazing at the Army man.

The Army man did. Leni sighed deeply and said, in English, "Yes, this film will be about goodwill between nations and peoples."

With the other reporters, the tone of the questions took a turn back toward the light and congenial, touching on her film career and her future beyond *Olympia*. Jäger then steered the session back to German, and Leni took a few more questions. When she was done, she drew applause from many of the journalists and stayed to sign autographs. She was amused to note that more than a few were for Americans. One was the young man who had teased Grantland Rice. He nodded toward Rice, in fact, and said, "He wants to turn everything into spectacle and everyone into gods." He nodded at the sheet with her signature. "Thanks very much!"

As she signed more autographs, including for the Americans, she wondered how many of them had met Glenn.

～

This is progress, Glenn thought as he climbed into back seat of the limousine while Kurt waited, poised, to close the door. This time, in another meeting set up by a note, Kurt not only shook his hand, he smiled. There wasn't much more conversation on the way, though. Glenn decided it was a combination of Kurt being uncomfortable speaking English; wanting to remain known for his discretion; and perhaps the habit of feeling lowly when driving around high-profile passengers. Whatever it was, Kurt wasn't going to let down his guard.

Glenn still had only foggy knowledge about the geographic layout of Berlin, but he figured out they had gone well past the Brandenburg Gate, going east. Kurt pulled over, let him out of the car and pointed to a building on the north side of the Unter den Linden. To Glenn, it looked like something that should be in Athens or Rome.

"Fraulein Riefenstahl will meet you in front," Kurt pronounced. "She should be here very soon."

Glenn angled his walk to be far enough away from the front of the building to take it all in. He was marveling at the portico and its six stone columns when he caught her approaching out of the corner of his eye and turned. Striding toward him purposefully, she wore a large, floppy hat and a baggy coat.

"Excuse me," Glenn called out as she approached, "can you help a helpless American visitor?"

She stopped about five feet short. "Yes, I believe I can," she said.

She opened her arms and waited for him. The hug, the sort with shoulders pivoting and memories summoned, wouldn't have struck anyone viewing it as passionate, and didn't draw the attention of many passers-by on the Unter den Linden. It was the hug of new lovers who were learning to be affectionate with each other. Glenn was shocked at how good it—a hug, just a hug—felt.

As they looked in each other's eyes, Leni said, "That was very nice. Is there anything else I can do for you, helpless American visitor?"

When they kissed, longer and more passionately than the embrace, Leni's hat fell off.

Now heads were turning. Leni long ago had become accustomed to the looks: "Say, isn't that . . . ?"

Holding Glenn's hand, Leni pulled him over to the hat. She picked it up and started to return it to her head with the one hand, but stopped. She said something in German—Glenn's uneducated guess was, "The hell with it"—and tossed it aside.

Then she led him toward the building. A few feet short, she stopped them. Her look at the building led Glenn to take another look. "Did Kurt tell you what this is?" she asked.

Glenn said no.

Leni sighed. "It was the guardhouse for the Crown Prince's home. It was not in good condition a few years ago, and it was rebuilt as a memorial to the men killed in the Great War."

"We have these, too," Glenn said. He thought of the famous "Spirit of the American Doughboy" statue in Colorado Springs he had seen on a trip for a track meet.

Outside, Leni pointed to the sculpture works in the pediment above the columns. "That's Nike, the Goddess of Victory, presiding over a battle," she explained.

Glenn thought: *I guess it didn't work in the Great War.*

Wondering what Glenn was thinking, she quickly added: "It was sup-posed to honor the Wars of Liberation . . . what others, I believe, call the Napoleonic Wars."

Leni led him past the columns, across the portico, through the doors. A circular skylight produced eerie light in the front room.

"This is where we reflect," Leni whispered. She turned to him. "In the Great War, your nation had many dead. My nation had many dead." She looked into Glenn's eyes. "We can never let it happen again."

"Agreed," said Glenn. "But I hope Hitler believes that, too."

After a couple of minutes of reflection, Leni led Glenn back to the por-tico. Her answer came as if the conversation hadn't been interrupted.

"I have told Hitler and his men that, Glenn," she said. "In my own way, I have. Sometimes we all forget that he was in the war himself. Right or wrong, he believes that he needs to posture and bluster and move short of war to give his nation the negotiating power we didn't have at Versailles. That's all."

She looked around. Confident she couldn't be overheard, she confided: "Half of Berlin knows that our troops would have turned around and come home the second there was any sign of reaction from France—or anyone else—when our troops marched into the Rhineland. How nobody else seemed to realize that is amazing to me."

Glenn shook his head. "Leni, I'm no expert in international affairs, but I think it's that nobody thinks the Rhineland was worth risking a war again— even a minor one. And if you're right, you're saying Hitler will stop there, anyway, right?"

Leni shrugged.

Glenn asked, "So why'd you bring me here?"

"Because, it will take Americans and English and French and Germans working together to make sure this"—she gestured at the memorial— "doesn't happen again. I don't want my brother fighting. I don't want you fighting. I don't want anyone fighting. And an Olympics film that shows all nations competing in an atmosphere of goodwill can help." She smiled. "And if a very handsome American is one of the heroes of the Games and the film, that is even better."

"Sounds good to me," Glenn declared.

They walked to a little café two blocks from the Memorial. The only sign was more of a tiny notice than an attention-getter. All is said was: "Café." There were three tables, and Leni and Glenn were the only customers. The proprietors, a fat man and his rail-thin wife, knew Leni and welcomed her. She introduced him in German—Glenn caught his first name and noted the omission of his last—and the couple nodded cordially.

Glenn noticed the woman went to the door and locked it from the inside. There would be no other patrons.

"What did you tell them?" Glenn asked.

"You are Glenn, a helpless American visitor. They know not to ask more." She laughed. "They also are savvy enough, so at some point during the Games when they see the newspaper and listen to the radio, they will say, 'Say, isn't that the man with Fraulein Riefenstahl?' Don't worry, though, as at the Café Halder, I have long ago figured out whom I can trust and whom I cannot. And there are fewer prying eyes here."

Glenn smiled. "I take it I don't get to see a menu here, either?"

"The horsemeat here is delicious." For an instant, she had him. Then she laughed and added, "There is no menu. There is only what they feel like making."

The vegetable soup with cabbage and the meatloaf were terrific.

As they were about to leave, Leni excused herself for a trip to the bathroom. Glenn was standing near the door when the wife approached him with a newspaper and a pen. It was the page with his picture on it from the recent *Berliner Tageblatt.*

Please sign, she pantomimed with the pen. Glenn obliged. He didn't mention it to Leni.

As they walked back to the cars, Leni seemed sheepish about needing to return to the Castle Ruhwald. "A crew and I are going to the gymnastics stadium," she said. "I can't miss it. I can't demand devotion from my people and not give it myself. I hope you understand."

He did understand. He understood this had been her way of showing there was more to this than sex.

⌣

At the Dietrich Eckert Stadium, the site of the gymnastics, she and her small crew, with Werner Hundhausen assigned as the lead photographer, went over the shooting angles for the various events. They knew that two Germans, Alfred Schwarzmann and Konrad Frey, were among the favorites, which might lead to some opportunities for highlighting home-nation triumphs in the finished film.

Leni trusted Hundhausen—both his skill and his judgment. So she was comfortable musing out loud as they walked from area to area.

"One of our challenges is going to be showing enough of the Führer and the German victories to satisfy Goebbels, but to preserve the film as an international work," Leni told the cameraman. "But if those boys"—Leni couldn't resist calling the slight, compact gymnasts boys—"do as well as they should, we can show them without being accused of overt nationalism. They will be gold medal winners."

"I'll make sure to get their interaction with the other competitors," Hundhausen said.

"Absolutely," Leni said. "The more we show the others congratulating our competitors, and our competitors congratulating others, the more we have that can highlight our status as fine sportsmen, acting in the spirit of goodwill."

Hundhausen laughed. "You should make a speech at the opening ceremonies! That all sounds so noble!"

"I believe it," Leni snapped. "Don't you?"

"Sure I do," Hundhausen said. "But have you thought of what you will do if one of our winners is the fencer?"

He meant Helen Mayer, the veteran fencer who had won a gold medal in the individual foil at the 1928 Games as a teenager, was half-Jewish, had moved to America and was teaching in California. Her inclusion on the German team was billed as proof that Jewish athletes weren't excluded in the tryout and selection process, and was cited in the campaign to prove to outsiders that the boycott movements were misguided.

"The *Mischling?*" Leni asked sharply, using the derisive term for "half-breed." "Yes, we will show her, even if she loses to the other Jewess—the girl from Hungary. It will be a very convenient way for us to prove our open-mindedness, will it not?"

"And what will Goebbels think of that?"

"My goal is that the first time he sees this, it will be at the premiere," Leni said. "If necessary, it will have to be impressed upon him that he needs to consider the bigger picture—as I am quite willing to do. Even if it means showing at great length the primitive American track and field athletes winning or a Jewess winning in the Fatherland's uniform."

Hundhausen laughed. "Good luck with that."

"I am thinking of Paris and New York, too," Leni said. "And so should Goebbels."

17

~

S.O.S. Iceberg

"Jesus," the Badger AOC man bellowed through the bullhorn, "we're never going to win any medals for marching! That's going to have to do!"

Glenn was relieved. "This was starting to get ridiculous," he told Walter Wood.

"Left, right, left, right," Wood said. "Not like it's hard."

Jack Torrance was drenched with sweat. "Somebody tell me . . . what difference does it make if we don't look like the guys at West Point?"

For an hour, the American men from all sports had taken several cracks at starting en masse at the end of the Village's practice track, walking down the front straightaway eight abreast and then curling onto the infield to reform as a group. It was difficult to take serious for several reasons, including because the American women—who would be marching behind them in the real ceremony—were miles away at their own village in the Reich Sports Field complex, and the U.S. officials who also would march weren't present, either. Plus, the jokes kept coming, both lighthearted and grim. Marty Glickman, seemingly half-serious and half-joking, suggested that all the Jews and Negroes should be on the inside of the lines on the track, and then at the far side of the group on the infield, as far away from Hitler as possible. Glenn Cunningham argued that if they did that, it was a form of segregation, anyway. So they just gathered, formed lines across the track, and marched. Despite several attempts to time the removal of the straw hats—the only part of their official outfit they were wearing—and the placement over their hearts, it still was more casual chaos than synchronization. Up front, flag bearer Al Jochim, a gymnast attending his fourth Olympics, never dipped the banner. In fact, he drew laughs in one run-through when, with feigned Herculean effort, he briefly raised the flagpole to a straight vertical angle as they reached mid-track and in theory were opposite Hitler. They'd all been given sheets with the "Official opening ceremonies Parade Instructions," clearly calling for all flag bearers to dip their banners, but Jochim knew he was expected to ignore that. Veteran water polo men Wally O'Connor and Fred Lauer, both also at their fourth Olympics, were the "color guards" on each side of him.

The Badgers said that Avery Brundage, while at the International Olympic Committee meeting that morning, would issue a statement pleading with the newspapers and radio reporters to emphasize that the Americans meant no disrespect for the host nation, but rather were following a time-honored U.S. Army protocol that had to be honored. Still, the athletes were warned that they might draw some catcalls and whistles for not dipping the flag, and were told not to respond or get flustered.

After the rehearsal, the trackmen for the most part remained in a pack, and Jochim—adopted as one of them because of his flag-bearer duty—was walking and talking among the group with another elder statesman on the squad, Glenn Cunningham.

Sam Stoller was indignant. "They're *still* acting like we should give a damn what the Nazis think."

With Jesse Owens by his side, Ralph Metcalfe offered thoughtfully, "Well, again, I don't think all the Germans in the stadium are Nazis."

"*Most* of them will be Nazis," Marty Glickman said with a snort. "That's how they're getting the tickets! And Hitler is Hitler."

Glenn thought of what Luz Long had said. "Don't you think we can do both?" he asked.

Metcalfe asked Glenn what he meant.

"We talked about this on the *Manhattan*, I think," Glenn said. "Whoever looks—eyes right—at the people on the stand is showing respect for the Olympic tradition and the host people, not Hitler. Nobody's going to be keeping score of who does and who doesn't. If you don't look over, that's your business. That's all."

"But the writers at least are going to trying to figure out what we're doing as a team!" Metcalfe said.

"We're going to look like a mob," Glenn said. "They won't be able to tell what angle Marty's—or anyone else's—head is. Or even if his eyes are closed or if he's looking down . . . or anything like that. It's the same with everybody. I think this is going to be fine."

Torrance jumped in. "We didn't dip the flag at Amsterdam eight years ago, right? Jochim, you were there! I bet you didn't debate it like a bunch of little old ladies playing bridge or some such shit."

"No, we didn't," confirmed Jochim.

"And I don't think the Dutch declared war on us," Torrance said. "This a whole bunch of worrying over nothing."

"In Amsterdam," Jochim said, "I think somebody said we didn't dip it to the king in London because some of the other Irish guys on the team hated England . . . and that was the start. I don't remember anyone saying anything about an Army rule."

Glenn decided Jack Torrance had the right attitude. It wasn't intended to be an insult to Hitler. Or to the Nazis. Or to the Germans. But if that's how they wanted to take it, that wasn't the Americans' problem.

The trackmen and the others had started to disperse when AP's Alan Gould chased them down.

"Need comment on two things!" he announced breathlessly. "Jochim . . . just confirming you're not dipping the flag, right?"

"Absolutely not," the gymnast said.

"Everybody support that?"

"Absolutely," Jochim said.

Gould looked around.

"Morris? That right? Everybody's behind it?"

"We didn't take a roll call," Glenn said carefully, "but I sure think so."

"Okay, second thing," Gould said. "Anybody have a comment on the 1940 Games being awarded this morning to Japan? To Tokyo? Cunningham?"

"If I go there, it'll be as a spectator," Cunningham said. "So I'm not the one to ask."

"Morris?"

"Seems fine to me. Spread things around."

Leni had the script for the opening ceremonies, with her handwritten notes on it, in one hand. It was called a script, but as Leni confessed to her cameramen and other staff, she knew it was more of an outline, because the parade of athletes of the various nations almost certainly wouldn't conform to the time schedule that organizers—and the stand-in members of the Hitler Youth Corps—followed at the rehearsal the day before. Among the delegations that already had "rehearsed" their entrances on their own, she was told, most were acting as if both suggested pace and formations were nothing more than that—suggestions. And only God knew what Glenn and those Americans would do, given all the blather about their flag protocol.

She used her other hand to gesture and point at the model of the Reich Sports Field, zeroing in on the stadium. She emphasized they needed to shoot the various delegations from the second they came into sight until they moved onto the infield, and how that required teamwork among the cameramen. They had gone over the rest many times before—from the athlete's oath, to Hitler's declaration, and the arrival of the final torch runner and lighting of the stadium flame. So this was a refresher.

She already had confided in Willi Hameister, in charge of the cameras in Hitler's box, that they should be prepared to remove them immediately after the Führer's brief speech, but that if they could get away with leaving them in place for the entire opening ceremonies session, they should. So she didn't bring that up in the mass meeting. But she did designate two other cameras on the lower levels to be looking up to Hitler and rolling as he spoke, just in case the cameras in the box malfunctioned.

"Or if they decide they don't want the cameras by the rostrum?" asked cameraman Kurt Neubert.

"No, that's not a possibility," Leni snapped. "We have taken care of that. With the only man who matters."

She rechecked her notes.

"I think that's all I have," she said. "Any questions?"

Camerman Paul Holzki asked, "How concerned should we be with how the spectators respond to teams—good and bad?"

"Concerned enough so that those of you shooting the stands get as much as you can, either way. That's not just tomorrow. We're looking for enthusiasm of foreigners for their teams, and if it's Japanese fans cheering at the ceremonies, we can plug that in for track and field events."

Finally, Guzzi Lantschner hesitantly asked what many of them were wondering. The former skier was a master of the smaller, relatively mobile handheld camera, so he would be entrusted with many of the key shots that required scrambling. "After the opening ceremonies, how much should we be worried about filming the Führer when he's at events?"

Leni waved it off. "First, we need to get through tomorrow," she said. "Then we need to see how often he shows up. He told me"—she paused just long enough to let that register—"that he probably would be too busy and wasn't enough of a sports enthusiast to attend much."

"But if he does?" persisted Lantschner.

"We film his arrival and his reactions, as much as possible," Leni said.

A young cameraman's assistant said something that made those around him laugh. Leni couldn't hear him.

"What's that?" she asked sharply.

"If this becomes an American niggerfest at the track, and he's there, that should be good cinema!" the assistant said.

Leni exploded. "All right, one last time! Some of you keep talking as if this film will premiere two weeks after the Games. It is going to be a long, long time before this is ready, and we can't have too much film. No matter what it shows. At some point, we might have different versions for different audiences. Germany, England, America, France . . ."

That got Hans Ertl's attention. It was the first time she had broached that possibility to the group. The star cameraman knew Leni well enough to know that she must have been thinking about this for months. He laughed darkly. "Like the English version of S.O.S. Iceberg?"

"Oh, shit, we must be better than that," Leni said with disdain.

Many in the crew—those who knew the English version's dreadful reputation—erupted in laughter.

After the meeting, Ertl approached her. Their friendship remained intact, even after Ertl had noticed the attraction between Leni and his friend, Walter Prager, and stepped aside, if with a bit of relief because he hadn't known how long he would be able to accept Leni's many demands. His question was sincere, not challenging. "Leni, hearing you talk about all of this again . . . you're not still planning on doing all the editing yourself, are you? That could take years!"

"For now, yes," Leni said. "The control has to be mine."

"I understand that," he said. "But as your friend"—and more, which they both knew always underscored their interaction—"I'm begging you to get more help than you had on the party documentaries. I know what that did to you, and there is so much more involved with this!"

"Thanks," Leni said, genuinely touched. She smiled. "Concern and suggestion noted."

Everything she did with *Olympia* needed to have the long-range future in mind. She *must* use it to be taken more seriously internationally. She *must* end up back on the screen, starring in her own films. And those films would be shown not just in the major cities in America and Europe, but in places like the town where Glenn went to school.

As Ertl walked away, Leni noticed Anatol lingering at a back table. He asked his question with his eyes. Leni gave a slight, yet emphatic shake of the head and began the walk to her office. There, she pulled out a sheet of stationery and wrote out another brief note to Glenn, enclosed it in an envelope, addressed it, and then pondered which runner to entrust with delivering it. As she had several times now, she considered trying to call Glenn on the telephone at the Village, but she knew he would have to be summoned to take the patched-through call and that was both complicated and likely insecure. She assumed all calls would be monitored. She knew her previous notes to Glenn hadn't gone unnoticed, so she had openly talked about sending a thank-you note to him for his "briefing about the decathlon" at the stadium that day. This time, she decided her approach would be that if she said anything, it would be that Glenn had become their liaison to the American team, and she was wishing him good luck in the upcoming competition. She picked out a different runner this time, a student named Heinrich, and told him it was absolutely necessary to keep this communication quiet because it might get Morris in trouble if it came out that he was helping out the *Olympia* crew.

Leni realized there were other possibilities for leaks, even if only relatively harmless, about the notes or her relationship with Glenn. She was willing to accept that—after all, they were both adults and Goebbels couldn't gripe because Glenn was Aryan—but there was no need to advertise it any sooner than necessary.

After dinner, Glenn decided to give the Village cinema a try, following the pack of other Americans—a mixture of trackmen, basketball players, and swimmers—to the Hindenburg House. A different film played at 8 each night and the Americans who had sampled the fare had said it was a comfortable way to pass the time. When Glenn entered the lobby of the building, though, the poster of the night's movie caused him to freeze.

He had spotted Leni, wearing a fur coat and looking frightened in the arms of a bearded costar, before he noticed the title: *S.O.S. Iceberg*. And then, also on the poster, the details: *In English. Starring Leni Riefenstahl, Rod La Rocque, Sepp Rist. Directed by Arnold Fanck and Tay Garnett.*

The Americans made up about half of the crowd. Glenn made sure he wasn't behind the mammoth Jack Torrance and settled in to watch. He sat through the seventy minutes, mainly trying to picture what it was like to film on the chilling Greenland locations. If he were seeing it in Denver or Fort Collins, he would have walked out wondering why she was billed as the star, since her character, Ellen Lawrence, spoke only a handful of lines. In the opening scene showing a pre-scientific expedition dinner, he kept waiting for her to say something as she sat next to her explorer husband, but she didn't. She didn't speak until far into the film, and Glenn wasn't even sure that was her voice. He better understood her desire to come up with a film and a role to give her more credibility in America and in the English-speaking parts of the world.

After the film ended, some of the Americans headed off to the community room for beers. Glenn was among the group returning to their own buildings when basketball player Joe Fortenberry said to nobody in particular: "Do you buy that deal saying it was filmed in Greenland?"

"Why would they make that up?" asked a swimmer.

"Just to make it sound more, I don't know . . . exotic? How do we know that wasn't a bunch of ice piled up on a set?"

Glenn couldn't resist. "They made part of it in Greenland and part of it in Switzerland, and the two versions—one in German, one in English—at once. That was all real."

Fortenberry looked at Glenn as if he had two heads . . . or had just given the Nazi salute.

"How do you know all that?" he challenged.

"I'm a movie fan," Glenn responded self-consciously.

Diver Marshall Wayne mused, "She looks even better in person."

Glenn was startled. "Who?"

"Leni whatever her name is," Wayne said. "She was at the pool the other day. Scouting out for the Olympics movie they're making. I guess she's a director and all that stuff, too."

"I'd let her direct me . . . to do anything she wanted," said another basketball player.

"I'm surprised they showed it to us," said a swimmer. "Considering she's a Nazi."

"She's not a Nazi," Glenn declared.

"Come on, the German guys said she made Hitler's propaganda films," the swimmer said, shrugging.

Glenn considered how to reply, without raising questions—and eyebrows. Finally, he said, "I hear the Nazis even brag that she's independent, not a party member. They—the Nazis—supposedly like that. It's the same thing with this Olympics movie. It's the International Olympic Committee's baby now, not the Nazis'."

Those *were* all things Glenn had heard. He didn't say from whom.

Back at the room, his heart jumped when he saw the envelope that had been slipped under the door, and jumped even more when he confirmed it was from Leni. Her note was innocuous enough. She wanted him to know she was thinking of him on the eve of the Games and wished him the best of luck in the upcoming competition. And she hoped they again would be able to talk about *The Blue Light* sometime. He caught the code. He laughed, though, knowing he had real questions he could ask about *S.O.S. Iceberg*.

The decathlon wouldn't be held until the final stages of the weeklong track and field competition, but Glenn already was nervous.

1 8

~

Opening Gambits

Saturday, August 1

Leni decided that her trademark white flannel jackets—which made her stand out in still photos, even the panoramic ones taken at the Nuremberg rallies—needed to be augmented at the Games. For the opening ceremonies, she picked out a gray flannel suit and blouse that could shield her a bit if the morning light rains kept falling. She already had it on when she strolled into the 6AM meeting.

"Why couldn't we just make it 05:00?" Guzzi Lantschner asked dryly. "Why this late? Ten hours to the opening ceremonies . . . isn't that kind of cutting it close?"

Guzzi was one of the few who could get away with impertinence. Leni smiled, signifying she knew he was teasing. Then she lectured. "Gentlemen, the time to sleep will come in two weeks. We won't get a second chance to be prepared. The first time we say, 'Oh, shit, we missed that,' we have failed. We can't just say, 'Take two!'"

She summarized the weather forecast—light rain off and on—and how they would adjust for various conditions. She reminded them they would meet again that night at 11 after the opening ceremonies to go over assignments for Sunday, and that would be the pattern throughout the Games. No more pre-breakfast meetings; they'd take care of the planning the night before.

"Now . . . everyone have a good breakfast," she said. "You all have your vehicle assignments, too. I want everyone at your positions by 12:00."

Later at the stadium, she was heartened to see that all seemed to beat her deadline. As the light rain fell, she made a round of the cameramen's assigned vantage points. Heinrich, the student and runner, was with her, in case she needed to dispatch messages. She had considered assigning Anatol to the role, but she knew that in addition to delivering notes, the runner might need to get involved in German discussion, and Anatol would be useless. He was assigned as an extra laborer and as a backup runner only when all he had to do was pass along a note. With fans starting to file in, Leni recognized an assistant cameraman hurriedly hustling toward her. "The rostrum cameras!" he yelled and pointed back over his shoulder.

Leni saw SS men gathered in Hitler's loge box, where the Führer would watch the ceremonies and ultimately declare the Games open. Much to her horror, two of them kept gesturing at the two cameras, which Leni's men had tied to the rail with rope, more to stake out their positions than to secure the cameras. The biggest one, a sound camera, would show Hitler's left side as he spoke. Leni's man, Wilfried Basse, appeared to be making the argument that the cameras belonged there.

As Leni made a beeline for the box, one of the SS men began tugging on the rope.

"Stop!" she yelled.

Startled, the SS men turned. They waited for her to storm into the box. She assessed the situation and concluded that the one who had tugged at the camera was the junior of the two SS men. So she addressed the other one, assuming he was supervising and issuing orders.

"The cameras stay!"

"Fraulein Riefenstahl . . ."

"So you at least know who I am!"

"Yes, but . . ."

"There is no 'but'! That camera . . . these cameras . . . stay where they are!"

The SS man was respectful, but unapologetic. "As I told your man here," he said, gesturing at Basse, "these cameras—especially this big one—are in the way. They stand out. The Führer won't . . ."

"The Führer knows! I spoke with him and he approved. He *wants* the cameras here."

The SS man said, "Minister Goebbels told us to make sure there wasn't anything cluttering up this area. He was clear that to have room for everyone who expects to be with the Führer at these ceremonies, nothing else can be here."

"You let Minister Goebbels tell me that himself. Do you want to be the man I point to when I tell the Führer he will not be shown in the film, declaring the Games open in the Reich, because some jackass ordered the camera moved?"

The SS man looked at his comrade, who shrugged. Finally, the lead SS man said, "We will wait. We will handle this when the Minister arrives. But if he orders us to take it down, we will have to do so."

"He won't," Leni said. "I won't let him."

～

With siren-screaming escorts, the nearly two hundred military buses moved in a caravan from the Village to the Reich Sports Field. The buses with U.S. flags on them were near the rear. On one of them, Glenn grabbed a window seat, and Walter Wood joined him.

Germans lined the final part of the route, at least several deep, and the greetings were a mixture of the Nazi salute and waves. Even the Nazi salutes mostly were accompanied by smiles. Glenn found himself looking around to see if either Marty Glickman or Sam Stoller was on this bus. They weren't.

The buses unloaded at the Glockenturm Plaza, and German organizers began herding the Americans athletes onto the huge May Field next to the stadium. Their spot was nearest the Bell Tower, at the northwest corner, again because of the marching order. The rain had stopped, but the skies still were overcast and more showers seemed possible.

"B-a-a-a-a," Walter Wood bellowed. "Let's go, sheep."

Glenn took in the awe-inspiring scene. In front of him stretched a throng of athletes, including the women who had made the hike from the Friesenhaus on the northeast side of the Sports Field grounds, in various national outfits. Spectators, many of them approaching from the adjacent train station, poured through the stadium's gates. Some walked around the concourse between levels. Majestic orchestral music carried across the field from the stadium speakers. The huge dirigible, the *Hindenburg*, was in the sky to the east of the stadium, on the downtown side.

German functionaries, including men in military uniforms—Glenn still wasn't certain which uniform went with each group and which initials— were intent on two things: One, keeping the teams in their national formations; and, two, keeping open a wide lane down the middle of the field, from the Bell Tower to the stadium. A railroad-type set of rails ran down one side of the wide lane. At the end nearest the Bell Tower, Glenn spotted a big flatbed cart mounted on the tracks. On it was a large film camera and a man Glenn assumed was its operator.

Leni's camera!

Glenn looked at his watch. It was a few minutes past three o'clock. Glenn Cunningham circulated through the trackmen. The team captain didn't preach about marching synchronization, but suggested at least a semblance of order. Cunningham paused among Glenn's group and looked toward the marathon gate.

"See that?" Cunningham asked.

"What?" asked Earle Meadows.

"Look . . . all those teams practicing the salutes."

Glenn looked down the field. The Bulgarians, Colombians, French, and Canadians, among others, were practicing salutes. But which salute? The Olympic salute was supposed to be given with the right arm extended at an angle to the side. The Nazi salute, as they had seen over and over, was made with the right arm extended straight ahead. The teams in question were saluting so imprecisely, the gestures could be interpreted either way. "That's not smart," Cunningham said, shaking his head. "Even the ones who think they're doing the Olympic salute don't get it—the Germans and the whole world for that matter will think they're doing the Nazi salute."

Near the Americans, the Germans, wearing white suits and yachtsman hats, milled quietly. Meadows nodded in their direction. "Guess they don't need to practice *their* salute," he said.

A Badger with a megaphone passed through the Americans' ranks, repeating his message. "Relax, ladies and gentlemen! We're going to be here at least an hour—probably longer!"

Glenn briefly considered sitting down, but realized it wouldn't look good to have grass-stained and wet pants as he marched.

Still poised and standing guard by the rostrum, Leni winced when she heard the voice behind her.

"What's going on here?" Joseph Goebbels asked. The slimy minister of propaganda stepped up to the ranking SS man. "Let me guess. She"—Goebbels hooked his thumb at Leni—"placed these cameras here, in the way of everything."

The SS man nodded.

Leni angrily stepped toward Goebbels. "Be careful, Herr Minister . . ."

"Don't you dare threaten me!"

The junior SS man stepped between them. Leni paused, only because—as angry as she was—she almost laughed. *He thought I was going to hit Goebbels! Well, I could pummel the little asshole if I had to.*

"The Führer approved this!" she shouted.

"I'm sure you misled him about the layout of this box and rostrum," Goebbels said sharply. "A camera here ruins the ceremonial atmosphere."

"It was fine with you when we did this for the Nuremberg films! Cameras like these recorded all the speakers—including, yes, the Führer! If you try to remove these, it is *you* who will have to answer to him. This is supposed to be a day of glory for him—him and the German people!—and you will force him to deal with something he thought was taken care of."

Goebbels waved around the vast stadium.

"I'm not ordering you to abandon filming this part of the ceremony," he said. "But there must be somewhere else you can set up your cameras and get it without cluttering up this area!"

"There isn't!" Leni snapped. Angry tears, long a major Leni weapon, began to form. "To get the sort of image the Führer deserves, the camera must be here—and only here. If you want to tell him he is so insignificant, we can get a tiny shot of him from far off, go right ahead! You don't believe he approved? Are you calling me a liar?"

"Again, I doubt he knew how crowded it will be," Goebbels said.

"I made that clear. He accepted that."

"All right," Goebbels said, "but if he arrives and doesn't like the setup, these cameras will be out of here, just like this . . ."

He held up his right hand and snapped his fingers.

"He won't object," Leni insisted. She turned to the ranking SS man. "You heard the minister. They're staying."

The SS man looked at Goebbels, who offered an almost imperceptible nod.

Suddenly, Hermann Göring, decked out in his white uniform, joined them in the box. Goebbels noticed him first and started hollering again, putting on a show for the portly Air Minister's benefit.

"You understand me, Fraulein?" He gave a little wave at the cameras. "Even if the Fuhrer allows *this*, you cannot do whatever you want during the Games. The decisions are mine! You hear me? Mine!"

"Whoa!" Göring bellowed. "What's this all about?"

Goebbels outlined the dispute, then added, "We'll see if the Führer has any objections here. But the bigger issue is that Fraulein Riefenstahl must realize—both now and in the upcoming days—that the Olympics are not being staged solely for her benefit. Our film can be useful, but we cannot have her intruding on the Games, on the Führer, or our guests!"

Göring turned to Leni. "Fraulein?"

"I have been preparing for months," Leni said, tears still visible. "He cannot undo months of planning and wipe away things that have been agreed upon months and weeks ago."

Goebbels protested, "She can't . . ."

Göring raised his chubby hand. "There is no sense in going back and forth about this. The points have been made." He put a hand on Leni's arm. "And you, girl, stop crying. There's even enough room here for my belly."

Leni laughed at that, making it a convulsing sob. *Good thing these two hate each other.*

As Göring moved to the other side of the box, Leni leaned closer to Goebbels. "There are going to be plenty of beautiful young girls around today—the ones participating in the medal ceremonies during the competition," she taunted. "You can just occupy yourself trying to feel up some poor little thing. But leave my cameras alone—or you *will* regret it."

"Don't *you* push your luck here," Goebbels hissed. "Remember who controls the money for your project. I do!"

"You do control the funding . . . only until I go to the Führer. I know he laughs at your stupid antics, but they aren't laughing matters when he has to deal with them. You'll be slitting your own throat if you sabotage this. All those reichsmarks for a sabotaged film! How would the Führer like that? And I would make it clear who did the sabotaging!"

Goebbels stormed off. Leni pondered whether it was safe to leave. Finally, she decided it was, but before she left, she told the cameraman to dispatch a runner to her the instant it seemed there might be any more problems.

The Little Prick wouldn't dare. But . . .

As the athletes waited on the May Field, Glenn noticed but didn't at first feel a light rain again falling. He thought: *These hats are good for something.*

"Get a load of that!" Walter Wood called out, pointing beyond the Bell Tower to the Glockenturm Plaza.

Armed Germans in various uniforms had gathered. Cars pulled up in the plaza, and one large limousine arrived at the foot of the Bell Tower. Adolf Hitler emerged from the back seat. Scattered shouts of greetings came from the few German civilians allowed in the area. Glenn was surprised at how quiet it was otherwise. Hitler, wearing a brown uniform and high black boots, returned the Nazi salute to an honor guard. Then he moved on to greet three men, and Glenn recognized two of them from the Americans' welcoming ceremonies—the chubby mayor of Berlin and Dr. Theodor Lewald of the German Olympic Organizing Committee. Lewald and the third man— Glenn assumed he was an Olympic official, too—wore long coats, high collars, and medallions draped around their necks on chains.

Soldiers filed down the corridor on the May Field, showily looking side to side as Hitler and his entourage followed. Hitler's group was perhaps seventy-five men—military officers, Olympic officials, and other functionaries. Glenn inched up, so close to Hitler's pathway that the soldiers brushed him. Then he saw Leni, squeezed onto the flatbed cart behind her cameraman, who was angled to catch the reaction of the athletes to Hitler. As she approached Glenn's vantage point, she spotted him. Their eyes met. As the cart went by, with her poised behind cameraman Walter Frentz, she gave him the start, the barest hint, of a smile. For a moment, Hitler was no more than ten feet away.

Marty Glickman ended up at Glenn's shoulder. He shook his head in wonderment. "Can you believe how close we were? Somebody could have . . ." He left it there.

The looks they exchanged confirmed they both knew Marty wasn't talking about getting an autograph.

As Hitler moved on, he didn't look to either side, despite scattered cries from among the athletes. Mostly, it remained eerily quiet.

Soon, though, the roar announced: The Führer had entered the stadium.

As Leni and cameraman Hans Ertl followed, Hitler was greeted in the stadium with a multiple-trumpet fanfare and the raising of a huge Nazi banner with the red swastika against purple. The Führer and his entourage walked down the marble stairs at the marathon gate end to the track. As she moved, Leni made sure her other camera operators were poised. She quickly glanced at the rostrum. The cameras and her men still were there.

Over one hundred thousand spectators filled the seats, most roaring, many offering the Nazi salute. On the track, Carl Diem's five-year-old daughter— Gudrun—stood alone, in a white dress, floral headband, and white socks and shoes. She offered Hitler a bouquet, which he cheerfully accepted.

Hitler and the entourage climbed to his box with the rostrum and settled in. The German crowd sang the anthem and the "Horst Wessel" song. Leni stood at the far edge, barely wedging her way in behind the big sound camera to Hitler's left and nodding at the nearby Albert Speer, Hitler's architect. As she watched sailors along the upper rim of the stadium raise the national flags of the competing nations, she hoped that one of the cameramen assigned to the pageantry had captured that.

At 4:14 PM—Leni marked the time—the Greek team came through the tunnel below the marathon gate and onto the track.

The parade was on.

When Glenn and the Americans neared the marathon gate, they saw the teams starting to form up in more ordered fashion to enter the stadium. The German with the national placard for each team would be five meters in front of the team's flag bearer. Another five meters behind the flag bearer came, in order, that nation's delegation officials, the women athletes and then the men. Most striking was the wide disparity in size of the delegations, and the one-man teams from Costa Rica and Haiti had become folk heroes in the Village.

The Americans followed Turkey. As he entered the tunnel, Glenn realized that he was on the side of the eight-across line that would be on the inside of the track, nearest the dignitaries—and Hitler . . . and Leni? Glenn and the American men were far enough back in the delegation that they still were in the tunnel when they heard the thunderous reaction to Jochim's entrance onto the track.

The first glimpse of the packed stadium stunned him. He had forgotten how, with the field and track dug far below ground level, the stadium looked big from the outside—but gargantuan from the inside. They turned right out of the tunnel, onto the track. Glenn noticed that some spectators, Americans he presumed, were standing, cheering and waving tiny red, white and blue flags. He peered ahead and followed Jochim's progress past the midpoint of the track, past Hitler and the dignitaries. Jochim kept the flag high. Glenn wasn't sure why he was so invigorated, since he knew that had been coming, and would have been shocked—and dismayed—by anything different. Still, he thought: *Good for Al!*

As the Americans passed Hitler's vantage point, a Wehrmacht officer wedged next to Leni grunted. "Disrespectful bastards," he said loudly, which meant Leni could barely hear him over the cheering. "We demeaned ourselves by begging them to come. I hope you don't even show their niggers."

Leni shrugged.

That was at the heart of why she was determined to again do most, perhaps all, of the editing herself—regardless of how long it took. It would enable her to adjust the content and tone, for the film in general and for the various versions, depending on the backdrop of unfolding European events over the next couple of years.

⌒

As Glenn and the men were in the first part of the front straightaway, stretching behind the women, the call came out from the front of the group: "Hats!" In something between unison and one-by-one independence, Glenn and the others doffed their white straw hats. Glenn could feel his against his heart as he moved, and he got out of control, skipped in his stride and almost bumped into the athletes in front of him. He did turn his eyes to the right, looking up at Hitler and the dignitaries. He guessed that he was the only American who noticed the woman at the side and back of the rostrum area, offering a couple of quick and tight waves with a hand in front of her shoulder. He nodded, uncertain she would be able to notice and hoping nobody watching would think he was nodding at the German leader.

As Glenn neared the turn, the stadium erupted. The Germans had entered the track. The band abandoned its generic martial marching music and again began playing "Deutschland uber Alles." The host nation's athletes offered the Nazi salute. The smiling Hitler gave it back. The roars continued undiminished as the Americans moved around the turn and eventually onto the crowded infield. Taking stock of the Nazi salutes, the yells, the passion, the fervor, all around the stadium, Glenn shook his head slightly and caught Walter Wood's eyes. *Jesus.* Suddenly, he knew that until this minute, he had been naïve about Hitler's hold on the German people. They had witnessed some of it since landing in Germany, but this was another level and confirmation. Not about its reach, so much, since he wanted to believe Luz Long's assertion that not all in the nation or even in the German Olympic uniform were fanatical Nazis. But this was about the emotional depth of those committed. *What would be in store for a German who sat quietly and didn't join in? What would happen to Luz Long if he won a medal and then spoke out? Or Leni, if she didn't make Hitler's films?*

After the Germans finished their triumphant loop and settled into the infield with the other delegations, attention turned to the rostrum. A scratchy recorded voice came through the speakers in French. "Baron Pierre de Coubertin, founder of the modern Games," the Badger closest to Glenn announced. "Competing, not necessarily winning, is the thing, he's saying."

"Try telling that to the folks back home," Earle Meadows said dryly.

Lewald stepped to the microphones. As the Organizing Committee executive droned on and on, Glenn caught enough references to Hitler to assume it was some sort of sickening tribute to the leader of the host nation. Finally, it was Hitler's turn. His pronouncement from his rostrum was brief, delivered in short bursts, and decisive.

The Games were open!

To tumultuous cheers, Hitler backed away, smiling. The huge Olympic flag was raised at one end of the stadium. Hitler Youth members released thousands of pigeons, and suddenly, Glenn felt a "splat" on the top of his straw hat and didn't dare immediately take it off to check as he heard others react—"Shit!" was the most common expression—around him. *One more thing these hats are good for.* Guns fired in salute.

All eyes, including Glenn's, turned to the East Gate. At the top of the lower bowl, a lanky runner held a torch aloft in his right hand. He trotted down the stairs, cut to his left, heading in what Glenn and the competitors considered the "wrong" direction on the track, and made his way to the other end of the stadium. He climbed Marathon Gate stairs and came to the huge bowl, balanced on a tripod, at the outside ground level entrance. After showing the flame to the entire stadium, he turned and held the flame inside the bowl, which ignited. The Americans and all those around them cheered.

The flag bearers for each nation were called out of formation to gather around a podium on the field as a German athlete—Rudolf Ismayr, a weight-lifter—took the Olympic athletes' oath, while grasping a part of the huge German flag on the pole at his left. Glenn and the Americans had been asked to study and even recite the English version, so they knew what he was saying: "We swear that we will take part in the Olympic Games in loyal competition, respecting the regulations which govern them and desirous of participating in the true spirit of sportsmanship for the honor of our country and the glory of sport."

Hundreds of young singers had moved in on the Marathon Gate stairs. Now, a gray-haired man was introduced. From their scripts, the Badgers told the athletes that the man was composer Richard Wagner and the song was going to be his new work composed for these Games, the Olympic Hymn.

After the final notes, Hitler and his entourage filed down the stairs and onto the track. There, the Greek 1896 Olympic marathon champion, Spyridon Louis, handed Hitler something.

"What's that?" Marty Glickman asked.

"Olive branch," a Badger said.

Glickman laughed darkly. "Lot of good that's going to do."

"At least he took it," Glenn mused.

"Probably didn't even know what it was," Glickman said.

As Hitler left, the chorus began singing again—a different song, the type that seemed to have verses easily repeated and could go on forever. The delegations on the field also began to file out of the marathon gate tunnel. This time, the Americans were early in the procession, and it was more of a mob scene than an orderly parade.

As Glenn emerged from the tunnel and blinked in the light, the thought struck him: *Wonder how Leni did with all that?*

Leni was exhilarated that after all the threats, her camera in the box had captured Hitler declaring the Games open. To her, that and the lighting of the flame were the indispensable shots, and all indications were that everything went well on both.

"Okay, the first lesson learned today," Leni said, facing the staff in the long room shortly before midnight, "is we're going to have to be on our guard every second to fight off interference. It was Goebbels today. It may be someone else tomorrow." She held up several sheets of Geyer Lab's film lab reports, summarizing the raw footage from each camera. "But if these summaries give us a fair picture, I think we got everything we needed. All agree?"

Heads nodded.

"Any observations?"

Guzzi Lantschner jumped in. "I heard some of the athletes complaining about the camera pits at the track," he said. "I couldn't understand everything, but I wouldn't be shocked if there are some objections tomorrow."

Cameraman Georg Lemki joked, "Maybe we can kill two birds with one stone—throw Goebbels into one of 'em and fill it in."

The laughter was sudden, and short. Every one of them was aware that in the Third Reich, sentiments expressed in private meetings—even one-on-one—could end up in reports. Friends became worse than enemies; they became informants. Leni waved that off, not in dismissal, but as a sign it was time to move on.

"I'll be going around with assignments for tomorrow. Let's try to make this as painless as possible, both now and every night. If we try to argue or debate every placement, we'll be here until dawn. If there's something you *must* get off your chest, or something you think I should know, speak up. But please don't waste my time—or yours—with whining or bullshit."

Leni started with Hans Ertl and his crew. Cameramen Leo de Laforgue and Werner Hundhausen, seated together, knew they faced a long wait. "Does she have any idea how inefficient this is?" de Laforgue asked. "Insisting on doing everything herself? Not delegating anything?"

Hundhausen had worked with Leni more than de Laforgue. "She knows no other way," he said. "She knows what she wants."

"Doesn't she trust anyone?"

"She doesn't trust us to read her mind," Hundhausen said. "And what's in her mind is the only right way to do it."

19

~

High Jump, High Drama

Sunday, August 2

Glenn decided to stay at the Village for training on the first day of track and field competition. Some of his teammates went to the Reich Sports Field, saying they would work out at the nearby practice track and then walk over to the stadium to watch some of the events. Glenn's theory was that he would be tempted to leave the practice track too early, trying to catch the high jump, with Cornelius Johnson the favorite, and the shot put, where Jack Torrance would hope to prove that his ballooning since becoming a police officer would help—and not hurt—him in his event. Seeing Leni, too, with all the conflicted emotions that would bring, would complicate matters and distract him on his final day of serious training.

At the Village practice track, despite light rain and cold, Glenn worked on the pole vault with Earle Meadows, Bill Sefton, and Bill Graber, in relative private. With the technique help and encouragement of the Americans, especially the veteran Graber, he was starting to feel more confident that he wouldn't have any problem clearing a minimal height—one at least high enough to avoid scuttling his gold-medal hopes.

"We keep working with you, we'll have you clearing fifteen feet by Tokyo!" Meadows teased.

Glenn laughed at that. "I'm pretty sure I'm going to be done with this stuff by then," he said.

Meadows walked off, leaving Glenn alone with Graber, the veteran of the group. "Can I make a suggestion?" Graber asked.

"Sure."

"No matter what you do, you could work out enough to stay in decent shape, maybe enter a few meets a year, then in a couple of years decide if you want to give it a shot for Tokyo, too. That's kind of what I did this time."

Glenn nodded. "Makes a lot of sense. *If* I do it, that's probably how I'll do it."

Graber balanced the end of his pole on his shoulder. "One other thing: If you have people telling you that you'll have all kinds of endorsement offers if you win and you can turn pro and you'll be rich . . ."

He paused, so Glenn jumped in and said, "No, the DAC guy and I are talking about a good job and *maybe* some other things, but nothing definite. And certainly not about getting rich off the Olympics. At least not off the Olympics, alone."

"Good," Graber said. "I can tell you there was a lot of bullshit flying in Los Angeles about what winning could do for anyone. Yeah, guys have good jobs and time to train, continue to compete for clubs in AAU meets . . . but endorsements and turning pro and making tons? That was bullshit. I mean, Eleanor Holm got a rich husband and a movie contract and so little came of that, Brundage couldn't even get away with declaring her a professional! And she had a couple of advantages we don't have."

Yeah, I remember that wet swimsuit.

Glenn thanked Graber for both the help and advice.

Ultimately, after six hours of off-and-on work at the track, Glenn toweled off his sweaty face, neck, and arms. As he pulled the sweatshirt over his head, the third pole-vaulter, Bill Sefton joined him. "German guys gave me the report on what's happened so far," he said. "Want to hear it or want to stay in suspense?"

"Go ahead," Glenn said.

"Jesse broke the world record this afternoon in the quarterfinals . . . 10.2."

"Wow!"

"That's the good news. The bad news is none of the shot-putters got a medal."

Glenn was shocked. "Not even Torrance?"

"Nope, fifth. Germans got first and third."

Glenn thought of the injured decathlon man. "Hans Sievert one of them?"

"No . . . don't think so."

"What about the high jump?"

"Still going," Sefton said. "They'll probably finish in the dark!"

⌒

For Leni, the stadium on the first day of competition was a studio, a stage, and the spectators were only bit players and a collective backdrop. She deliberately dressed a bit frumpily, almost matronly, with an especially conservative and baggy suit with long skirt and white hat, to emphasize her seriousness as the woman in businesslike charge.

In the afternoon, Jesse Owens lined up for his second race of the day, a quarterfinal heat. As she had been for Jesse's easy win at the morning session, Leni was on the infield, near the finish line, with Erich Nitschmann and a big tripod camera. She was perched underneath the camera, looking up. She knew one of her crews was stationed in the pit along the outside of the track, at the corner past the finish line. She was gratified to see several of her cameramen, as ordered, again focusing on Owens at the starting line area, from the outside of the track and from the inside. Watching him run for the first time that morning, she had noticed that rather than concentrating as if he were wearing blinkers, he sensed the cameras' presence and even played to them. Leni always had maintained that cameras invigorated—rather than distracted—true "performers," including athletes and leaders speaking at podiums. She pictured the cameras' film of the powerful Negro, tense as he moved into the set position and then broke at the sound of the starter's gun. Owens won easily, and the judges announced his time was a world-record of 10.2 seconds. As he had at his morning race, he found a camera after the finish and walked right at it, smiling.

Leni was thrilled: *The nigger is a showman!*

She was mildly surprised to see the Führer arrive in his box during the afternoon. He already had backed down from his resolve to skip the frivolity of athletics after the opening ceremony! After Owens's race, she looked up at Hitler's box to see if the Führer had a noticeable reaction to the runner's dominance. He didn't seem to be paying attention.

For the next three hours, as she hustled from position to position, checking in with cameramen through the women's javelin, shot put, 800-meter heats for the men, and the 5,000-meter finals, one of the Führer's aides breathlessly caught up with her, saying Hitler asked that she visit him at some point. She could see that Göring was in the box with the Führer, but she didn't see Goebbels. After she climbed the private stairway under the stands, she went through the room and into the box. Hitler spotted her and brightened.

"Fraulein, we can see you running around down there faster than the athletes—except the niggers, of course."

"I'm glad you changed your mind and came," Leni said.

"I decided that when there aren't more pressing matters, I can play the good host for the athletes . . . at least most of them."

Göring said, "And we have started off with a bang . . . two German gold medals already!"

Leni smiled with the rest when the two German winners—shot-putter Hans Woellke and women's javelin thrower Tilly Fleischer—showed up together in the box, shaking hands with and accepting backslaps from the Führer. That drew thunderous cheers from the crowd. As they walked through the room behind the box, Woellke grabbed one of the many extra programs, came back in the box and asked for Leni's autograph on the cover. She wrote her name across Glenn's face. Then, much to Leni's surprise, all three Finns who swept the medals in the 10,000 meters also were brought to the box. Hitler was outgoing in greeting them, joking to Göring and Leni that the Finns could have put on Luftwaffe uniforms and looked perfect!

Leni noticed that the high jump seemed to be in its final stages. This is going to be the first test, she thought. She could just stockpile the film, including of the Negroes, and decide later how to handle it in *Olympia*; for the Führer, the choice about whether to visit with the winners, which she knew was really no choice at all, had to be made instantly. She pointed down to the field and told Hitler and Göring, "I need to get back down there to get the end of the high jump."

"Will a nigger win?" Hitler wanted to know.

"I'm not completely sure how it works," she said. "But it's possible."

Hitler looked to the western horizon. Then he looked at his watch. "I might have more pressing matters in a bit," he said.

Leni hustled down to the field and, from her camera pit, saw Cornelius Johnson win the gold before the event continued with a three-man jump-off for second and third. Eventually, another Negro American, Dave Albritton, claimed the silver and USC student Delos Thurber finished off the sweep for the USA by edging a Finn for third.

A few minutes before the medal ceremony started, Leni spotted Hitler departing his box. It wasn't a run to the lavatory, either. He was heading out of the stadium. There would be no visit to the Führer's box for these medalists.

⌒

Glenn was in his room reading—he had knocked off another hundred pages in *Of Time and the River*, with only a little cheating—and Walter

Wood was writing a letter when the knock came and decathlon man Jack Parker poked in his head.

"Hey, guys, they say the high jumpers are back and they've got their medals in the dining hall," Parker announced.

Glenn looked at Wood. His wordless question: *Think we should?*

After waiting a few seconds, Wood said, "Well, I'm going to go look. . . . I'm never going to get one of those myself."

Glenn stood. "How about if we go, but don't touch them? Don't want to jinx ourselves!"

"Sounds like a plan," Parker said.

"You guys can do that," Wood said. "I'm going to hold it like I just won it!"

A couple of minutes later, the three of them heard voices as they approached the dining hall. Johnson, Albritton, and Thurber were seated as a crowd of teammates both stood and sat around them. For weeks, Glenn knew, the Negroes had been teasing Delos Thurber that with a name like his, Hitler would think he was one of them, anyway. The three Americans' medals were on the table, next to what looked like a tree seedling in a tiny pot. The group included nearly a dozen other white boys and most of the other Negroes, minus Owens and Ralph Metcalfe, who had the 100-meter semifinals and finals coming up the next day. Glenn Cunningham and Bill Graber seemed to be the ringleaders.

"Is it bad to ask to see them?" Walter Wood asked.

Corny Johnson picked up his open case and handed it to Wood, who was wide-eyed.

"Wow," he exclaimed, taking it out of the case.

Glenn couldn't resist looking, too.

On one side, next to a Greek figure, the lettering said:

XL
Olympiade
Berlin
1936

Wood turned it over, and there the design showed a Greek athlete being carried off on the shoulders of others, with no lettering.

The three shot-putters—Sam Francis, Jack Torrance, and Dimitri Zaitz— all were there, too, and they were being good sports after missing out on medals themselves. The only complaint came when Torrance joked, "We should at least get little ribbons or something . . . you know how hard that was to make sure we finished fourth, fifth, and sixth, right in a row? That's almost as hard as you guys finishing first, second, and third!"

Jack Parker pointed to the pot on the table. "Let me be the eighth guy to ask . . . what's with the plant?"

"You're not the eighth," Johnson said, smiling. "You're about the twentieth. It's an oak tree. The gold-medal winners are supposed to take them home and plant them. Supposed to be a sign of international goodwill."

Albritton said, "But there's a limit to their goodwill, of course. They'll give you a tree, but not a handshake."

"Why, what happened?" Cunningham asked.

"Hitler called all the winners up to his box today . . . except us. I know there were only four finals today and a couple of the winners were German, but it's funny how he had the Finnish runners up there after the 10,000 meters, too, and then all of a sudden he was gone right before we got our medals. It wasn't *that* late or anything."

"Think it was deliberate?" Cunningham asked.

Albritton laughed. "What do *you* think? Not that I wanted to meet that jerk, anyway, but if it was going to be part of the Olympics here, I would have gone, just to show them we're not as rude as they are."

"It doesn't really bother me," Johnson declared. "I didn't want to meet him, either."

Albritton said, "I even asked the German movie lady—Leni whatever—where her Führer went and if he didn't like the high jump or something."

Glenn tried to be low-key. "What'd she say?"

"She said he couldn't stay any later or he'd be mobbed if he tried to leave when everyone else was. She spoke really good English. But she did ask why we had to take so damn long between jumps and make it run so long. I laughed, but I'm not sure she was kidding."

Glenn thought: *She wasn't.*

Albritton added, "She seems really intense. From what I saw, running all over, giving orders, jumping down at that camera pit with her crew, I'm not sure I'd like to work for her. But she was nice enough to us."

That's Leni, all right.

Cunningham jumped in. "Okay, guys, see what you think," he said. "It doesn't matter if they say it was an accident or bad timing. If he snubs any more of our winners, none of us—first, second, third, whatever—will go up there, even if invited. Sound right to everybody?"

Glenn joined in the nods and words of agreement.

"Start spreading the word," Cunningham said. "Now let's win enough gold medals to make this an issue!"

"Jesse'll force their hand tomorrow," Albritton said. "And ours."

Glenn thought: *Better be at the stadium.* He knew the heavy part of the track and field schedule the next day—including the 100-meter semifinals and finals and the hammer throw—wouldn't begin until 3PM, so he would work out in the morning at the Village, and then head over.

20

~

Leni's Tantrum

Monday, August 3

Glenn wore his warm-up suit, but not his official uniform, to the stadium. The noncompeting Americans who attended the Sunday events passed along the news that even during the competition, there was room to lounge around on the infield, but more notably, at the open areas at corners of the track. Glenn took one of the tunnels from the dressing-room area under the track and emerged in the infield. The 400-meter hurdle heats had started, and he watched American Dale Schofield—Glenn knew him from his college days at Brigham Young University—run second in his heat to advance to the semifinals the next day.

Then he spotted Leni. She wore trousers, a blouse, and a scarf, and she was watching one of her cameramen—Glenn didn't know it, but it was Guzzi Lantschner—working a camera set on a cart that was moving on rails, back and forth near the hammer-throw ring. Glenn and the American hammer throwers had joked about which of their events was more obscure in the United States, and the hope was that one of them—Bill Rowe, Donald Favor, or Henry Dreyer—would sneak into the top three and earn a medal.

One of the Germans uncorked an impressive heave, but even he turned before the weight landed when he noticed the furor behind him. A supervising official rushed up to Lantschner and shoved him. "What do you think you're doing?" the man demanded. "Pick up your toys and get out of here! This is not a playground."

Lantschner was stunned, and before he could react, Leni had grabbed the official's coat.

"What do *you* think you're doing?" she asked sharply.

"Fraulein . . ."

"You heard me, you miserable bastard. This was approved long ago. The athletes know about it and are fine with it."

A second German hammer thrower jumped in. "That's right, sir, Hein and I knew about this, and we asked the other competitors about it. They all said it was fine. Finns, Americans, Swedes—all of them." He smiled. The three Americans were lounged on the grass nearby, and the German competitor called out to them in English. "Camera," he said, pointing, "is all right?"

Rowe laughed and gave a thumbs-up gesture.

Favor said robustly, "Sure!"

The German who had just thrown joined his teammate and the confab. "My throw was awful, but the camera didn't have anything to do with it," he said. "Leave it!"

"You don't run this event," the official said. "We do. So I must say . . ."

"You must say *nothing*," Leni ranted. "Shut your goddamn mouth, let the men throw, and let us shoot them." She held out an upturned hand, gesturing at the filled seats. "Those people came to watch these men, we came to film them, and nobody gives a damn about watching you be an asshole!"

Glenn was too far away to hear all of that, and he wouldn't have understood the German, anyway. But he figured out the gist, and he resisted the temptation to rush over and try to help. The official tore away from Leni and huddled with three other men. Leni stayed with Lantschner, glaring at the officials. Finally, the first one returned and said, "Your conduct is unacceptable, Fraulein Riefenstahl."

At least the miserable son of a bitch knows who I am.

The man continued, "We discussed it and decided that you can use this gadget through the first two rounds of throws here in the semifinals, but then you must get it out of here."

"No!" Leni said. "I need at least part of the finals!"

"But all distances carry over," the man said, frustrated. "The winning throw might even be in the first round of throws!" The man pondered, and then sighed. "We need to get moving here," he said. "All right, you can photograph the six finalists for one throw apiece. We will not go any further than that."

Leni looked at Lantschner. He shrugged. "All right," Leni said. "But this is ridiculous. It's like none of you idiots know who's in charge, and those truly in charge aren't around while you clerks try to run things."

The official walked away. Glenn joined the three American hammer throwers. "What was all that about?" Glenn asked as casually as he could.

"They tried to kick out that camera contraption," Bill Rowe said. "I don't think they knew the wild woman came with the camera."

From her vantage point nearby, Leni turned. Spotting Glenn, her eyes widened—at least Glenn noticed—and she walked over to them. "Thank you for supporting me," she said in English.

She wiped away a tear.

Henry Dreyer told her, "Anything that helps hammer men get attention, we're all for."

Leni introduced herself, not making a move to shake hands. Dreyer returned the favor for himself and the other two hammer throwers. "And this," he said, gesturing at Glenn, "is Glenn Morris, who isn't talented enough to be a hammer thrower. He is a decathlon man, meaning he's trying to decide what he's good at."

Leni reached out, offering her hand to Glenn. As they smiled and looked in each other's eyes, Leni thought: *Oh, I know what he's good at.*

"Hello, Miss Riefenstahl," Glenn said.

Leni excused herself, saying, "I must get back to work, with the runners this time. I believe Guzzi has this under control . . . now."

She backed away, waved, and turned, heading toward the starting line area for the 100 meters.

"Jesus, Morris," Rowe said, watching her depart, "that look meant to meet her under the stands in fifteen minutes."

"Oh, come on," Glenn protested.

As Glenn watched the hammer-throw competition continue, Leni talked with her cameramen near the starting line. A uniformed member of the Honorary Youth Service materialized and handed her a note. She read it, then looked up at Hitler's box. The Führer wasn't there, but several men were— and one of them was the gerbil whose signature was on the note—Goebbels. She thought of ignoring the summons, but decided she should get it over with before the 100-meter semifinals began.

Upstairs, in the room behind Hitler's box, Goebbels went on the offensive.

"I saw that commotion down there and then was told that you had been disrespectful," he roared. "Who do you think you are? Your crew can stay . . . you can't."

Leni's angry tears began as she said, "I told the idiots there, we had permission in advance from the track and field officials and from the competitors."

"That's another issue! You can't be attacking judges down there on the field as you're representing the Reich. We can shut down the shooting now!"

"You wouldn't!"

The tears now were a torrent.

"Oh, Jesus, you're always performing," Goebbels said derisively. But then he softened. "You can knock off the crying and go down there and apologize to the judge you attacked, and we will consider it your warning."

Leni didn't say anything, but kept sobbing.

"Did you hear me?"

"I will apologize to the asshole," she said, "but not to you. If we are going to make this film and make the Reich's investment worthwhile, you will have to support me—not continue to try to fuck me over!"

"Fraulein . . ."

"You heard me! Stop trying to fuck me over. Because in the end, if you do that to me, you ruin the film and I can't imagine you trying to explain that to the Führer! We can't be having these ridiculous arguments at every step of the way!"

"You have to stop fighting reasonable limits on your filming! And I will check on this and be watching . . . you must apologize to that man!"

"Why would you sign off on this—with all the reichsmarks involved, I remind you—if you weren't going to back this? Answer me that!"

"I wish I hadn't," Goebbels snapped.

"Are you going to tell me, too, that we can't come here to shoot the winners the Führer invites up to congratulate them? I will have someone here once the medals start being awarded!"

"That's moot now," Goebbels said.

"Why?"

"The International Olympic Committee man has asked—told—the Führer that the tradition isn't for the heads of state of the host nation to receive the winners," Goebbels said. "He said that would be all right, but the Führer cannot be selective. Either he greets all the winners or none of them."

"Because of what happened with the American high jumpers yesterday?"

"Of course. But the Führer now has an excuse—as if he needed one—not to meet with the niggers the rest of the way. No one can whine about him snubbing them."

"Which, of course, he will be doing," Leni noted.

"Of course," Goebbels said smugly. "He's been diplomatic with the Olympics officials in his presence, but he's making it clear to the rest of us that the Americans should be ashamed of letting the niggers win for them. We could go to the jungles for slaves, too, and have them win for us here. But that would not be a celebration of our nation's character, either."

Leni nodded, and the agreement seemed to lighten the mood.

Goebbels continued, "The Führer said he might still have some competitors come up here, but he will not do so in his loge. It will be here, in this room, and it will not be publicized."

Leni was halfway out the door and passing the SS guard when Goebbels called out: "Fraulein?" She stopped. "Don't think I have forgotten," he said. "I will be watching and checking to make sure you apologize to the official."

"I should just tell him to go fuck himself," Leni muttered.

She noticed a hint of a smile on the SS man's face. It hit Leni halfway down the stairway that the SS man might have thought she was talking about Goebbels.

With a feigned rueful smile, Leni addressed the hammer-throwing judge. "I am sorry I grabbed you, but I hope you understand my passion for this project," she said sheepishly.

The judge nodded, then they both turned, drawn by the commotion in the stands. Adolf Hitler had arrived in his box.

Next up were the 100-meter semifinals. The top three in each of the two races would make the finals run ninety minutes later. Leni went back to the starting line area and grabbed one of her cameramen, Sepp Ketterer. "Sepp, I want shots of the Negro Owens getting ready to run after digging his holes," she ordered. "His thighs, his buttocks, all the evidence of a primitive, but powerful, creature."

Ketterer nodded. Leni scurried along the infield, past the finish line and allowed herself to be helped down a small ladder, joining cameraman Walter Frentz in the pit at the corner of the track, outside the lanes as the lime markings curved into the turn.

In the first of the two heats, Jesse Owens ran from lane seven, with nobody outside him. Frank Wykoff was in lane four. They easily ran one-two, with Owens winning, and he looked to his inside after he crossed the finish line and almost didn't cut left in time to avoid falling into the camera pit. The track official chasing down Owens to tell him his placing passed the edge of the pit said, "Hey, this might not be a good . . ."

From a few feet away, Owens—while not understanding the German, but getting the gist—called out. "It's my fault," he said. "I didn't follow the curve."

Satisfied, the official held up one finger for Owens and told him his time—10.4 seconds. Owens looked at Leni, who yelled out in English: "Thank you!"

She meant it. *I didn't need another fight!*

Owens waved as Wykoff joined him. Knowing they both were advancing, they patted each other on the back. Five minutes later, Ralph Metcalfe won the second semifinal, but the big news—at least to the crowd—was that German Erich Borchmeyer ran third, qualifying for the final. A German would be running up against the three Americans, including two Negroes, in the race for the medals.

"Drama!" Leni exclaimed to Frentz. "We have drama. The fastest of the white race against the primitives!"

She stayed with Frentz through the first round of 100-meter heats for the women, taking note of the young American, Helen Stephens, who broke the Olympic and world record in winning easily. She was tall, blonde, and flat chested.

"If she ran for us, Goebbels would love her," Leni said.

"Are you sure? She's not a beauty."

"Walter, we all know you have very high standards," Leni said, smiling. "And compared to the Pole, she's a picture of womanhood." She meant Stella Walasiewicz, Stephens's major challenger for the gold and a dark-haired runner who—as Leni had heard in her wanderings—was the subject of many raised eyebrows and rumors about whether she should have been in the men's events. To the Americans, she was Stella Walsh, because she trained in the United States, where she simplified her name.

"I'm also pretty certain Miss Stephens likes girls," Frentz said dismissively. "And I mean the way *I* like girls."

"And we know you like girls . . . especially the Italian runner!"

"Oh, don't believe everything you hear," Walter said, smiling.

To Leni, that confirmed the Castle rumor: Walter not only had managed to sneak into the Friesenhaus with a pretty Italian runner, a significant accomplishment amid the security, he had stayed the night with her and got back out the next morning without being detected.

Glenn went to the locker-room area under the marathon tunnel to see if a trainer could rub down his slightly sore right shoulder. A grizzled trainer for the U.S. team named "Sparks"—Glenn wasn't sure if that was his first or last name; he'd never heard the man called anything else—obliged, kneading out some of the knots. As Glenn emerged in the hallway, he ran into Owens, Metcalfe, and Wykoff heading to the track for the 100-meter final. He joined them on the walk.

"Good luck, guys," Glenn said. "Hope we sweep!"

To Glenn, Owens seemed calm and relaxed, the other two tense and nervous. At the track level, the first person they saw was Eleanor Holm Jarrett, wearing a skirt, blouse, and hat. She displayed a press card, but Glenn still wondered: *How'd she get here . . . on the field?*

Eleanor greeted them as a group, and then asked Owens if she could ask him a couple of questions for her column.

"*Now?*" Owens asked nicely.

"Just a couple. . . . I know it will be messy after and I need to run this by one of the guys writing it for me."

She had neither a notepad nor pen. Glenn and the other two sprinters left Owens and Eleanor alone. But they were able to hear Eleanor ask her first question, about the sprinter's reaction to his time of 10.2 the day before not being confirmed as a world record because of excessive winds behind him— winds that weren't measured, but only vaguely and instinctively judged as excessive by race officials.

"She was serious, wasn't she?" Wykoff asked. "I wonder if someone tried to interview her at the pool before her races in Los Angeles."

"Knowing Jesse, it'll just keep him relaxed," Metcalfe said. "He might fall asleep on the grass before they call us to the starting line."

Glenn joined a pack of Americans in the lower-bowl section reserved for the athletes next to the dignitaries' area. Among the group were the two "extra" sprinters, Marty Glickman and Sam Stoller. From the higher vantage point, Glenn noticed how one of the cameramen—Leni's, he assumed— seemed to be fascinated with shooting Jesse Owens's every move, even maneuvering to be behind him.

"So what you think?" Walter Wood asked Stoller. "Any way Jesse loses?"

"It's a longshot," Stoller said. "But his lane's beat up and a little wet, and if Ralph gets off to a good start, it's not automatic. But it would have been worse if they hadn't moved everyone out a lane and left lane one open. Even Jesse would have had trouble winning from there."

"Jesse wins easy," Glickman declared.

"That's what I think, too," Wood agreed.

Thinking about Eleanor Holm distracting Jesse and maybe him being too relaxed, Glenn grinned and asked Wood: "What odds will you give me if I take the field for a buck?"

"Anybody but Jesse?"

"Yeah."

"Three to one?"

"Five to one," Glenn countered.

"Okay, deal," Wood said.

"I'll put a dollar on that, too, Walter," Stoller said.

"Sure."

They shook on it.

Jesse got off to a great start, but for an instant, as Metcalfe closed in the final strides, Glenn thought he had a chance. But after Jesse crossed the finish line a stride in front, Glenn turned to Wood: "I'll pay you back at the Village."

The official results were posted. Owens's time of 10.3 seconds tied the old world record—the one that still stood because of the judges' decisions about the wind the day before. Holland's Martin Osendarp was third, claiming the bronze medal; Wykoff fourth; and the German hero, Borchmeyer, fifth.

Glickman pointed out, "They can't even say the German was the fastest white man! Now we see if the bastard snubs the Negroes again."

Glenn Cunningham added, "And what happens after that."

"They're saying that's not an issue anymore," said hammer thrower Bill Rowe, who had finished fifth in his event, the best placing among the three Americans.

"Meaning?" Cunningham asked.

"Hein—he won the hammer—said the coaches told the Krauts that the Olympics people told Hitler he couldn't congratulate the winners in his box unless he brought them all up," Rowe said. "So they couldn't be mad if the Führer didn't pat them on the back in public. This is secondhand, through Hein, and he doesn't speak English all that well."

"Besides," said Stoller, "he has to be careful about what he says."

"At least this doesn't force our hand," Cunningham said. "Sounds like it's not going to be an issue. But . . . like we decided last night, nobody's going to see him, right?"

The Americans nodded.

"Everybody's passing the word, right?"

Wood laughed. "Thanks, Glenn," he said.

"What for?"

"For acting like I have a chance to win!"

Cunningham grinned and patted Wood on the back. "Stranger things have happened, Walter," he said.

Glenn Morris decided that it actually took some pressure off. There was enough on him, already, as he went for the gold in an event in which only Olympic gold was noticed, but now he didn't need to worry about what he would say to an invitation to meet Hitler in his box. Deep down, he knew there were some people in Simla and Fort Collins who might be impressed and jealous, rather than offended, but now he didn't need to be concerned about negotiating that minefield.

Glenn decided to stay until the end of the day's competition. He wasn't as concerned with watching the remaining events—heats in the 800 meters and the steeplechase, plus the women's 100-meter semifinals—as he was with possibly being able to talk with Leni. Buses back to the Village ran until midnight, mainly in case the athletes visited the Strength Through Joy restaurants or beer halls on the Reich Sports Field grounds.

With some help, Leni climbed out of the camera pit and went to the medal stand area to watch the ceremony. She thought: *The primitive Americans get their awards!* She also caught herself repeatedly focusing on Jesse Owens's powerful rear end and upper thighs. Glenn wasn't the only American who noticed Leni.

"I think the movie lady likes Jesse, too," Rowe said.

"No way," said Glickman. "She's Hitler's pal, remember."

"She at least likes to look," Rowe said.

"She's doing her job," Glenn found himself saying. He knew that could be taken several ways. "When filmmakers film things, they're doing their jobs."

"What the hell does that mean?" Rowe asked.

"In documentaries, they just shoot film and see what they end up with."

Glenn was relieved when Rowe didn't press him.

A few minutes later, Glenn laughed when the German girl involved in the ceremony handed Jesse the same type of tree seedling and pot that Corny Johnson had displayed the night before. "What's Jesse going to do with all those trees?" Glenn asked nobody in particular. "I mean, he might get . . ."

Glenn stopped, realizing that might be a sensitive subject for Glickman, who still was awaiting word on whether he would be included in the relay.

"If he gets three, great," said Glickman. "If he gets four, I'll be . . ."

Stoller interrupted. "Did you see that?" They looked at him, and he was pointing at Jesse, who had walked away from the medal stand and was beneath the box seats and Hitler's loge. "He just nodded and waved up at Hitler!"

Wood scoffed, "How do you know he was waving at Hitler? There are a hundred thousand people in this stadium. Could have been at the writers behind Hitler. Could have been someone else."

"I could tell!" Stoller claimed.

Rowe said, "He could have been saying, 'Take that, asshole!'"

Cunningham said, "I guess we'll just have to ask."

Owens was swept up, though, to go and speak with the writers, so the question was going to have to wait.

∽

Glenn returned to the infield for the steeplechase heats and made a point of moving to the outside edges of the infield and cheering on the three Americans—Harold Manning, Joe McCluskey, and Glen Dawson. He laughed to himself, thinking that if everyone decided he was the consummate teammate, maybe more of them would show up to root him on in the decathlon.

Suddenly, during the last heat, Leni was standing next to him, a half step back—Glenn assumed, to make it less obvious. She seemed to have shaken Rolf Lantin, her still photographer shadow. As the runners went past and then were on the other side of the track, she said, "If you can, meet the car in the platz underneath the Bell Tower at 19:30 . . . 7:30."

"But . . ."

She was gone.

2 1

~

Leni's Idea

Kurt was his driver again and he gave Glenn a jacket to put on over his American team sweatshirt. The elevator operator was a different man than before, though, and Glenn again realized Leni was counting on the discretion of many folks in her life.

After his knock, she called out for him to come in, and it sounded as if she was in another room. Opening the door, he stepped inside and saw a bottle of wine on the dining-room table with two glasses. "I'll be there in a moment," she called out.

When she came in, she went right to the door and locked it.

"You are my captive," she told him, smiling.

She hadn't changed clothes from the stadium, but she looked as fresh as if she had stepped out of the bathtub an hour earlier. By now, Glenn understood that once she got into high gear—and that seemed to be often—her energy was boundless. Her kiss and hug were emphatic, but short of being a sign to Glenn that they would be rushed. She motioned for him to take off the jacket, then threw it on a chair in the corner and stood back, looking at him.

"My, my, my," she teased, nodding at the lettering on his sweatshirt. "A very handsome representative of the USA. They must be so proud of you back in Colorado."

"They'll be more proud if I win Saturday," he said. "If I don't, I'm yesterday's news."

Leni was confused. "What is 'yesterday's news'?"

"Washed up," Glenn explained. "A has-been. A nobody."

Leni's look remained blank, so he tried again.

"A failure."

"Really? Is Herr Blask a failure because he finished second in the hammer toss today—and to his own German countryman? Is your Metcalfe a failure because he didn't get the gold and your Owens, did? With all the athletes here competing, you are saying that winning the gold is all that matters?"

"Well, how else am I going to get in your film?" he asked with a grin.

Leni poured wine into the two glasses, handed one to Glenn, then raised hers. "To the Olympics and your gold," she said.

"To the Olympics and your movie," Glenn said as they clinked.

Glenn sipped. Leni drank.

Then Leni asked, "What do you think your America will think of Negroes winning your gold medals?"

"What do you mean?"

Be careful. "Will the high jumper and Jesse Owens now be able to drink from water fountains in your country? Or eat in all the restaurants? That is all I meant."

"Maybe it will help us make some progress," Glenn said. "I also think if Hitler had met Corny—the high jump winner—or Jesse, it might have helped Americans think he isn't so queer."

"He had to leave before the high jump winner was free and they told him he couldn't receive the winners any longer," Leni said. "None of the winners."

"Yeah, that's what we heard," Glenn said. "Would he have congratulated the Negroes, anyway?"

"I don't know," she said slowly. "I can tell you, though, that the director of German Sport was telling the Führer that he should meet the Negroes, and then the Führer could ask if the leaders of any of your Southern states would do the same thing."

"*That* would have made things more interesting," Glenn admitted. "But . . ." When he paused, Leni signaled for him to continue. He said, "But then Jesse might have asked him about the Jews." Glenn thought: *Actually, I'm not sure Jesse is a real political guy, but . . .*

Leni smiled darkly. "*That* would have made things more interesting," she said, gently mimicking. "But I'm told that his security men really did say the Führer should leave before the end of the competition for the day."

"I'm surprised you were able to come home, the way you were running around, all the work you have to do."

"Oh, you wouldn't believe all the shit I've put up with the past few days," she said. "I probably crossed the line a little bit. I forgot I should be concerned about my parents, too. I deal with some very petty people. I needed to get away for a few hours before I said or did anything more. I'll say I was at the Geyer Film Lab, but just run by there on the way to the Castle for the meetings with the cameramen."

"My teammates have noticed you," Glenn confessed with a grin. "I hope you don't mind. I think a couple of them wanted to ask you to dinner."

"Mind? When they stop noticing, that is when I know I must become what your people call a 'character actress,'" she said with a laugh. "When I get back to dramas, I will want to be the lead! I hope I have a few more years."

"I think you're safe," Glenn said.

"Are you hungry?"

Glenn admitted he hadn't had anything since a quick snack at the noon hour. Leni told him dinner was on the way from another of her favorite cafes. "It will be wonderful, but I have been assured they will not send too much food. Are you down to your competing weight?"

"Just about," Glenn said. "Maybe a few more ounces."

"Well, you're still in your practice clothes," Leni said. "You could just go out and run a kilometer or two after eating!"

"Not a bad idea!"

She laughed and pointed. "What's underneath that sweatshirt?"

He lifted up his sweatshirt to reveal the shirt that said: "PROPERTY OF COLORADO AGGIES ATHLETICS."

"What's 'Aggie'?"

"Short for Agricultural. We're Aggies . . . and damned proud of it."

"If that's something to be proud of, I commend you," Leni said, smiling. "I asked because I'd say we could be sitting here when they bring in the food, but if they see your sweatshirt—or even that T-shirt—it might be too much to expect the man to keep quiet. The men working in this building, I trust. They lose their jobs if they don't respect the privacy of the residents. One man from a café might find it too tempting."

The knock came moments later. Leni pointed to the bedroom, so Glenn moved there and closed the door behind him. He heard the conversation in German in the dining room, noticed it had stopped and heard the front door close. He poked his head out. On the table was a small-portioned three-course dinner on platters, with an empty plate for each of them.

"Looks great!" Glenn said.

"It is."

"But where's dessert?" Glenn teased. "No apple strudel?"

"Your weight, remember? We'll just have to come up with our own," Leni said.

They did. In bed after, Leni perched on an elbow and looked at Glenn.

"Was that better than a run on the street?"

"Oh, yeah."

She inhaled a couple of times and seemed about to say something. She waited. Finally, she said, "You are proving to be quite a distraction."

"That's all?"

Touching his face with a finger, she said, "I said I wouldn't fall in love again. Couldn't get hurt. Couldn't be distracted. Couldn't end up having my lover saying choose between him and my art, which is what happened—even if they didn't see it that way. They should have known, I don't do things by halves."

"I understand that."

"I love you," she said.

Did I hear that right?

Softly, she continued, "So what about you?"

"What do you mean?"

"It isn't a hard thing to say, Mister American Hero. You can say it: 'I love you, too.'"

He paused, thinking of the meaning, thinking of Karen, thinking of the complications . . . and then thinking of the moment.

"I love you, too."

They kissed, and the lovemaking this time was more tender.

Glenn sat at the dining room table an hour later, drinking water, as Leni rushed around, getting ready to leave. She joined him and poured herself a glass from the pitcher.

"We need to face something here," she said.

Glenn waited.

"This is very powerful," she said. "If you think I will be able to say good-bye and that's it, you are wrong."

Glenn didn't know what made him say it. He at least smiled. "Is that a promise or a threat?"

Leni looked hurt. "You think of it that way?"

He reached out and took her hands in his. "I was joking! That's what we Americans do when we are embarrassed. Leni, you keep forgetting I'm a Colorado country boy. If anyone had told me even last week, and for sure last year, that something like this could happen—with someone like you—I would have laughed in their faces."

"All right," Leni said, wiping away tears.

"I don't know what happens, either," he said. "But I'm sitting here thinking you'll be able to go back to your life—your busy life, your famous life—the second I leave Berlin, and if I pretend anything different, I'll be the one hurt. And you do forget, there is a girl and a life back home for me."

"Again . . . do you love her?"

"I thought I did. Now? I'm not so sure. If I loved her, would I be here? Maybe that's trying to rationalize. But my world has changed quite a bit."

"Enough that that you'd thinking of moving here to be with me?"

"*What?*"

"Americans live in London," Leni said. "Americans live in Paris. Americans *have* lived in Berlin. Some of them have done it for love . . . or their art. They are not turning their backs on the country."

"But here? Now? It's *different* now!"

"I know that!" Leni exclaimed. "But this saber rattling, this talk, all will calm down and we will find—I am hoping, at least—that even Hitler wants peace. He will settle for restoring order and prosperity. He is a lot of things, but he is not stupid. This maneuvering is to strengthen his hold on power. He wants to make sure the world lets him continue to rebuild the armed forces—putting us on equal footing with the rest of Europe again. That's all. It's the same with his Jewish policies. He will step away from the extremes."

"That's all a little over my head," Glenn said.

"Oh, stop playing the farmer boy," Leni said. "You are not ignorant."

"I'm not. But I'm trying to tell you . . . I'm trying to sort it all out."

"So . . . hear me out. You stay or you go home, take care of some things, come back to Germany. With me. I put together this film. Glenn Morris in *Olympia*."

"What if I don't win?"

She ignored that. "And we have a love story of our own in the making," Leni said. "A love story we can proudly share with the world."

"You didn't answer me. What if I don't win?"

"You will. I know you will. But you think that's important to me?"

"Yeah, I do. What kind of story do we have if I finish fifth?"

"You're underestimating yourself." After a few moments, she asked, "So will you at least think about what I say?"

"Of course I will. For one thing, you're asking me to—no matter where it leads—walk away from the girl back home."

"That was part of your old life. You just said your life has changed. It will change more in the upcoming days. You've made no promises to her, have you?"

Glenn said no, and then thought a moment. "But I'd be telling her it's over for something that's only a 'maybe' with you. Didn't Marlene Dietrich move to America? Why can't you do that? Then we see what happens."

"She just acts, Glenn. She is not a filmmaker. She left before the Führer came to power. It would not be as simple to leave now. I don't know what has become of her family, but I will not turn my back on mine here."

"And me moving to Germany wouldn't be turning my back on *my* family?"

"It wouldn't! You could go back and forth. That is fine with Americans. Here . . . well, once everything stabilizes, we could go back and forth."

"But when will that be? Can you promise me you know when that will be . . . or that it will happen at all? Or that it won't get worse?"

Leni's reddened eyes bore in on his. She said nothing.

"So you don't know those answers," Glenn said.

"No, I don't. I also am saying I am willing to let it play out—with us together."

Glenn sighed. "We have plenty of time to think about this. Can't we just leave it here for now? That we think about it? You're right. A lot can happen in the next week or two."

"Some things might change," Leni said, standing. "This won't." She leaned over to kiss him.

Glenn made it back to his room at about 11. Walter Wood was reading. "You keep carousing, you've got no chance at gold," he said.

Glenn interpreted it as teasing with a point. "Carousing?" he asked. "Just eating there by the stadium, that's all, after everything was over."

"In your sweat suit?"

"Sure! Half the guys there are dressed like this, you know that," Glenn said.

"How was dessert?"

"Fantastic!"

"If you talk about strudel in your sleep, I will suffocate you with your pillow. If you talk about the movie lady again, I'll be taking notes."

As he was climbing into bed a few minutes later, Glenn told Wood, "I did meet her today."

"The movie lady?"

"Yeah," Glenn said. "I was talking to the hammer throwers and she came over to thank them because they'd gone along with her putting some gadget camera by the hammer ring. So I got introduced, too."

"Did you tell her you'd already dreamed about her?"

"I sure didn't," Glenn said with a laugh. "But I think she might have been able to tell."

Leni was distracted as she went through her meticulous notes and instructions for each camera crew at the Castle. Only Guzzi Lantschner, Walter Frentz, and Hans Ertl knew her well enough to notice, and each asked—in his own way—if anything was wrong. She had told them that the infighting about access and everything else, thinking all was set and then finding out that wasn't the case, was testing her patience and endurance—and that was as true as far as it went.

When he could approach her alone, Ertl asked, "I know what's wrong. What's his name?"

"Stop it!"

He did, but he patted her hand.

After the meeting ended, Anatol still was lingering in the hall. His eyes asked the question. Again, Leni shook her head.

2 2

~

The Führer's Box

Tuesday, August 4

When lanky American Helen Stephens won the 100 meters in a rout, finishing well ahead of Stella Walsh and Germany's Käthe Krauss, Leni was by the broad jump pit with Walter Frentz, eagerly awaiting the final rounds of jumps in a gold-medal showdown between Jesse Owens and German hero Luz Long. Leni shook her head in regret, thinking of the terrific footage she could have gotten of the white American girl if officials hadn't ordered her shooting trench at the end of the track filled in. All the other trenches remained, so she decided to accept one small defeat.

Soon, an SS man she recognized as a member of Hitler's security entourage hustled across the track. "Fraulein Riefenstahl," he said forcefully, "I have been ordered to bring you to the Führer's box. Now."

She thought: *Here we go again.* Giving the SS man a pained look, she asked, "Is this from Goebbels?"

"No, Fraulein," he said. "Herr Hess. The American woman sprint champion was about to meet with the Führer, and Herr Hess said she asked about you and seemed very interested in meeting you, too."

"I've seen her down here," Leni said impatiently. "She's seen me. I'll be happy to introduce myself to her if she comes back to the field. But I shouldn't leave here now—not with Long about to compete!"

"Please! I have been told not to take no for an answer. It shouldn't take long."

Leni shrugged at Frentz. "I'll be back as soon as I can."

With the SS man, she went up the private stairway to Hitler's loge area and into the room behind the box. The Führer was in a rage, screaming at a photographer Leni didn't recognize. He turned to his SS men. "Get him out of here! Destroy his film!"

Stephens, a towel around her neck and tucked inside the top of her USA sweatshirt, watched, dumbfounded. Rudolf Hess, the deputy Führer, was with the American, and Leni wedged herself next to Albert Speer in the back of the room. The guards shoved the photographer through the door.

"What's this all about?" Leni asked Hitler's architect.

"He photographed the Führer and the American girl," Speer said. "There weren't supposed to be photographers in here."

Suddenly, as if the switch went back off, Hitler softened and smiled at Stephens, who still seemed confused. He spoke to her in a flurry of German words. "You are such a big, strong woman," he said. "Blonde hair. Blue eyes. You should run for Germany!"

Stephens turned to Hitler's translator and listened. Then she responded, "Thank you, Mister . . . Chancellor. But I like America fine!"

The stilted small-talk conversation continued, with the translations going back and forth. Hitler congratulated her on setting a world record. Helen giggled and told him records were made to be broken. He asked her what she thought of Berlin, and she said it was very clean and nice. Then, incredibly, Hitler asked if the tall American would like to come to visit him at Berchtesgaden—his Bavarian retreat—over the upcoming weekend.

The American coach, apparently nonplused, explained that Helen still would be training for the Monday relay and needed to stay in Berlin. Helen thanked him for the offer. Hitler smiled, shrugged, reached out and pinched Helen's rear end, turned and left the room. The runner looked surprised, not offended.

Much of the tension seemed to leave the room with Hitler. Hess nodded at Leni, motioning her to meet with the runner. As Leni moved forward, she called out, "Miss Stephens . . ."

The American turned and brightened. Leni introduced herself. "Oh, I know!" Stephens exclaimed, enthusiastically pumping her hand. "I've seen you on the field. Jesse said you were Mister Hitler's favorite movie person and that I'd get to meet you if I won. He was right."

"Congratulations on your victory," Leni said.

"Am I going to be in your movie?" Stephens asked, wide-eyed.

"Oh, I certainly think so," Leni assured her, smiling. "You were very impressive."

Noticeably flattered, Helen said, "Thanks!"

The woman American coach interjected: "Helen, you need to talk with the writers now." She turned to Leni. "I hope you don't think that's rude."

"Oh, no," Leni said, hoping her relief wasn't obvious. "I understand. I need to get back to my crew—and see if your Jesse can beat Luz Long!"

Walter Wood sought out Glenn at the Village practice track and suggested heading to the stadium to catch the end of the day's events.

"You sure you want to go?" Glenn asked. "You need your rest for tomorrow."

Wood waved that off. "If I throw my lifetime best, I *might* crack the top ten," he said.

Gordon Dunn, Ken Carpenter, and Wood were the American entrants in the discus, set for the next day. Dunn, known to his teammates as "Slinger," was the favorite, with Carpenter considered his top threat. Deciding there was a happy medium between not going to the stadium at all and hanging out there for hours, Glenn agreed to go. They wore slacks and USA sweaters, but not their sweat suits. At the stadium, they came out of the dressing room tunnel and walked around the outside of the track, and entered the athletes' section of the stands.

"Hey, decathlon man!"

Glenn looked in the direction of the dignitaries' boxes.

"Decathlon man!"

Thomas Wolfe was waving and smiling. The blonde German woman, the newspaper artist, was with him.

"Come on up, decathlon man!"

Glenn and Wood briefly debated whether they could get over the railing that set off the boxes from the athletes' seats to join Wolfe and the woman.

"What the hell," Wood said. "If somebody stops us, they stop us."

Glenn and Wood took seats directly behind the novelist and the German woman. Glenn introduced Wood to Wolfe and Thea, and also shook hands with what turned out to be a couple of functionaries from the U.S. Embassy. These were Ambassador Dodd's seats, Wolfe explained.

Wood got Glenn's attention, nodded at Wolfe and mouthed: "He's drunk."

Glenn nodded. Standing and cheering as the runners came down the stretch, they watched Glenn Hardin win the 400-meter hurdles, with fellow American Joe Patterson finishing fourth.

"Nice to know a Southern white boy can win for us!" Wolfe bellowed.

As the 800-meter runners warmed up and the broad jump qualifiers—including Jesse Owens and fellow decathlon man Bob Clark—prepared for the final rounds of jumps, Wolfe turned.

"So what you think, boys? Will Owens beat this German fellow?"

"Absolutely," Wood said.

"I sure hope so," Glenn said. "And John Woodruff is going to win the 800, too."

"He's a Negro, too, right?" Wolfe asked. When Glenn nodded, the writer hooked his thumb toward Hitler's loge, barely seventy-five feet above them. Hitler was seated, near the rail. "Not sure Mister *Mein Kampf* up there is going to like that," Wolfe said.

In the 800, the tall Woodruff weaved in and out of traffic. At one point, he had to virtually put on the brakes to drop back and maneuver out of a box of other runners. Despite running farther than anyone else because of his wanderings, the University of Pittsburgh student won the race, ahead of Mario Lanzi of Italy and Phil Edwards of Canada. The other Americans, Chuck Hornbostel and Harry Williamson, were fifth and sixth.

"What a race!" Wolfe exclaimed. "Never seen a runner give ground like that and come back!"

Wood and Glenn cheered almost as lustily for the quiet, but popular Woodruff. "You might have to put him in your next book!" Glenn teased Wolfe.

"I might, at that," Wolfe cheerfully conceded. As they sat down, the author asked. "So, Morris, how's your reading going? Do I get a good review?"

"So far, so good," Glenn said.

Wolfe was offended. "That's all?" He gestured around the stadium. "Hell, Morris, one of the reasons I'm here is that probably half the people in this stadium have read my German editions. And you think that's because they're 'good'?"

"Okay . . . so far the book is *great!*"

"That's more like it."

As the broad jump drama unfolded, Wolfe loudly cheered each Owens jump. Glenn watched Leni scrambling around the infield, from cameraman to cameraman. After Owens uncorked a final jump of 26 feet, 5 inches, beating Long by 7 inches, Glenn and Wood cheered and clapped, but Wolfe outdid them. The author jumped up and roared: "Way to go, Jesse! Atta baby, Jesse! That's the way to show them!" Several at the front of Hitler's box—including the Führer himself—looked down, glaring. Wolfe turned and, with his hands still forming the megaphone, yelled in the direction of Hitler and his entourage: "They might be darkies, but they're *our* darkies!"

Naoto Tajima of Japan was third, and Bob Clark—despite a terrific leap of 25-2—finished sixth.

~

Leni was shocked to see Long's reaction to finishing second. He raised Owens's arm overhead, saluting him as the champion, and embraced him. In the next few minutes on the infield, and openly as photographers—including Leni's—snapped away, the two men lounged on the grass and cordially talked as if they had grown up in the same neighborhood, at one point huddling heads so close no prying ears could pick up the conversation. They also headed off the track, to the dressing room area, together, with Long taking the lead to make it arm-in-arm. Leni checked. It was hard to tell from this far away, but the Führer didn't look to be paying attention.

Leni thought: *Maybe Luz Long knew that. Maybe he didn't. Either way, this is not the smartest thing he has ever done, and now I understand why there are rumors that he is not enthusiastic about the cause.*

As it had all week, the spectators' reaction surprised Leni, too. Mostly German, of course, they were enthusiastic about the success of Owens and the other American Negroes, cheering them and chanting "Yess-ee, Yess-ee" and "Ow-ens, Ow-ens" to honor the man who had won two gold medals and perhaps would win one or two more.

She wondered if they would cheer Glenn Morris this way, too.

~

A spirited conversation was in progress when Glenn and Walter Wood arrived in the dining room for a late snack, and to join what had become a nightly gathering of the American track athletes.

"It was my fault," Glenn Cunningham said ruefully. "I didn't even think about making sure the women knew, too."

"No," said Ralph Metcalfe, "none of us thought of it, either. Plus, she must have known what had gone on—and she still went up there. That's *her* fault."

"You're being a little unfair," Jesse Owens said. "She's a nice girl. How old is she? Eighteen? I really don't think she thought she was doing anything wrong. If she heard anything about it, she probably thought we were talking about him congratulating winners in front of the crowd in his box—not in private."

Glenn Hardin, hours removed from winning a gold, said, "Hey, she came back down and was talking about it. She wasn't trying to hide it. I don't think she had any idea she wasn't supposed to go up there."

Marty Glickman, red-faced even before he'd said a word, snapped, "But that's the point. She didn't know. But she should have."

"Well, I'm going to blame the women's coaches and the Badgers," sprinter Frank Wykoff said. "They knew the deal, too, and didn't keep her out of trouble."

Hardin summed it up. "It's *all* their fault," he snapped. "Helen said Coach Boeckmann was with her the whole time."

There was a brief silence, so Glenn Morris jumped in. "Congratulations, Jesse—again!"

"Thanks, Glenn," Owens said. "It'll be your turn soon."

"We'll see," Glenn said. He paused. "Sorry, but what are you guys talking about? Something with Helen Stephens?"

Glenn Cunningham spoke softly. "She didn't get the word that we agreed we weren't going to go up to Hitler's box . . . even if we were invited."

"She got invited," said high jump gold medalist Corny Johnson. "She went. She even got his autograph!"

Confused, Wood said, "I thought they told Hitler he either had to have all the winners up to the box—or none of them."

Hardin said, "This wasn't in the box. It's like Jesse was saying. It wasn't a ceremony. It was in a room behind it. Least that's what Helen said when she came back down."

"What happened?" Glenn asked.

"She said some German soldier came up to her and the coach after the ceremony and told her Hitler wanted to meet her," Hardin said. "She even said she held them off and went and did the radio interviews first, and the Kraut was getting all nervous, like Hitler was going to have him shot if she didn't show up."

"But she went?" Wood asked.

"Sure as hell did," said high jumper Dave Albritton.

A guy Glenn didn't recognize spoke up. "Can a swimmer say what he thinks?"

"Sure," said Cunningham. "By all means."

"Sounds like you trusted word of mouth on this—even getting to the women's village," he said. "And I think it's reasonable to think there's a dif- ference between meeting him in his box in front of the world and meeting him in a private room in something that's not a real ceremony. My God, guys, he *is* the head of a country. How often do we have chances to meet heads of countries?"

"Jesus," said Albritton. "Why don't you just spit in our faces?"

"I'm just saying what others might think," the swimmer said.

"I still think you're making too much of this . . . at least about Helen," Owens said as he got up and stretched. "She was pretty close to being the first to congratulate me yesterday after the 100 meters. Today, she wasn't that far behind Luz Long. They said Hitler called Long to the back room, too, and I don't blame him for going. And that's why I'm going to meet him now in his building."

"You're meeting the German?" Metcalfe asked incredulously. "You think they'll let you in? What are you going to talk about . . . the Master Race?"

Jesse waved dismissively as he started to the door.

"Life," he said. "Just life." He stopped and turned. "Besides, I'll say this again—for people who are supposed to hate us, these Germans are being a lot nicer to us than a lot of folks back home. I've signed more autographs here than I do at home. These people want to touch us wherever we go. They cheer us and they mean it. Some of the same people who wanted us to boycott the Olympics don't want us to eat with them or stay in their hotels or, God forbid, go out with their daughters. Any of you guys thought about that?"

"What I think," said Dave Albritton, Jesse's roommate and pal from Ohio State, "is that you just had a long day today with the 200 qualifying and the broad jump, and a long day tomorrow with the 200 semifinals and finals . . . so you better get your ass to bed. Soon."

"Keep the light on for me," Jesse said with a grin.

Glenn went to the food line and as he grabbed an apple, Marty Glickman was at his shoulder.

"As much as I like Jesse, I don't think he gets it," Glickman said, as if Glenn were a sounding board.

"Not sure I know what you mean," Glenn said carefully.

He took a bite out of the apple and stopped. So did Glickman. This didn't seem like a conversation to take back to the tables.

"Hitler despises the Negroes," Glickman said. "But the masses don't hate 'em as much as they dehumanize them. The Negroes here are like animals on display in the zoo to these Germans. That's insulting and disgusting, too, but I'm not sure it's as hateful as Hitler wants it to be. Now, us . . . the Jews . . . for a lot of them, even the same people cheering for Jesse and asking for his autograph, that's hate."

Glenn didn't argue. Instead, he asked, "Any word on the relay?"

Glickman chuckled darkly. "Get different answers from everybody," he said. "And straight answers out of nobody. We've been practicing the hand-offs in just about every combination possible with Draper, Stoller, and me. I think Wykoff's a sure thing. It just comes down to whether they stick in Jesse and Ralph—and who they'd replace."

At Castle Ruhwald, Leni was going over paperwork and the film reports in her office before beginning the late-night meetings with each cameraman and his crew.

Across from her, Walter Frentz was reading *Der Angriff*, hot off the presses. "Listen to this," he announced to Leni, then changed tone to make it clear he was reading. "'If America didn't have her black auxiliaries, where would she be in the Olympic Games?'"

Leni scoffed. "They'll have a lot of white winners, too. Even had one to-day. The hurdler. There will be more." As casually as she could, she added, "Like the decathlon man, Morris. Goebbels could put him in an SS uniform and put him on a poster. He could stay here after the Games and be a star here. Even as an American in Berlin."

Frentz didn't seem to understand that she was floating an idea.

"But Owens might even win two more golds!" Frentz exclaimed.

"As long as he keeps smiling at the camera and lets you people shoot his rear end and legs up close, that's all right with me," Leni said. "And it will be good for the film internationally if we can show we'll put the stars in the starring roles . . . even the primitive men from Africa."

Ernst Jäger knocked and came in.

"Need anything from me before I go home?" he asked.

Leni thought a second. "What's the tone in the press tribune from the Americans?"

"Jesse Owens, Jesse Owens, Jesse Owens," Jäger said. "He's just about all the Americans are writing about, but the poor scribblers are spending a lot of their time trying to see if he and the Führer at least waved at each other. But the strange thing is that they're looking to pass judgment, and they're writing like they're trying to please Goebbels. I'm told that the most famous American sports journalist of all—Grantland Rice, he was at your press session—today wrote that it's a 'darktown parade' and another from New York, Joe Williams, said it was a 'darktown strutters' ball.'"

"Did they think they were writing for Streicher?" Leni asked dryly.

Frentz squinted at Jäger and asked, "How do you know what they wrote already?"

Jäger chuckled. "It's actually kind of funny to watch, because everybody's figured out what's going on," the publicity man said. "Half the people in the press tribune and work areas are Gestapo in plainclothes. They hear, they see, they read. So the word gets around. Even before it gets published."

23

~

Vaulting into the Night

Thursday, August 6

On the eve of the decathlon's first day, Glenn, Bob Clark, and Jack Parker
ran and stretched together at the Village practice track. They paused to
watch a "race" the coaches staged among Foy Draper, Sam Stoller, and
Marty Glickman, theoretically to prioritize them in the final selection of the
400-meter relay team. Stoller won, Glickman was second, and Draper third.
But some of the suspense seemed to have been taken out of it because coach
Lawson Robertson had announced the day before that Jesse Owens wouldn't
be on the team, and that led to the widespread speculation that the foursome
would be Stoller, Glickman, Draper, and Frank Wykoff.

Glenn ran slowly over and patted Marty on the back as he gathered up his
sweats. "Nobody's going to beat you guys," he said.

"I'm still not sure I'm running," Glickman said. He gestured toward
Stoller. "Or Sam, either."

"But Robertson said . . ."

"Until it happens, I'm not going to count on it," Glickman said. "They
might want to get Jesse another gold, and they might not want us—Sam
and me—running here. Nobody's convinced me that Brundage isn't against
that."

Glenn shrugged. "It's going to work out."

Brutus Hamilton checked in with the decathlon men. "I've been thinking
about final advice," the coach said. "You and your own coaches know your
strengths and weaknesses better than I do. The only thing I can really come

up with is that I've seen guys get caught up in the Olympic atmosphere and the thinking that this is their one shot, so they go all-out in everything. They come in knowing that they need to preserve energy if they can, but they forget it in the Olympics. So especially in the field events, think about whether you can back off a bit once you think you've done about the best you could."

Clark laughed. "Well, one thing we've got to hope for is that we don't go as long in the pole vault as the regular pole-vaulters did last night."

"No way you can go *that* long," Hamilton said with a smile. "Then you'd be running the 1,500 in the middle of the night."

Most of the Americans hadn't even known the pole vault results when they went to bed the night before. Many of them had seen, or heard of, the other Wednesday results, including Jesse Owens winning his third gold medal in the 200 meters, with Mack Robinson winning the silver. Ken Carpenter upset Gordon Dunn in the discus, but they finished one-two, with Walter Wood—living down to his own expectations—coming in thirteenth. Most of the Americans advanced through early heats of the 100 hurdles and 1,500 meters. But the pole vault seemed to be interminable. They got the word at breakfast on Thursday morning: The event hadn't ended until nearly 11 the night before, with Earle Meadows winning the gold ahead of the Japanese, Shuhei Nishida and Sueo Oe. Bill Sefton and Bill Graber came up just short of medals.

When he heard the results, Glenn's first thought was: *Wonder if Leni's people had been able to get all that.* His second thought: *Too bad for Sefton and Graber.* His third thought: *Well, the Japanese seemed like good guys, too.*

Going back to the dormitory, Glenn ran into Graber. "Should I congratulate or console you?" Glenn asked.

Graber chuckled. "Under those conditions? Night? Cold? I did as well as I could. Every minute it went on, the more advantage the younger guys had. I'm just glad it's over, and now we're going to some nightclub tonight to toast it all. You should come! We're going in and having dinner, then heading to that club. It's called 'Resi' or something like that. Bunch of the guys already have been there, say it's great."

"Do you have to bring a pole to get in tonight?"

"Well, you've got one . . ."

"Even if I don't really know what to do with it."

"Still . . . I think you'd be allowed to join us."

Glenn thought about it—but only for a second. "Wish I could . . . but I can't," he said. "Competing tomorrow and all that . . ."

"I figured that."

Back at the building, one of the messengers was waiting with another sealed note from Leni.

Remember, good fortune smiles on those who deserve it. You deserve it!
And then maybe after—
Love you,
L

～

Glenn divided his afternoon between walking around the grounds and reading in the community hall, to avoid just sitting in his room. As he walked near the wooded area with the lake, he laughed about the Australians at the practice track complaining that the German maidens stopped showing up in the woods once the Games started.

"For God's sake, the swimmers, divers, boxers, rowers . . . all of 'em, had another week to kill until they compete," one Aussie said. "The Krauts could have had an even better Olympic team in 1960!"

As near as Glenn knew, no Americans had taken advantage of the opportunity . . . or at least admitted to it.

At dinner, a Badger came in to summarize the afternoon results from the track stadium and other venues. Glenn Cunningham finished second to New Zealander Jack Lovelock in the 1,500 meters. That drew groans, but the Badger said: "I'm told it was a terrific race. Lovelock set a world record!" Fingering his sheet, he added that Archie San Romani was fourth and Gene Venzke ninth. No Americans medaled in the javelin or hop, step, and jump, but that wasn't a shock.

The Badger seemed to be done, so someone asked, "What about the high hurdles?"

Just as the man said, "Not in yet," another Badger rushed into the room. The two Badgers whispered back and forth. "All right, boys, in the hurdles . . ." the first said. He paused and waited for silence. "Gold—Forrest Towns!" Cheers rang out. "Bronze—Fritz Pollard!" More cheers.

After Glenn finished dinner, he approached the two Negroes scheduled to compete in the 400-meter semifinals and finals the next day—Archie Williams and Jimmy LuValle. "Hope the track's in decent shape for us tomorrow," Glenn said.

"Should be," said Williams. "It was okay today during the heats. Don't think the weather's supposed to be too bad."

LuValle said, "My biggest worry is getting to sleep."

"Same here," Glenn said with a smile.

"Mr. Morris?"

Glenn turned and was facing a well-scrubbed member of the Honorary Youth Service.

"Yes?"

"I have been asked to have you come to the office at the front gate," the young man said.

"Why?"

"You have a visitor there."

"Who?"

"I don't know," the young man said. "They just said to get you. And that it was important."

Glenn's guess was right. Leni, still wearing a light jacket, was in the superintendent's office, alone. She signaled Glenn to close the door behind him, and when he did, held out her arms and waited for him to come to her.

"I've missed you," she said breathlessly as they kissed.

"Missed you, too," Glenn managed to say.

When they were hugging, Leni began slowly. "It's been too long," she said.

"Not that I'm complaining," Glenn said, "but why did you come now?"

"Can't I wish you good luck for tomorrow in person?" she asked.

"Sure, but . . ."

She admitted, "I do need to ask one favor. For the film."

"What?"

"All day long today, we were bracing for the film report from last night. When I got to Ruhwald tonight after the events, the report was on my desk saying the pole vault film was—as we feared—not acceptable. It went so late, and the lighting was horrible."

"That's too bad," Glenn said. "I hear it was all very dramatic."

"Today, when we were thinking about the possibilities, your officials said you're pretty good friends with your vaulters. I didn't even bring your name up. They did."

"Well, sure . . . they're good guys. They've helped me."

"And the Japanese?"

"I've met them."

"Can you introduce them all to me?"

"I thought we weren't supposed to know each other!"

"Glenn, you were introduced to me! I have talked with many of the Americans, from Jesse Owens to your girl sprinter. For us to know each other now isn't scandal."

"Why do you want to meet them?"

"To see if we can get them back to the stadium to re-create the final jumps. We'll set up floodlights next to the pit and runway, get each to make a couple of jumps, get them up close . . ."

"Why can't you just use some of their earlier jumps, when it was lighter?"

"Yesterday, I went to the yachting in the morning," she said. "I should have been there. They got some wonderful shots of the early vaults, but that's what they were—early vaults. All the writers were saying how dark it was when they finished. Someone will remember that when the film comes out and say something. More important, this way we can actually control the conditions and make it even better than the real thing. I'll have them talking with each other, the camera in front of them as they start down the runway . . . things like that. All in the dark, but with our lighting. This can be an opportunity."

"When?"

"Tonight, if we can get the vaulters there. My people already have notified some officials to be ready. The second we confirm this, the calls will go out again and they will go to the stadium. They know I will make it worth their while."

Glenn was flabbergasted. "*Now?*"

"I'm told the Japanese trackmen are leaving for home once that part of the competition is over. And you already said some of you are going to other parts of Europe for exhibitions, too. I know we could do it now. I don't know about next week or any other night."

"Well, there's at least one problem . . . our vaulters aren't here now."

"You know that?"

"Yeah, Bill Graber told me the three of them were going to dinner and then some nightclub."

"You know which nightclub?"

"Residence . . . or something like that."

"Resi?"

"Sounds right."

Leni grabbed her coat. "I'll have my runner find the Japanese, and see if they're game. Let's go find your Americans."

"Leni . . ." He waited until she had turned. "I'm competing tomorrow. It's going to be one of the two most important days in my life. I can't be running around Berlin! That's twenty miles from here!"

"All right," Leni said, "you go in and tell the boys the story, and if they're agreeable, have them come out to meet me. I'd go in, but it will be a commotion, believe me. I will send you back here to the Village in the car. You will be back here in ninety minutes. You can tell them—and I will do so, too—this probably is their chance to star in the film. Two or three jumps, some close-ups, and they're back to the nightclub. And I will make a call, and their bill for the entire night at the club will go to me."

Glenn couldn't resist laughing. "Well, knowing those guys . . . that might swing it," he said. "But do you have any idea what that might cost you?"

"It's not my money . . . and it'll be worth it," Leni assured him.

Glenn knew he wouldn't be able to get to sleep for at least a couple of hours, anyway. "Okay, as long as we stick to that plan," he said. "I can't be gone too long. But we also need to hope they haven't had too many beers already. I don't think you want any of them to get killed trying to clear four-teen feet drunk." As he was getting ready to leave, he thought of something else he had been aching to bring up. "This might sound stupid, but sometime I'd like to see how you look at and edit the film, too. Of this or anything else."

"Sure," said Leni. She smiled and lightly touched his face. "It's the least I could do."

⌒

Much to Glenn's surprise, it worked better than planned, because the American vaulters still were in the lobby of the nightclub, waiting to be shown to a table.

Graber saw Glenn first. "Well, look who's here!" he exclaimed.

Glenn quickly explained the situation to Graber and Earle Meadows, the most important target because he had won the gold medal. He explained Leni was trying to line up the two Japanese medalists, too.

"How long will it take?" Meadows asked.

"Half hour once you're dressed and out there," Glenn said. "Maybe an hour. Do your acting thing under the lights, smile a lot, then you're back here. This place stays open 'til dawn, or something like that. And she says your entire bill is on her."

Their reactions showed that was the clincher.

Glenn asked, "Your equipment's still there, right?"

"Yeah," said Graber. "But we'd need to get into the equipment room."

"I think she has ways to get anywhere she wants in the stadium. I don't think that'll be a problem."

"And how are we getting there?" Meadows asked.

"There are two limousines out there now for you," Glenn said.

"It might be kind of fun," Meadows said. He paused. "But how'd you get in this, Glenn?"

"She came looking for you guys at the Village and I was there. I said I knew where you were and I'd help. And . . ." Glenn shrugged. "Well, I've got to get back. She's in her own limo out there, waiting for me to tell her you're doing this!"

"She's here?" Meadows asked, incredulously.

"Sure is," Glenn said. "And she's counting on you."

Glenn started to leave, and Graber followed closely. He said it as if there were no doubt. "You and her have something going," Graber said.

Glenn tried to sound incredulous. "Leni Riefenstahl?" he asked.

"No, Greta Garbo. . . . Of course, Leni Riefenstahl!"

"Don't be ridiculous."

"Right, I'm being ridiculous. Twelve hours before the decathlon starts, you're her errand boy to find us and beg us to help her."

"You're reading too much into this," Glenn said. "Why don't you come out with me and I'll introduce you, and then I'm out of here and it's out of my hands. I've done my part . . . and not because anything's going on with her, okay?"

"Stick to your story, Glenn," Graber said with a laugh. "That's fine with me."

Outside, Glenn introduced Graber to Leni through the open window. "Thanks so much, Mister Morris," she said, smiling warmly at Glenn. "I will see *you* at the stadium tomorrow."

After spotting his familiar limo and Kurt, Glenn climbed in and was in bed ninety minutes later.

The five vaulters, two Japanese plus three Americans, were stunned when they emerged from the dressing-room tunnel and took note of the nearly dozen white-jacketed track and field judges and officials who had barely beaten them to the well-lighted pole vault pit. Bill Graber approached Leni. "Ma'am, you sure have a lot of pull," he said. "This is amazing."

Leni squinted, unsure of what "pull" meant, and then decided whatever it was, she had it. She had left it up to others to line up the officials, and she knew that not all of them had worked the pole vault event itself. But all they had to do was look as if they knew what they were doing, accept the reichsmarks handed them, and not stick out their tongues at the camera at the wrong moment.

Over the next two and a half hours, Walter Frentz and three other cameramen, working from various vantage points, filmed everything. First, each of the five vaulters in turn stood poised, at the beginning of the runway, holding their poles, rocking back and forth on their heels to toes. She told them to look pensive or determined—or however they usually looked in real competition—as they pondered their upcoming vaults. "I know this is fun," she told Bill Sefton, "but you have to stop smiling!" Sefton immediately adopted an overly dramatic, and a bit sarcastic, scowl, triggering laughter from the other vaulters.

Leni thought: *It's going to be hard to find frames of these boys looking serious enough. But we'll make it work.*

After that was finished, she announced: "All right, we need three jumps— two unsuccessful and one successful—from each of you."

Bill Graber spoke for all of them. "The misses, those'll be easy," he said, grinning. "But if you want us to clear something now, you better put the bar at about thirteen feet."

Leni didn't smile. "I want it as high as we can get it and still have you make it," she said.

As they took turns vaulting, Leni kept praising them, egging them on. Nishida, the veteran who knew a little English, joked, "She should be coach!"

Finally, after what seemed an eternity to the vaulters, she had what she needed, including a shot of Meadows clearing his "winning" height—at a real height that, shown from the lower angle, at least could pass for what earned him the gold medal in the dark the night before. The others had cleared respectable, but lower heights.

"Man, you don't know how hard that was," Meadows said, rejoining the other vaulters as they lounged on the grass, with blankets over their shoulders.

"All right, the hard part is over!" Leni told them. "Officials, you can go!"

"You mean there's more?" Sefton asked.

Leni outlined what she needed next and supervised as they played their parts. Each of them in rotation shook hands with the other four, showing that good Olympic sportsmanship. They pretended to be "watching" others vaulting as they remained on the grass. Individually, they looked to be contemplating their next vaults as they waited in the cold. Finally, an official handed Meadows one of the wreaths made of oak leaves presented to medalists, and Leni coached him into pretending he was listening to the U.S.

national anthem as he stood atop the medal stand. So Meadows smiled and saluted as the cameras rolled.

"Wonderful!" Leni proclaimed. "We're done!"

Graber laughed. "Good thing," he said. "The decathlon guys will be out here in about fifteen minutes."

Actually, the early morning start still was a few hours off, but even Leni laughed. She shook hands with all five vaulters and thanked them individually. As they gathered up their gear, Meadows tried to keep his voice down, but Leni heard.

"Her and Morris . . . there's something there," he said.

Graber laughed. "You just figured that out?"

Leni decided she didn't mind. At some point, she knew, it would come out as something other than whispers. Perhaps even on her terms. In headlines. And then on screen.

24

~

Decathlon, Day One

Friday, August 7

Glenn didn't like coffee and rarely drank it. He made an exception this morning in the dining room after awakening at 6. The early morning bus from the Village was only half filled, and as he walked down the aisle to an open seat in back, Glenn nodded at the other passengers. Most were his decathlon competitors, and in addition to Jack Parker and Bob Clark, Glenn knew a few others by name—including Olle Bexell of Sweden, Jan Brasser of The Netherlands, and Armin Guhl of Switzerland. They nodded back, with tight smiles.

During the ride, he read his small stack of telegrams. One was from Karen, and that triggered guilt pangs.

GOOD LUCK, DARLING
LOVE, KAREN

Others were from Harry Hughes, his landlady, his car dealer-employer, plus one adorned with over one hundred names, beginning with those of Colorado Governor Ed Johnson and Denver Mayor Ben Stapleton. Then he came to one from the former heavyweight champion of the world.

SIMLA SENSATION:
HOPE YOU SCORE A K.O.
SIGNED, THE MANASSA MAULER

Bob Clark passed him a copy of the official decathlon entry sheet, finalized the previous day. Several tentative entrants had dropped out, and Hans Sievert hadn't magically reappeared on the list. So at the outset, before the inevitable withdrawals during the competition, there would be a total of twenty-eight men going for the decathlon gold. Scanning, Glenn didn't see anything to change his opinion that the major threats to the three Americans were the Dutchman, Brasser, and the friendly German, Erwin Huber, who wasn't on the bus. Glenn also noticed that in his first event, the 100 meters, Huber also was in his three-man heat—getting the head-to-head competition going right off the bat.

Arriving in the dressing-room area, Glenn had another cup of coffee, then was on the field to warm up by 8:15. He was surprised that quite a few fans already were in the seats. Despite the talk about how the Europeans were fascinated with the decathlon, he had expected the event to be a private affair for most of the day. The men's 400-meter heats began at 3PM, and until then, the decathlon was the only event in the stadium.

He was startled to see Leni emerge through the doors at the bottom of the dignitaries' boxes, with a pack of about five of her cameramen who kept going, heading to their shooting stations. Leni lingered behind and seemed to be looking at him, inviting. Glenn pondered. They wouldn't be in the middle of the infield, but they'd be visible. Still, he went over and greeted her. By now, he could be just another of the many prominent athletes in her film who had met her. She held out her hand. "Good luck," she said as he shook it.

"Did you just stay here all night?" Glenn asked, smiling.

"Two hours of sleep at the Castle," she said. "That's enough."

"How'd it go?"

"Very long, but very well. They will not win any acting awards, but once they got out there, they enjoyed themselves." Leni looked around, then said, "Come back here for a second. I didn't properly thank you last night."

Glenn followed her through the doors, under the seats, and up a few stairs of the private stairway that led to Hitler's box. There, she stopped and, while on a step above him, drew him into a passionate kiss and embrace.

When Bob Clark easily won his 100-meter heat in 10.9 seconds, Glenn was reminded his American teammates were going to be tough to beat. *You're not running against the guys in your heat; you're running against the stopwatch and all the others.* Clark was shaking his head as he came to the area outside the track on the corner and picked up his sweatshirt. He told Glenn, "For what it's worth, either these guys are bad timers or the track's definitely slower than Milwaukee. I felt good . . . thought it'd be 10.7 or so. When the guy said 10.9, I was shocked."

Glenn had to wait through eight other heats. He loosened up with Er-win Huber, who said it was a pleasure to compete against the world-record holder. Glenn at first wondered if he was being set up for overconfidence with flattery, but Huber's smile again was warm.

By then, to Glenn's amazement, there were perhaps 30,000 fans already in the seats at the early-morning hour, and he told Huber how surprised he was.

"This was a very popular ticket!" Huber said. He pointed at the section nearest them. 'Look! Half the people there are writing down the times when they are announced! At what other event are you going to see fans keeping tabulations like that? There are *zehnkampf* fans up there who will be able to plot this better than our coaches!"

Indeed, many of the fans seemed to have pen and paper in their hands.

The other runner in their heat was teenager Josef Klein of Czechoslovakia. In the middle between the two Europeans, Glenn got a good start and pulled away from Huber and Klein, but was shocked and alarmed when the officials told him his time—11.1 seconds. *Now I know what Clark meant!* That was a full four-tenths of a second slower than what he had run at Milwaukee, so not only was he going to be behind Clark after one event, he would be far off the pace of his world-record score in the Trials.

The broad jump, Clark's specialty, was next. As Glenn tried to visualize a perfect jump, he and Clark had a light moment when they noted that the press seats, dignitaries' boxes and the competitors' section were virtually de-serted, standing out among the otherwise filling-up stadium.

Glenn felt the pressure mounting when Clark's first jump was measured at 7.67 meters, or a shade over 25 feet. When Glenn was told his initial attempt converted to 21 feet, 9 inches, he lectured himself that he couldn't leave it there. *If I do, Leni's going to be filming Clark on that top step.* On his third try, he planted his right foot on the board, hitting it almost perfectly, and felt an extra spring as he took off, landed, rolled over and got up to assess his mark in the sand. *Better!* The judge told him 6.97 meters, and considering he had been shooting for 7 meters, he was satisfied with that. In a few seconds, Ham-ilton told him the distance converted to 22 feet, 10 inches, 4 inches better than his best at Milwaukee, so Glenn breathed easier. He was acceptably close to Clark through his two strong events.

There was a break of a couple of hours before the shot put began, and Glenn—starving after having only a light breakfast hours earlier—ate a small steak brought over from the Strength Through Joy Village. He pondered whether drinking more coffee would help or hurt, but decided he might as well be all in and had a couple more cups.

The shot put was a mixed blessing. Glenn shrugged off a warning from a judge, who signaled that he was taking too much time in the ring, shoving the shot put back and forth from his right hand to his left as he pondered his throw. Finally, he settled it next his jaw, slid across the ring and got off a toss of 46-3, the top effort among the entire field, but more than a foot less than his distance at Milwaukee. After three events, he still was second to Clark—2,534 points to 2,436.

In the high jump, as he rocked back and forth and prepared to take a run at the pit, Glenn noticed one of Leni's cameraman a few feet away, rolling film, and lowering his sights to focus on Glenn's legs. For the first time ever in his athletic career, a photographer left him a bit discomfited. He took a deep breath, told himself to ignore it and again looked at the bar. Although his steps were a bit fouled up and he had to stutter-step as he neared the bar, he cleared 5-11 with his scissors-style jump. He shook his head, knowing he barely had gotten over the bar, and sensed that on this day, in part because he couldn't get the approach timing and steps right, he wasn't going to match his 6-foot-1 leap at Milwaukee. He turned out to be correct, and he tried to follow the mandate to conserve energy. The good news was he still was part of a three-way tie for second among the decathlon men in the high jump, behind only Jan Brasser, and ahead of Clark and Parker.

During the finals of the 5,000 meters, Glenn paid attention only until the top American hope, Don Lash, fell out of contention. After sweeping the 10,000 meters earlier, the Finns came up just short of duplicating the showing in the shorter race, with Gunnar Höckert winning and countryman Lauri Lehtinen second. Sweden's Henry Jonsson claimed the bronze, and the top American was teenager Lou Zamperini, who closed strong, but still was only eighth. Lash dropped all the way to thirteenth.

Bob Clark watched the distance race more intently than did Glenn. "Looked like Lash was either going to win the damn thing or die trying," Clark said, shaking his head. "He shouldn't have tried to stay with those guys. They might have come back to him."

A short time later, Glenn found himself again with Huber, preparing for the last event of the decathlon's first day, the 400 meters. "I'm starting to wonder if anyone's going to deserve to win this," Glenn mused to the German.

"Whoever has the most points will deserve to win," Huber said, shrugging.

Brutus Hamilton signaled Glenn over to join him with Clark and Parker.

"Come on boys, let's pick up the pace," Hamilton said. "Let's show the fellow with the moustache what Americans are made of—again."

Glenn looked up to the loge box. Yes, Hitler was there.

As Clark was running in the third heat, Leni took advantage of the diverted attention to wave Glenn over to her spot in the infield. "I am not an expert on this competition," she said, "but I think you look as if you are doing calculations in your head on every step. Why not just stop worrying about those things and just compete?"

She walked away. Pondering, Glenn decided she was right. *Stop worrying and just go for it.*

In the fifth heat, Glenn again was with Huber and Klein, plus Franz Sterzl of Austria. He was assigned the inside lane in the staggered start, so the other three were ahead of him at intervals and to his right. *Don't worry about splits. Don't worry about the others. Just run. And remember, you're done for the day after this.*

For the first time ever in competition, he ran a 400 as if it were a 100-meter dash. He made the other three look is as if they were running in sand, pulling away as he quickly made up the "stagger" and more. From only about 150 yards into the race, he had no competition. As he came into the straightaway, he wondered: *Did I blow this?* Fighting for air as his head bobbed, he tried to ignore his tightening legs, slowing but pushing on. Completely expended at the finish, he didn't bother with his usual run well beyond the line. He slowed to a walk quickly and considered cutting over to the grass and dropping to the ground. But he stayed up and heard the official tell him his time—49.4 seconds, over a second better than his time in the Trials.

Clark approached him and slapped him on the back. "I'm no math guy," he said, "but I think we're pretty much tied."

When the totals were posted on the huge board in the end of the stadium, Clark's impression was confirmed:

CLARK—USA 4194 PUNKTE

MORRIS—USA 4192

PARKER—USA 3888

Jan Brasser was the Americans' closest pursuer, fifteen points behind Parker.

As he still was warming down, Glenn stayed to watch the 400-meter finals, and saw American Archie Williams win the gold, edging Godfrey Brown of Great Britain, with Jimmy LuValle of the USA third. Near the finish line, Leni again was kneeling, and then laying on the infield grass, underneath the lens of one of her photographer's huge standing film cameras. She said something to Williams, and the runner smiled. Glenn recalled how bothered Williams was when Glenn congratulated Max Schmeling. Archie apparently wasn't thinking Leni was a disloyal German for congratulating him.

Glenn considered trying to talk more with Leni, but after the whirlwind of events of the last two days, he knew he would be crazy to do anything other than head right back to the Village, have a light dinner and be asleep by 10 . . . maybe even sooner. He'd see Leni soon enough, in the morning . . . on the biggest day of his life.

Walter Wood came down from the athletes' section to pat Glenn on the back, and he said he was joining a group of Americans having a few beers at the Strength Through Joy Village after the competition for the day. So he wasn't with Glenn on the way back, but Williams and LuValle were. When Glenn congratulated them, Williams said thanks and added: "That's six now!"

"Six what?"

"Six golds for the American auxiliaries!"

Wood tried to be quiet when he arrived back at the room at about 1 in the morning, but Glenn had just finished telling himself: *Last time I chug coffee for anything.*

Trying to be silent, but noticing Glenn stirring in the dark, Wood whispered, "Jesus, sorry!"

Glenn didn't whisper. "Don't worry about it. I was awake."

"Well, then, get to sleep!"

"I'll give it my best shot."

Wood bumped into a chair.

Glenn said, "Hey, don't break something. Turn on a light."

As Wood got undressed, Glenn asked, "Have a good time?"

"Yeah," Wood said. "A bunch of guys showed up. We went downtown for a bit, too."

"I kind of guessed that."

"Sorry . . ."

"Sorry? There's nothing wrong with that, okay? Just don't throw up in the middle of the night."

When Wood was in bed and had turned out the light, his question came out of the dark.

"You nervous?"

"Of course I am," Glenn said. "Weren't you?"

Wood laughed. "Actually, not at all," he said. "Maybe that was part of the problem."

About minute later, Wood spoke again. "Maybe I shouldn't say anything, but . . ."

He stopped.

"But what?"

"Naw, you've got enough on your mind."

"But *what?*"

"Do you want to know what some of the boys are saying about you or would you rather not know?"

"Walter, you can't bring it up, then drop it. Go ahead."

"A few guys asked me if something's going on between you and Leni Riefenstahl. Other guys said they know there is."

"What did you tell them?"

"I said I think you had met her and you might have got a boner like everybody else has when looking at her, but I said I thought that's all it is."

"Thanks."

"But you know I was lying. I know something's going on."

Glenn didn't say anything.

Wood said, "I guess that's my answer."

"No, it's *not* your answer," Glenn snapped. "Your answer is I have a girl and a life back home, and this all isn't part of it."

"You at least feel guilty?"

"None of this leaves this room, right?"

"Of course not."

"All right," Glenn said. "Mostly no. I'm done trying to talk myself into it. Does it make me an asshole to say except for a few seconds here and there, like when I look at Karen's picture, or read her telegram, or think about the last couple of years, I really don't feel guilty?"

"Do you want to know what I really think?"

"There you go again . . . say it."

"It's still like I said the other night. I think you're forgetting that this is Germany. She's part of that, and you can't ignore that. Even if we aren't here that long. Even if you never see her again."

"Damn it! She's been forced into doing things for them! She's no Nazi! She's an artist, a professional. She makes films."

"You *really* believe that?"

"Yeah, I do."

"And you believe she was a virgin, too, I suppose."

Glenn made a move to jump out of bed. "Shut up!"

Wood sighed. "Look, it's the beer talking some. Sorry. But I'm your friend now, right?"

Glenn thought a moment. "Yeah. Of course you are."

"Glenn . . . no matter what you do with her, don't be an idiot. This is not some cute actress in Hollywood."

"You don't know her!"

"You're right, I don't. But look around! Look around that stadium! Look around these streets! Doesn't that tell you enough?"

"I get it. This is some smart Cornell guy telling the Colorado hick he's stupid."

The pause lasted longer this time. "No," Wood said. "I'm not."

"Let's drop it. I'm going to sleep."

Glenn rolled onto his side, turning away from Wood. He settled in, with one arm around the pillow. He decided he had one more thing to say.

"Walter . . . No matter what, you have to understand something."

"What's that?"

"You're wrong about her."

2 5

~

Decathlon, Day Two

Saturday, August 8

Alan Gould of the Associated Press was waiting, with pen and notebook poised, when Glenn and Walter Wood—their tension the night before was, while not forgotten, at least off limits—got off the bus outside the stadium. Walter, though hung over, insisted on coming to the stadium with Glenn. "I feel like I have a stake in this now," he said. They sat near the back of the bus, so they were among the last off.

"Morning, Morris," Gould said. "Can I talk with you for a second?"

"*Now?*"

He was thinking: *Who do you think you are . . . Eleanor Holm?*

"I need a quote for the early story . . . especially if this thing drags out as late as some people seem to think it might."

"Well, there's not much I can say now. Just that I hope we push each other to a sweep."

There. That's one quote.

Gould persisted. "Is the pole vault going to be the key?"

"Every event is important," Glenn said. "No one more important than the other. That's what the decathlon is."

"But if you can get through the pole vault . . ."

Glenn laughed. "I'll get through it. I don't know what height I'll clear, but I'll get through it. Maybe with a broken arm or a broken wrist, but I'll get through it."

Gould scribbled, then put down his notebook. "That'll do!" he said. "Thanks."

"Welcome," said Glenn.

Gould gestured at the bus. "I was waiting for the relay guys, too," he said, "but none of them were with you, looks like."

"On this bus? No. I think I saw Marty Glickman going into breakfast when I was leaving, but that's it."

Gould looked at his watch. "Glickman's not running. Neither is Stoller."

"Who is?" Glenn asked incredulously.

"Draper, Wykoff, Metcalfe, and Owens. Robertson told me last night. I wrote it for the morning papers in the states. He and Cromwell decided that's the team, for the heats today, finals tomorrow. He told Owens and Metcalfe last night, too, so they'd know to get some rest, and he was going to tell all the boys right after everybody was up this morning."

"Why?" Glenn asked.

"Robertson and Cromwell said the Germans have been hiding some guys out, have a tough team and want to steal the gold on the final day to end this thing," Gould said. "They said we had to put our absolute best team out there, and that means Owens and Metcalfe."

"And not Glickman and Stoller?" Wood asked.

"And *not* Glickman and Stoller," Gould confirmed.

Wood tapped Glenn's elbow. "You should get going," he said.

They said good-bye to Gould and headed into the dressing room tunnel. They talked as they walked. "Well, Jesse will get a fourth gold medal," Glenn said. "That's good."

"But at the expense of two guys who worked hard, too," Wood said. "I bet Brundage made a deal with the Germans. No Jews running."

"I don't like Brundage, either," Glenn said, "but that doesn't make sense—since they replaced them with two Negroes."

"Okay, look at it this way: The Negroes have won a bunch of events. That's embarrassing enough for the Germans, so what difference does another gold make? Not much. So now if we come at them with two Jewish fellows, and they're standing on top of the medal stand on the final day, that's a *bigger* embarrassment for the Nazis."

"But the German team will lose with Jesse and Ralph running!" Glenn said.

"They could put *you* on the team with Marty, Sam, and Draper, and we'd win. The Germans know that. If we don't drop the baton, we're getting the gold; they aren't. No matter what."

They were at the dressing room. Walter told him someone in their Village room had to win a gold medal, so he was counting on Glenn. Then he said that with the track and field competition virtually over after today—only the relays and the marathon would be run Sunday—the weight men were organizing a junket to the Essen Haus again.

"It's going to be a celebration for you, too," Wood said. "You won't have to buy a thing."

He nodded in the direction of the athletes' section in the stadium. "I'll be the guy up there screaming the loudest . . . unless Wolfe is there and drunk again!"

The first decathlon event of the day was the 110-meter hurdles and Glenn knew that, as a former college hurdler, he needed to not only pass Bob Clark and move into first place in the standings, he also needed to take as large of a lead as possible. As he dug his starting holes, he told himself to think of this as a dual meet against Wyoming or a relays meet in Boulder at the University of Colorado. He needed—wanted—not only to win, but also to blow away his competition. As he stood and looked over the crowd—again, surprisingly large given the early hour—he laughed as it hit him that the way for a decathlon man to maximize his points would be to add a "real" competitor in each event to his heats, at least in the running events. If he were running against Forrest Towns in the hurdles, for example, it might push him to a better time. He would have to make do with running against Erwin Huber and Josef Klein again, though.

By the first of the ten hurdles, he was a stride ahead. *Push yourself!* Leading over each hurdle with his left leg and having his steps work out perfectly, he pulled away. Landing after the final hurdle, he leaned forward and drove through the finish line, leaving the track and ending up near the restraining wall at the bottom of the seats. When he curled back and walked onto and across the track, a smiling Huber was waiting with an outstretched hand. "I had a good view from behind," he said. "You drive over the hurdles. I float!"

Glenn's time of 14.9 seconds matched his effort at the Trials and was the best among all the competitors, a tenth of a second better than Jack Parker and eight-tenths better than Bob Clark. He had hoped for better, but settled for it, especially because he had taken the lead in the competition with four events to go.

Between their events, the decathlon men watched the Americans' relay team—with Owens leading off—rout the field in its heat, with a time of 40.0

seconds. He turned to Clark. "That's just not right," Glenn said. "Marty and Sam should be in there."

Clark nodded agreement.

Glenn had mixed feelings about his performance in the discus. He never felt comfortable with the mechanics of his "spin," but he was thrilled with his distances, including one toss of 141 feet, 2 inches that was more than 6 feet better than the next-best throw in the field. He decided Walter's tip at the practice track had made the difference. As in the earlier field events, he took kidding from his fellow competitors for wearing his watch into the ring. "You need to be somewhere?" Clark asked.

On paper, he now had a secure lead. Yet the eighth of the events, the pole vault, was—at least to Glenn—ugly, menacing, and potentially devastating to his gold-medal hopes. As Glenn awaited the vaulting with dread, he and the other two Americans again lounged on the ground. All three wore their sweat suits, with towels around their necks. Parker and Clark were on a spread-out blanket. Only Glenn's head was on the blanket, the rest of his body on the grass. Parker was writing in point totals on an entry sheet, ostensibly to see if anyone had a bona fide chance of preventing them from sweeping the top three spots.

Suddenly, Erwin Huber was standing over them—with Leni. Glenn had spotted her earlier, again moving from cameraman to cameraman. She was wearing baggy white trousers and a matching jacket, a checked blouse, and a headband. Glenn rose up, resting on his right elbow, as Huber plopped down on the blanket, too. "American boys," he said with a disarming smile, then pointed up. "For those of you who don't know, this is Fraulein Leni Riefenstahl, our cinema star and director."

"Hello, American boys," Leni said.

Huber pointed at each, in turn.

"Clark, Parker, Morris."

"Of course," Leni said, smiling.

Leni dropped to the grass next to Glenn. She pointed at the sheets spread in front of Parker. "Erwin said you would know the way the results are developing," she said.

Huber said good-naturedly, "I meant you would know if I might win a medal. After I did so terrible in the discus."

"How does it look?" Leni asked.

"We'll just have to see," Parker said, grinning.

Leni looked at Glenn. "If what you do the rest of the day is going to be in my film," she said impishly, "you need to clean yourself up!" She reached into a pocket, pulled out a handkerchief and with her left hand, tenderly ran it across his forehead, brushing back his hair, too, as she and Glenn looked in each other's eyes. Parker turned and watched, grinning. After a few moments of awkward silence, Leni said, "Well, good luck to all of you the rest of the way. And from what Herr Huber just told me, you, Herr Morris, just need to again relax a bit in this next event and you will be fine."

Glenn looked at Huber, who shrugged.

Then Leni reached out and brushed Glenn's forehead again. "I know all three of you will provide fine drama," she said.

With that, she pulled herself up and gave Glenn a knowing look down that he realized Clark and Parker couldn't have missed. Then she said a cheery good-bye and was gone, heading for the starting line for the relays.

Parker returned to his numbers. From behind Glenn, Clark said, "I thought she was going to go right after it in front of all these people!"

A few minutes later, the bar at the end of the pole vault runway looked about 20 feet high to Glenn. And it was only set at 3.1 meters, or roughly 10 feet, 2 inches—the opening height for the decathlon men.

At the end of the pole vault runway, Glenn ran through it in his head. *Up, over, turn, let loose of the pole, fall. What's so damn hard about that? What did Leni say? Relax! What the hell . . .*

He cleared it easily. Instantly, much of the pressure was off. When the bar got to 3.5 meters, he told himself to go for it, that if he didn't make it, it wouldn't be a problem, that he really had nothing to lose. It all came together as he planted the pole, and a second later, he felt like pumping both fists in the air after he landed in the pit. He was over, he had hit his goal, and he had managed not only to avoid complete disaster, but also get a decent point total for the event.

Then he got cocky. He thought of accepting 3.5 meters and not jumping any more, but he decided against that. First of all, he felt great, fresh, and sharp. Second, he felt he had at least one more perfect—for him—vault left in him. Third, he didn't let anyone know this, but now he was starting to think more about what he had talked about in his Village letter to George Whitman—becoming the first man ever to crack the 8,000-point barrier. That almost certainly would require a few more points in the pole vault.

So he stayed in the competition and took three tries at 3.6 meters—but missed all three. On the third, in fact, his hand slipped off the pole, he didn't even get turned and came down, still facing forward, after crashing into the bar.

Well, that was real smart.

When the decathlon men had just started the javelin event, Leni again was summoned to Hitler's box. This time, there was no sense of urgency in the SS man's voice, so she wasn't worried.

As she arrived, Joseph Goebbels was waiting for her at the top of the stairway.

"So now it's the American decathlon man, this Morris?" he asked, leering.

Maybe he just saw us on the field.

"Since you are staging your own little athletic events with him," Goebbels said, "it is a tribute to him that he still is leading this competition!"

She glared at him. "Your jealousy flatters me," she said. "Thank you very much."

"I supposed we should not be surprised," he said. "But it should make this even easier for you. The Führer just arrived and would like you to give him some information on these three white Americans. For some reason, he has become fascinated with the decathlon. Time permitting, I believe he will want to meet these Americans after the competition—in private, of course."

She went into the box. A chair was shoved to Hitler's left, slightly behind him, and it was obvious that was where Leni was supposed to station herself for this conversation. After the greetings, Hitler said, "You were right. The Americans don't need niggers in everything. Tell me about this boy Morris."

Leni long ago had stopped marveling at Hitler's memory, but she also realized it could be selective, too. He could forget—or pretend to forget—what he didn't want to remember.

"He is what you see!" Leni exclaimed. "He's from a farm in the all-white, all-Christian middle part of America. He was a fine athlete in other sports, too, and he was elected president of his university's students. He already holds the world record, and he will improve on it by the end of the day! They say that the winner of this event is the world's greatest athlete, and he will be a star everywhere!"

"It sounds as if you already are a fan," Hitler said.

"I am a fan of anyone who can make my film better," Leni said.

Hitler's slight smile let her know he realized there was more to it than that.

⁓

Watching the 3,000-meter steeplechase off and on, Glenn tried to consider it inspiration for the decathlon's upcoming 1,500 meters, or the "metric mile." The decathlon men joked that all Finnish distance runners looked exactly alike and ran alike—which wasn't far from the truth. Finns again ran 1-2 in the steeplechase, and Clark, who had been paying the most attention to the other track and field events, declared that meant runners from Finland had won all the golds and silvers in the 5,000 meters, 10,000 meters, and now the steeplechase.

"Did they have the Olympics in Finland like twenty-four years ago or something?" an Australian decathlon man asked.

Clark said, "Don't think so, but why would you ask that?"

"Just wondering if they had all their pretty maidens breed with the distance runners at the Olympic Village," the Australian said, laughing.

A while later, Glenn was second-guessing himself more for taking so many attempts in the pole vault. His best javelin throw—178 feet, 10 inches—was nearly 5 feet short of his Trials effort. But at least he hadn't scratched all three times.

The decathlon's 1,500 meters was pushed back because a time-filling gymnastics exhibition ran long. None of the competitors minded the wait. Glenn had 7,305 points, leading Clark by 217 points and Parker by 401. Because of attrition over the two days, the field was down to seventeen competitors, and Glenn was in the last of the three heats. After Clark posted a time of 4:44.4, giving him 513 points, in the second heat, Wood rushed down. Breathlessly, Wood said he had done the math and determined that Glenn needed only to crack about 5:25 to win, and that anything under 4:34 would enable him to break his own world record.

"You sure?"

"Checked it three times."

"So I don't have a chance at 8,000?" Glenn asked.

"Sure you do," Wood said, straight-faced. "If you run like Glenn Cunningham . . . not Glenn Morris."

Brutus Hamilton approached with an update, too, and the coach's differed in one important way: He said Glenn would need to run 4:32—or two seconds better than Wood's estimate—to break his own world record. "So if you want my advice . . . play it safe, nice easy pace, come in at five minutes—and you win," Hamilton said.

After the coach left, Glenn placed a hand on Wood's shoulder. "Walter, my best time in this is 4:48. . . . So what you think?"

Wood thought for a second. "Logically, I should tell you Hamilton's right."

"That's the Cornell in you. What do you *really* think?"

"Don't do anything really stupid, like sprinting the first 300 meters . . . but go for it!"

"If I play it safe, I might foul it up," Glenn said, nodding. "And besides . . . what if the math's wrong?"

Wood feigned outrage. "It's right, you dumb Aggie! But I say win it in style!"

Thinking, Glenn leaned over to retie his right shoe tighter. When he stood up, he announced: "It's a deal!"

Wood shook his hand and headed back to the stands.

In his heat, Glenn was with Huber and Klein again, plus Maurice Boulanger of Belgium and Lyuben Doychev of Bulgaria. As they got ready to start, Huber tried to make it clear to the other competitors that because Glenn had so much at stake, the one thing they should all avoid was tripping him. Glenn winced, because as well-meaning as Huber was, and as appreciative as he was, he wondered if the one way to guarantee a collision was to make everyone conscious of trying to avoid it.

On the field, Leni checked her watch. It was shortly after eight o'clock, and the sun had been down about an hour. This wouldn't go as late as the pole vault, and she believed the stadium floodlights—plus the single light she had received permission to erect near the finish line—would be good enough to leave her with some usable footage of this final race. This race would confirm Glenn Morris's stardom—in both her film and her life.

2 6

~

1,500 Meters

Glenn was in lane two, and he caught the grins from the other runners when he dug holes for his toes and went into a sprinter's stance. But he wanted to get out fast to avoid that traffic. He got to the lead about thirty yards into the race and settled into what he thought was a pace he could maintain until going all out in the final 150 meters or so, and perhaps even better his best time in the event by a few seconds. Judging from the times Brutus Hamilton called out each time he crossed the finish line, he was on track. In the last lap, as he tried to push himself toward a "kick," he thought his lungs were about to collapse and his legs were about to stop moving.

Boulanger did him a huge favor on the final backstretch. The Belgian passed Glenn and quickly opened up a short lead. There was something about winning the decathlon, but not crossing the finish line first in the final event, that bothered Glenn. That had happened at Milwaukee, and he didn't want it to happen again.

He also heard the crowd. The roar was for him; he just knew it. He was 200 meters from a gold medal, and those on the scene—mostly Germans, a few Americans, others from around the world, including athletes in the competitors' section and on the infield—were pulling for him, exhorting him, cheering him. He owed them, and he owed himself, a heroic finish worthy of the international roar. He didn't ignore the pain in his legs and his stomach; he fought through it. He pushed harder, overtaking the Belgian coming out of the final turn.

~

Leni alternated between watching Glenn running and watching Adolf Hitler rock back and forth in his chair. As the American came into the homestretch, the Führer stood and rooted on the American down the stretch as if Glenn had a swastika on his chest. In Glenn's final strides, the Führer pounded a fist into his other open palm. Huber, the game German, was about ten yards back in third, also behind Boulanger. For a second, Leni wondered if Hitler was cheering on Huber, but she realized he was cheering for a man he would consider an Aryan champion.

The finish tape loomed. Glenn's legs and lungs tightened even more. He drove on. Finally, he brushed the tape aside. Everyone seemed to be coming at once, and he cut over and to the infield and dropped onto the grass. A race official, bending over, told him his time—4:33.2. Other teammates had joined Walter Wood on the field, and the pack congratulating Glenn included Clark, Parker, Ken Carpenter, and Gordon Dunn. Huber, the good sport, said it had been a pleasure to compete with him.

Within a minute, Brutus Hamilton said that Glenn had indeed barely beaten his own world record and finished with 7,900 points. *Should have known that Wood had the math right!* For an instant, Glenn was disappointed that he hadn't reached 8,000, but then thought: *It's just a number!*

As the public address announcers said the same thing in a succession of languages, United Press sports editor Stuart Cameron rushed through a "bulletin" that would be on the wire, coming across teletypes in newspaper offices, in minutes.

Berlin (UP)—Glenn Morris, 24-year-old automobile salesman from Fort Collins, Colo., Saturday was crowned the world's greatest all-around athlete when he smashed all records in winning the Olympic decathlon on the next to last day of track and field competition.

The Colorado boy even had Adolf Hitler excitedly rocking back and forth like a coxswain coaching a crew as he led the throng of 90,000 in cheering the American down the stretch of the 1,500 meters.

A Badger explained to Glenn, Clark, and Parker—the three medalists—that because of the late hour, the medal ceremony would be held at the start of the session the next afternoon. The events in the stadium would be the women's high jump, plus three relay finals—men's and women's 400 meters and men's 1,600 meters—and the start and end of the marathon. "By the time they'd be ready for the ceremony now, the stadium would be all but empty, so we think this is the right decision," he explained. "So you'll have to come back one more time. But the stadium will be full."

The three American decathlon men looked at each other in turn. Each nodded. They were disappointed, but understood. Walter Wood announced the Americans were headed for the Essen Haus. "You guys won't buy a beer all night!" he said. "But get your asses there as soon as you can!"

A Badger stepped up to claim Glenn. "Okay, Morris," he said, "you'll have the radio interview first and then you meet with the writers. Some of them are rushing to get their stories in afternoon papers back home, so we need to hurry a bit."

Twenty minutes later, as he got up from the table in the radio room, he congratulated himself on remembering the right people to thank. Including Karen.

"Okay, now the writers," the Badger said.

Perhaps thirty writers, most of them American, gathered around him. He answered the predictable questions—"How do you feel?" "When did you know you had it won?" "Did you know Hitler was cheering for you?"—with grace.

Paul Gallico was on the fringe. When the gathering was breaking up, he congratulated Glenn, too, then said, "But I do have to say you have to liven up your comments to us scribes. You didn't give us stuff as good as Marty Glickman's today!"

"The relay?"

Gallico nodded.

"What'd Marty say?" Glenn asked.

"Said it was all politics," Gallico said.

"Did he explain what he meant?"

"He said Dean Cromwell wanted Draper and Wykoff on there because they're all from USC."

"Yeah, but . . ."

Glenn stopped. He decided he'd better say, "We're just talking now, right?"

"Absolutely," Gallico said.

Glenn said, "Sure looked to me today that any team we put together, even minus Jesse, would win. As long as they get the handoffs right. They knew that. They kept Sam and Marty off, anyway."

"Because they're Jews?"

"That's my guess," Glenn said.

With furrowed brow, Gallico responded, "Might be something to that. But there's something else here, too. Jesse Owens is a very fine young man, but I'm pretty sure he's played both sides of the fence on this one."

"How so?"

"Robertson said Owens was all for it when they told him last night, but he supposedly acted at the meeting this morning like this was the first he'd heard of it and they should leave Sam and Marty in it. I think that was for show. Jesse wants that fourth gold medal. There's nothing wrong with that. I wish he'd just say it, though. It'll make him more money when he turns pro . . . like ten seconds after the Olympics are over."

"Interesting theory," Glenn said.

As he walked away, he was thinking: *Jesse and Ralph should have said nope, they weren't running. We supported those guys; they should have supported Sam and Marty.*

An older man was waiting at the press box door, and he waved as Glenn and the Badger approached. It took a second for Glenn to recognize him. *Leni's press agent.* Ernst Jäger reintroduced himself and explained his connection to "the Olympic film" to the Badger.

"Congratulations, Mister Morris," he said. He turned to the Badger. "May Miss Riefenstahl and her crew please have Morris now for an on-camera interview downstairs?"

The Badger, looking at his watch, clearly didn't want any part of this.

Glenn thought: *He must be missing a party!*

"It's okay," Glenn said. "I can get back to the dressing room."

"You sure?"

"Yes, sir."

The Badger appeared relieved and Jäger led Glenn away.

"I didn't know you did interviews on camera," Glenn said.

"We don't," Jäger said with a dark laugh. "I'm told we have a matter that requires some diplomacy we have to discuss with you. Something your man didn't need to know."

Glenn didn't know whether to be excited or worried.

"Do you know what it's about?"

As they walked, Jäger looked at him, calculating. Making a decision, he said, "It's about the Führer wanting to meet you."

"Now?"

"Oh, no," Jäger said. "He's gone now. It was too late and everyone realized it would take too long to arrange . . . even if it could be arranged. Leni has been asked to schedule something else."

Great.

Jäger led Glenn back to track level, to the dignitaries' lounge behind the box seats—the same room he had brought Glenn to meet Leni on the day the Americans arrived in Berlin. He knocked, opened the door and said something in German, then translated: "I just told her the world's greatest athlete had arrived!" That still sounded strange to Glenn. *Mel Ott, Lou Gehrig, Bronko Nagurski . . . now those were athletes. But you'd better get used to that!*

"Thank you Ernst," Leni said in German. She was alone, reading from a notebook, with several pencils on the table to its side.

Jäger waved Glenn in, said congratulations again, and asked Leni, "You're good now?"

"Yes," Leni said with a smile. "Go home to that beautiful wife of yours."

A second after the door was closed, Leni rushed into his arms and kissed him ravenously.

"You were marvelous," she whispered.

"Thanks," Glenn said.

She guided his hands inside her blouse. A minute later, their hands and mouths still wandering, he managed to wedge in whispers. "Leni . . . We can't . . . I mean . . . They're going to be looking for me . . . and here?"

"I know," Leni whispered back. "I know." She stepped back.

"Wow," Glenn said, shaking his head in wonder, "you turn me into a lunatic!"

"What's that? 'Lunatic'?"

"I was saying you make me crazy."

Holding both his hands in hers, Leni said, "Lunatic is a good word . . . better than crazy. I'll have to remember that one!"

Glenn took a deep breath. He decided it would be better to bring it up as a question than to suddenly dig in his heels.

"So what's this about me and Hitler?"

"He wants to meet you, perhaps tomorrow after your medal ceremony or later in the week—here at the stadium or elsewhere, away from the crowds. Perhaps even at the Chancellery."

Glenn's words were measured, his tone careful, yet decisive. "Leni, I can't meet him. I'm sorry if that's a problem for you, but I can't. I just can't. Not tomorrow. Not another day. Not at all."

Leni seemed genuinely shocked. "Why not? You would shake his hand and nod your head when he says nice things about you. That's all. No more than what you did with Max Schmeling! Or Erwin Huber!"

"Leni, they're not Hitler! Our team agreed that we wouldn't meet with him after he wouldn't meet with our Negroes when *they* won. It's a team thing. Plus, I still don't know when I'm leaving. They're still not telling us who's in the meet at London Saturday, and where guys are being sent after that. There might even be other meets sooner than that."

Suddenly, she looked vulnerable, reminding Glenn of his high school dance date, looking down and speaking softly.

"So you're saying you could leave any day now?"

"Unfortunately, yeah."

"You're not going to sneak off, are you?"

"I'll sure try not to."

"Please don't." Leni sighed. "Now I need to get back to the crews and then the Castle." She paused and obviously trying to brighten the mood again, asked, "And what *are* you doing to celebrate?"

"It's just the relays and marathon tomorrow, so everyone else is done," Glenn said. Leni nodded. She knew all that, of course. "So there's a pretty big group going to the beer hall again," Glenn said. "They're probably already there! Same place we went before the competition started. The Essen Haus. Should be fun . . . and I really need to go. And go back with them to the Village."

Glenn tried to read Leni's smile. The tension hadn't disappeared, but had lessened.

"Why, Mister Morris," she began, "you say that like I was going to insist on you spending the night with me tonight."

"Well . . ." Glenn began tentatively. Part of him very much wanted to do just that. Part of him wanted to avoid her—because of the issues that would come up.

She held up a hand. "I understand," she said. "I have to be at Ruhwald. There is a lot of work to do and things to go over for tomorrow. We'll be all over the marathon course, and that's going to be quite a challenge."

"Those guys are crazy!" Glenn marveled.

"Perhaps," Leni said, "but I know others who say men who do ten events in two days are the crazy ones!"

"They might be right," Glenn conceded.

"I hope I can be at your ceremony. If I can't be, though, I know some people who will film it for me . . . and the world."

"I'll be sure to smile," Glenn said.

"Now don't get so drunk tonight you miss it," she said with a laugh.

She leaned closer and said softly, "I'm proud of you. We'll work out the other things. We'll get through them. Now go!"

When Glenn entered the Essen Haus, it was jammed, and he was shocked to see Luz Long with the Americans. The German broad jumper was with a huge man Glenn didn't recognize, and within moments, Glenn knew he was German shot-putter Hans Woellke, the gold medalist.

Soon, Glenn was on his second beer, and he was beginning to wonder if it might be a good idea to take a nap on the table. Mostly, the Americans stood. They started with toasts to not just Glenn, but also to all the other American track and field gold medalists—present or otherwise. Then Glenn toasted Bob Clark and Jack Parker—"as good of teammates as you can have in the decathlon!" Next, the vanquished Jack Torrance led the toast to Woellke and also paid tribute to Long as "a silver-medalist broad jumper, but a gold-medal sportsman!"

Glenn felt a tap on his shoulder.

It was Erwin Huber.

"Can I join this party?" he asked, yelling.

Glenn ended up sitting down with Huber. It was hard to hear, but Glenn still found the conversation pleasant. They joked that they both nearly died in the 1,500 meters. Soon, Long joined them. The broad jumper toasted Glenn's triumph, too, then said: "You're so well-known now, you have company."

"Lots of it," said Huber, gesturing at the other Americans.

"That's not what I mean," Long said, looking at Huber. "I mean . . . Gestapo."

For a second, Glenn was worried that Long was going to mention Leni. For an instant, he was relieved that he didn't. Then it hit him: *Gestapo?*

"Secret police, right?" he asked Long.

Long nodded.

"There's a man at the second table over in the gray jacket . . . Gestapo," Long said conspiratorially.

Glenn tried to look without advertising it. The man was nondescript, perhaps a qualification for the job.

Long added, "And the man over there by the wall, black jacket . . . Gestapo. That's the one who was following *me*."

"Following you? Why? Because you were so nice to Jesse Owens?"

Long laughed, pretending to be involved in a lighthearted story. "I might have *two* following me after that," he said. "That wasn't the smartest thing I've ever done—being so open about it. But they've been following me off and on for about a year."

"Why?" Glenn asked.

"Too complicated, Herr Morris. But now, at least for the rest of your stay here, it looks like you will have the same honor! The one in the gray coat followed you in. And he even went to the lavatory once at the same time, am I not right, trying to make sure you weren't escaping?"

"I didn't notice if he did."

"He did."

"So why would they be following me?"

Long stared at him, gauging whether Glenn truly hadn't figured it out. Finally, Long said slowly, "She is not a Nazi—that is technically true, I suppose—but she is very important to them."

Long then changed the subject to tell Glenn what to expect at the medal ceremony the next morning.

Glenn realized Long hadn't even said her name.

2 7

~

Glenn's Gold

Sunday, August 9

Glenn didn't feel good when he awakened at mid-morning. He was amazed he wasn't worse. At lunch in the dining hall, he accepted congratulations from the athletes who hadn't gone to the Essen Haus the night before, including many swimmers gearing up for the start of their competition on Monday, and additional congratulations from many who had been at the beer hall.

Glenn Cunningham was touching, saying he always knew Glenn had it in him and he had made the Glenns—Hardin, Cunningham, and Morris—two-for-three gold-medal opportunities. Glenn assured Cunningham that a silver medal in a 1,500-meter race in which the winner set a world record wasn't anything to sneeze at.

The runner smiled. "You'd trade your gold for my silver then?"

Glenn didn't know what to say.

"Didn't think so," Cunningham added with a warm smile that erased any bitterness. Back at the room, as ordered to do for the medal ceremony, Glenn put on the white slacks and the blue jacket, plus the red, white and blue tie. He didn't mind that, but he thought it a little strange that all the other winners received their medals while wearing their uniforms—or at least their sweat suits—and the decathlon men will look as if they just left church.

Glenn couldn't get the tie knot right on the first three tries.

"There's no pressure on you," Wood teased. "Your grandchildren will be looking at this picture someday."

"Thanks a lot."

Wood waited quietly while Glenn tried again and was satisfied with what he saw in the mirror. He turned and showed Wood. "How's that?" he asked.

"Now *that's* a gold-medal knot," Wood said.

The decathlon men again rode the same bus to the Reich Sports Field, taking gentle teasing from the other Americans among the passengers for being dressed-up.

"Some guys just have class," Jack Parker boasted.

Glenn took stock of all the passengers, looking for and not finding the Gestapo man from the night before, and then wondering if another of the men in street clothes on the bus might have been his replacement for the day. But then Glenn told himself that was silly—if only because the Gestapo knew where he was going and didn't need to follow him.

At the stadium, they checked in at an officials' kiosk in the dressing room tunnel, and were told the ceremony would be right after the marathon started and the runners left the stadium for their excursion through the streets of Berlin, and just before the 400-meter relay finals. The official checked his watch. "The best thing would be for you to stay right here," he said in only slightly accented English, "and you will be escorted out for the ceremony."

As they waited, Jesse Owens emerged from a dressing room. Owens carried a baton in his right hand. Switching the baton to his left hand, he reached out with his right to Glenn.

"Congratulations!" he said warmly. "Remember on the ship when that writer asked who would be deserved to be called the world's greatest athlete?"

Smiling, Glenn said he *did* remember.

"Well," Jesse said, "I'm looking at him!"

"Hardly," Glenn said. "Four gold medals to my one?"

"Three now," Jesse said. He lifted the baton. "And we have to make sure we don't drop this before I get another one."

Owens also shook hands with Clark and Parker, and then headed to the track.

When he was gone, Parker spoke what was on the minds of all three. "Good guy," he said. "But he shouldn't be running today."

Clark's brow furrowed. "I was thinking of something else, too," he said. "He's wanting to cash in, and I don't blame him. But I bet if he had said publicly he wouldn't run in the relay because Marty and Sam should, and he didn't let the coaches tell him any different, he'd be even *more* popular."

Glenn shrugged. "I agree with you guys about Marty and Sam," he said. "But I bet before long, we'll just be saying Jesse won four gold medals and won't care about the technicalities. Four gold medals sounds better than three."

An official hustled them toward the track.

Soon, Glenn accepted his encased medal from an IOC official and then bent forward, allowing a young German woman in white to place an oak-leaf wreath on his head. Then he was standing, looking at the three American flags side-by-side and listening to the "Star-Spangled Banner." He told himself: *Remember this moment.* The song was recorded and instrumental, but he could *hear* the words.

What so proudly we hailed . . .

His eyes drifted, took note of the hundred thousand spectators—including the athletes in their section of the seats—standing for the anthem, listening respectfully. They were from around the world, and they were all acknowledging his—and his two teammates'—accomplishments.

O'er the ramparts we watched . . .

Leni was off to his right, beaming, as Guzzi Lantschner filmed.

. . . the bombs bursting in air,

Glenn checked Hitler's box. The Führer wasn't there.

For the first time in his life, Glenn didn't want the anthem to end. But it did. He mouthed the final line himself: *O'er the land of the free and the home of the brave.*

After he also accepted one of the familiar potted oak seedlings, he reluctantly stepped down from the stand, only because it seemed as if they were expected to do so.

Leni approached the three Americans, smiling and reaching out a hand demurely to Parker first and congratulating him. Then Clark. Then Glenn. She and Glenn were a few steps from anyone else, but she was careful. "That meeting issue we discussed yesterday?" she said.

By now, he wasn't as angry about the Hitler issue—it wasn't Leni's fault— as he was determined to stick to his guns. He wasn't going to betray his teammates, even if others didn't view meeting the Führer as that sort of betrayal. So he shook his head and said, "I still . . ."

She stopped him. "They aren't pressing for it today," she said. "He's got too much company, I think."

"Good."

"They might still ask for later in the week."

"My answer's going to be the same. If I'm still here."

"I understand that," Leni said. "You can say no. But I can tell them I asked."

She noticed Clark and Parker waiting. "I've got to go straight to the pool after the relays," she said softly. "We're having problems there. I trust my people to get the end of the marathon here. But the next few days are going to be crazy because everything after the track and field is so spread out, all over the area."

Glenn nodded in sympathy. She leaned even closer. "You have to promise to let me know if you find out when you're leaving," she said.

"I promise. Nobody's said anything. The earliest I could leave is Friday . . . and that's only if I'm going to London."

"Good. See if you can come to the pool Tuesday. The diving is fun to watch and I should be able to get away afterward for a while."

"I'll try," Glenn said. Noticing Leni's crestfallen look, he added, "Unless something comes up they haven't told us about yet, I'll be there."

Leni smiled and then raised her voice as she looked toward Clark and Parker. "Good luck to the Americans in the relays!" she called out.

Glenn offered a meaningful nod and a little wave as he left. The Americans rushed up to the athletes' seats, heading toward a block of their teammates. Glenn felt a little self-conscious about carrying the oak-tree pot, but he couldn't think of a viable option. Clark was a little ahead of them. Catching Parker looking at him strangely, Glenn asked, "What?"

"It's true, isn't it? The way she reacted yesterday. And I don't think that was a talk about camera angles."

"Jack . . . drop it."

"Okay, but I'm not the only one saying . . ."

"What a bunch of old ladies!"

"Have it your way, Glenn."

Marty Glickman was a few rows higher than the other Americans, close enough to be considered part of the group, but by himself. Glenn considered joining Marty, but Walter Wood signaled that he had a seat saved for him, among the pack. Glenn also wondered what he would say, and decided that Marty might want to be alone. Quickly, Glenn scanned the rest of the section and didn't spot Sam Stoller.

Glenn whispered to Wood. "You're not talking to anyone about . . . you're not, are you?"

"No, I'm not," Wood whispered back. "But I'm being asked about it more every day."

"Shit."

The starter's gun fired, and Jesse Owens broke from the starting line in the 400-meter relay and into an instant lead. Although Owens's baton pass to Metcalfe wasn't efficient—Jesse actually passed his teammate before Metcalfe gathered in the baton and got going—the Americans won easily, beating the Italians and Germans by ten meters. When the results were posted, the winning team's time—39.8 seconds—drew both gasps and cheers from the Americans. Glenn turned to look behind him. Glickman was motionless, but Glenn Cunningham was with him, off his right shoulder, saying something. Redirecting his gaze past the two American runners, farther to his right, Glenn checked the loge box. Hitler was in his seat, talking to other uniformed Germans. If Owens's latest triumph bothered him, he seemed determined to avoid showing it.

Tapping himself on the chest, Glenn made sure the case holding his gold medal was in his inside pocket. He took it out, opened it and looked at the medal again. "They're not going to take it back," Wood teased him. He gestured at the oak-tree pot, too, sitting on the cement at their feet, and added, "Not that, either."

Glenn told himself: *Marty should be getting a medal, too.* He stood up and turned, intending to go tell Marty just that. But the sprinter was gone. Glenn realized he must have gone up the aisle, past the security guards and onto the concourse level. Glenn Cunningham was moving down to join the group. When he arrived, Glenn asked the distance man: "How was Marty?"

"He handled it better than I would have," Cunningham said. "Said Jesse's the greatest runner ever and it gave him goose-bumps to watch. But when he saw how far back the Germans were, that set him off."

"Why?"

"Because the coaches swore the Germans had something up their sleeves and we needed to have Jesse out there to beat them. No way that was true."

"What'd you tell him?"

"That we were always going to be his teammates and we were proud of him, including he way he handled this," Cunningham said.

A few minutes later, the German women were leading the 400-meter relay when they botched the final exchange, dropping the baton. Glenn quickly turned and saw Hitler plop back into his seat and slap himself on the leg with the gloves he held in one hand. The Führer didn't seem to consider it solace that, with the Germans out of the race, his American acquaintance, Helen Stephens, roared down the stretch to secure another gold medal.

When the American men—running a team of second-tier quarter-milers—finished second to the British in the 1,600-meter relay, Glenn and those around him noticed and discussed the contrast with the approach in the shorter relay. Neither Archie Williams nor Jimmy LuValle, the gold and silver medalists in the 400 meters, were on the relay, and that didn't seem to bother anyone. "Guess none of those guys who ran were Jewish," Walter Wood said.

During and between the races, Glenn noticed that Leni again was a whirlwind, moving from cameraman to cameraman, animatedly giving instructions and framing shots with her hands.

After the 1,600-meter event, Glenn decided he had seen enough and wouldn't wait around for the end of the marathon. Wood agreed, snatching up the oak tree himself to help, and their movement started a mass exodus of the Americans out of the seats and down the aisle.

As the marathon runners approached the stadium, Leni was in the dignitaries' lounge behind the boxes, and below the Führer's loge. Hermann Göring had been talking with the King of Bulgaria, and summoned Leni via an SS messenger when the monarch said he would love to meet her. After that formality was out of the way, the king headed up to join Hitler in the box for the end of the marathon. Göring said he would follow in a moment, and gestured Leni to a private corner.

"How are you getting along with Goebbels now?" the air marshal asked. "Is he still plaguing you on this project?"

Leni reflected a second. With Göring, there was no need to sugarcoat anything about Goebbels, but she didn't have the time to list all the problems. She settled for, "He's not making it easier."

"I asked the stupid bastard how he could sign off on your funding and then try and sabotage you at the same time," Göring said. "He should be asking you what you need, not telling you what you can't do."

"Exactly! That's what I've been telling him, too! Many times!"

"How is the filming going otherwise?"

"Very well," Leni said. "I am trying to monitor it as we go, but it's difficult to keep up. So I know there might be some surprises when we get to the editing."

"Well," laughed Göring, "the American niggers will win there, too. At least you won't have to decide whether to show the American Jews." He noted her quizzical look. "The Jews, their relay runners."

"There aren't any, as far as I know. The relay teams just ran."

"I know, that's what I mean," said Göring. "They removed the Jews. Goebbels saw to it that American Olympic officials were told that in exchange for being so tolerant of the niggers winning, we asked for only one thing in return. Not let the Jews—I understand there were two—run on their sprint relay team. I am told there was one American official more than eager to see that it was done. And it was."

28

~

Unwanted Company

Monday, August 10–Thursday, August 13

As the second and final week of the Games progressed, a running joke among the American track athletes was that they should have gone into hiding the second the track and field competition ended on Sunday. And stayed hidden until it was time to leave for London on Friday, the 14th, the day before the dual all-relays meet against the British.

After the relays and the marathon concluded the track and field portion of the Olympics, the Badgers claimed the highest-profile runners, including Jesse Owens, Ralph Metcalfe, Jimmy LuValle, and Glenn Cunningham. The runners divided in two groups, appearing at meets in five cities—four in other German cities, plus one in Prague, Czechoslovakia—in a span of three days. Owens was the biggest draw, of course, and Jack Torrance jokingly theorized that the AOC knew that any day now, Jesse would declare himself a professional performer, commanding his own large fees for exhibitions and appearances, perhaps even on the vaudeville circuit. Torrance argued they were sending him out and making money off him while they could.

All the Badgers would say was that the additional meets in London and Stockholm were set and everything else still was uncertain, and that all the details and itineraries would be announced in the next few days. Brutus Hamilton let it slip that he knew Glenn was down to compete in the three-day meet at Stockholm. "Think of what events you want to be in," he said. Glenn was relieved that meet organizers apparently weren't trying to put together a decathlon. That would be a little much.

Glenn had mixed feelings about not going to London, but he still was tired; recovering from decathlons took time. Looking ahead, the no-pressure competition on the other parts of the tour might be a small price to pay for seeing more of the continent. After all, who was to say when they'd get another chance? What bothered Glenn the most, though, was the Badgers' complete lack of self-consciousness or concern about the haphazard nature of the planning.

On Tuesday, Glenn opened another cable from the Denver Athletic Club's George Whitman, who alluded to "possible additional opportunities. Will discuss upon your return." Other telegrams from promoters mentioned possible clothing or watch endorsements, with no dollar figures mentioned.

Getting away from some of the tumult, he enjoyed going to the pool and watching University of Michigan graduate Dick Degener win the 3-meter springboard diving, especially because even a trackman could see why Degener was known as "the Fred Astaire" of the sport. He spotted Leni supervising her cameramen at the side of the pool. From the athlete's section of the seats, he caught her eye at one point and nodded decisively, confirming he would be able to do what she had suggested in a note that morning—meet her after the end of the session at the little unnamed café near the war memorial.

Over dinner, he said he was almost certain he would be in Berlin through the closing ceremonies.

"That's great news!" she said, beaming.

For the first time since he had met her, Leni looked fatigued. He asked Leni if she was all right, and she sighed. "It's just always having to go here, go there, answer questions and tell people what to do," she said. "The crews on this are the best, but they still need guidance. And then there always is some official who wants to upset the plans. I'll try to get more sleep the next few days. I get so wound up in it, I lose track! I'll be glad when the Games end. Well, except for . . . if you leave."

She let that hang.

After the meal, they rode together in Leni's limousine to her apartment. Even there, completely in private, the conversation around the lovemaking was comfortable, mainly because Leni didn't bring up the vexing questions of their future and didn't say anything about Hitler's folks pushing for a meeting with Glenn. But she did bring up something they had discussed earlier. "Do you still want to see how I look at the film?" she asked.

"Sure," Glenn said.

She squinted in thought, pondering the schedule.

"How about if Kurt picks you up at 19:00 Thursday and brings you to the Geyer Lab?" she said. "I'll show you the editing room and we can look at some footage in the reviewing room, too."

"That's fine," Glenn said, wondering where else it might lead.

Leni fell asleep in his arms. Although she had mentioned she needed to be back to the Castle Ruhwald fairly soon, Glenn didn't have the heart to wake her up. He was drifting off, too, when Leni awoke with a start. Checking a clock, she playfully shoved Glenn, saying, "All right, world's greatest athlete, up and dressed—fast. We need to go. Klaus will drop me off at Ruhwald, then take you back to the Village."

As they left together, Glenn briefly wondered whether he should be concerned about her apparent reluctance to allow him to remain behind in her apartment alone—even for a few minutes. He decided he was being petty.

Glenn, along with Wood and some of the other trackmen, checked out the boxing competition and more swimming. He also spent a lot of time sifting through the new telegrams, which included invitations to appear on radio shows in New York after their return. Also, four letters from Karen arrived at once. The dates indicated they all had been written before the opening ceremonies, and he realized that if she kept writing, other letters likely would make it to Berlin after he was gone. He read the expressions of her support and the depth of her affection, and again the lack of guilt surprised him. It was as if that was another life shoved over in a corner, perhaps to be resumed.

On Thursday, Kurt the driver finally was comfortable enough to act as more of a guide on the way. He pointed out several of the sites this time, and eventually announced over his shoulder: "Now we're in Neukölln. Another borough."

Five minutes later, as they pulled in front of a nondescript building, it was as if he hadn't paused. "And this," he said, "is the Geyer Film Laboratory."

A stocky young man, half-bald and tired-looking, and very nervous, greeted Glenn as he entered. What also caught Glenn's attention was that there were three men in the familiar black uniforms—SS?—and two other men in plainclothes, seemingly on watch in the lobby. Gestapo?

The man introduced himself as Stephan. "I am Fraulein Riefenstahl's editing assistant." Even the simple phrase in English was a struggle for him, though, so Glenn decided it would be futile to ask about the security. He took Glenn to a room where Leni was bent over a strange-looking machine, with what appeared to be a lens in the middle and film sticking out of each side. Other filmstrips were strung around her neck like unclasped necklaces. Still more—many, many more, perhaps hundreds—were draped from hooks on the wall.

Leni hadn't heard them.

"Fraulein?" Stephan asked.

Leni turned and lit up. She started to shed the filmstrips. "Welcome to my world, Glenn," she said, smiling tightly. With Stephan watching, she came and gave Glenn a hug that could have been between coworkers, so Glenn followed that lead. But then she kissed him—lightly, but real enough.

Guess there are going to be no secrets. Better keep practicing that speech. "Sure, I've met Leni Riefenstahl. She's making a movie about the Olympics, and I'm in it!"

"I barely beat you here," Leni said. "I was at the pool all day . . . and your Americans are not doing well!"

Glenn had heard that the Japanese and Dutch were dominating the swimming so far. "They'll get going," he said.

Stephan lingered, and Leni didn't seem interested in chasing him out of the room. For the next fifteen minutes, she and Stephan demonstrated how they ran filmstrips through the viewer and marked them. They were looking at footage from the swimming from the day before. Leni said, "Stephan has put together a selection of what we have from you competing—very raw, but I'm sure an indication of what you will see in the final film—and the relays from yesterday and we'll watch it in the viewing room down the hall."

She nodded at Stephan, and he left without saying another word. This time, the kiss was deeper. That was fine with Glenn, and he was still holding her and their eyes were only inches apart when he asked: "What's with everyone out in the lobby?"

Leni hesitated.

"Oh, oh," Glenn said. "I'm not going to like this, am I?"

She locked on his eyes. "Do you love me?"

"Here and now, yes."

"That's cold," she said, wounded.

"You know what I mean!" he said, moving his hands to her shoulders. "Come on, if people looked at this, damn near every one of them would say *you'll* be the one to decide it was fun while it lasted and tell me it's over."

"I have been talking of more. I thought you were thinking about it!"

"I am. I will." He paused. "But you changed the subject. What's going on here?"

"The Führer," she said.

When she didn't continue, he prompted, "The Führer is . . . ?"

"Coming here."

"Now?"

She nodded, a sheepish confession. "To meet you . . . and watch some of the film."

Glenn backed away. "You set me up!" he shouted.

"Wrong! They found out you were coming here to see the footage. I don't know how, but they did. Perhaps I told too many people. The Gestapo is all over."

"I know it is."

"How?"

"Doesn't matter now," he said, and then made a move toward the door, his intentions clear.

"Stop!" she shrieked.

He did—involuntarily, with his hand on the doorknob, without understanding why.

"You can't do this for me?" she asked.

"I can't!"

"Because of my family and my work, I need to do what these people ask me to do—within reason, of course," she said. "I am *not* a Nazi issuing an invitation. I'm someone who loves you asking you to help me."

Stepping away from the door, Glenn folded his arms and looked at the ceiling. "They probably know everything, don't they? *Everything!*"

Leni shrugged. "I'm not sure. What I know is the Führer's adjutant said they would join us." That had been on Tuesday, but she didn't tell Glenn that. "Can't you see?" she implored. "I had no choice!"

"You could have gotten word to me not to come!"

"Kurt was on his way to get you. And even if I had reached you, they would have known I warned you off."

"I could have been sick, I could have had a meeting, or I could have been told I couldn't leave the Village. We would have come up with something."

"They would have been able to check your story . . ."

Glenn slapped his head with both hands. "This is great," he said sarcastically. After a long pause, he added, "At least tell me this is going to be a secret!"

"I will try to see that it is," Leni said. "But you are acting like no other athletes have met the Führer! They have. More than you know, I am thinking. They have come up to the room behind his box, they have shaken his hand, and they apparently have not felt guilty. They are meeting the leader of the host nation. That is all."

Glenn took a deep breath.

"Please do this," she pleaded.

Glenn said tentatively, "You're saying no pictures or reporters or announcing it to the world, right?"

"He was angry when someone took a picture of him with your woman runner. He *wants* the meetings with the athletes to be private."

"But if . . . if . . . it ever comes out, you have to back me that I didn't know this was going to happen," he said.

"Yes."

"And don't expect me to act like I'm his biggest fan. No 'Heil Hitler' from me."

"Glenn, just be civil," she said. "They'll just think you're nervous."

"And you think I won't be?" He thought a second. "How many people is he going to have with him? And who?"

"I'm not sure," Leni said. "SS guards, for sure. An adjutant. I don't know who else." She was thinking: *As long as it's not Goebbels.* "He might not even have his translator with him. I wasn't told much except they were coming."

There was a knock on the door. Leni spoke in German. Stephan stuck his head in. Glenn didn't understand him, but he knew what he said. From his tone and his anxiousness, it was obvious.

"They're pulling up," Leni said. "We'll meet them in the viewing room."

The room, down the hall, was a small theater with five rows of slightly tiered and anchored seats—functional but short of plush. The door was at the side of the room, with the projector showing in a hole in the wall at one side and the screen set up at the other. Leni left the door and as they waited, she tried to take Glenn's hand, but he pulled away and backed up. She looked hurt, but then their attention returned to the door as Stephan entered first, showing the way. Then came the three SS men who been waiting in the lobby. They nodded at Leni and surveyed the room. Glenn assumed they already had checked it earlier. He also wondered how he'd react if they tried to search him. They didn't.

One SS man returned to the door and stepped into the hall. Glenn could see him nodding, and then another man in uniform entered. The adjutant, Glenn assumed. And then the Führer strode through the door, with more SS men in his wake. Glenn's heart raced. The Führer wore a brown uniform with a red belt around the jacket, and black boots. Glenn's eyes were drawn to the medal pinned to his left breast pocket.

Hitler first went to Leni and briefly took her extended hand in both of his. The ensuing conversation allowed Glenn to assess. The smiles and demeanors seemed cordial and familiar, but short of affectionate. Hitler was even shorter than he expected. Remembering the frequent derisive comparisons to Charlie Chaplin's Little Tramp quelled his nerves a bit. He decided it wouldn't be good if he burst out laughing, either.

With her upturned right hand and a smile, Leni introduced Glenn. He caught the word *zehnkampf*—decathlon—and his name. Suddenly, they were shaking hands, and Glenn at that instant regretted that he wouldn't be able to say for sure if he did or didn't make Hitler reach first. Hitler's grip in the quick shake was loose and clammy, but his smile seemed sincere as he locked on Glenn's eyes. Glenn couldn't resist doing the same. With his head slightly turned to Leni, making it clear she was expected to translate, Hitler spoke for about fifteen seconds.

Leni waited until she was certain he was through.

"The Führer congratulates you on your gold medal and says you were heroic," she told Glenn. "He found it quite exciting to watch you, especially in that last distance race."

"Thank you," Glenn found himself saying. "I was very fortunate."

When Leni translated that, Hitler gave a dismissive wave before saying something about Glenn, America, and Germany. That much, Glenn could tell. He also noticed that Hitler's adjutant and even one of the SS men smiled. Leni translated, "You are a fine representative of your nation, and America should be proud of you for what you have done here in Germany." Glenn sensed Leni had left something out—perhaps something that prompted the smiles from the others—but he wasn't about to press the issue. His guess was that he was being congratulated as a champion of the white race.

"Thank you again," Glenn said, looking at the Führer and trying not to stare at the moustache. "All athletes owe your nation thanks for doing such a great job of putting on the Games."

Your nation. Not you.

Hitler's ensuing spiel mentioned both countries, this time with animated hand gestures punctuating his message, and he also nodded toward Leni and the projector showing through the opening in the wall at the back of the room.

Leni said, "The Führer hopes that in my film, your performance will serve to remind many that our nations have much in common. And that it would be tragic if we don't strive to remember that moving forward."

Glenn stared at Leni, again trying to read whether she had left something out. He wondered if Hitler had said anything to acknowledge that he knew about their affair.

"I know this film will honor the spirit of friendly competition and sportsmanship," Glenn said. "I'll be proud to be in it."

Leni spoke in German, gesturing at the seats. One of the SS men acted as an usher, directing Glenn to the front row. Glenn sat, and two of the men in plainclothes joined him, flanking him. Hitler and his adjutant went into the middle row, with SS men on each side. Out of the corner of his eye, Glenn noticed that several men remained standing.

When the lights went out and the film began, Leni sat at the end of the front row. In the shadowy light from the projector, she caught Glenn's eyes briefly. It began with prefacing shots of the stadium and then the decathlon men, including Glenn, gathered in the corner of the track, loosening up and picking through their gear.

He heard the side door open and noticed the brief flash of light from the hall. He turned slightly, noticing two more uniformed men escorting a woman into the room. Blonde, young, plain . . . that was all he could tell without turning completely around and making it obvious. He could tell, though, that she slipped into the back row with her escorts on each side.

He turned his attention back to the screen.

The footage stunned him. Glenn had seen himself in pictures, of course, including from football games and track meets, but never in film this clear, this close up, this illuminating, from so many different angles. *Leni really is brilliant!* He laughed silently, thinking that for a moment, he had forgotten that not only was he on the screen, but that Adolf Hitler was ten feet away, watching the same thing.

Brief blank, black interludes in the film showed how it was a rough cut, spliced together, but it was in chronological order over the two days. Glenn was discomfited when the camera showed his looks of steely concentration, especially in the field events, where he shifted the shot put back and forth from hand to hand and looked out over the landing area. *Yeah, I should have taken off the watch.* As the passages continued, the shifting of the camera up and down, showing his legs as he was about to get off throws or jumps, made him feel as if he was about to break into a cold sweat any second as he watched.

That embarrassment became a feeling of exultation, though, as he watched his best vault, giving him the height he was perfectly satisfied to accept. And he hadn't realized how extensively he had demolished his competition in his heats of the high hurdles and the 400 meters.

Hitler clapped in several places—or at least Glenn assumed it was Hitler—prompting others behind him to join in. The Führer's periodic comments were indecipherable for Glenn.

The footage showed only seven of the ten events, and was missing the climax—the 1,500 meters. When he thought that was coming up, in fact, they suddenly saw shots of Helen Stephens, both getting ready for and then running in the 100-meter final, and on the victory stand. Next, she ran the final leg of the relay, storming down the stretch and securing another gold medal—after the Germans dropped the baton. Glenn wondered if whoever decided to show that would be in trouble, so he was shocked when he heard applause behind him again.

He thought it came from the back row, too.

That's weird.

Then, to Glenn's surprise, there were shots of the opening ceremonies, including several glimpses of Hitler responding to the salutes of the athletes parading on the track. Glenn waited for the American entrance and procession, wondering if he could spot his near-stumble. But his team wasn't shown before the film returned to Hitler, shown close up from his left, pronouncing the Games open. In the Geyer room, there was applause for that, too. Glenn didn't join in. Then the screen was black and the projector light went dark. The lights remained out, though, as additional applause came and Glenn sensed movement behind him. He turned slightly and noticed the woman and her escorts heading to the door, and then out into the lighted hall. He didn't get much of a look at her before she was gone and the lights came on. Glenn blinked to adjust to the light, but stayed seated. Two rows behind him, Hitler stood. Leni moved to be next to Glenn. Hitler spoke quickly to both of them—first to Glenn, then to Leni. Glenn could tell she thanked him, and then she turned to Glenn to translate. "The Führer said it was even more inspiring on film than in person," she said.

"Thank you," Glenn said. *Just keep saying that. That's all.*

Hitler pointed at the screen and spoke again, and Glenn inferred from the words he caught that the Führer was talking about the shots of him at the opening ceremonies. Hitler was nodding, so he seemed to be approving. Leni didn't translate that. Then, with no warning, Hitler turned and followed his security entourage down the row and out of the room. Glenn was surprised and relieved that there wasn't another round of handshaking.

Soon, Leni and Glenn were alone. She threw her arms around him. He tried to resist, but she was shivering and crying. So he hugged her, too, and as she sobbed, Glenn found himself whispering, "It's all right."

"Each time he looks at anything I have done, I am trying not to fall apart," she said. "You don't know how careful I must be. Goebbels hates me so much, the second the Führer wavers about allowing me to be independent, all will fall apart. And my family will be hurt."

"I'm figuring that out," Glenn said. "But that's the problem. That's the life you want me to think about joining. What happened to the talk about how it's all maneuvering and bluster, and it will not turn out to be policy? That he isn't the monster some say he is? Why are you so scared then? If you're so scared like this, how can you say you are independent? Look at you! He controls you!"

"Those are two different things," she said, still sniffling. "His policies *will* turn out to be more moderate and I won't have to worry about my independence being taken away . . . or held against me. The people don't want another war. They want our prestige and prosperity restored. He is giving them that."

"But the Jews . . . ?"

"The Olympics have helped! With the world coming here, they stepped away from many of the Nuremberg measures. They're realizing there's no need to go back to them."

They returned to the editing room, where Glenn picked up his jacket.

"You don't have to leave yet," Leni protested.

"Yeah, I think I should," he said.

"You didn't say what you thought of the film . . . at least what you saw."

"It looked pretty good to me," Glenn said. "The right man won."

Leni smiled. "Thank you."

"But I have to admit some of that—like going up and down my legs—made me feel a little weird."

"It's the art of film. The human body is part of art—sculpture, painting, photography, film. It is like that when I'm on the screen, too. You saw that."

"Yeah, I did." He paused. "But none of that stuff is important. The important stuff is that I promised I wouldn't be a part of meeting Hitler . . . and I was. I did. And you were part of it. The life you have here—was part of it. We can't ignore that. *I* can't ignore that."

"So what are you telling me?"

"I need to think about it. We're supposed to find out tomorrow what plans they have for us, too. I'm still thinking I'll be leaving Monday or Tuesday."

"You'll let me know, won't you?"

"I'll try," Glenn said. Glenn walked off without kissing her. As Kurt pulled the car away, Glenn looked back at the Geyer Building. Leni was outside, watching, her arms folded, sobbing.

"Stop!" Glenn called out.

He jumped out of the car, walked back to Leni and held her as she cried. At first, he was glad he had returned, but then he sensed it was a mistake. She probably thought it was a sign of concession, a change of mind.

So he kissed her quickly on the forehead, pulled away again and rushed back to the car.

∼

Walter Wood was waiting for Glenn in the room.

"They handed out the list for London," Wood said, pointing at a sheet of paper on the desk. "Maybe half the team. We're not on it. None of us discus guys, not you or Parker, either. Clark's in the broad jump. They're all leaving tomorrow."

Glenn took a look at the list. "No surprises here," he snapped. "It's a stupid relay meet."

Noticing the edge in his voice, Wood said carefully, "They said we should know what they've got in store for the other places tomorrow."

Wood waited, but Glenn didn't respond.

"So how was the movie?" Wood asked.

Glenn had told Walter he was going to see the raw footage of the decathlon at the lab and that, yes, he would see Leni. The two men hadn't known each other long, but Glenn marveled at how little he had to tell his roommate for Wood to figure out so much.

"It had a sad ending," Glenn said.

"So it's over?"

"I think so."

"Your doing or hers?"

"Her doing, my decision."

"You going to tell me what that means?"

"Nope."

After an awkward silence, Wood seemed relieved to be able to change the subject. "Not that this is as important . . . but the Badger press guy came by to tell you Joe Williams would be by about 10 in the morning to interview you. He heard you weren't going to London. He said to make sure you knew it would be for the Denver paper, not the New York one."

"I was thinking of going to the rowing tomorrow—see those guys from Washington win."

Wood laughed. "Just talk fast," he said.

When the light was out and they were in their beds, Glenn spoke quietly. "Walter . . ."

"Yeah?"

"It was supposed to be so simple. You win, you celebrate, you go home, you're all excited because everyone knows who you are, you get on with your life."

The pause was so long, Glenn wondered if Walter had decided against saying anything. But then he broke the silence. "Glenn, no matter what happened . . . nothing says you can't still do that. You know, a lot of guys wouldn't understand why this is bugging you. You scr . . . you'll be with a famous lady for a couple of weeks, and then you'll go home. That sounds good to a lot of guys here. Some guys are as jealous of that as they are of your gold medal. You know all of that, don't you?"

Glenn didn't answer.

29

~

The Spirit of What You're Saying

Friday, August 14

Glenn's racing thoughts were worse than fifteen cups of coffee, so he spent much of the night between consciousness and sleep. He tried counting Walter Wood's ordered breaths to put him to sleep, but that didn't work, either. As early as he thought decent, with Walter still dozing, he headed to the dining hall for breakfast, not so much because he was hungry, but because he didn't want to stay in bed and be tortured.

There, he took his food over to a corner table and sat alone. But within a couple of minutes, swimmer Al Vande Weghe, competing in the 100-meter backstroke finals that day, approached the table. All he had on his plate was fruit and one piece of toast.

"Can I rub your gold medal for good luck?" Vande Weghe asked as he sat down.

"We'd have to get it in the safe," Glenn said with a tight grin.

After taking a couple of bites, Vande Weghe squinted at Glenn. "Man, you look beat," remarked the swimmer. "It was supposed to get easier after you were done!"

When Glenn left the dining hall, he decided to go for a walk. Without having a sense for where he was headed, he wandered between the long lines of dormitory buildings, watching the athletes from the other nations emerge. He nodded to many of them and accepted congratulations from a few, including a pack of about five Japanese. Eventually, he came to the practice track, a reminder of how much his life had changed. He walked a full lap.

A week ago, he was a would-be decathlon gold medalist; today, he was the champion, sorting through some of the complications that came with it.

That's the first thing you have to face: If you hadn't won, her attitude might have changed awful fast. She'd say not, might even believe it, but it's true.

He lectured himself about why the events of the night before had been so telling. Leni always would have to be concerned about staying in Hitler's good graces. Regardless of all else, that was the overriding reality.

She's made a deal with the devil. Doesn't make her a Nazi. It means you can't ever become part of her world. It's time to throw cold water on your face. Karen's your real world. Even if you just told Leni we'll play it by ear and see what happens, you'd have to tell Karen it's over. And that wouldn't be right. You've got a life back home and it's time to start leaving this—Berlin, Leni—behind.

He checked his watch. He'd been walking for almost two hours and was late for the appointment with Joe Williams.

One of the Honorary Youth Service stewards—they all could pick out the decathlon champion now—caught Glenn as he was about to enter his building. He called out Glenn's name, then handed him a telegram. Glenn decided to open this one right away. In it, George Whitman of the DAC said:

> PARADE BEING PLANNED IN DENVER UPON RETURN
>
> WILL BE IN TOUCH ABOUT SCHEDULING
>
> THURSDAY DENVER POST SAYS YOU IN SWEDEN ALREADY.
>
> ASSUMING THAT'S INCORRECT.
>
> WHIT

Glenn shook his head in wonderment. *Sweden now? Where do they get this stuff?*

Williams was talking with Wood when Glenn got to the room.

"I couldn't talk him into telling the world about a guy who finished thirteenth in the discus," Wood told Glenn. "So you'll have to do."

"Hey," Williams told Wood, "maybe in 1940!"

Wood laughed. "I fully intend to have an office in a skyscraper by then. If I got to Tokyo, I want to be one of the fat Badgers along for the ride. That's the way to go!"

"Or as a sportswriter!" Glenn couldn't help adding.

"Hey, I don't need any more competition," Williams protested.

Wood shook hands with Williams again and said he'd leave them alone. At the door, he turned and told Glenn, "I didn't tell him you talk in your sleep."

"He does?" Williams asked, thinking he was only playing along with a joke.

"To beat the band," Wood said. He laughed. "But it's all in French!"

The discus thrower waved and left. Glenn felt relieved.

Williams apologized that the responsibilities of covering the Games for the *New York World-Telegram* had prevented him from spending much time providing copy about Glenn for Denver's morning tabloid, the *Rocky Mountain News*. "But we'll take care of that now," he said. "This will be a nice 'follow' piece for the folks back home in the mountains."

Glenn resisted the temptation to point out that like the *Denver Post's* pieces, the *News's* stories on him in recent months were filled with hokum. And Glenn didn't bother to point out that none of those he considered his "folks back home"—in Simla, Denver, and Fort Collins—lived in the mountains.

"When will it be in the newspaper, Mr. Williams?"

"I'm guessing tomorrow . . . Saturday morning," Williams said. "They're so many hours behind us, it shouldn't be a problem for me to get it done for 'em and wire it in. I can get you a carbon if you want . . . like if you go to the closing ceremonies. You going to be around still?"

Glenn explained that as far as he knew, he would be leaving for Stockholm on Tuesday, but added there were all sorts of rumors flying about other possible exhibition meets being scheduled at the last second. "I mean, the way it seems to be going, an AOC guy could knock on the door and tell me I'm leaving for Munich or someplace in fifteen minutes."

Williams pointed at Glenn's desk, where two things were prominent—the potted oak and Karen's picture. He asked what plans Glenn had for the tree.

"Not sure yet," Glenn said. "The governor asked in his telegram if it could go to the State Capitol, but I'm thinking he'll understand if I give it to my college or high school."

"So you're not putting it in your backyard?"

"Kind of hard, since I don't have a backyard," Glenn with a laugh.

"Are you going to *get* a backyard someday? With . . ."

He reached over and briefly lifted the picture.

"With this young lady, I assume?"

"At some point, yes."

"Getting married, I take it?"

"At some point, probably."

"And her name is?"

"Karen."

"Let's start there," Williams said. "You've got her picture here, so it's safe to say she's your inspiration?"

Glenn didn't respond right away.

She's in the life you have back home. She's a great girl. She's . . .

"Morris, if you don't want to talk about her, we can find something else for the folks back home."

"No, it's not that, Mr. Williams. I'm just thinking about how to say it."

He told Williams about meeting Karen, about her help during his training, especially with his diet, and her support as he became devoted to trying to make it to Berlin in the decathlon.

As had happened in the shipboard interview with Paul Gallico, Glenn found himself slowing down or even pausing in mid-sentence in the early stages as the writer scribbled only a few words of notes for each answer. Williams noticed. "Don't worry about me getting down every word," he said. "We're just talking. I'll be able to capture the spirit of what you're saying— better than you're saying it. Don't sweat it." He laughed. "Babe Ruth and Lou Gehrig never have complained. Okay?"

They talked about Karen and Harry Hughes's roles in his life and training, about how Glenn gravitated to the decathlon and his improvement over the past year, and about the competition in Berlin. When Williams pressed him about his future, Glenn emphasized that it was less than a week since he accepted the gold medal, certainly not enough time to sort things out. He did mention that he likely would move to Denver.

Williams tried to press Glenn about his reaction to Jesse Owens all but announcing he wanted to make as much money as he could, as fast as he could, in the wake of his Olympic triumphs. Glenn responded, "Jesse's a very smart guy, I think he's trying to sort things out, too. That's all. Can you blame him for that?"

"No," said Williams. "But he's got to be realistic about how many chances a Negro is going to have."

～

The University of Washington rowers, the decathlon men's tablemates at the send-off dinner in New York, came from behind to edge Italy in the final 500 meters to win the 2,000-meter, eight-oared event on a lake at Grünau, on the southeastern side of Berlin. Stunned that a huge crowd overflowed the abundant bleachers and jammed the side of the lake, Glenn and Wood were thrilled to have a great view near the finish line in the small athletes' section. Glenn was even more gratified when coxswain Bob Moch spotted him after the race, thanked him for coming and said his gold medal must have brought them good luck.

At the pool, Hans Ertl noticed Leni's angst as he went about his own stress-filled task of shooting the lead footage of the swimming competition. As Leni moved from camera position to camera position, she kept looking up at the athletes' section, hoping to spot Glenn and concoct a way to corner him for a talk—or at least arrange for one later. Americans Adolf Kiefer and Al Vande Weghe finished 1-2 in the 100-meter backstroke, triggering flag-waving celebration among the U.S. athletes and fans in attendance, and because Leni had heard Glenn mention both of them, she was surprised he didn't show up to watch their triumphant moments. *Or he's here and he's hiding from me.* After the medal ceremony, Ertl cornered her.

"I've never seen you like this," he said. "This is your moping at the Castle magnified."

"You've seen me tired before," she said.

"No . . . this American has you all crazy."

"Does *everyone* know?"

"Oh, you know how gossip travels."

Solicitously, Ertl put a hand on her shoulder. "I should be jealous that you didn't act like this when it ended between us."

She thought a second. "Who said it was over with him?" she asked.

When Glenn and Wood returned to the Village, copies of the updated schedule and the several sheets listing individual assignments were posted on the bulletin board at the entrance to the dormitory building, and also slipped under their door.

The first sheet read:

UNITED STATES MEN'S TRACK AND FIELD MEETS—UPDATED
Mon, Aug 10—at Cologne (COMPLETED)
Mon, Aug 10—at Dresden (COMPLETED)
Tue, Aug 11—at Hamburg (COMPLETED)
Tue, Aug 11—at Prague, Czechoslovakia (COMPLETED)
Wed, Aug 12—at Bochum (COMPLETED)
Sat, Aug 15— at London
Mon, Aug 17—at Glasgow, Scotland

Mon, Aug 17 and Tue, Aug 18—at Helsingfors, Finland
Mon, Aug 17—at Prague, Czechoslovakia
Tue, Aug 18—at Vienna, Austria
Wed, Aug 19; Thu, Aug 20; Fri, Aug 21—at Stockholm, Sweden
Thu, Aug 20—at Joensuu, Finland
Thu, Aug 20, Fri Aug 21, and Sat Aug 22—at Oslo, Norway
Sun, Aug 23—at Karlstad, Sweden
Sun, Aug 23—at Paris, France
Mon, Aug 24—at Helsingfors, Finland
Tue, Aug 25—at Hamburg, Germany
Wed, Aug 26—at Oslo, Norway
RETURNS
Wed, Aug 19—SS President Roosevelt from Hamburg
Wed, Aug 26—SS Manhattan from Hamburg
Thu, Aug 27—SS Manhattan from Havre and Southampton
SEE INDIVIDUAL MEET ASSIGNMENTS AND DEPARTURE SCHED-
ULES ON FOLLOWING SHEETS

"Man, what did they do? Just throw darts at a map?" Wood asked incredulously. "Look at that! We're split up at three places on a couple of those
days! Okay, I understand why the Finns might want us for those meets, so
they can cheer their medal-winners from here. But do they like track that
much in Oslo?"

They quickly flipped to the sheets listing their names and assignments.
Glenn and Walter both were going to Prague and Vienna. That surprised
him a bit, since Jesse and his troupe had passed through Prague, too, earlier
in the week. Next, Glenn would head for Stockholm, Karlstad, Helsingfors,
and Oslo; and then catch up with the SS *Manhattan* at Southampton. After
the meets at Prague and Vienna, Wood was down to compete at Paris and
then meet the ship at Havre. "You—and those Scandinavian women—are
just going to have to do without me," he joked, but with underlying tone of
regret that the roommates and new friends soon would be separated.

By far the biggest U.S. roster for a single meet would be at the relays
event in London. Some of that group would be through after that meet and
be on the *Roosevelt*; some would move on to Scandinavia; still others would
return to the European mainland. The assignments seemed as chaotic as the
scheduling. But the most important detail was that Glenn was down to leave
Berlin Sunday.

30

~

On Tour

Saturday, August 15–Tuesday, August 18

On Saturday morning, Glenn debated whether writing a letter to Leni was a good idea, since it would have to pass through other hands to reach her. Deciding that was ridiculous at this point, he sat down, grabbed the stationery and wrote the longest letter of his life. He explained he was leaving for Prague and Vienna on Sunday, traveling on to Scandinavia from there, and then heading home. He said he wasn't saying good-bye, though, because as unlikely as it might seem, maybe they would see each other again—if she visited America or if he came to Germany again. He tried to make it clear he wasn't angry, just realistic. He accepted that she had very difficult choices to make, choices of the sort he couldn't even grasp. And as wonderful as it had been, he knew that because they would so drastically complicate each other's lives, continuing this was impossible. She understood that now, too, he assumed. He thanked her, said he never would forget his time in Berlin, and his time with her, and he knew he always would love her. He stuffed the sheets into the envelope, addressed it to Leni at the Castle Ruhwald, found the Honorary Youth Service steward and handed it to him to get the delivery in motion.

~

Joe Williams' story indeed ran in the *Rocky Mountain News* on Saturday morning. It began:

Glenn Morris to Marry Sterling Girl,
His Inspiration, On Return Home
By Joe Williams
News Staff Correspondent
    BERLIN—Glenn Morris admired the little oak tree that they gave him for winning the Olympic decathlon.
    He fingered the prized Olympic medal—one of the trophies that went with the honor of winning the distinction of being the world's greatest all-around athlete.
    But all the time he faced a picture on his dresser. He eyed it proudly and smiled:
    "I bet she's happy. She said we would win; we couldn't lose. She's the swellest girl in the world, Mr. Williams."
    The handsome Colorado athlete is in love, and when he gets back to Colorado next month he and Karen Wiley, Sterling, Colo., school teacher, are to be married.
    "Karen was my inspiration," Glenn said, as we sat in his quarters in Olympic Village. "She was the inspiration which made me champion. She was my trainer and coach and offered me encouragement when others were inclined to scoff at my inspiration to win the Olympic decathlon."

The morning tabloid did an inspired job of packaging, asking Karen to come to Denver to be interviewed for an accompanying story. Karen was pictured smiling above the story on her, and next to the one on Glenn. That story began:

Sweetheart-Coach Tells How
She Trained Olympic Champion
Miss Karen Wiley, on Visit to Denver, Gets News
Of Her Forthcoming Marriage Thru the News
    Karen Wiley, pretty 21-year-old fiancée of the world's greatest athlete, felt Friday night that as if she were being rushed into something—but she didn't mind it a bit.
    Miss Wiley, blue-eyed Kappa Alpha Theta from Colorado State College of Agriculture and Mechanic Arts at Fort Collins, is credited by Glenn Morris with being his trainer-coach and inspiration during his two-year preparation for the 1936 Olympics.
    Morris told Joe Williams, correspondent for The Rocky Mountain News, that he and Karen would be married when the decathlon champion returned to Colorado in September.

"We hadn't really set any date," Miss Wiley said, as she read an early edition of The News for information about the man she is going to marry.

"We didn't know how Glenn would come out over there in Berlin. We were going to wait and see. I was going to teach home economics and Spanish in the Fountain high school this fall. It takes so long for us to get word back and forth to each other. Glenn writes to me every day, but some of the news of him comes first from newspapers.

"Where does it say we are going to be married as soon as he gets to Denver? When will he get to Denver?"

At the swimming stadium Saturday, Leni again kept looking for Glenn. She was so preoccupied, in fact, she missed an older American tourist woman—Carla de Vries—audaciously asking for and receiving an autograph from Adolf Hitler, seated in the front row of the stands, and thanking him with a kiss on his cheek. Several minutes later, Hans Ertl found Leni, chortled and told her that he had gotten "it" on film.

"What's 'it'?" Leni asked.

When he decided she was serious, he explained what had happened, saying reporters apparently quickly had determined it was a wealthy woman from Los Angeles. "The film's going to be great!" he said.

"She could have had a gun," Leni said, "and then you wouldn't be smiling." She caught Ertl's look and added, ". . . or maybe you would."

A little later, Leni approached one of the male American swimmers. She introduced herself.

"I know," said the 400-meter gold medalist who was about to go for another victory in the 1,500-meter freestyle. "I'm Jack Medica."

Leni waved at the athletes' section of the stands.

"I don't see any of your track and field athletes," she said. "I heard many of them were going to London . . . but all of them?" Hastily, she added, "I needed to check on something with them."

"Pretty sure most of them are gone," he said. "Maybe all of 'em. They were talking about being sent all over the place! Morris is going to Prague, I know that."

She thanked him and walked away, and hadn't gotten far when it registered that she hadn't specified whom she wanted to know about. That didn't bother her. What bothered her now was that he hadn't contacted her. The way things stood now, she wouldn't have a chance to win him back before he left for America. She didn't try to fool herself. It hurt.

Glenn's letter was on her desk when she passed through Sunday morning. She knew it hadn't been there the night before. She went to the door, slammed it shut, took a deep breath, slit open the envelope and froze. She was both angry and anxious. It clearly had been written the morning before and the fact that she didn't have it in her hands until now meant either Glenn delayed in sending it, or someone had been negligent in not getting it to her faster. Finally, she slid the sheet out of the envelope, unfolded it and read.

By the time she was done, a falling tear had smudged a couple of lines. She realized it was too late to try and catch up with Glenn. He was gone. Leni couldn't remember the last time she had cried when alone, when it wasn't for show, when it was real.

Glenn, Walter Wood, Ken Carpenter, and 400-meter hurdler Dale Schofield were on the train to Prague. Glenn had left behind the oak-tree seedling, assured by the Badger in charge of Village checkout that it would be labeled and returned to him on the SS *Manhattan*. On the train, Wood quizzed another escorting Badger, noting the original listed squad was larger, but couldn't get a straight answer about why the group was so small. The Badger said he probably would be able to tell them more after their arrival. Wood joked that if he was forced into throwing the javelin, for example, the Czech fans might demand their money back—or somebody might be impaled after his wild toss.

"Don't worry about it," the Badger said. "These people know we have two gold medalists—Morris and Carpenter—and we're Americans. They had a great crowd for Jesse Owens and the runners the other day, and that's why we're back . . . they wanted more. Supposedly, they're big on the decathlon, so they're all excited to see you, Morris."

After they stepped off the train and into the main part of the terminal, they waited, with the Badger assuming that the next official-looking fellow through the doors was going to be their guide. Their bags and clothes announced they were Americans, and they drew curious looks. After fifteen minutes, the Badger went outside to check.

Carpenter spoke for all of them. "Great goddamn system," he said.

A skinny older man in a fedora approached the Americans. His English was heavily accented, but understandable. "Hello, American athletes," he said. "I am sorry I am late. Told incorrect time."

Wood leaned toward Glenn and muttered, "That surprise you?"

The Czech escorted them outside, where the Badger still was scanning the street. Spotting them, the Badger rushed over. A rushed exchange established that the hotel was close enough to walk to, so there was no bus or need to take taxis.

Close enough to walk turned out to be about five blocks, easy under normal circumstances, but not when hauling suitcases and bags of uniforms and equipment.

"Great goddamn system," Carpenter repeated.

The solemn closing ceremonies, with Hitler present but not speaking, made Leni misty-eyed. Rather than scrambling around, she spent most of the ceremony watching and reflecting. The flame was extinguished, the Olympic flag taken down, a hymn—"The Games Are Ended"—sung. The stadium, overflowing because authorities had let it be known that tickets weren't going to be checked in order to guarantee a full house, became a choir loft, with most in the audience singing, or at least joining in the linked arms and rocking in time to the music. Leni decided, though, it would make better film—and be better, period—if at future Games, teams were encouraged to keep their athletes at the site through the entire fortnight and make marching in the closing ceremonies as important as in the opening ceremonies. Under those standards, Glenn would have been there.

In Prague, Glenn and the boys had a nice dinner at a small restaurant near the hotel, scraping together just enough of the local currency—obtained in exchanges at the hotel—to cover the bill. "Where's the Badger when you need him?" Glenn mused.

Carpenter laughed at that. "Wouldn't have mattered. He would have figured out what he owed. Right down to the penny, or whatever the hell this stuff is."

Schofield brought up a good point: They hadn't even been told what time the meet started the next day and what events they would be in for sure. Or whether anyone else was coming. "Anybody else starting to get a bad feeling about this?" he asked.

"I've always had a bad feeling about this," Carpenter said.

The next morning, the Badger announced to them in the lobby that the Vienna meet the next day was canceled, and they would be heading over to the city of Pardubice instead for an exhibition Tuesday. "That's only eighty miles or so, so we'll stay based here," he said. "Then you'll go on from here— to Paris or Stockholm."

"What happened with Vienna?" Carpenter asked.

"They decided they couldn't meet our guar . . . well, they decided to cancel," the Badger said. "We had some idea this might be coming. That's why we brought only you four yesterday. These two days will be just a few events, strictly exhibitions against the Czech boys they've rounded up."

Carpenter shook his head. "Great goddamn system."

On Monday afternoon in Prague, the stands were barely half-filled, but the crowd was enthusiastic. The Americans competed in only four events, and the Czechs didn't seem bothered. It helped that Carpenter had a terrific toss in the discus, a shade over 174 feet, 1 inch, or better than he had done in winning at Berlin. In fact, was less than an inch short of German Willie Schroeder's world record. "If I'd know that," he said with a touch of seriousness, "I would have put a little more oomph in it!"

Walter Wood was second, at 161-11, at least out-throwing the Czechs in the field.

Schofield won the 100 meters, in 10.7 seconds. "These poor people," he said. "They probably thought I was the guy who finished second to Jesse or something."

Glenn was more comfortable in the 110-meter high hurdles than he thought he would be. His winning time of 14.8 seconds was better than what he ran in Berlin. The Czech organizers begged the Badger to have Glenn take a few jumps in the high jump, too, and he cleared the equivalent of 5-10 7/8—nothing flashy—and finished second to a Czech.

On Tuesday, the Americans traveled to Pardubice and back in cars. In the exhibition meet against the token competition provided by local Czechs, Schofield won both the 100 and 200 meters, Glenn won the hurdles and Carpenter and Wood were one-two in the discus.

In Berlin, the wrap-up dinner that night saluted the German athletes and the German Organizing Committee officials. Leni was assigned to sit next to Hitler. On the other side of him was javelin gold medalist Tilly Fleischer. The others near them included Göring and a visibly jealous Goebbels; organizing committee leaders Carl Diem and Theodor Lewald; and other German track and field gold medalists, including javelin thrower Gerhard Stöck, hammer thrower Karl Hein, shot-putter Hans Woellke, and discus thrower Gisela Mauermayer.

Hitler was engaging with Fleischer and the nearby Mauermayer, who both looked as if they could have come off posters for the Aryan ideal. Tilly especially was amazingly relaxed and unintimidated. Hitler talked with Leni off and on through dinner, saying he knew her film inevitably would bring even more glory to the Fatherland, immortalizing the spirit with which the Germans embraced the Games.

Eventually, he asked out of the blue: "And what of your American friend?"

Leni knew it would be ridiculous and even counterproductive to play coy, so she said, "He is headed to Sweden and Finland."

"And then . . . ?"

"Then home."

"Am I not correct that he is an important part of your film . . . and more?"

"Yes," Leni said.

"Could he be a friend of Germany?"

"In what way?"

"As someone who either lives here or visits you and appears not in just this film, but perhaps others. Someone who serves to emphasize the common elements in our nations."

She was flabbergasted. It was as if he had read her mind. "Well," Leni said slowly, "I have thought of proposing that."

"Do it! He also can be paid handsomely from the treasury for his labors and commitment. It could come from the Reich Film Board or from a company, if that would make him more amenable. You have my backing. I will communicate that to Minister Goebbels."

With that, he turned to Tilly Fleischer, who had been listening to all of this—and pretending she wasn't. As the dinner broke up, Fleischer smiled at Leni. "Ohhh, the American is handsome!" she said. "Good luck with that!"

Back in the comfort of her apartment, and alone, Leni thought it through, and by the time she was ready for bed, she had a plan.

31

~

Glenn, Meet Eva

Wednesday, August 19–Sunday, August 23

Glenn and Ken Carpenter headed for the Prague airport early, but the weather turned terrible, with thunderstorms. The delay meant they had a lot of time to kill. Finally, Carpenter said what was on his mind. "You notice I haven't asked you about *her* yet," he said.

Glenn winced.

"Hey, don't get the wrong idea," Carpenter said. "Wood wouldn't tell anyone a damn thing. Not that we didn't try. He also made me promise that I wouldn't press you about anything. Said it was a sore subject and I should mind my own business. Sorry . . . I *tried* to mind my own business."

"Don't worry," Glenn said. "It doesn't matter anymore."

"So you're going to tell me all about it?"

"That's not what I said," Glenn said. "I said it doesn't matter."

After finally making it to Stockholm, Glenn and Carpenter rushed to the stadium, but the events at the first day of the three-day meet were over. A handful of Americans remained in the dressing room. "Well, look who decided to grace us with their presence!" Earle Meadows teased.

"Did the fans miss us?" Carpenter asked.

"Don't worry about it," deadpanned sprinter Foy Draper. "I signed all the autographs 'Glenn Morris.'"

"And I signed 'Ken Carpenter,'" chimed in shot-putter Sam Francis. "They all went away happy!"

⌒

On the track on Thursday, Glenn was taken aback when young Swedish boys and girls jammed down near the front rail of the bleachers and over the tunnel leading out from the dressing room, calling for his autograph. At first, he thought it was simply a case of just screaming at the Americans, but then he picked up the repeated calls of, "Morris! Morris!"

Glenn Cunningham came over. "See why they were upset when you weren't here yesterday?" he asked with a grin. Then he turned sheepish. "I don't know how I got roped into this," he said, "except somebody had to do it . . . and it's better than having some Badger telling us what to do." He explained that Jesse Owens's coach, Larry Snyder, had been ticketed to serve as the supervising coach on this trip, but Jesse's withdrawal and his coach's trip home with him fouled up those plans. "I've got you down for the high hurdles and, just to get you in a field event, the broad jump today," Cunningham explained. He smiled and nodded in the direction of the nearby Dave Albritton, the high jump silver medalist. "Actually, our two broad jumpers will be you and Albritton. He said he'd give it a try, too."

"Just hope neither of us hurts himself," Glenn said dryly.

"Tomorrow, how about if you try the 400 and the discus?"

Glenn laughed. "I guess so, that's as good as anything," he said.

He felt awful and sluggish as he warmed up, and he teasingly begged Towns not to completely embarrass him in the hurdles. When the gun sounded, though, he was surprised how suddenly the juices flowed again. He finished fourth, behind Towns, a Swede, and a Canadian, but again, he was impressed with his own time—14.7 seconds, or 0.2 of a second faster than his showing in Berlin and 0.1 of a second better than in Prague.

He watched as Cunningham ran away from the field in the 800 meters, and the crowd's reaction was tumultuous when the announcement came that the American veteran had just set a world record—1:49.7, breaking John Woodruff's record by 0.1 of a second. In fact, it was over 3 seconds better than Woodruff's winning time at Berlin in the wild, strategic race. Hearing the time, Glenn and his teammates mobbed Cunningham.

In the broad jump, Glenn wasn't paying attention as he left the pit after his second jump, stepped on the board holding in the sand and twisted his ankle. He didn't fall, and the pain was only a minor flash, but it was significant enough to leave him with a slight limp. He told Albritton and an official that he would pass on his third jump. The Badger who had been in Prague, apparently still feeling as if he was Glenn's monitor, followed him into the dressing room. "Can't you do that after your last jump?" the Badger inquired as Glenn asked a Swedish trainer for ice.

Foy Draper, who was changing after winning the 200 meters and showering, heard that. "Man, do you guys ever quit?" Draper challenged. "It doesn't do anyone good to have Morris limp down the runway and jump twelve feet. Come on, they came to see him . . . and they did."

The next morning, his ankle was sore as he joined Glenn Cunningham and Ken Carpenter for breakfast. He vacillated about whether to compete, especially since he had missed the first day in Stockholm, but Cunningham assured him that he—as acting coach—would say he insisted that Glenn sit out the day's activities. After all, his scheduled appearance in the 400 would come against Olympic-caliber Scandinavian runners, and limping through it wouldn't do anyone—including the fans—any good. Cunningham asked only that Glenn suit up in his uniform, smile through an introduction to the crowd and sign autographs and socialize with the fans. The goal would be for him to be at full-strength for the upcoming stops. From Stockholm, Cunningham and three others were heading for a meet at Paris, and four other Americans were joining Glenn for the meet at Karlstad in the western part of Sweden. Then it would be on to Finland and Norway.

"Deal," Glenn said.

"Can I get the same deal?" Ken Carpenter asked mischievously.

A bellman called: "Mister Morris! Mister Glenn Morris!"

Glenn raised his hand. "Here!"

"Mister Morris, we have a radio call for you," the bellman said.

Glenn looked at the other two Americans, shrugging.

A minute later, Glenn wasn't surprised to hear Leni's voice. "Hello, Glenn," she said.

"Hello, Leni."

"I've missed you."

"Leni . . ."

"I got your letter—a day late," she said. "Most of it was nice. I don't agree with all of it, however."

"I know."

"I wish you had come and found me and told me all that," she said.

"It would have made it harder. I thought you'd see it before I left, anyway."

He waited.

"I need you to come back to Berlin," she said.

"We went through that."

"No, I need you to come back for more filming. Our plane will be there tomorrow to pick you up and bring you back here."

She explained that the previous evening, while again going through the footage of the final event, the 1,500 meters, at the Geyer Film Lab, she confirmed how inadequate it was because of the lack of lighting and intimacy. "I want the type of extra film we got after the pole vault. It will help me, and it will help you, if we can get that kind of footage of you. Erwin Huber has agreed to be a part of this, too, and he said we should be able to find the Czech boy who competed with you."

"Leni, what are you talking about? I've got all these meets coming up . . . then home. I can't just quit, pull out of the meets, and come there."

He didn't mention his ankle injury.

"You can," Leni insisted. "Your American Olympic people already have approved this. They know the more you're in the film, the better it is for them. It's better than a few Swedes and Finns and Norwegians seeing you in the discus or something on that silly tour."

Glenn could see the Badger nearby, waiting. He was reading another telegram.

"Leni, hold on a second," he said. "I'll be right back . . . I promise."

Noticing Glenn's approach, the Badger held up the telegram. "Looks like you're heading back to Berlin tomorrow! Your air passage is all set, says right here. Be at the airport at . . ."

"What about the rest of the tour?" Glenn asked sharply.

"You're injured!" the Badger said, grinning. "Now, be at the airport at . . ."

Glenn already was on his way back to the phone. There, he said to Leni, "You didn't even ask me? You at least could have done that first."

"I needed to move fast . . . and make sure it was possible."

He had made the break and faced the realities of Life after the Olympics, Life away from dreamland. This would make it so complicated again. Hell, there probably were complications he hadn't even thought about! For an instant, he told himself he would be able to resist temptation with Leni, but then he knew that was both unrealistic and impossible—if she still wanted him. And she *was* Leni.

"Glenn?"

"I'm here."

"If it has to be business, it will be just business. One of your Americans already lectured Ernst Jäger about what we had to do to make sure you remain an amateur for the next Olympics. Just expenses, nothing more, we are told. And then you go home on the ship."

"From where? I was down to leave from Southampton."

"That still can work," she said. "The plane can fly you there. Or I suppose you could go over to Hamburg and catch it there . . . if we're done."

She didn't tell Glenn that to get him out of rest of the tour, she had agreed to pay the American Olympic Committee an astounding five thousand dollars, plus compensate with smaller checks the organizers of the meets in Karlstad, Helsingfors, and Oslo.

On the rocky plane ride, Glenn again tried to think it through. By returning, he knew he was jumping right back into involvement with Leni. He wasn't fooling himself into thinking he could reject her and turn this into all business. Unless she was determined to be coldly professional, the relationship was resuming for at least a few more days. If she could live with that, he could. But then he would be gone.

Leni and Ernst Jäger met him at the airport Saturday, and her initial hug was between circumspect and affectionate. But when her publicity man went with the driver to stow his bags—one suitcase and one athletic bag—in the limousine, she abandoned all reserve and the kiss answered the question of whether she expected this visit to be coldly professional. As they pulled up to the Hotel Adlon, Glenn laughed. He explained to Leni that he knew this must be a great hotel because it's where all the American Olympic officials had stayed. "They only go first class," he said.

"You settle in," she said. "Kurt will pick you up and bring you to the restaurant. We'll go over the schedule then."

A bellman rushed to take Glenn's bags. Jäger got out of the car and gave him a key. The driver also stepped out and stretched his arms. Leni leaned over. "I'm glad you came," she said. Before Glenn could react, she added, "Now go. We have plenty of time . . . to talk."

At the small, but elegant restaurant several miles from Central Berlin, Glenn was relieved when Leni told him she wouldn't press about the future. "I am not promising I'll never bring it up," she said. "I will. Sometime. But I'm happy we're not leaving it as it was after our last meeting. If we have to say good-bye, we will say good-bye. But at least it would be face-to-face this time."

"Leni, no matter what happens here, I don't think anything can change
. . ."

"Stop! Let's not ruin now."

"Let me ask you," Glenn said slowly. "Do you *really* need to do more film-ing? You'd seen the film of the 1,500 before hadn't you?"

"Yes, I had," she said. "The more I looked at it and thought about it, the more convinced I was that it wasn't good enough. I could have gotten by without replacing it, but this *will* be much better." She smiled at him. "Don't get a big head, but if it hadn't been you, I wouldn't have thought this neces-sary. I admit that. You are going to be a star, Glenn. You are a handsome American, and if the filmmaker of this was a fat man named Heinrich, rather than me, he would say the same thing, because it will help the film."

Leni said they would have at least two sessions with the cameramen—one the next afternoon, Sunday, with just Glenn as the subject in the daylight at the stadium; and then one at night, with Huber and the other athletes, re-creating the climactic 1,500-meter heat. "We are hoping for Tuesday night, but that's not certain," she said. "We need to make sure we're set on our crew and track officials, too. We'll set up the same lights we had for the pole vault and it will be wonderful footage."

"What are we doing in the daylight tomorrow?" Glenn asked.

"Close-ups of you looking very masculine as you get ready to do various events or maybe relaxing on the infield grass," Leni said with a smile. "That shouldn't be difficult for you."

"I'll do my best."

"And after that, re-create you receiving your medal, the wreath, and the oak," she said. "We have people set up to do those honors."

"So I'd change into my blazer and tie and all that—like the real cer-emony?"

"I think it would be better in your competition uniform. That's the way it was for most of the presentations. But if we decide to, we can do both. We now have enough time to try several things."

Glenn chuckled. Leni slapped his hand. "I mean in the filming, young man," she said.

After spending the night with Leni at her apartment, Glenn didn't make it back to the Adlon until late Sunday morning, and that was to pick up his bag with his uniform, sweat suit, and shoes on the way to the stadium. There, when Glenn emerged from the dressing-room tunnel in his white

USA uniform, with his Number 801 still pinned to the front and back, he was impressed to notice that Leni's attention to detail was so complete, she had arranged for stadium workers to relight the Olympic-flame cauldron. Yet after the excitement of the competition and the huge crowds in the stadium only two weeks earlier, it seemed eerily quiet. Leni, wearing billowing gray slacks and a blouse with a sweater over it, teased him, "Here we have the hitherto unknown American and the favorite in this event, Glenn Morris from Colorado." Glenn couldn't resist smiling, in part because it was the first time he'd ever heard anyone *say* "hitherto."

She directed him to the shot put ring, where two movie cameramen, Albert Kling and Werner Hundhausen, and still photographer Rolf Lantin waited. He went through the motions of several throws, and then took a break with his hands on his knees as Leni stood over the heavy steel ball on the ground. "Appears easy to me," she said brightly and, with great effort and mock grunting, picked it up, cradled it in both hands and handed it to Glenn.

While he continued throwing, Glenn thought back to her crew shooting at the pre-Olympics practice at the Village track, and it seemed to him that this was a bit of a repeat. As if she was reading his mind, Leni said, "Glenn, just keep in mind that no matter what, we can't have too *much* film of anything."

For the next two hours, they shot footage and pictures of Glenn in various spots around the track. About halfway through, a blonde woman wearing the outfit of the medal-ceremony wreath presenters emerged from the dignitaries' area of the stands at mid-track, but what struck Glenn more than the appearance of the woman herself was that two SS men and one plainclothesman were with her. There was something familiar about her, but he couldn't place her. Finally, they moved to the medal-stand area and the woman and her entourage joined them. Leni explained to Glenn that she realized they couldn't re-create the entire ceremony without the other two medalists and the Olympic officials presenting the medals, so all she had in mind was Glenn being draped with the oak-leaf wreath and then pretending to be looking at the American flag as the anthem played.

Leni led Glenn by the hand to the woman. She was more handsome than beautiful, but a nice-looking woman with noticeable makeup applied, perhaps in her late twenties. In German, Leni introduced him, and then said, "And Glenn . . . this is Eva."

Eva smiled, shyly. "Hello, Glenn Morris," she said. That seemed to be the extent of her English.

Leni said, "Now that you two have met, let's get on to the ceremony. Glenn, top step, lean down, and Eva places the wreath on your head. You smile and say thank you, then turn to look at the flagpoles."

She repeated what seemed to be similar instructions to Eva in German. Eva giggled and asked something in the same language. Smiling, Leni clearly told her no. They went through the presentation three times for the still photographer and a couple of times for the two film cameramen. Glenn noticed that every time, the shooting came from behind Eva, and he realized they weren't getting anything of her face.

Leni announced in both German and English that the next take would be it. This time, as Eva placed the wreath on his head, she delivered a quick kiss to his forehead. Glenn and others laughed. Leni didn't.

With Eva and her escort watching, Leni then coached Glenn through the pretend anthem playing as he looked at the flagpoles at the end of the stadium. "You have just won the gold medal, you have accepted it and the wreath, and now you hear your anthem!" she said.

Even without the music, without the flag, and without the crowd, Glenn had no problem remembering and re-creating the moment. He was wearing his uniform, not the blazer and necktie this time, and despite that and the other differences, he was amazed at the feeling.

When Leni pronounced the filming ended, Eva took an Olympic program from one of the SS men and extended it to Glenn. She spoke German, but he got the message: She wanted an autograph. Glenn signed his name, then thought to add, "To Eva," above the signature. She thanked him and left with her escorts, heading toward what Glenn assumed was a tunnel exit from the dignitaries' section.

As they walked toward the dressing-room tunnel, Glenn asked Leni, "So who's Eva? She seems familiar."

Leni didn't answer. Then the light went off in Glenn's head.

"That night! At the Geyer Lab! She was the woman who came in late. Behind . . ."

"That's right," Leni said.

"But what . . ."

"That's all I'm going to say!"

In the dark later, in bed, he tried to raise it again.

"Let me guess about Eva," he began.

He felt Leni tense up. "I don't know the whole story, either," she said. "So stop it! I mean it."

She came up with something—again—to take his mind off Eva.

32

~

Leni and Glenn

Monday, August 24–Thursday, August 27

Leni sheepishly admitted to Glenn that lining up enough German track and field officials and making all the arrangements for the night filming was taking longer than she expected—and hoped. But Erwin Huber indeed had found Josef Klein, who ran with them in so many of the decathlon heats, including in the 1,500 meters, and Klein would arrive in Berlin that afternoon. They weren't having luck locating the other two runners from the heat, Maurice Boulanger of Belgium and Lyuben Doychev of Bulgaria, and Leni said, if necessary, they would recruit other athletes to fill the field. She told Glenn that Huber and Klein were meeting them for dinner that night at another of Germany's finest restaurants, Ludtke's, and they all would talk about what they would be trying to do in the filming.

Glenn knew he should have been flattered if Leni was deliberately drawing out the shooting, but he again reminded her he *had* to be on the SS *Manhattan* before it left Europe, catching it at Hamburg, Havre, or Southampton.

"We'll have you on that boat somewhere," Leni promised.

Glenn realized he was enjoying his stay, had come around to completely rationalizing it, and for more than the energetic lovemaking. He was looking forward to returning to the States and Colorado, reveling in the glory of his gold-medal victory, and seeing what opportunities might be out there. Yes, he still assumed Karen would be part of it . . . eventually. But this was an exhilarating interim, and Leni seemed to have accepted that.

In the afternoon, they watched her first film, the silent *The Holy Mountain*. Her face filled the screen in the opening, and then she, as Diotima, danced on the jagged rocks by the sea.

"When was this?" Glenn asked.

"Ten years ago," she said. She laughed. "I was very young."

"You're prettier now," he said. Indeed, she seemed a girl on the screen; now she was a woman. He was tempted to ask if she'd had work done on her teeth, but he knew that would be ungentlemanly. She didn't bother to translate the title cards, except when she was shown on cross-country skis, bidding farewell to her beau, about to race. "It says, 'Come back a winner, and I'll grant you a wish,'" she said.

"That sounds familiar," Glenn said dryly.

He was impressed that she looked to be an excellent skier. "No faking it there, is there?" he asked.

"That's all me!" she said.

Suddenly, he recalled the *Time* cover, with her on skis and wearing a bathing suit. *No, no faking it.*

At the end of the film, when the awaiting Diotima got word of her beau's death on the mountain after his selfless act of sacrifice in remaining with a fallen climber, tears dripped down her cheek. Diotima walked out the door of the mountain cabin, and the tale—with brief flashes of shots of the mountains and sea—ended.

"That was my first break," Leni said. "It got me around Doctor Fanck. I was just learning how to act, but to see the film being made, all the challenges, all the opportunities, that was what attracted me."

They took a walk, holding hands, through the Tiergarten, then headed to dinner at Ludtke's, where Huber and Klein were waiting. They had a corner table, but Glenn at first still wondered if they were being reckless, especially when Leni let it slip that American journalists dined here. None seemed to be present, and then Glenn also realized even the American Olympic Committee folks knew and approved of what he was doing, so on most levels, there was nothing to hide. Officially, he was here, with a German and a Czech, and perhaps more, to do supplemental filming.

Glenn was reminded what a gentleman Huber was. The German had rallied on the second day to finish fourth and didn't seem at all envious of Glenn's gold. Glenn decided one reason was that after Hans Sievert's injury, not even his own countrymen expected much out of Huber, who at twenty-nine was considered to have seen his best days in the event. Klein still was a short, stocky teenager who spoke only Czech, but his smile was infectious.

Over dinner, Leni explained in both German and English, and pantomiming to Klein, that she wanted to re-create the actual race under her bright lights in the dark, but wouldn't make them run the entire distance. "We'll get the start, the jostling during the race for position, and Glenn coming down the stretch and finishing as the Olympic champion," she said. "And then we have you two congratulating him and we see the beauty of sportsmanship all around."

⟿

Leni finally broke the news that the filming indeed would have to be delayed until Wednesday night. "For many reasons," she said. "All logistics. It was easier when everyone was here for the Games."

In the apartment, they watched Leni in *Die weisse Hölle vom Piz Palü*, or the *White Hell of Pitz Palü*, when Maria/Leni and her husband were rescued from certain death when stranded on a mountain ledge. An aviator spotted them and summoned rescuers. Leni explained that the pilot, Ernst Udet, a Great War ace, played himself. Her running commentary during the film was minimal, mostly about the ghastly—but realistic—conditions of the filming. After the film ended, she stood and turned off the projector. Standing over Glenn, she asked, "Now, after the last two days, do you see why I wanted to control my own destiny in the dramas? That led me to *Blue Light*. And do you see why I want to go back to that?"

"You never told me how *Blue Light* happened."

"I wrote the story out, perhaps five pages of narrative. Together, we formulated a script from that, improvising, though, as we went. I was proud of the way it turned out."

"You should be. I loved what I saw of that." He smiled. "The parts I saw."

Leni went to her second bedroom, which she had made her office. She came out with several sheets of paper. "You have to promise me you won't react right away . . . that you will think about this," she said.

Oh, oh.

She handed him the sheets. The first thing he noticed was the writing was in German. The second thing he noticed was the title at the top.

Leni und Glenn: Die Schauspielerin und der Athlet.

"*Leni and Glenn: The Actress and the Athlete,*" she explained. "It is a feature film linked to *Olympia*. *Olympia* is a documentary; this is a story. German filmmaker and actress—me—meets and falls in love with an American Olympic athlete—you. I play me. You play you. It's our story." She looked in his eyes. "It will be as big in Chicago and Los Angeles and New York as it is in Berlin and Munich."

Glenn pondered the implications. "I assume we'd be telling everything?"

"At least hinting of it, yes," she said. "Lots of hand holding and kissing. But remember, it is a script, a story. We can make it say anything we want." Leni paused. "I would perhaps use less of the decathlon in *Olympia* than I envisioned, and we can use a lot of that footage of you in *Leni and Glenn.* So we already have a head start!"

"Interesting," Glenn conceded.

"There's one other thing you are not thinking about," she said. "You want to take advantage of your fame, don't you?"

"Well, yeah, but that would be with a good job. And maybe some endorsements."

"I can assure you what you could make from acting, in this film, and then maybe others, would be better than any job in Colorado," she said. "However the movie is financed and structured, I am sure the other producers would go along with providing a very handsome salary for you, and that's just to start with."

She named a reichsmark figure that meant nothing to Glenn. Her eyes rolled to the ceiling as she calculated, and she came back: "Perhaps fifty thousand dollars."

Glenn couldn't help it. "Wow!" he exclaimed.

That was more than Jesse Owens was being offered for his vaudeville work.

"Acting and film know no boundaries," Leni said. "It would open other doors, but you would be even more famous after this is made. We would get American partners, as with *S.O.S. Iceberg,* and either make English and German versions or make one film with separate soundtracks, whatever we have to do."

Despite it all, he couldn't resist a dark laugh. "How's it going to end?"

"We'll just have to see, won't we?"

Glenn got up and paced. "I'm going to have to think about this," he said slowly.

"You should do more than that," she said. "You should do it."

"You're also assuming I can act."

"You don't have to, not in this one. Just play yourself!"

"And no matter what, I have to be on that boat back to America. I have to go home to see everyone I need to thank, whether I've decided or not."

And I'd have to tell Karen.

"All right," she said. She took back the sheets. "And that is all we are going to say about it until after the filming."

Much to Glenn's shock, she stuck to that.

～

The next morning, Wednesday, Glenn went with Leni to the Geyer Film Lab and watched her work at the editing machine, looking through the raw footage of field hockey; the championship basketball game between the Americans and Canadians, played outdoors and on a muddy court; plus fencing and swimming. He was fascinated with the process, including Leni's patience. He wondered: *Could she really do this for a year, getting a film ready?*

That night at the stadium, all was finally ready, with many of the German meet officials on hand, the lights set up at several vantage points, and the atmosphere eerie. They hadn't found the other two competitors in the heat, but another German athlete lined up with them for the start of the 1,500 meters, far enough outside so the camera wouldn't show his uniform. Leni directed Glenn to start from the inside lane, dismissing his mild argument that he had broken from lane two in the real race. She noted it would be much easier to focus on him with nobody between him and the camera. Glenn dug the holes for his feet and broke from a sprinter's position, as he had in the real race. At first, he worried that his ankle wouldn't hold up to it, but he found that it was fine. Leni filmed several takes of the start, but they only took a couple of strides. Then Leni's strategy became clear as she had them run around the track. She used Huber and Klein to re-create the dramatic moments in the race, showing Glenn passing Klein and then holding off Huber when the German challenged him. *Close enough*, Glenn thought. And then, with the lights shining on the finish line, he crossed it in a blaze of glory. They also filmed an official placing a blanket around his shoulders, and then Huber and Klein separately shaking his hand. Finally, she had him don the oak-leaf wreath again and look off in the distance, as if he were peering at the U.S. flag again, explaining that she might want a shot that appeared to be in the dark after the race. But when Glenn again pointed out that the medal-ceremony had taken place the next day in the daylight, when he was wearing his blazer and tie, Leni repeated they she just wanted to have as many options as possible. "But in every one of them, you still win!" she said.

They finished after midnight. As they packed up, Glenn called over the still photographer and had him take a picture of him with Huber and Klein, arms around shoulders and smiling.

When Glenn was in the dressing room, Huber approached Leni, close enough so nobody else could hear him. "You're not fooling yourself with Morris, are you?"

"I don't believe so, Erwin." After a few seconds, she added, "But what do you mean?"

"When—or if—if he goes home, he's not coming back. You know that, don't you? I know he can't hurt you, I'm just saying you are treating this as a farewell, too, aren't you?"

Leni pondered how much to confide. "I'm offering him a life far better than what he would have in America. He will realize that. He would have a job in industry, a meek wife, four children, and an unexciting life. If he continues to compete, it will be as an amateur—a pauper. If he doesn't compete, he might be paid to be in advertisements, but that won't last, and there will be occasional banquets where he is saluted for what he once did. And soon his countrymen will forget even that."

Huber said, "You've got this all figured out, don't you?" His grin lightened the mood. "If you two have children, will you at least name the first-born son Erwin Morris?"

Over breakfast, Leni reached out and put her hands on Glenn's.
"Stay."

He shook his head. "Leni, I'm not a dog."

This time, she pleaded. "Please stay. With me."

"I can't!"

"You say that like you couldn't ever go back to America. I'm asking you to stay here. Now. With me. You said you'd think about it. And us."

"I *am* thinking about us! I said I'd think about coming back. So tell me how that would work."

She laid it out. The first thing he would do after returning would be to participate in the additional filming for *Olympia*'s prologue, playing Myron's sculpture of the Discus Thrower come to life. "What do I wear, my American uniform?" he asked.

"No," Leni said, "you wear a loincloth."

"And?"

"That's it. A loincloth. You are an ancient Greek, after all!"

"Wow," Glenn said, wondering if he was blushing.

Leni said she would depart from her usual procedure and enlist aid in editing and putting together *Olympia*, so she could work on a script for *Leni and Glenn* and move forward on that film. Her goal would be to have *Olympia* out first, whetting the appetite for the love story, and then to premiere *Leni and Glenn* soon after, perhaps in early 1938.

As she talked it through, she congratulated herself on her ingeniousness. Instead of following through on the plan she hadn't told many about—a two-part *Olympia*, perhaps four hours long—she would pare down the documentary and essentially make *Leni and Glenn* the second part. That is, if Glenn went along. The more she thought about it, the more she liked the idea of perhaps becoming the highest-profile multinational married couple in the world. Together, they would be far greater than alone—or than they would be with anyone else.

"If you stay now, Glenn, it will be so much easier," she said.

"Now you're just thinking like a director," he countered.

"Stop it! It's part of what I am, but this is what I would be saying if there were no films," she said. "I would be saying . . . please stay. We could be husband and wife and lovers and partners and . . ."

"Wow," Glenn said.

"I'm not saying we get married tomorrow. Sometime. But for now . . . stay."

"I can't."

He got out of his chair and looked out the window.

Unless something comes up you haven't heard about yet, there might be some one-time endorsements and then you're going to have a nice job in Denver. Hmmm. Work in Denver, probably marry Karen; or be a movie star, on both sides of the Atlantic, and be with . . . maybe even marry . . . a famous and exciting woman. God knows what's going to happen in Germany, but if Leni is right? It could work, and you wouldn't have to be a Bad American to do it!

He turned. "Leni, I have to go home first," he said. "I have to see my family. I have to see Karen. No matter what I tell her, I still have to see her. I have to say thanks to the people who helped get me here in the first place. If I don't, it probably closes every door in America . . . and for you, too, in a way, right?"

Leni was sobbing. He joined her on the couch.

She rode with him to the airport. They held hands on the way. When they arrived, Leni's face looked as it did in the climactic moments of *The Holy Mountain*, tears running down her cheeks. Her driver circumspectly got out of the car and, with some help, carried Glenn's bags inside as Glenn and Leni embraced and kissed.

"Are you coming in? Glenn finally asked.

"I don't think I can," she said. "I'd fall apart. This is best."

She paused and said, "I love you."

"I love you, too."

"This won't be farewell," she declared. "You will be back. Think of the life we will have together."

"I'm thinking about it," he said.

They embraced again. Finally, Glenn pulled away, looked her in the eyes one more time and, suddenly, slid out of the car. But he leaned back in and smiled.

"Thanks for everything," he said.

"Tell me you will be back."

"I will be back."

And then he was gone.

33

~

Triumph of the Will

As Glenn waited at the Southampton dock, he was surprised to see Foy Draper, Bill Graber, Ken Carpenter, Gordon Dunn, and Forrest Towns arrive, too. Then he realized they competed in Oslo the day before.

"Hey, you guys look a little blue at the gills," Glenn teased.

"I'm not even sure where that place was we stopped," Carpenter said. "But getting here was worse than that flight from Prague to Stockholm."

As Glenn expected, Carpenter got him off to the side, to talk. "Nobody believes that stuff about extra filming because it was dark," the discus thrower said. "Graber said she did that with them, but right away."

"Well, it's true," Glenn said sharply. "One day in the light, one day at night. Me and Erwin Huber and the Czech kid."

"Okay, okay, don't get mad," Carpenter said. "I'm just telling you . . . you're going to have guys asking you, or looking like they want to ask."

When the SS *Manhattan* pulled up, Walter Wood was waving from the rail. The reunion was warm, with back slaps, and Walter led them to their room. Along with the oak-tree seedling, Glenn had a thick stack of telegrams, mail, and notices waiting for him on one of the little dressers. He opened his suitcase and, in it, found a surprise—a thick folder of pictures. A quick look confirmed it was filled with prints of still photos Leni's photographers took both during the Games and the "extra" sessions after his return to Berlin. She'd had them slipped into the suitcase as his going-away present. Walter noticed. "Let me guess who gave you those," he said. Glenn didn't say anything as he put the folder back in the suitcase.

"So what happened?" Walter asked. "Anything you need—want—to tell me?"

"I'm not ready . . . yet."

A couple of the telegrams were from Karen. One said:

I ACCEPT YOUR PROPOSAL!!!

LOVE, KAREN

As he sifted through, he found that her parents, his parents, Karen herself, Harry Hughes, and his own brother and sisters all considered him headed for the altar virtually the instant he arrived back in Colorado. Between the lines, though, Karen also seemed to be hurt that he wasn't writing more often. He was perplexed and had a churning in his stomach, but he finally opened a letter from George Whitman dated August 15. Inside were two clippings from the *Rocky Mountain News*, and Glenn scanned them first, increasingly flabbergasted as he continued.

That's not what I said! He put words in my mouth! I've never said "swellest" in my life!

He handed the clippings to Walter. "Well," the Cornell man said after reading them, "this makes things more interesting."

Briefly, Glenn was angry with Karen for her presumptuousness, but then he realized the position she had been put in. As his own experience with the Joe Williams story reemphasized, too, Glenn couldn't even assume that Karen had said exactly what was attributed to her in the paper.

Before he fell asleep, he again went through it all in his mind. The one thing he knew: He couldn't just go home, nod about all this wedding talk, set a date and then write to Leni and ask: "Okay, when do we start filming?"

If it was going to be with Leni, he had to be all in. He knew she wouldn't stand for anything else.

The voyage home was uneventful and he accepted the barbs and even leers without responding, and he opened up to Walter with the barest of outlines about his return trip to Berlin. Otherwise, his strategy came to be telling his official story once—he had gone back to Berlin for supplemental filming with other decathlon men and nothing more—and then not respond again. Jack Torrance, whose sense of humor hadn't been dulled by his disappointing showing in Berlin, announced that as a duly sworn officer of the law in Louisiana, he would arrest the next man for harassment who tried to press Glenn for details.

Of course, the first time Torrance was alone with Glenn, he said, "You can tell *me*, you know." Glenn's pained look caused Torrance to guffaw. "That's all I need to know," he said.

A day out from New York, as Glenn walked around the deck, he came to his decision: It would be Leni. It would be daring, but . . . *You only live once.* Now the trick would be to figure out how to tell everyone, including Karen.

As catharsis, he wrote a letter to his older brother Jack, knowing he wouldn't be able to mail it until they landed. The brothers weren't close, but it was more drifting apart than estrangement, so Glenn felt as if he could confide in Jack—at least face to face. In the letter, he talked about the trip to Czechoslovakia and Sweden, and of the grand way his teammates were treating him on the return trip. He left it that he also had "many, many experiences" he would tell Jack about when the brothers got together. He also gently informed Jack that a newspaper guy had gotten carried away, and that his marriage wasn't imminent.

As the SS *Manhattan* moved to the pier in New York on September 3, as a band played aboard one of the waiting ships, as thousands waited and cheered, Glenn realized he hadn't walked on American soil in seven weeks, and he again marveled at how much his life had changed since. When reporters accosted him on the dock, he said the Olympic experience was wonderful; no, he likely wouldn't return to his job as a car salesman; but, no, he didn't know what the future held. The Badgers assured the Olympians planning to stay at least overnight in New York that their baggage—plus the winners' oak-tree seedlings—would be sent along to the hotel. The AOC would pay for one more night; after that, the athletes were on their own.

At the Battery, they met many of their teammates who had returned on the SS *President Roosevelt* a week earlier. One was Jesse Owens, and Glenn rushed over and got in a quick hello. Jesse said about half of the trackmen from the earlier return had hung around New York, or lived close enough to return, for the parade.

"We had to wait for you big lugs!" Jesse joked.

The parade caravan went up Broadway, into Harlem, and eventually to Randall's Island. Glenn was stunned by the reaction as he sat on top of a back seat in an open car with Dale Schofield and waved. New Yorkers lined the street and leaned out of windows, waving and cheering, dropping and throwing ticker tape and other bits of paper. At the Randall's Island stadium, Glenn was the first to meet Mayor Fiorello LaGuardia, who presented him with one of the commemorative New York medals he handed to the entire team as perhaps 2,000 gathered in the stands. Glenn was a bit taken aback, and he was surprised by the grumbling, when the athletes figured out that the New York medals weren't the same for all—silver medals went to all Olympic medal winners, bronze medals to those who didn't place.

Walter Wood was headed home for New Jersey, so the roommates had to say good-bye.

"Thanks, Walter, you've been great," Glenn said. "A real friend."

After they hugged, Walter said, "Your secrets are good with me . . . but call me if you need to talk. Don't be a stranger."

"I won't be."

They shook hands again and Glenn headed to the bus. As he walked and was trying to decide whom he'd call first and how he'd proceed, a Badger tapped him on the shoulder. "Got a national radio appearance for you," he said. He introduced Glenn to the man with him, a Ralph Something who worked for the Columbia Broadcasting System. He was an athletic-looking man in a suit and hat and could have been mistaken for a recent Olympian himself. Ralph said he'd escort Glenn to the network studio and then to the hotel.

"Shouldn't take long," he said.

"Do I have to?" Glenn asked politely. "I'm awful tired."

Ralph Something said, "I guess not, but I would think you'd want to." He laughed. "If you don't stay an amateur, the more your name is out there, the more . . ." He rubbed his thumb on two fingers. Money.

"All right," Glenn said.

In the taxi, the radio man asked about the food in Germany and about the Olympic atmosphere. He said he was proud to be an American when the boys did so well. They got out at a building on 49th Street, just after they had crossed Lexington Avenue. Something wasn't feeling right. There were no indications, no signs, that this was CBS's headquarters. Noticing Glenn's uneasiness, Ralph reached into his inside coat pocket and held up a wallet badge. "FBI," the man said. Before Glenn could react, two other men—dressed the same, looked the same—joined them, nodding at Ralph.

"What's the story here?" Glenn stammered.

"Someone needs to see you," Ralph said, still amiably.

"I take it I have no choice."

"You have no choice."

Glenn's heart started pounding.

They took him to what seemed to be a freight elevator at the back. On the eleventh floor, there was a reception-type area with a desk and a man at it right off the elevator, and a hallway running down each side.

"This way," Ralph said, taking him down to the end of the hall to the right and knocking on the door.

"Come in," a husky voice said.

The room was a huge office, with a large desk devoid of any pictures or other adornments. Nothing was on the wall behind it, either. Another door was behind the desk. In the other end was a conference table. One man, in his fifties, was sitting behind the desk. A second, in his forties, was standing. He had a notebook in his hands.

"Thanks for coming, Mister Morris," the younger man said.

Glenn didn't respond.

The older man moved out from behind the desk, carrying a single sheet of paper. "First of all, congratulations on your victory in Berlin," he said, reaching out with his hand. Glenn shook it, warily. The older man gestured at the conference table. "Sit," he said. It was not a suggestion. On the other side of the table, the younger man kept the notebook below table level, on his lap. The older man had his single sheet folded in half vertically and still in his left hand.

"So what's the FBI want from me?" Glenn asked.

"Oh, we're not FBI," the younger man said. He gestured in the direction of the hallway. "Those men are. We're not."

"Then who are you?"

"You don't really need to know."

"Yeah, I do."

"Okay," the older man said with a laugh. "I am Mister Smith." He pointed at his compatriot. "He is Mister Jones. And when you walk out of this office, you will forget even that, and you never will have been here."

The younger man—"Jones"—leaned forward. "Near as we can tell, you got laid a lot in Berlin," he said. "Big movie star, famous woman. Wham, bam, go home. Hey, if that's all it was, more power to you. We're jealous, as a matter of fact."

Smith said softly, "But if you think it can be more than that . . ."

Jones jumped back in. "Playing house with Miss Swastika herself?" He looked down at his notebook and read aloud, sarcasm dripping from his voice. "Reich Film Board memo, translated. *Leni and Glenn: The Actress and the Athlete*. To be financed in entirety from the Reich Treasury, with funds transferred to a company formed to preserve the appearance of independence. Glenn Morris to receive fifty thousand U.S. dollars, half immediately, half upon the completion of filming."

Jones looked back up and locked in on Glenn. "How stupid can you be?" When Glenn didn't respond, Jones snapped, "I'll tell you how stupid . . . it's gonna take a few hours to tell you."

Smith put his hand on Jones's shoulder. "You're being a little harsh there," he said. Next, he clasped both hands together on the table in front of him and looked at Glenn. "It was easy to lose perspective over there. You lost your perspective. You can get it back."

Smith raised his hand. A signal. Two men—not the FBI agents—hustled in through the door behind the desk. One shoved a cart with a movie projector on it and set it up at one end of the table and plugged it in. The other set up a screen at the other end. Another man entered—scholarly, distinguished, looked as if he had forgotten his pipe—with a stack of papers and sat at the far end of the table, nearest the projector. He also had a flashlight.

The lights went out. The man turned on the projector. For over a minute, just grainy darkness was on the screen, accompanied by dark orchestral music. Then the menacing Nazi eagle on a stone perch, and a scroll below it to:

Triumph des Willens

"Triumph of the Will," intoned the man at the end of the table. As the words and numbers appeared on the screen in German, he again translated: "The Documentary of Reich's Party Convention 1934. . . . Produced by order of the Führer. . . . Directed by Leni Riefenstahl. . . . Twenty years after the outbreak of the World War . . . sixteen years after the onset of German suffering . . . nineteen months after the beginning of the German rebirth . . . Adolf Hitler flew again to Nuremberg to review his faithful followers."

Glenn felt a lump in his throat and had to swallow.

For nearly two hours, they watched. Glenn felt worse and worse. He kept trying to tell himself: *This is what she told me. She had to do it. This is her job. She had no choice.*

For the speeches, the translator was reading from a transcript and delivered the English almost simultaneously. In the opening session in the convention hall, the Nazi figure identified as Julius Streicher intoned: "A people that does not maintain the purity of its race will perish."

Glenn told himself: *A lot of people in America feel the same way.*

As he watched, he decided that what she had said in so many ways was true: There wasn't continuous venom, no point-by-point recitation of the hateful party program—the one Leni had told Glenn would be toned down. But he knew: She had to *believe* to make this. She had to.

He saw Hitler's motorcade after his arrival in Nuremberg, the band concert, the Labor Service Rally, the SA Torchlight Parade, the Hitler Youth rally, the review of the troops, all shown from the perspective of reverence . . . and agreement. The film came to Hitler's speech on the closing night, when, at least according to the translator, he said: ". . . and with the best racial quality of the German nation, its proud self-esteem, we boldly claim the leadership of the Reich and the people. . . . One who feels himself the bearer of the best blood, and knowing this has risen to lead the nation, is resolved to hold this leadership, fulfill it and never give it up. . . . It is only part of a people that constitutes genuinely active fighters. More is demanded of them than of the millions of other countrymen. For them, merely declaring, 'I believe,' is not enough. Instead they vow, 'I will fight.'"

When Hitler was through, Rudolf Hess led the "Sig Heil" salutes to Hitler. Then came the haunting "Horst Wessel" song.

The lights came on.

"Yeah," Jones said, "just a nice little documentary by a lady letting us make our own judgments, right?"

Glenn was afraid it wasn't.

"So when were you going to look at *this?*" Jones said. "She showed you all the fairy tales, right? She showed you all your own glorious moments in the decathlon—with Hitler sitting right behind you, clapping, and thinking you show an American can look like a storm trooper. How come she didn't show you this?"

How did they know?

Smith said softly, "Morris, most of us know—or think we know—what happened. She's captivating. She's charming. She can say exactly what needs to be said at any given time and believe it. Then she can say something completely different five minutes later and believe it, too. By the way, just curious: How old is she?"

"Never asked her," Glenn said. "The *Time* story during the Winter Games said twenty-eight. So twenty-eight or twenty-nine."

"She turned thirty-four on August twenty-second," Jones snapped. "You were fucking an old lady. Ten years older than you! You were a damn college boy a year ago . . . and she was using you. Like she uses everyone else."

Smith nodded at the translator, who read from another sheet:

"Leni Riefenstahl, July 1936, Berlin, meeting with two members of the Reich film board to discuss rerelease of *The Blue Light* and the board's instruction to remove her Jewish partners from the film's credits.

"Board President: 'So how many are there?'

"Fraulein Riefenstahl: 'Three. Balazs, director and writer, Mayer, writer, Sokal, a producer. All were in consultation and subordinate to me, of course.'

"Board president: 'Their names must be removed from the credits.'

"Fraulein Riefenstahl: 'They deserved no credit from the start. *The Blue Light* was mine. Sokal put up some money and as a Jew, he expected more back and I have no doubt that, as a Jew, he swindled me. The other two helped me, but no more than nominally. And they have made claims that it was much more than that!'

"Board president: 'This surprised you?'

"Fraulein Riefenstahl: 'Nothing Jews do surprises me. Not now. Once I was naïve and was taken advantage of, but I am smarter now. The Führer helped me see things for how they are. I never again will let Jew vermin manipulate me.'"

The translator looked up. "End of transcript."

After a long silence, Jones tossed out: "We just obtained that transcript. But so you know, that was the morning after your first little afternoon tryst in the apartment."

Glenn faked more defiance than he felt. "You can just make that stuff up," he declared.

Smith said softly, "You just saw that film. You think we made it up?"

Glenn was afraid they hadn't.

Jones said, "We've got another film of the Nazis that Fraulein Riefenstahl made the year before. It's called *Victory of Faith*, and it's a nice little story—except Hitler had one of his costars, Ernst Röhm, murdered soon after it came out, so that was a bit of a problem. That's why you won't see it in Germany any more. But Fraulein Riefenstahl showed how wonderful those Nazis are."

Smith asked quietly, "Need to see that, too?"

Glenn shook his head.

After a knock, another man entered. He dropped Leni's gift—the folder of photos—on the table. "This was in his bag," the man said to Smith. "We took pictures of all of them, so we'll have copies. But thought you might want to see this."

"Hey, you had no right!" Glenn protested.

"Sue us," Jones said. "Besides, don't sweat it. We already sent your bags—and your Nazi tree—on to the hotel."

For a minute, Smith leafed through the prints, with Jones watching. Smith stopped the longest at the one showing Leni and Glenn at the shot put ring during his return trip. Leni was standing over the shot put and Glenn was bending over, his hands on his knees and looking at her. Smith and Jones didn't say anything, but exchanged meaningful looks. Finally, Smith flipped the folder closed and slid it across to Glenn.

"These are quite good, I have to admit," Smith said. "She and her people know what they're doing." He stood and looked down at Glenn. "You know how much credit we're giving you, I hope. If we thought for one second you are, or could be, a Nazi yourself, or at least go over there and along with that kind of thinking without goose-stepping in the parades, we wouldn't be taking this approach."

Jones snapped, "Because then we'd be thinking you might just run right back across the Atlantic and back into her bed, and say America is misunderstanding this fine fellow Adolf."

Smith said, "We think you're a better man than that. Are we right?"

Glenn again nodded.

Jones stood up, too. "All right, Morris, here's what we're going to do . . ."

Smith cut him off. "Let me take this, okay?"

Jones nodded.

"Look, Morris," Smith began, "we're not going to debate politics with you or anyone else. We know some congressmen would watch that film and deep down be saying, 'Good for them.' The way we treat Negroes in our country can make us look like hypocrites when we say these Nuremberg Laws are disgraceful. We know all of that. But the point here is that the son of a bitch is going to drag this world into another war. Anything that gives him hope that we'd stay out of it—even something as unimportant as a movie about a famous German and a famous American playing house—will embolden him even more. We've tried to get that across to Mister Lindbergh. And Mister Ford, too."

Jones said, "So you know, we even talked about having you go back to be our eyes and ears." Noticing Glenn's startled look, Jones continued, "We know it wouldn't work. You're an amateur, you wouldn't have enough direct access, they'd have their eyes on you as an American, and the first misstep . . . well, you wouldn't be found in the Rhine, but you'd probably be expelled at the very least, or have a sudden and shocking fatal heart attack at worst."

Smith jumped in. "We decided it would be the best for everyone—you included—if we simply showed you the real Miss Riefenstahl and scuttled this little relationship. Just in case you weren't going to come to your senses before you got home to Colorado and before you broke the news to your girl."

Glenn was stunned, but not so stunned to realize they must have had someone on the inside at the Film Board; plus at the Castle Ruhwald, at the Geyer Film Lab, at her apartment building . . . maybe all three.

Jones piped up again. "We were going to list all the others she's . . ."

Smith cut him off. "That's not necessary now, Mister Jones."

With a dismissive wave, Jones said, "All right . . . we wouldn't have had enough paper, anyway."

After a nod from Smith, Jones got up and left the room.

"You'll be out of here in a few minutes," the older man said reassuringly. "But you'll be picked up at your hotel at 9 in the morning, and you'll spend an hour or two, maybe three, meeting with some folks who will want you to tell them everything you can about your meeting with Hitler, and maybe about anything else you saw. Sometimes we don't even know what's important until later."

"What if I refuse to go?" Glenn asked.

"Come on, Glenn, that wouldn't be smart," Smith said. "Or patriotic. You help us . . . we'll help you. You want to be in the movies? We at least can get your foot in the door there. If you're bad, we probably can't make them ignore that." He laughed darkly. "Well, I shouldn't say that, either, because there are a lot of bad actors out there with their names on marquees and making a lot of money. But movie people can be encouraged, shall we say, to look at you. Radio network folks here can be prompted to maybe put you to work in the interim. If you're cooperative."

Glenn put his head in his hands, and then brushed back his hair.

"Hey, I know it's all overwhelming," Smith said. "But we know you're a good American, you'll stay a good American, and the most important thing is that it can work out for the best for you. To start with, your hotel will be paid for, for as long as you want to stay here in New York . . . although we know they've got those big welcomes planned for you in Colorado next week. And speaking of that, you can call your girl—or anyone else . . . in this country, at least—from the hotel and we'll take care of that, too."

Smith stood and raised one hand. Again, Glenn wondered how anyone could see his gesture. But the door opened, and the three FBI men popped in. "They'll get you to the hotel," Smith said. "And I know this goes without saying, but you'll just complicate matters—for yourself or anyone you tell—if you talk about *this* with anyone."

At the hotel, Glenn had to call Karen's parents in Sterling to get her phone number at the boarding house in Fountain, the small town where she had just started her teaching career. Her mother gushingly congratulated Glenn—and it took a second for him to realize she was talking about the engagement, not the gold medal. But she got to that, saying they were *so* proud of him. For a few seconds, he felt about two inches tall. But then he reminded himself: The reason Karen was in Fountain was that he wasn't ready to get married, and she knew that. And that was before Leni had come into the picture.

Yet when he talked with Karen, the feelings came in a flood. It wasn't "guilt" as much as the renewed realization that, minus the embellishments, what Joe Williams had said of his attitudes in the story was true. She had been an important part of his life the previous two years, she had encouraged him to pursue what at one time had seemed outlandish Olympic dreams, and while she had taken the teaching job when he dragged his feet, she hadn't given up on him—in more ways than one.

And, yes, he loved her. Her pride in him rushed through the phone line. At first, it was as if they were trying to catch up on everything in a few minutes on the phone. They both laughed, realizing that wouldn't work. "This is going to cost you a fortune!" Karen exclaimed. Glenn briefly pondered saying the government—as far as he knew, it was the government—would pay for the call as a reward for his gold medal, but he decided against it. But he did swallow hard and say, "Honey . . . I saw the newspaper stories. It's not your fault, but the writer in Berlin kind of twisted what I said. I never said we were getting married right away."

She didn't say anything, and Glenn could picture the downcast look he was accustomed seeing when Karen was hurt.

"Honey," he said again, and paused. He realized he never had called Leni "Honey," or anything like it. She was, "Leni . . ."

"What are you saying?" she asked.

"Honey, don't take that wrong. . . . I just mean when we set a date, it's going to be after we talk about it. Okay?"

"Okay," she said shakily.

When they hung up, he told her he loved her and was looking forward to seeing her soon. He meant it.

He spent much of his travel time back to Colorado debating himself, mostly about whether he would have realized there could be no future with Leni even without the session with the shadowy Smith and Jones in New York. Glenn also thought of whether there was a middle ground—conceding he was through with Leni, but realizing that his rationalization of his relationship with her showed he wasn't yet capable of complete commitment to Karen . . . or maybe not to any woman. Not yet.

He practiced the speech. *Honey, there's so much going on, so much coming at me, so much changed, you're just starting your career, maybe we better back off a bit. Maybe even date others.*

When he saw her, he didn't lose the nerve to say it. Instead, he decided he didn't want to.

3 4

~

Homecoming and Hollywood

The night before the Denver parade and celebration, Glenn and Karen spoke with *Denver Post* reporter Frances Wayne in George Whitman's living room. Wayne, a middle-aged society writer wearing a huge hat, gushed: "You two look so wonderful together! I can tell how much you're in love."

Glenn told Wayne that he would be leaving later in the week for a multiple-city tour with other Olympic gold-medalists on behalf of the AAU. *He thought: Guess they haven't made enough money off us yet.*

"After that, what?" Wayne asked.

"Perhaps Hollywood!" Glenn said.

Wayne switched her gaze to Karen. "How would you like that?"

"I wouldn't presume to tell Glenn what to do, or what not to do," Karen declared. "I couldn't say whether I would like Hollywood. I mean, I really don't know much about it . . . except what I've seen in the movies."

George Whitman walked into the room, carrying Leni's gift—the folder of photos. Glenn had handed them to Whitman in his den and explained they were from the famous filmmaker Leni Riefenstahl, who was making a movie about the Olympics. He didn't explain that he had removed the shot of Leni and Glenn together, and that was safely tucked away.

"Excuse me, Miss Wayne," the businessman said, and then turned to Glenn, holding up a tight shot of an intent Glenn preparing to throw the javelin. "These—all these—are great! Amazing stuff!"

The reporter asked who took them.

"Lena Riefenstahl," said Whitman.

Glenn didn't correct him—either on the name or about the fact that Leni generally didn't take her own pictures.

"Who's that?" Wayne asked Glenn.

"She's a German actress and director making a movie and maybe a photo book about the Olympics," Glenn said as matter-of-factly as he could. "She and her people took miles of film and a ton of pictures—of a lot of us—and they've also got the right to use anything in others' newsreels. She said the decathlon might even be in the prologue."

Karen raised her eyebrows and smiled. "Is she pretty?"

"I didn't notice," Glenn deadpanned in a tone making it clear he did, but wanted to come off as teasing. As in: *Of course she is, but no big deal, honey.* Karen laughed and hit him with a couch pillow.

She was at his side the next day. They rode in a parade through downtown Denver, and were honored in a ceremony carried on national radio and attended by 10,000 at the University of Denver football stadium. The only tense moment between Glenn and Karen during the proceedings was when Glenn told Chet Nelson, the perpetually red-faced *Rocky Mountain News* sports editor, that Joe Williams had "misquoted" him. He explained that he and Karen *were* engaged, but they didn't know when they'd be married. Glenn tried to take the sting out of that with a quick arm around her and hug. He scoffed when Nelson asked him whether Eleanor Holm Jarrett's ouster from the team was fair. "Well, she got kicked off, didn't she?" he asked. He didn't mean to be as harsh as it sounded, but he decided he'd be digging himself in deeper if he tried to explain the nuances of his position.

Karen left for Fountain, insisting that she had signed a teaching contract, needed to honor it and didn't want to let down her students. Glenn said he understood.

That night, the Denver Athletic Club paid tribute to him at a banquet, and Glenn found himself choking up when he went to the microphone and faced Whitman and the audience of businessmen. "You stood behind me before I'd even tried the decathlon," he said. "You showed faith in me and gave me a chance. I'll always be grateful, no matter where life takes me. You helped me realize how proud I am to be an American, how proud I am to be from Colorado, and how proud I am to have represented you all!"

He got a standing ovation.

In Fort Collins, Glenn was greeted as a returning Aggie hero, and he presented the oak tree seedling to Colorado A&M president Charles Lory.

In Simla, he was saluted on his "Day," culminating with a town barbeque. As he spoke from the hotel balcony, he spotted his very first love—the girl who had cried for an hour after the first time for them both. She had two little children and a husband with her. She looked more like a discus thrower than a runner now.

～

In Berlin, Joseph Goebbels's secretary called Leni and declared that the propaganda minister needed to see her. She knew it would be counterproductive to balk. When she arrived, Goebbels with obvious pleasure immediately told her that he was going to order German reporters to not mention her or the Olympic film project for the foreseeable future.

"Why not?" Leni erupted.

"Until we have a handle on the way you are spending the money allotted for this, and that you will not remain out of control and wasting money for your personal *pleasures*, we will pretend that this film is not being made. It won't be as embarrassing if we decide to shut down this project completely. We'll carefully audit your records and expenditures and decide how to proceed from there."

"You can't be serious! You don't want to fight with me on this! The Führer is all for it! And for the other film, too!"

"The *other* film? Fraulein, if I were you, I wouldn't even bring that up any more. But if you wish, I will inform the Führer also that the American athlete made you look so foolish. He led you on, he got what he wanted from you, and then he walked out on you and went home to get married."

"You're just jealous," she snapped. "Of everything he has. I *knew* there was a girl in Colorado. He told me. I even know he said nice things about her from here that a reporter distorted, and that was before he came back here and we talked it through. He is going to be coming back to me."

"You think so?"

"Yes, I do."

He handed her a stack of sheets. On top was a wire photo of Glenn in his Olympic blazer and slacks, with Karen. They were warmly hugging each other in an outdoor pose for the photographer. It didn't appear to be forced affection. "That was taken yesterday. As you see, he is rejecting her," Goebbels said sarcastically. "They probably went into the bushes and fucked right after the photographer was done."

Beneath the picture, a long sheet of newsprint, folded in several places horizontally, was a wire-service story, and a quick glance told her it was a rewritten German version of Glenn's homecoming. Another stapled stack of sheets contained typed and translated versions of all the Denver newspaper stories. "Go ahead, read at your leisure," Goebbels taunted. "You'll see . . . he forgot about you the second he left your bed. You tell *me* if that sounds like a man coming back to you. You tell *me* if you want the Führer to know all this. The Führer seemed to like the fellow and he thought you could work your magic on him. And I'm starting to think you must be boring in bed, because you can't hold on to any of these men. I have decided you don't tire of them; they tire of you. As I'm sure I would have!"

Leni didn't give him the satisfaction of seeing her cry. She broke down in the car, though, in bursts of both sadness and anger.

Against his better judgment, wondering if the letter would be either intercepted or read before it left the country, Glenn wrote to Leni a month later. He didn't apologize; he explained. He said he regretted the way it all unfolded, and he wanted her to know he meant what he said before he left Berlin. He was sure, he said, that she had come to accept how unrealistic they both had been, and this would be for the best.

He still occasionally tried to convince himself that the shadowy Americans who confronted him had made up her anti-Semitic rant. He still tried to convince himself that she could make the Nazis' films without embracing the National Socialist agenda.

He couldn't pull it off, but he kept trying.

Glenn's letter arrived just before Leni left with her friend, Margot von Opel, for a quick trip to the resort on the island of Sylt in Northern Germany. Leni spent much of the stay confiding in Margot, saying it would take months for her to get over the American athlete. The story she told Margot was Leni's Truth, with embellishments she believed as she listed them. She had Glenn swearing to her that there hadn't been a girl back home. She said he *promised* to return and marry her by the end of the year. And then one just popped into her head. Pretending embarrassment, she claimed she had advanced Glenn the $25,000 first part of his acting payment for *Leni and Glenn*—and that she realized his desertion meant he had stolen the money from her.

On the second day, Leni joined Margot in the hotel café and apologized for being late, explaining she was checking on arrangements for Willy Zielke to film extra material for the prologue on the shores of the Baltic Sea. Erwin Huber was set to step in for Glenn as the Myron Discus Thrower.

A man billing himself as a handwriting expert was going from table to table, hustling work. His act was one of the café's trademarks. Mostly, customers scribbled samples for him, and his interpretations sounded similar to those of Gypsy palm readers. As he neared their table, Margot asked Leni if she still had Glenn's letter. Leni did, but she pointed out that it was in English. Margot talked her into pulling it out, anyway, pointing out that the man would interpret the handwriting, not the words.

Margot handed it to the man. He looked at it, winced, and then dropped it on the table. He insisted he couldn't interpret it, but Margot pressed him. After poring over it for a minute, he declared that the man who wrote it had a dark side few knew about, with violent, sadistic, mean-spirited and unstable elements that would take over his life—and anyone around him. Margot thanked him and gave him a sizable gratuity. The man nodded and moved on. Leni appreciated the gesture, but she knew Margot must have huddled with the man before she arrived and told him what to say if she handed him a letter written in English. She appropriated the man's message as Leni's Truth, too.

In December, Glenn was living in New York and working for NBC Radio as a liaison for sports broadcasts, and preparing to compete for the New York Athletic Club, when he and Karen were married at her parents' home in Sterling. She gave up her teaching job and moved with Glenn to Manhattan. That month, he also was named the winner of the Sullivan Award as the nation's top amateur athlete for 1936, and he angered AAU officials when he reacted honestly, saying to the reporter who informed him of the news: "If I won, what happened to Owens? I thought he'd get it." He knew many of the voters were holding it against Jesse that he quickly had declared himself a professional after the Games, and Glenn was especially sheepish because he didn't intend to remain an amateur much longer, either.

In mid-1937, the call came from Hollywood, and the AAU declared him a professional, too, for "cashing" in on the fame Olympic competition had brought him. Karen marveled that he didn't even need to take a screen test for the film moguls, but Glenn explained to her that his agent—a Mr. Smith—had given copies of his Olympic photos to a producer, and that was enough to get his foot in the door. He didn't mention that Leni Riefenstahl had given him the pictures. He and Karen went to Los Angeles, where he first played himself in a brief MGM newsreel-type feature, *Decathlon Champion: The Story of Glenn Morris*. A small Los Angeles college served as

Colorado Agricultural College during his playing days,, with some other contrivances used to represent Simla. He enjoyed making the film, but he knew how much better *Olympia* would be—and how much better *Leni and Glenn* would have been. There was no word from Berlin about when *Olympia* would be released, and it was as if there was a curtain drawn over the project. Glenn was unsure and uneasy about how Leni would treat him in the film after all that happened, but if she still showed him prominently, he hoped it would generate other opportunities . . . especially if the film made it to America.

Producer Sol Lesser signed him to play Tarzan in the upcoming *Tarzan's Revenge*, an independent production to be shot at Twentieth Century Fox. The publicity department announced that he stood to make $250,000 in the next five years under his contract with Lesser if all went as expected. Glenn knew that was hogwash and that the deal was conditional and year-to-year, even picture-to-picture, but he went along with the story. He had two shocks about the assignment: One, when he discovered his only line in the script was, "Cynthia, I am Tarzan"; and, two, when Eleanor Holm—minus the "Jarrett"—was signed as his costar and romantic interest. His first reaction was to laugh darkly and wonder if her shipboard offer was still open. He also guessed that Smith and Jones had talked with her, too, and that the government had a hand in the casting.

The filming began in early October 1937 and lasted only five weeks. Glenn did several interviews on the set. One Associated Press story distributed nationally noted that he said: "It's a crazy business. But it's better than selling cars."

Eleanor frostily set the tone, and they didn't speak to each other except when absolutely necessary. Although they never talked about it, he assumed she had heard that he didn't sign the petition to protest her ouster from the Olympic team, and perhaps also had gotten wind of what he said to the *Rocky Mountain News* about her case.

At first his line in the shooting script was changed to "Eleanor, I am Tarzan," because producers decided to change the name of his costar's character. One day, he heard some of the crew joking that it was changed to Eleanor's real name so the stupid former athlete could remember his line. Bruised and angered, he considered asking them what they'd ever accomplished, but kept his mouth shut. Ironically, two of his biggest scenes were when Tarzan went swimming with Eleanor—including in the movie's ending.

The film was released in January 1938, and even Glenn admitted as he saw it at the premiere that it was wincingly awful. Though he was allowed to be athletically heroic in foiling villians, his adjusted dialogue turned out to be saying "Tarzan" twice, plus "Eleanor" and "good" once apiece.

Glenn was cast in a bit role in Twentieth Century Fox's upcoming *Hold That Co-Ed*, a light comedy starring some big names, but he knew that wouldn't advance his career, either. He assumed Smith and Jones felt they had done their part, and now it was up to him. He still was a popular invitee on the party circuit, though, both in Twentieth Century Fox circles and outside. "Meet Glenn Morris . . . you might remember, he won the track and field decathlon in front of Hitler!" Feeling like he was on display, perhaps even wearing a breechcloth, he started to ignore his previously self-imposed limits of two beers or one cocktail. He also began drinking at home, something Karen chided him about. He worried about money, since nothing of note had come in during 1937. Karen began crying at night. She argued that if nothing happened soon, they should move back to Colorado. Glenn could use his Denver Athletic Club contacts to land a job in the business world, she said, and she could return to teaching. They argued about it almost every night. He never hit her, but grabbed her several times, in his mind trying to shake sense into her.

In early March, Glenn got a call from a man who introduced himself as Hubert Stowitts, who said he was a former dancer and actor at MGM now making a living as a painter. Halfway through his second sentence, Glenn knew he was a homosexual, but he had come to accept that it was common in Hollywood and wasn't bothered. Stowitts did surprise him, though, when he added that he had been the track captain at the University of California before getting into dance. He told Glenn that it was complicated to explain, but he had met Leni when he participated in an art exhibition and Leni had asked him if she could use some of his artworks of athletes in her prologue. He had stayed in Berlin nearly two years, and when he returned to Los Angeles, Leni had entrusted Stowitts with a print of *Olympia*—scheduled now to open in Germany shortly, Stowitts said—and asked him to screen it for selected and private audiences in Los Angeles. Leni's goal, he confessed, was to get influential Americans to stand behind the film and lobby for its U.S. release and distribution. Stowitts said he had set up a showing for selected American Olympic athletes from the area at the Wilshire Ebell Club.

"Have you seen it?" Glenn asked.

Stowitts said he had, and confided that Glenn and the decathlon were prominently featured in the second part, *Festival of Beauty*. "You'll want to see it," Stowitts said. He laughed. "Trust me. She didn't hold a grudge. Or at least you couldn't tell it from the film. You're a star in it!"

Great. He knows, too.

Stowitts emphasized, though, that her instructions to him were specific: The Wilshire Ebell Club showing would be only for the athletes, nobody else. No wives, no girls, no coaches, no friends . . . and certainly no reporters or reviewers. Everyone had to agree to sit through the entire four hours and not leave once his or her event was shown. "Hitler hasn't even seen it yet!" Stowitts exclaimed. "It has to be kept quiet. Agreed?"

Glenn preferred it that way.

It was great to see a lot of the boys again, including Ken Carpenter, Earle Meadows, Bill Graber and a handful of the swimmers and divers. There was awkward small talk, but before long, it was as if they were back in the Olympic Village, teasing. Glenn even took it good-naturedly when Carpenter teased that if he didn't win an Academy Award for *Tarzan's Revenge*, there was no justice in the world. Glenn did notice, but didn't ask about, the absence of any of the Negro trackmen who lived in Southern California. Nobody questioned him about Leni before the film started.

Standing at the front of the room, Stowitts again explained that it was two parts, *Festival of Nations* and *Festival of Beauty*, and that this soundtrack was in German, but it would be replaced with an English one for the eventual North American release. "If there is an eventual North American release," he added. He repeated that Hitler hadn't even seen this yet, as far as he knew, and absolute discretion about the film's content was both requested and expected.

They hooted during the erotic prologue, showing the Greek ruins, nude women dancers, and eventually Erwin Huber nearly nude as Myron's Discus Thrower. Glenn was the only one who recognized him, and he also was all but certain he saw Leni, shown only from behind, in the artistic shots of the nude women. Then came the opening ceremonies, with the Americans marching in near the end and with the Olympians in the screening room trying to spot themselves. Most of them jeered when Hitler pronounced the Games open. Then they came to the events, with the excited German announcer providing narration as if he was watching the events live. The "restaged" pole vault footage looked obviously contrived to Glenn, especially because Meadows and the Japanese appeared as if they were about to burst out laughing any second during their close-ups at the end of the runway. Glenn looked at Meadows and Graber, who chuckled, but they seemed to be the only ones who thought it looked a little strange. Otherwise, Glenn was stunned at how even-handed the film seemed to be with the Negro athletes, especially playing up Jesse Owens.

"Man," Ken Carpenter said to Glenn, "your lady friend might be in trouble for this."

The decathlon didn't show up until about a half-hour into the second part. But for about twenty minutes, Glenn truly was the star, in close-ups and in the events. Carpenter and Graber especially teased him when the camera panned up and down his legs. He had seen much of the footage in the theater at the Geyer Film Lab, so he resisted the temptation to blurt to Stowitts that it wasn't true that Hitler hadn't seen this yet. But he saw the footage of the restaged 1,500 meters for the first time, and it looked ridiculous to him, as if someone was following him around with a flashlight as he circled the track or shook hands with Huber. He noticed that Eva wasn't in the film, and that all that was of him reaping the spoils of victory was his restaged peering at the flagpoles, with the wreath on his head. There was nothing from the real medal ceremony in the daylight.

When it ended, the athletes rose for a standing ovation, feeling a bit silly doing so, but doing it nonetheless.

The trackmen adjourned to the club's bar to talk about it, and the consensus was that it was both better and more seemingly objective than they had expected. They agreed it had taken them back to 1936. Graber finally asked him what they all were wondering: "Did you guys just break it off when you left or what?"

"Don't know what you're talking about," Glenn said in a tone that made it clear he knew exactly what he was talking about.

"Hey, you can tell us now!" Graber protested.

Glenn sighed. "I haven't seen her since I left Berlin. And you guys seem to forget that I got married a few months later. Does that answer your question?"

"Not really," Carpenter said. "It just raises some more."

That's all they got out of him.

Driving home, Glenn was excited. Thanks to Leni, he would be back in the international spotlight when this finally was released—as a hero, not as a guy with four words of dialogue in a terrible movie or a guy standing around on the fringe of the huddle in a football comedy. After it came out, he hoped, the offers would get better. He convinced an agent, Eddie Hanson, of that, and signed on with him, asking him to find work for him beyond the conditional work from Lesser. He had given up on Smith and Jones.

He filmed his small part in Hold That Co-Ed, and then settled in to wait. During his many arguments with Karen, he tried to get the point across that when Olympia finally came out, it might open doors for him. Each time he mentioned Leni, Karen's looks got sourer.

Glenn was crestfallen when he read in Daily Variety that the premiere was being delayed until April 20, 1938—or Hitler's forty-ninth birthday. The Germans claimed it was to honor the Führer, but the assumption was that the Germans' march into Austria in March had something to do with it. After it opened, though, the dispatches from Europe made it clear that the two-part film was a triumph, praised even by non-Germans. As it premiered in other European nations, too, Leni repeatedly drew praise for her treatment of the American Negroes and for showing triumphs of all nations, not just Germany.

Glenn kept waiting for confirmation that *Olympia* would be distributed in America. The trade papers ran periodic pieces about American studios and theaters balking. The four-hour, two-part configuration was an issue. But mostly, it went beyond art. Germany was increasingly bellicose. Leni was wrong: Instead of moderating his anti-Jewish stands and practices as time passed and the world knew he was there to stay, Hitler and the Third Reich turned even more hateful. That became increasingly clear with each dispatch from Germany, and movie moguls understood it was bad business to make any sort of financial commitment or otherwise be linked with the Germans. Then Glenn read a story in the *Hollywood Reporter* saying Leni hoped to come to America to plead her case, including about the film being an International Olympic Committee and not a Third Reich project. She wanted to bring prints designed for the U.S. market, with an English soundtrack and, presumably, fewer shots of Hitler and displays of German nationalism.

His agent, Hanson, got nothing done. Glenn fired him in June, deciding that he would find a new representative when *Olympia* reached the United States and he was a hot property again.

Leni's letter came in August. Glenn was glad he beat Karen to the mailbox. The letter was neither coldly formal nor warmly intimate, perhaps written with the assumption that Karen might see it. She hoped this letter found him well and happy, and on the verge of Hollywood breakthroughs. She thanked him for his cooperation on *Olympia* and said the reaction—in France even!—was rapturous and that the segment on the decathlon was drawing much praise. Glenn was a star in Europe again! She confirmed she would be coming to New York in the fall and hoped to eventually make her way to Hollywood. Perhaps by then, she said, it would be unnecessary, and that exhibitors and others would have seen the light, but she feared that might not be the case and she would be staging private showings, hoping to convince all that this was not a German film, but an international one. She said she would be honored if he could attend a showing or a premiere and would be in touch after her arrival in America to update him. She also would be grateful if he spread the word in his Hollywood circle that she was no Nazi and that the film was art, not propaganda. He noticed she made no reference to Stowitts's private showing for the athletes. It was if she thought the stipulation about discretion for that showing involved her, too. As he thought about it over the next few days, Glenn found himself stepping away from the uneasiness and revulsion he felt in Smith and Jones's office, and wondering if he had been unfair.

About a week later, when Glenn returned from a local high school and running—he was trying to stay in condition, at least for the screen and not competition, given his "professional" standing—Karen had Leni's envelope in her hand. "What's this?" she challenged.

"Letter about *Olympia*," Glenn said. *True enough!* "Go ahead and read it," he said, assuming she already had.

She looked it over long enough to make it seem the first time.

"Written in July," she said. "Why didn't you tell me about this? Or show it to me?"

"Why should I have? There's nothing in there I haven't been talking about," he said. "To you and to everyone else. You've *heard* me talking about it! She's a filmmaker. I'm in her film. She wants me to promote it. I can either promote and hope it helps, or we can be evicted from this place in a month or two."

"That'd be all right with me," Karen said, starting to cry.

"Honey," he said, surprised he still could call her that as he grabbed her shoulders, "we have to play this out."

She looked up at him. "Glenn, you've talked about her in your sleep."

"What?"

"I've never said anything. I've known for a while. You talked about her in your sleep—or to her. And you're not making a movie."

"Oh, don't be . . ."

"Stop it! I know. Okay, it was in Germany, I guess during the Olympics. And then you came home. I was willing to live with that after I figured it out, and I did. In all of this, even during the fights, have I ever said anything about it? But now . . . if she's coming here . . . you have to give me your word it's over."

"Karen, nothing ever . . ."

"Stop it!" she sobbed.

He stepped away and went to the window. After a minute, he came back. He took her hand. "I was stupid," he said. "It's over. But . . ."

"But what?"

"I still have to try to get that movie seen here. For me. For us! Do you understand that?"

"If you say so," she said. "But this can't go on forever. We can't go on like this. We can't keep arguing here. We should go home . . . to Colorado . . . soon."

"We'll talk about that. We have a screening to go to, remember."

His part in *Hold That Co-Ed* was embarrassingly minor, so he wasn't excited to see it at the screening a month in advance of its release. But at the pre-showing reception, each time someone asked him what he was up to, or what was next, or even when he was asked about the stories in the trade papers, he pounced. Fewer and fewer Hollywood folks seemed to know who he was without being prompted. Yes, Olympic glory could be fleeting. But he forcefully advanced the theory that his prominence in *Olympia*—at least that's what he had heard—and the treatment of his Negro teammates, showed that "Miss Riefenstahl" wasn't under the thumb of the Nazis and that Americans should give her film a fair chance.

"You're starting to sound like a Nazi, Morris," one second-tier actor said from the fringe of the group.

Karen pulled him away. "He's right. Especially when you talk about *her*."

"I'm talking about the film," he said sharply.

He reintroduced himself and Karen to two of *Hold That Co-Ed*'s stars, John Barrymore and George Murphy, and when each asked him what he was up to, he brought up *Olympia* and stated his—and Leni's—case. Karen was seething, but smiled bravely. Barrymore seemed to be looking past Glenn. The affable Murphy at least listened and said he would keep an open mind. An older woman Glenn recognized waved at Murphy.

"Isn't that Sophie Tucker?" Karen asked.

"Yes," laughed Murphy. "The Last of the Red-Hot Mamas! Come on, I'll introduce you." But as they walked over to the corner, Murphy leaned into Glenn's ear. "Whatever you do, don't bring up any of that German shit with her . . . or with any of the other Jews here."

In making the introductions, Murphy joked that Tucker "made me look good in *Broadway Melody of 1938*."

"I certainly did," she said with a straight face. "And they had me about eighth in the credits! Below George here and Robert Taylor and Buddy Ebsen and Eleanor Powell and even that girl Judy Garland!" Murphy was smiling, but Glenn and Karen weren't sure how to react, and Sophie noticed and burst out laughing. "At my age," she said, "I'm just glad to be under any man . . . even one as homely as ol' George here!"

⁓

Glenn drove them home, and there were several problems with that. One, he was drunk. In the Hollywood of matching drink for drink, he was in way over his head. For years, from Simla to Berlin, he had been careful. But around movie people, moderation was damn near impossible. Two, he still was embarrassed over having to watch his fringe role as a football player at the screening. And three, nobody among the movie folks had promised better things were in the works, or given him any hope of support in getting *Olympia* into an American release.

Karen, who'd had too much champagne, too—a rarity for her—started crying again. "Now you're flaunting it," she said bitterly. "You know, probably six people there tonight told me you must have fucked her, the way you talk about her. And six more said they *know* you fucked her."

He'd never heard Karen say "fucked" before.

"Well, I hope you're proud, you got it out of me," Glenn said bitterly. "But I remind you, we weren't married then."

"You are now! Everybody there thinks you're going to be in her hotel room, fucking her, the second she gets to Los Angeles. Hope you do a better job with her than you've been doing with me lately!"

He took his right hand off the wheel and, as hard as he could, gave her a backhanded slap to the face.

"Shut up!" he yelled. "Shut up!"

"The truth hurts," said Karen, crying harder and rubbing her face. She had a cut at the corner of her eye, and blood was streaming down.

"I never should have married you!" he said. "You tricked me into it after that idiot sportswriter put words in my mouth! You've hurt my career out here, dragged me down, told me I'm horseshit and we need to get out of here."

"Well, you are a horseshit actor," she screamed. "You are! You have to get that in your head!"

For the next few miles, silence. When they got home, Karen raced into the bedroom and barricaded the door. Glenn went into the second bathroom, washed his face and looked at himself in the mirror. He was drunk, but not too drunk to be horrified. *Forget everything else. You hit her!*

He went to the bedroom door and tried to nudge it open. He knew if he took a run at it, he could get it open, but decided against it.

"Karen?"

Nothing.

"I'm sorry. I drank too much. I said stupid things. I'm sorry for hitting you."

Nothing. He slept on the couch.

The next morning, she came out of the bedroom with a suitcase. "I'm going home," she said.

"I said I was sorry!" Glenn said, jumping up from the couch.

"You said things you can't ever, ever take back, too. You can say you didn't mean them, but you did."

"Well, what about you? You said things, too."

"Yes, I did," she said. "I've stopped trying to fool myself. You used to be such a good man! Even after I figured out what happened over there, I still thought that. I don't anymore."

Her father came back out with her to Los Angeles a couple of weeks later, and she filed for divorce on September 9, 1938. Even the Denver papers turned on him with a vengeance. The filing claimed that he had punched her, pulled her hair and thrown her against the door, knocking her unconscious. And that he had given her a black eye on another occasion. The papers noted they were only allegations, but played them up with huge headlines and a judgmental tone. The filing claimed he had made $18,000 in 1937 and asked for $700 a month in alimony and $2,000 to pay her attorney fees.

I pay her $2,000 so her attorney can make things up?

On September 22, they saw each other in Los Angeles Superior Court. They didn't talk, at least not to each other. Glenn told the judge he couldn't afford to pay alimony. As near as he could remember later, the wire-service story quoted him semi-accurately: "Since my wife and I separated on August 28, I have been living off the bounty of friends. I have borrowed fifty dollars—borrowed it in dribs and drabs, sometimes as little as two dollars at a time." He told the judge that, yes, he had made about $18,000 in 1937, but the money had disappeared because of the payments on their house, the high expenses of living in Los Angeles, and his practice of sending money to his parents every month. He said he had made $975 so far in 1938. He admitted he even had tried to return to his former profession and get a job as a car salesman, but had failed, and was starting to sell insurance on commission. He insisted, though, that there still was hope for him in the movie business. He didn't mention Leni or *Olympia*. The judge denied Karen's immediate alimony request and said he would hear the case in October.

The next week, Hanson, the fired agent, sued Glenn for $288,000, alleging breach of contract. Glenn laughed at that at first, wondering what the point was—except for publicity and to embarrass the former client. Hanson knew how little he had made. But then he decided it might even be a good sign: Hanson seemed to think Glenn might make some money in the future in the business. Maybe *he* had heard about *Olympia*.

～

Desperate for money, Glenn agreed to play for the Hollywood Stars semi-professional football team, against the Los Angeles Bulldogs on November 1. He didn't embarrass himself, and it planted the idea that returning to that sport might be a possibility in the future, perhaps in the National Football League—if he trained seriously, got back into football condition and went to a training camp with a team. But the semi-pro money was minimal and the chance of injury too great if he still hoped to get his acting career going. So he put football back on hold.

～

One night out of the blue, Karen called him. She said her father and lawyer had insisted that the filing needed to be "jazzed up" a bit to provide a case for alimony, and that if she had known how carried away the newspapers would have gotten, she wouldn't have gone along with it. But she said she was withdrawing the divorce request from the Los Angeles court.

"Oh, honey . . ." Glenn began.

"Glenn, I'm not coming back to you," she said. "I need to come out there to straighten some things out, but you won't see me if I can help it. Too much has happened. I'll get a divorce a different way, not with the whole world watching. And it might not even be for awhile."

"I don't know what to say," he said.

"Glenn . . ."

"Yes?"

"She ruined you. You won a gold medal, but now I wish you'd fallen down during the trials. You'd be coaching, I'd be teaching, we'd be happy. She ruined you."

35

~

Olympia, U.S.A.

Leni stepped off the *Europa* onto the New York docks on November 4, 1938. Ernst Jäger and Werner Klingeberg, Carl Diem's underling on the German Olympic Committee, accompanied her. She had made many friends among the affluent Americans on board, and they made a show of flashy good-byes to her as they departed and she spoke with reporters. After one of the interruptions, one of the reporters, hollering, asked if she was "Hitler's honey."

"We're just good friends," she said, smiling.

Soon, she would wish that she had just pretended not to hear the question.

In his nationally syndicated column, Walter Winchell snidely called her "pretty as a Swastika," and that helped set the tone for derision from the press that increased when she too hastily dismissed—or even denied—the reports in the wake of the horrific state-sanctioned *Kristallnacht* violence against Jews across Germany on November 9. Initially, she said the reports must be exaggerated and that they slandered both Germany "and the greatest man who ever lived." Later, she would claim that she wasn't aware of the true extent of the carnage and violence until she returned to Germany. That, of course, was Leni's Truth.

From coast to coast during her visit, she encountered adulation and positive receptions many places and even rave reviews of *Olympia* from writers who not only watched it at screenings, but also watched it with an open mind. The grudging nature of some of the positive reactions strengthened her case, but she couldn't overcome the odds stacked against her. "Good

299

friends" and "greatest man who ever lived" repeatedly were thrown back into her face. Even those naturally inclined to support her, including Avery Brundage in Chicago, Henry Ford in Detroit, and Walt Disney in Los Angeles, couldn't justify backing her publicly. Brundage arranged for an *Olympia* showing to a small audience at the Chicago Engineers' Club. After seeing it, Brundage wrote to American Olympic Committee member William May Garland in Los Angeles, calling *Olympia* "the greatest sports film ever made." But he couldn't do more than that. Like other titans, he feared the backlash.

Leni never could get America to accept that it was an IOC production, not a Reich film, and that she was independent. The view remained that in the wake of *Kristallnacht* especially, to embrace Leni and *Olympia* was to support Hitler and the Nazis. She was a Hitler crony who had made what came to be considered a wonderful and surprisingly "fair" film, but that wasn't enough to get it into theaters or in the pipeline for national distribution.

But for two months, she kept trying. She arrived in Los Angeles on November 24, America's Thanksgiving Day.

Reports of Leni's travels in the papers, including the *Hollywood Reporter* and *Daily Variety*, shook up Glenn. He read the "good friends" and "greatest man who ever lived" comments, too. He realized the chances of *Olympia* making him a national hero again—instead of a wife-beating bad actor— were dwindling.

Her phone call on the day after Thanksgiving didn't surprise him. The conversation was awkward at first. It had been more than two years since they parted at the airport. Two years since he said: "I will be back." As the small talk about her trip and her first impressions of Los Angeles unfolded, Glenn guessed that part of the awkwardness was that she wondered if Karen was standing next to him, listening.

"Leni," he said, "I'm getting divorced. Karen's back in Colorado."

"I'm sorry," she said. "What happened?" She didn't mention that she had seen several accounts in the German papers, because he still was considered big news—and now more than ever in the wake of *Olympia*'s release.

"Too long a story," he said. "At least for the phone."

She invited him to come to her bungalow at the Beverly Hills Hotel on Sunday for lunch. They'd talk, catch up, and see if there was anything they could come up with together to aid the chances of *Olympia* finally breaking through the obstructions being placed in its path in America. She sounded friendly, but also businesslike. Glenn kept thinking back to Smith and

Jones's office, as he had thousands of times since. He remembered how offended and hurt he had been when confronted with her Nazi films and her anti-Semitic comments, how he had lectured himself for being so naïve and heard himself called stupid. Now, if anything bothered him, it was that he realized that everything said in that room was true . . . yet he still wondered how it would have turned out if he had shrugged it all off and returned to Leni anyway.

On Saturday, Glenn went to the Southern California-UCLA football game at the Los Angeles Coliseum, meeting Ken Carpenter and Bill Graber, the USC graduates. At the March screening of *Olympia*, they promised one another they'd get together more often, and they'd pulled it off a few times. He teased them by wearing a blue UCLA sweatshirt to the game. As they settled into the seats, they double-teamed him. Carpenter asked, "You heard from Leni Riefenstahl yet?"

Glenn sensed pretending was a waste of time. So he admitted he was having breakfast with her Sunday morning.

"So how many times have you said good-bye to her?" Graber asked pointedly. "I mean, really good-bye? And you keep going back!"

Glenn shrugged. He knew both men knew about his problems with Karen, and her—or at least her lawyer's—accusations. But they didn't bring those up, either at the game or after.

The Bruins and Trojans played to a 7-7 tie, sending only the neutral away happy.

On Sunday, Ernst Jäger answered the door. He greeted Glenn warmly and introduced him to Klingeberg, who seemed genuinely excited to meet a decathlon champion. Leni emerged from the bedroom, smiling and holding her arms out. Thanks to the correction in Smith and Jones's office, he knew she was thirty-six. She looked her age now. As pretty as before, maybe even more, but unquestionably much more mature. The embrace was nice, but wasn't one of lovers. The four of them sat at the table and ate scrambled eggs, and Glenn mostly parried the questions about the state of his movie career. Then Leni asked him what he thought of *Olympia* when he saw it at the private screening.

"I couldn't understand a word your announcer was saying, but other than that . . . Leni, it really is good. You should be proud. I'm proud to be in it."

Jäger spoke up, looking at Glenn. "It is a film about sport, and a wonderful one at that. Why can't your people understand that?"

Leni spoke in German to Jäger, and touched his hand.

She turned to Glenn. "I told him I couldn't have said it better myself."

When they were done with lunch, the other two men made their excuses and left. Glenn didn't move. She leaned forward.

"It took me six months to get over you, Glenn Morris," she said slowly. "Six months! It was a knife. You stuck it in. Then Goebbels twisted it. It gave him *such* pleasure to show me the stories about you returning home to your girl and putting a ring on her finger and all that."

"I'm sorry, Leni. The reason I'm getting divorced is that I couldn't hide that I knew I made a mistake marrying her and not going back to you. Plus, she's a smart girl. She figured it out. And she had a lot of other people telling her, too."

"You talked about me in your sleep, didn't you?"

He couldn't help himself. He laughed darkly. "Well, yeah."

"So whatever happened to Alice?"

"Alice?"

"The girl you talked about in your sleep with *me*."

Alice was his first, the Simla girl who cried.

"I saw her in Simla at Glenn Morris Day there. Two kids. Fat."

Leni stood. "Good," she said. They still hadn't touched after the initial hug. "So, Glenn Morris," she said, "you said you know you made a mistake. So what did you decide would have happened if you had done what you promised to do? If you had come back to me?"

"I'm not completely sure, but we . . ."

She cut him off. "Let *me* tell you what would have happened," she said. "*Olympia*, a one-part *Olympia*, would have opened a year ago, in Europe. It would have been before the *Anschluss*. It would have been before *Kristallnacht*. The film—and Leni Riefenstahl—would have been embraced around the world. *Leni and Glenn*, a joint German-American production, would have come out earlier this year and we would be basking in it. It would be loved in both countries . . . and more. It would have been, and it would *be*, a real-life love story, the sort the world loves. It would be better than the Duke and Duchess of Windsor! There would have been some obstacles, but we could have overcome them and set in motion what couldn't be overturned. Nothing Hitler has done the last few months would have changed anything. Now, the world would be debating what you and me, the lovers, would do if it becomes apparent that our nations are going to war again. Then they'd go back and see the film again."

Glenn tried to take that all in. "Okay," he said slowly. "Maybe."

Leni said it slowly, for emphasis. "That *is* what would have happened," she insisted.

"Nothing we can do about that now," Glenn responded, shrugging. "The question is: What now?"

"Can we agree that we both want *Olympia* to get national distribution in America?"

"Absolutely," he said.

"Then you and I appear at a press briefing here at the hotel next week. Whenever Ernst thinks best. You say you've seen the film and then you say what you think of it. The truth. You say you believe the American people are being cheated out of a chance to see a wonderful film. You refuse to get into politics, and you say that's the point. This is about friendly competition and goodwill and art, not politics."

Glenn could see the wheels turning in Leni's head. By now, he knew what she was. He knew how manipulative, phony, conniving and even hateful she could be. Yet that all sounded good to him. He could say all she suggested he say. He believed it, too. For all her faults, she had made a good film. And one that could help him to climb out of the pit his life had become.

That night, in Leni's bedroom, Glenn talked about Alice in his sleep. Alice again was sixteen and skinny and crying.

Leni shook him awake. "I should be offended," she said. "But I guess I have it coming."

Leni told him she had meetings scheduled for Monday and Tuesday, and that it was best if he didn't know whom with. He returned home Monday morning, to await Jäger's call about the press briefing at the hotel, or Leni's summons to return.

He had two beers and got out the photos Leni had given him. He had a third beer as he flipped through the prints. He was starting to feel uneasy again. He knew what Leni was. *What are you getting into? Maybe this isn't such a hot . . .*

The doorbell rang. When he saw who it was, his mouth dropped.

"Hi, Glenn," said Mr. Smith, who had become grayer in the past two years.

"Hi, Tarzan," said Mr. Jones, who had become no less insolent in the past two years. "Where's Jane?"

Glenn tried closing the door, but Jones, with a decisive reach, prevented that. "Now what kind of hospitality is that?" he asked. "We have things you're going to want to see . . . and hear! And we've come a long way to enlighten you!"

Smith said, in what bordered on the soothing, "It's either here or we find a reason to be able to take you downtown."

Glenn stepped aside.

For three hours, with Glenn anchored to the couch, they read horrific summaries, news stories, and transcripts of eyewitness accounts of *Kristallnacht*. Setting up a projector, they showed him film of Nazi thuggery, saying it was both from *Kristallnacht* and earlier. They apologized for the quality of the film, noting it had to be taken surreptitiously and smuggled out of the country. Glenn repeatedly asked what it had to do with him, and they ignored him. They plowed on, and it was mind numbing.

When the film ended, Jones walked over to turn on the lights. "That's the regime and the movement your Fraulein is in bed with," he said sharply. "'Greatest man of all time,' she said. Her 'good friend,' she said. She used to be at least a smart cookie; now she's just a fucking bitch who thinks we're all stupid on this side of the ocean."

Smith said, softly, "She really thinks she can talk Ford or Disney to step up for her, the poor persecuted and misunderstood artist."

Eventually, the two men set up a phonograph and began playing a record. It was Leni's voice, muffled and unclear at times. She was speaking English and the conversation was with, apparently, an American. He sounded older. Smith explained that they left the man on there just enough to prove this was a conversation. Glenn didn't recognize the voice.

Leni ranted that the Jews had it coming. They had betrayed the Fatherland for so long, ruined the Fatherland, twisted the aims of the Fatherland for their own selfish purposes. And here in America, it was no different, and when were they going to do something about it? The American said it wasn't that simple in this country, but allowed it was a problem. The Jewish cabal, he called it.

"And now your fucking Jewish *cabal*," she said, "is making sure *Olympia* will not be distributed and shown in your theaters. I was so careful to make it an international film. And that's what it is! The rest of the world gets it. The rest of the world sees it. I believe most of America would understand that. But your Jewish bastards are going to make sure, with blackmail and economic leverage and their own power, that this film is not seen here. It is bad enough here, but I know it's going to be even worse in Los Angeles . . . Hollywood. I will try, but I know what I will be facing."

The other voice asked: "How will you try?"

Smith quickly said, "We cut out some passages here. About who your Miss Riefenstahl would see here. You don't have to hear that. What you need to hear is . . ."

Leni's voice was back, and it was dripping with sarcasm.

"And I will parade Glenn Morris in front of the reporters to say that even as a patriotic American, he recognizes the genius of the film and beseeches America to embrace the principles of free speech and artistic expression to give this a chance. Just give it a chance. Let America see it and vote with their money! When America realizes what a true masterpiece this is, how fair it is, how free of Third Reich control it is, Americans will fill the theaters."

"You trust him to say all that?" the other man asked Leni.

"Well, we'd have to have him practice a few times. He has become a drunken fool now. An asshole who hits women. We have to hope the reporters won't ask him about that, but he can say that he is unable to talk about it but the truth will come out. And to think I was so in love with him. To think it took me so long to get over him."

"So you're glad he didn't stay with you in Germany?"

"I didn't say that! I would have molded him. We would have made a wonderful love story—in two languages. He wouldn't have fallen apart, as he has. He can't act, but that wouldn't have mattered. And I am telling you"—there was a blip there, and as stunned as he was, Glenn was able to infer she had said the man's name—"it could have brought Germany and America closer together. I don't know how that would have affected events, both up to now and in the future, but I think it would have. I really do. I think *he* knows all that. That is why he has fallen apart. He knows he fucked up."

"Why don't you just make *Leni and Glenn* now?"

"That window has closed. In every way. It has to be *Olympia*."

"You really think he'll do your bidding now?"

"He will," she said. "Even if I have to fuck him again to get him to do it."

The record went to silence. Smith turned off the phonograph.

Glenn sat in stunned silence, leaning back, deep into the couch.

Jones asked Smith: "Think we need to show him the pictures now, too?"

"Probably not," Smith responded. He paused. "But let's do it anyway. After all, he *has* shown an ability to rationalize."

Jones pulled two folders out of his satchel. "Okay, I'm going to show you some of *our* pictures," he said. "You look, you hand 'em back. Okay, first one . . . one of your German friends coming out of the Gestapo headquarters."

The picture he pulled out of the first folder and handed Glenn was of Kurt, the limousine driver.

"Kind of careless, I guess you could say," Smith said.

Glenn dropped the picture on the floor. Okay, so the guy driving him was in the Gestapo, too. Not great, but…

Unfazed, Smith said, "The funny thing is, as near as we can tell, the Gestapo had about three of her cameramen on the payroll, anyway, so they were keeping an eye on her from a lot of angles. I guess we should be a bit insulted that they didn't know we were doing the same thing . . . if to a little lesser extent."

Reaching out with another picture from the first folder, Jones said, "Speaking of which . . . this was the man talking to us. Or at least the *one* we can tell you about now."

The next shot was of Stephan, Leni's young film editing assistant, on a Berlin street. Smith said, "When they figured out he was reporting to us, they picked him up, tortured him, got out of him what they could—which wasn't all that much, other than that he'd told us some things about your Fraulein and the Führer's visit to that film lab—and then they blew his head off. That's one I truly feel bad about. What he told us in the big picture wasn't all that important. And we had bigger plans for him."

Glenn wondered, "Like . . . ?"

Smith shrugged. "Something bigger."

Jones raised the second folder, showing it to him as if he were challenging him to guess what it held. "Okay, here are the last ones," he said. "Go ahead. They're an eyeful." He dropped the folder on the coffee table. Glenn wanted to simply wave a hand and announce he wouldn't even look at them, but he couldn't resist. As Glenn reached for the folder, Jones said, "If it's any consolation, this is from last year . . . and we don't think it started until then."

For perhaps thirty seconds, nothing was said as Glenn was frozen, holding the closed folder in his hand.

The two men waited.

Finally, Glenn sighed and opened the folder. He flipped through a small stack, looked at each one, growing sicker each second. Suddenly, he dropped the pictures, jumped up and ran toward the bathroom as fast as he had on the track at Berlin.

He didn't make it in time.

~

Epilogue

Glenn Morris didn't make another movie.

His wife obtained a quickie Nevada divorce in August 1939, when she was about to begin a teaching job in Wyoming. She married a Denver business-man in November 1940.

In 1940, at age twenty-eight, Morris made the roster of the National Football League's Detroit Lions as a reserve end. The Lions' young star was another Coloradoan, Byron "Whizzer" White. By then, Morris was so unheralded that the wire-service lineup information appended to game ac-counts listed him as "Morse" for his first two games. Glenn played in six of the first eight games, starting two. His only statistic was one interception, for twenty yards, and he also made a tackle that produced a safety in a 43-14 victory over the Chicago Cardinals. But with the Lions out of champion-ship contention with a 3-4-1 record, Detroit pared the roster with three games remaining, and Glenn was one of five Lions released on November 5, 1940. The Associated Press story that ran in the Denver newspapers didn't even mention his Olympic accomplishment. As the season wound down, he briefly joined the Columbus Bullies of the American Football League, one of several operations using that name over the years. That was the end of his pro football career.

After returning to Colorado, Glenn sold insurance in Denver.

At thirty, he enlisted in the U.S. Navy in October 1942 and became a lieutenant junior grade on the attack troop transport USS *Banner* in the Pacific. Although he often showed officers clippings of his Olympic glory, he mostly was aloof. A beachmaster, he went ashore during battle in the Philippines and seemed to crack up, accusing fellow navy men of stealing his gas mask. In truth, he had left it on the landing craft. He also was involved in landings at Okinawa. Most who knew him felt he came out of the service emotionally scarred, and some—perhaps not realizing how bruised emotionally he already was when he entered the service—later would say it was post-traumatic stress syndrome. After leaving the Navy in 1947, he lived mostly in Northern California and worked as a steel rigger for the Atomic Energy Commission and at construction. A heavy smoker and drinker, his health deteriorated and he was diagnosed with emphysema, high blood pressure, and an enlarged heart. Another marriage didn't work out. When he was inducted into the Colorado Sports Hall of Fame in 1969, it was said he was too ill to travel and attend the banquet. By early 1974, he was in a veteran's hospital full-time. He was sixty-one. He looked eighty. His hair was silver; he was overweight and constantly short of breath. He died on January 31, 1974. He is buried in Skylawn Memorial Park in San Mateo.

～

In 1940, after World War II had begun, Leni Riefenstahl began filming *Tiefland*, envisioning it as her triumphant return to feature films. She was producer, writer, director, and star. Incredibly, given the cost of the war effort, the German government put up seven million reichsmarks for the project. Filming continued in fits and spurts until 1944, and Leni used Gypsies interned in concentration camps as extras.

After the end of the war, she was detained under house arrest for several years by the Allies and interrogated, most notably by the very skeptical writer Budd Schulberg, working for the Office of Strategic Services. She claimed to have known nothing of Nazi atrocities until after the war. She was tried several times, but received only the relative slap on the wrist of being labeled a "fellow traveler" of the Nazis.

She managed to complete *Tiefland* and it was released in 1954.

Two years later, she was seriously injured in a truck crash in Kenya while looking for possible filming locations for a feature film that was never made, and was in a coma for a time, but recovered.

In later years, her reputation was somewhat rehabilitated as she turned to still photography, shooting such figures as Rolling Stones lead singer Mick Jagger and animal trainers-magicians Siegfried and Roy. She spent considerable time living with the Nuba Tribes in Sudan and published best-selling books of her photos of them in 1974 (*The Last of the Nuba*) and 1976 (*The*

People of Kau). Also in the mid-1970s, she obtained a scuba-diving license, lying about her age to do so, and also released several books of marine-life photos and a 2002 film, *Impressionen unter Wasser*—or *Underwater Impressions*.

She was married twice, first to German officer Peter Jacob from 1944 to 1946. Then, on her 101st birthday on August 22, 2003, she wed her driver, photographer, and companion of thirty-five years, Horst Kettner. She died seventeen days later in Pöcking, Germany.

~

Author's Afterword

In May 2010, I heard from former newspaperman Tony Phifer, a senior writer for Colorado State University's Division of External Relations. Tony and I share an appreciation of history and serve together on the selection committee for the Colorado Sports Hall of Fame. Tony suggested that an upcoming ceremony on the CSU campus in Fort Collins might be in my wheelhouse for a *Denver Post* story. CSU was going to plant an oak-tree seedling to salute Glenn Morris, the school's former student-body president and football and track star who won the 1936 Olympic decathlon at Berlin. I had heard of Morris, knew of that gold-medal accomplishment, was aware he was from the small Colorado town of Simla, and had looked at the display honoring him in the Hall of Fame, located in the Denver Broncos' stadium. I knew that one other successful athlete was from Simla—former University of Colorado All-American and ex-San Francisco 49ers punter Barry Helton, who earned a Super Bowl championship ring when his NFL team routed the Denver Broncos in Super Bowl XXIV. But I had to admit, to Tony and myself, that I didn't know much about Morris beyond the highlights.

Why an oak tree?

Tony explained that the German Organizing Committee officials handed out seedlings for the gold medalists to take home and plant, preferably in their hometowns or at their universities. As the trees grew, they would be reminders of the Olympic spirit. Less trumpeted was that they also could be considered links to mythology's Thor and his "Donar Oak." Tony found a picture that proved Morris presented his tree to CSU president Charles Lory

311

in September 1936. By the twenty-first century, though, nobody seemed to know where it had been planted, if it had been planted at all, or what had happened to it. Tony wrote stories for university publications on the mystery, and he hooked up with Don Holst, the 1968 Olympic team's decathlon coach and an Olympic historian who lives in Chadron, Nebraska. Holst sought to trace the few known surviving Berlin trees, produce second- and third-generation oak seedlings, and then replant them at various sites tied to the 1936 Olympians around the country. In May 2010, it was CSU's turn—in honor of Morris.

I did considerable preliminary reading about Morris, most of it on microfilm in the *Post* library. Tony suggested I contact Dr. Morris Ververs, who at Simla High from 1967 to 1984 first taught and later served as principal. He was retired and living on a small ranch just outside of town. His wife, Verna, was related to Morris—her father was Morris's first cousin—and Dr. Ververs had become a trustee and advocate of the Olympic champion's legacy in his hometown. My plan was to visit Simla several days before the Fort Collins ceremony and write a profile of Morris in advance, then attend and plug in information from the tree-planting ceremony, and file the story for the next day's paper.

At Simla High, Ververs took me to the glass-covered display cases honoring Morris outside the gym. Next, we went to Ververs's home, where we spoke at length. He showed me Glenn Morris's gold medal, held in trust by the school district. Eventually, Ververs popped a VHS tape into a TV-VCR and showed me the segment of Leni Riefenstahl's famed documentary *Olympia* that featured Morris and the decathlon.

I went to the CSU oak-tree ceremony the next week, and my story appeared in the newspaper on May 11, 2010. I also did a blog with additional information. In both, I mentioned the Morris-Riefenstahl affair. I saw a couple of pictures of the two them together during the Games; much later, I would see more, including several I eventually concluded almost certainly were taken during his return to Berlin for supplemental filming and pictures. Those pictures, and many others of Leni or Glenn separately, are all over the Internet. I was aware of Riefenstahl and *Triumph of the Will* and *Olympia*, but had seen only snippets of those films. Ververs told me that he and his wife visited Glenn's brother, Jack, in San Diego in the late 1970s, and that Jack passed along that Glenn had confirmed the relationship in brother-to-brother discussions. "Jack told us that when Glenn died, he said on his deathbed, 'I should have stayed in Germany with Leni,'" Ververs told me. Glenn also told Fort Collins businessman Sparks Alford, one of the athlete's sponsors during his college days, about the affair with Riefenstahl.

While writing that 2010 newspaper story, I committed the sin of assuming archival pieces were correct. In many cases, I was to discover, they weren't. Sportswriters wrote few personality profiles of college athletes in those days, so there wasn't much on the record about Glenn during his football and track career at Colorado Agricultural College. In the rush to tell America about this man who seemed to come out of nowhere to decathlon prominence, reporters seemed to buy into any fairy tales tossed their way about Morris. Multiple-part series about him in the Denver papers in 1936—one as the Olympics approached, one after—read like Jack Armstrong novels and, curiously, only indirectly and unreliably quoted Glenn himself. That started a cycle of myth that continued as other writers, including me, later used the clippings as reference material.

In April 2011, I returned to the CSU campus to attend another ceremony honoring Morris. The school renamed the South College Field House, where Glenn did much of his track and field training, the Glenn Morris Field House. Ververs that day loaned Morris's gold medal to CSU, where it's now stored. In his remarks during the ceremony, CSU president Tony Frank acknowledged that Morris's life was troubled after his Olympic accomplishments. But he also was correct when he told me of the renaming decision: "Like most universities, we typically name things in response to philanthropic contributions. But we also name things for accomplishment. . . . I don't think anybody can question Glenn Morris's accomplishments. I think he was fairly unarguably the greatest athlete in Colorado State University history. If we're not going to name a facility after that level of accomplishment, especially involving something as historic and symbolic as that gold medal at that Olympic Games, then I don't know where you're going to set the bar."

By then, a book about Leni and Glenn was on my short list of possible projects.

In the many books written about the 1936 Berlin Olympics, Morris usually is minimally mentioned. More recent works at least usually added Riefenstahl's disclosure of the affair in her 1987 memoirs, translated into English and published in Great Britain in 1992 and the United States in 1993. To start with, she claimed that Erwin Huber introduced her to Morris on the second day of the decathlon, that she was "transfixed" on first sight, and that the attraction was obvious and mutual. Several of the most-often seen pictures of Leni and Glenn together are similar and were taken in one photo siege during the decathlon. Those shots show them lounging on the ground with Jack Parker and Bob Clark. The one used on this book's cover, showing her reaching to Glenn's forehead, was obtained from the National Archives via Double Delta Industries. Leni also said that she subsequently called upon Glenn to help line up the pole-vaulters for additional filming the day after their event—or, actually, the next night in an attempt to duplicate (with her extra lights) the conditions that existed when Earle Meadows ultimately claimed the victory in the poorly lit stadium. She said Glenn went to the dance hall and "dragged" the pole-vaulters to her at the stadium.

Although her timetable often has been parroted in books, there's a major problem with it. The pole vault was on August 5. The decathlon was on August 7 and 8. Glenn couldn't have helped Leni the night after the pole vault if he didn't meet her until two days later. I wrote this on the theory that Leni was correct about the pole vault filming taking place the next night, and that Glenn was involved as an intermediary, which means she met Glenn sooner than during the decathlon.

Leni's claim in her memoirs that Morris received his gold medal after the decathlon ended and then tore off her blouse and kissed her breasts in front of a packed stadium was ludicrous, and not only because if her narrative was to be believed, this was *before* their physical relationship began. Nobody in the stadium, including the many journalists, noticed? It couldn't have been *that* dark. She said she realized he was a "lunatic" then. That's why I use that word in my passage about what happened that night. (I also should note that I'm realistic about the perils of translation from German to English.) So she thought he was a lunatic, yet she subsequently contacted him in Sweden after the Games, arranged travel for him back to Berlin, and *then* began an affair with him? As you read her accounts, the natural reaction is to marvel at the gall of Leni, the storyteller. Does she really think we're going to believe this? Yet in her own way, *she* arguably believed it as she typed. That's the way she was. Plus, she was writing (and all indications are that she did the writing herself) about incidents of a half century earlier. So even if she had *wanted* to be truthful and get the little details and timetable correct, that would have been impossible, absent a detailed journal or diary.

The decathlon medal ceremony, in fact, was delayed to August 9, the day after the completion of the event, and the three Americans involved wore their blazers and ties. Later stories, including mine in the *Post*, said that Eva Braun presented Morris with the gold medal and/or wreath, but I came to understand that the picture cited—it's taken from behind the woman, and you can't tell who it is—wasn't taken at the actual ceremony, but later. In that picture, taken in the daylight, Morris is wearing his uniform, not his blazer and tie. The German public didn't know of Eva Braun's existence, much less her role in Hitler's life (whatever it was), so at the very least, her involvement in any presentation to Morris wouldn't have been flaunted.

I decided that when Leni brought Glenn back to Germany from Scandinavia after the Games, it wasn't just to do extra shooting—or maybe not even *mainly* to do extra shooting, both film and still. It was to *restart* an affair that began during the Games. After all, the supplemental film, when included, hurt the credibility of an otherwise amazing documentary. The restaged sequences of the pole vault and decathlon 1,500 meters looked more absurd each time I viewed those scenes in *Olympia*. Leni acknowledged there was electricity and passion between her and Glenn during his return to Berlin, to the point where they almost forgot to do the shooting before Glenn's departure date arrived, and she said it took her six months to get over him.

I never seriously considered writing a "Glenn Morris biography." Former Fort Collins newspaperman Mike Chapman's *The Gold and the Glory* about Morris came out in 2003. In roughly sixty pages of text, he laid out what he could find through interviews and research. He was especially dogged in coming up with information about Morris's military service and his crackup during the Philippines landing. He brought up Morris's affair with Riefenstahl, and even sent her a letter, asking about the relationship, not long before her death. As he explained in his book, the return letter said she stood behind what she said in her memoirs about the American athlete. Understandably, that tended to be her stand about everything in her tome, which runs 656 pages in the North American editions.

Even after I started a young-adult novel planned to be the first book in a series, I sporadically did additional exploratory research about Leni and Glenn and another project on my short list when the mood struck. I made an additional trip to Simla, visited Ververs again, and listened to the tape of his visit with Jack Morris in San Diego. At that point, I still was thinking that if and when I did *Leni and Glenn*, it would be nonfiction with an asterisk—meaning that I would allow myself considerable leeway to speculate, hypothesize, and even entertain within that format. Eventually, though, I reached a group decision with Rick Rinehart and Kalen Landow of Taylor Trade. I might as well go all out. I would do *Leni and Glenn* as a speculative narrative, within the framework of my research. Mostly, I decided there was a story to tell here, questions to raise and try to answer, gaps to fill in, and it would be impossible to do it within the traditional parameters of nonfiction.

I put aside the young-adult novel. I dived into this, knowing from the start that I wouldn't have or find all those "answers." I approached the research hungrily, in much the same fashion as I did my nonfiction books, which I am proud to say have drawn praise for their thoroughness and in at least two instances—*Third Down and a War to Go* and *Horns, Hogs, and Nixon Coming*—involved the unearthing of much revelatory material.

Once I started writing, documented fact was my outline. Of course, I used dramatic license, primarily in unleashing my imagination. I let it play out in my head, seeing and hearing it as I consulted my gathered material, and typed. Much of the dialogue comes from or is at least suggested by what was said in newspaper stories of the time. The outline of Glenn Morris's life—pre-Olympics, post-Olympics, post-marriage—is as it happened. That includes his one-season NFL stint with the Detroit Lions. The oft-repeated lore was that the hard-luck Morris suffered a broken leg in the first game of the 1940 season. Some online databases have him down for playing four games, but a game-by-game perusal of the Lions' season and additional checking of microfilm showed that Morris in fact played in six games—and then was unceremoniously released with three games remaining before he joined the Columbus Bullies. The more I learned of his stunning "fall," the more I was saddened. Yet this was a story, essentially with a life of its own, taking me where it wanted to go.

I wrote quickly for two reasons. One, I had a deadline. But, more important, I wanted to see how this story would turn out.

I have changed a few names, including that of Glenn Morris's wife.

Leni Riefenstahl did appear at the Telluride Film Festival in 1974 and faced a reception that matches what I have here. Her quotes come from a story by *Post* film critic Rena Andrews. I rewrote the information about Leni's appearance from Rena's story and elsewhere into my own piece, by a fictitious bureau reporter.

Riefenstahl did go to Los Angeles in November 1938, seeking to rally support for *Olympia*, when Glenn Morris—who had been in the headlines for his marital problems and abuse allegations—still was living there and attempting to make it as an actor. Hubert Stowitts indeed showed a copy of *Olympia* to Los Angeles–based Olympic athletes earlier, in March.

I have the Glenn Morris artifacts on display at the Simla school several years before Ververs oversaw the installation of a first case in a different part of the building, before a new gym was built and the display was moved to the gym lobby. For a few days, I felt guilty when I nudged Thomas Wolfe's arrival in Berlin up a few days. But his interview for the *Berliner Tageblatt*, his relationship with caricaturist Thea Voelcker, and his attendance and actions at the Games' track and field events, mostly were real. (They later were fictionalized in Wolfe's *You Can't Go Home Again*.) Also very real was Glenn and Walter Wood's jog for photographers with Max Schmeling. The Associated Press picture of the encounter appeared in publications around the world, and that photo is one of many that served to suggest incidents in this narrative. In many cases, I was writing "around" actual pictures. Another example was a famous picture of Helen Stephens's post-race visit with Hitler. Glenn's interview with noted sportswriter Joe Williams actually happened and the *Rocky Mountain News* story here is genuine, although slightly cleaned up. Other journalists—including Alan Gould, and then others in Denver—wrote what I have them writing.

Yes, I have drawn other historical figures, such as Jack Dempsey, Damon Runyon, Paul Gallico, and William Shirer, into this, but in credible situations. In Shirer's case, I used his books *Berlin Diary* and *Nightmare Years* for background.

The track and field competition, whether in Berlin or on the various post-Olympic tours, is reality based, as is Glenn's itinerary after the Games, including his "injury" in Stockholm and disappearance from the Scandinavian tour at that point. No, I'm not convinced the "injury," cited in the wire-service reports of the Stockholm meet, was genuine, but I went along with that here. That timetable at least gibes with Leni saying in her memoirs that he returned to Berlin from Sweden.

Those post-Olympic tours indeed were chaotic, and the 1936 newspaper stories—disclosing dates, locations, participants and results—don't always match up with the "official," but sometimes erroneous American Olympic Committee Report, a very self-serving, historical record published in hardback form and sold to the public. I've used discretion and common sense in piecing this together. For example, Jesse Owens's coach, Larry Snyder, said before leaving for the United States that some athletes were scheduled to go to Czechoslovakia and Austria, but had that trip pulled out from under them. I've let the problems with that part of the schedule help explain why only Glenn Morris, discus gold medalist Ken Carpenter and two others (Walter Wood and runner Dale Schofield) made a scaled-down swing through Czechoslovakia. Also, Brigham Young University's Sports Hall of Fame biography reports that Schofield not only won the 100 meters in the August 17 meet at Prague, as documented in an AP story also noting the performances of Glenn, Carpenter, and Wood, but also says that Schofield won the 100 and 200 in another meet in the same country. Some of the secondary meets apparently didn't make the wire services. The AOC required athletes to sign forms by July 20—when most of them were on the SS *Manhattan*—requesting "leaves of absence" to compete in the exhibitions, and the tours in theory were voluntary, but that seems to have been a formality designed to obligate them. I was amused to note that Daniel Farris, the AAU official, wrote in the AOC *Report* that he would recommend skipping such future tours after future Olympics, because he had found that the athletes had been enthusiastic in advance of the Games about participating in post-Olympic tours but that enthusiasm dwindled by the time the tours actually took place. I assumed that meant the AAU and AOC didn't make enough money. Regardless, I read plenty of references that made it clear that the athletes who signed the forms felt as if they were being ordered around and had little choice in the matter.

As I continued my research about Riefenstahl, reading of her in the wide selection of books available and also in her own memoirs, I gradually understood why it was unwise to assume she told the truth about anything. That's not a newsflash. Her many biographers made that disingenuousness a cornerstone of their works. Yet there almost always is *some* truth in what she said, amid the rationalizing, twisting, dissembling . . . and lying. I came to think of it as Leni's Truth. I did note and use what she said in her memoirs in forming the outline for this story, but I was judicious, selective, skeptical, and open eyed.

I believe there was some basis to her "lunatic" story at the stadium tied to Glenn's victory, especially when considered in the context of their physical attraction and relationship. In her memoirs, Leni also told the story about a "graphologist" analyzing Glenn's handwriting. Again, I don't believe she told the whole truth, and I've speculated what that whole truth was. Her memoirs repeatedly and so brazenly massaged the facts, it became laughable. But the massaging almost always was done to make her look better, which is why her "confession" about being enamored of Glenn and even dreaming of marrying him before he returned to the United States and to his "fiancée" was unusual. At that point, she was the one "rejected." Given her track record, that was at least surprising—or a surprising admission. Glenn Morris broke Leni Riefenstahl's heart. She got over it and, in my mind, even got revenge later, but the American athlete managed to break the heart of a shameless opportunist who often seemed to be heartless. Although I don't buy all of her story, and don't believe she told it all, I find it enlightening and credible *enough* to be additional confirmation that an affair took place.

I watched her as an actress in The Holy Mountain, The Blue Light, and S.O.S. Iceberg. This is grudging, but especially in the context of how women were treated professionally at the time, her work in getting The Blue Light made on a relative shoestring budget and doing a lot of the directing on location is especially remarkable, and it truly is a fascinating film—and now easier to judge because of English subtitles on the DVD. That she later be-trayed her collaborators and hogged more credit than she deserved for the film doesn't change the facts that her contributions were trailblazing and the film was well done for its time.

Of course, I watched her documentaries—the rediscovered Victory of Faith, plus Triumph of the Will and Olympia. And I came to regard a stunning

1993 German television documentary, *The Wonderful, Horrible Life of Leni Riefenstahl*, as both illuminating and invaluable. She "cooperated," but she all but convicted herself. Watching her react, squirm, complain, rant, and tell what obviously are lies or half-truths—while probably believing it all—for the first time had me thinking I was beginning to know her. She was in her early nineties when the documentary was filmed.

She was not a "sympathetic" character, and I didn't want to make her one. But she also was complicated, with multiple dimensions. That ability to rationalize and adapt for her own advantage meant she could be many different things, while convincing herself she was genuine, regardless of the swings. I wasn't going to portray her as devoid of feeling and affection. She wasn't. She wasn't absent of charm, either, which helped her somewhat "rehabilitate" her reputation in later years. But in following her selfish agenda, she was both capable of evil and, even more, of embracing and tolerating evil, if that's what served her at any given moment.

To bring this full-circle: The oak tree mystery brought me into this, and that remains unsolved. Had I continued the novel's narrative beyond 1938, this is what I would have said: After Glenn Morris moved to Denver in 1940, with his marriage failed, with his movie and football careers over, with his life disintegrating only four years after his victory in Berlin, he went to Fort Collins and cut down that damn tree.

—Terry Frei
Denver, Colorado

~

Appendix

1936 United States Track and Field Roster

Men

Albritton, Dave (High Jump-Silver)
Bartlett, Lee (Javelin)
Brooks, John (Broad Jump)
Brown, Billy (Hop, Step, Jump)
Brown, Tarzan (Marathon)
Cagle, Harold (1,600 Relay-Silver)
Carpenter, Ken (Discus-Gold)
Clark, Bob (Broad Jump, Decathlon-Silver)
Crosbie, Ernie (50K Walk)
Cunningham, Glenn (1,500-Silver)
Dawson, Glen (Steeplechase)
Deckard, Tom (5,000)
Draper, Foy (400 Relay-Gold)
Dreyer, Henry (Hammer)
Dunn, Gordon (Discus-Silver)
Favor, Donald (Hammer)
Fitch, Alfred (1,600 Relay-Silver)
Francis, Sam (Shot Put)
*Glickman, Marty (400 Relay)

---

*Listed on roster, but did not compete.

Graber, Bill (Pole Vault)
Hardin, Glenn (400 Hurdles-Gold)
Hornboster, Chuck (800)
Johnson, Cornelius (High Jump-Gold)
Kelly, Johnny (Marathon)
Koegler, Ernest (50K Walk)
Lash, Don (5,000; 10,000)
LuValle, Jimmy (400-Bronze)
Mangan, Albert (50K Walk)
Manning, Harold (Steeplechase)
McCluskey, Joe (Steeplechase)
McMahon, Billy (Marathon)
Meadows, Earle (Pole Vault-Gold)
Metcalf, Malcom (Javelin)
Metcalfe, Ralph (100-Silver, 400 Relay-Gold)
Morris, Glenn (Decathlon-Gold)
O'Brien, Edward (1,600 Relay-Silver)
Owens, Jesse (100-Gold, 200-Gold, Broad Jump-Gold, 400 Relay-Gold)
Packard, Bob (200)
Parker, Jack (Decathlon-Bronze)
Patterson, Joe (400 Hurdles)
Pentti, Eino (10,000)
Pollard, Fritz (110 Hurdles-Bronze)
Robinson, Mack (200-Silver)
Romero, Rolland (Hop, Step, Jump)
Rowe, William (Hammer)
San Romani, Archie (1,500)
Schofield, Dale (400 Hurdles)
Sefton, Bill (Pole Vault)
Smallwood, Harold (400)
Staley, Roy (110 Hurdles)
*Stoller, Sam (400 Relay)
Terry, Alton (Javelin)
Thurber, Delos (High Jump-Bronze)
Torrance, Jack (Shot Put)
Towns, Forrest (110 Hurdles-Gold)
Wood, Walter (Discus)
Venzke, Gene (1,500)
Wilkins, Dudley (Hop, Step, Jump)
Williams, Archie (400-Gold)

Williamson, Harry (800)
Woodruff, John (800-Gold)
Wudyka, Stanley (10,000)
Wykoff, Frank (100, 400 Relay-Gold)
Young, Bob (1,600 Relay-Silver)
Zaitz, Dmitri (Shot Put)
Zamperini, Lou (5,000)

Women
Arden, Alice (High Jump)
Bland, Harriett (100, 400 Relay-Gold)
Burch, Betty (Javelin)
Ferrara, Evelyn (Discus)
*Hasenfus, Olive (400 Relay)
Kelly, Kathlyn (High Jump)
O'Brien, Anne (80 Hurdles)
Pickett, Tidye (80 Hurdles)
Robinson, Betty (400 Relay-Gold)
Rogers, Annette (100, High Jump, 400 Relay-Gold)
Schaller, Simone (80 Hurdles)
Stephens, Helen (100-Gold, Discus, 400 Relay-Gold)
*Stokes, Louise (400 relay)
*Warren, Josephine (400 Relay)
Wilhelmsen, Gertrude (Discus, Javelin)
Worst, Martha (Javelin)

~

Resources

Books

Bach, Steven. *Leni: The Life and Work of Leni Riefenstahl*. New York: A. Knopf, 2007.

Bachrach, Susan D. *The Nazi Olympics: Berlin 1936*. New York: Little, Brown and Company, 2000.

Baker, William J. *Jesse Owens: An American Life*. New York: The Free Press, 1986.

Chapman, Mike. *The Gold and the Glory: The Amazing True Story of Glenn Morris, Olympic Champion and Movie Tarzan*. Newton, IA: Culture House, Books, 2003.

Cigaretten-Bilderdienst. *Olympia 1936*. Hamburg, Germany: Cigaretten-Bilderdienst, 1936.

Cunningham, Glenn. *Never Quit*. Lincoln, VA: Chosen Books, 1981.

Dempsey, Jack. *Dempsey*. New York: Harper & Row, 1977.

Donald, David Herbert. *Look Homeward: A Life of Thomas Wolfe*. Boston: Little, Brown and Company, 1987.

Evans, Richard J. *The Third Reich in Power*. New York: Penguin Press, 2005.

Glickman, Marty. *The Fastest Kid on the Block: The Marty Glickman Story*. Syracuse, NY: Syracuse University Press, 1996.

Hart-Davis, Duff. *Hitler's Games: The 1936 Olympics*. London: Century Hutchinson Ltd., 1986.

Hilton, Christopher. *Hitler's Olympics: The 1936 Berlin Olympic Games*. Stroud, UK: Sutton Publishing, 2006.

Hirn, John. *Aggies to Rams: The History of Football at Colorado State University*. Loveland, CO: Vision Graphics, 2009.

Infield, Glenn B. *Leni Riefenstahl: The Fallen Film Goddess*. New York: Thomas Y. Crowell, 1976.

Kershaw, Ian. *Hitler: 1936–45 Nemesis*. New York: W.W. Norton & Co., 2000.

Large, David Clay. *Nazi Games: The Olympics of 1936*. New York: W.W. Norton & Co., 2007.

Magi, Aldo P., and Walser, Richard, editors. *Thomas Wolfe Interviewed: 1929–1938*. Baton Rouge: Louisiana State University Press, 1985.

Owens, Jesse. *Jesse: The Man Who Outran Hitler*. Plainfield, NJ: Logos International, 1978.

Riefenstahl, Leni. *Leni Riefenstahl: A Memoir*. New York: St. Martin's Press, 1992.

Riefenstahl, Leni. *Olympia*. New York: St. Martin's Press, 1994.

Rother, Rainer. *Leni Riefenstahl: The Seduction of Genius*. New York: Continuum, 2002.

Rubien, Frederick W. *Report of the American Olympic Committee: Games of the XIth Olympiad, Berlin, Germany, August 1 to 16, 1936*. New York: American Olympic Committee, 1936.

Salkeld, Audrey. *A Portrait of Leni Riefenstahl*. London: Pimlico, 1997.

Schaap, Jeremy. *Triumph: The Untold Story of Jesse Owens and Hitler's Olympics*. New York: Houghton Mifflin, 2007.

Shirer, William L. *Berlin Diary: The Journal of a Foreign Correspondent*. New York: Knopf, 1941.

Shirer, William L. *The Nightmare Years: 1930–40*. New York: Little, Brown and Company, 1984.

Speer, Albert. *Inside the Third Reich*. New York: MacMillan, 1970.

Trimborn, Jurgen. *Leni Riefenstahl: A Life*. New York: Faber and Faber, 2007.

Tunis, John R. *The Duke Decides*. New York: Harcourt, Brace & World, 1939.

Walters, Guy. *Berlin Games: How the Nazis Stole the Olympic Dream*. New York: William Morrow, 2006.

Other Publications

Film Culture, Spring 1973. Many articles in a section labeled "A Tribute to Leni Riefenstahl," pp. 90-226.

Time magazine, uncredited story, "Games at Garmisch," February 17, 1936.

Many newspapers, including *Denver Post; Rocky Mountain News; Simla Sun; New York Times*

Films (All Available on DVD)

Riefenstahl as Actress:

The Holy Mountain
The Blue Light
S.O.S. Iceberg

Riefenstahl's Documentaries:
Victory of Faith
Triumph of the Will
Olympia

On Riefenstahl:
The Wonderful, Horrible Life of Leni Riefenstahl: A two-part documentary, originally
  made for European television. Directed by Ray Muller. 1993.

Morris as Actor:
Tarzan's Revenge